10/18

CRA

KT-461-602

The Whisperer

WITHDRAWN

B000 000 025 0166

ABERDEEN LIBRARIES

ALSO BY KARIN FOSSUM

Broken
I Can See in the Dark

The Inspector Sejer Series

In the Darkness
Don't Look Back
He Who Fears the Wolf
When the Devil Holds the Candle
Calling Out For You
Black Seconds
The Murder of Harriet Krohn
The Water's Edge
Bad Intentions
The Caller
The Drowned Boy
Hellfire

The Whisperer

KARIN FOSSUM

Translated from the Norwegian by Kari Dickson

Harvill *Secker*

LONDON

1 3 5 7 9 10 8 6 4 2

Harvill Secker, an imprint of Vintage,
20 Vauxhall Bridge Road,
London SW1V 2SA

Harvill Secker is part of the Penguin Random House group of companies
whose addresses can be found at global.penguinrandomhouse.com

 Penguin
Random House
UK

Copyright © Cappelen Damm AS 2016
English translation copyright © Kari Dickson 2018

Karin Fossum has asserted her right to be identified
as the author of this Work in accordance with the
Copyright, Designs and Patents Act 1988

First published with the title *Hviskeren* in Norway
by Cappelen Damm in 2016

A CIP catalogue record for this book is available
from the British Library

penguin.co.uk/vintage

ISBN 9781787300941 (Trade paperback)

Typeset in 12.25/15.7 pt Sabon LT Pro
by Integra Software Services Pvt. Ltd, Pondicherry

Printed and bound in Great Britain by Clays Ltd, Elcograf S.p.A.

Extract on p.vii from *Act of Passion* by Georges Simenon, translated from
the French by Louise Varèse, published by Penguin Books UK in 1965.

Penguin Random House is committed to a sustainable future
for our business, our readers and our planet. This book is
made from Forest Stewardship Council® certified paper.

 MIX
Paper from
responsible sources
FSC
www.fsc.org   FSC® C018179

The Whisperer

Monsieur Ernest Coméliau
Examining Magistrate
22 bis rue de Seine
Paris (VII)

Your Honour:

I should like one man, just one, to understand me. And I would like that man to be you.

We have spent many long hours together during all the weeks of the preliminary investigations. But at the time it was too soon. You were a judge, you were my judge, and I would have seemed to be trying to justify myself. But now you know, don't you, it has nothing to do with that?

Georges Simenon, *Act of Passion*, 1947

Chapter 1

She wasn't beautiful, and she was of course perfectly aware of it. She moved timidly across the floor in the way that most shy women do, with an apologetic expression. With no desire to take up space, no hope of making an impression or being believed, or, for that matter, being taken seriously at all. For well over forty years the mirror had taunted her about this lack of beauty, and she had bowed her head and accepted the judgement. If a spark had come blowing on the wind, she would presumably have gone up in flames – her hair was as dry as straw and she was pale as paper. She was wearing a green nylon coat, with big, deep pockets that contained nothing, as they had long since been searched and emptied. There was a logo on the breast pocket, over her heart, with the word 'Europris' embroidered in big letters. She had an ugly scar across her throat, left by a wound that had not healed well. She was underweight and perhaps anaemic, with red hair and freckles. And yet, despite her lack of colour, the blood was still coursing through her veins, especially now that she was standing in front of him, there to explain herself. Her hands hidden in the thoroughly inspected coat pockets. She was waiting for permission to sit down, was not presumptuous enough to make herself comfortable. Sejer had questioned many people over the years, but no one like her.

She pulled the chair out carefully, so it would not scrape on the floor – the noise might bother someone. She had never had anything to do with the public prosecutor before, must not irritate or provoke him in any way, make him angry. Only now did she notice the inspector's dog over by the window; it stood up and padded across the floor. The dog, Frank Robert, was a small, fat Shar Pei and rather charming with all his wrinkles and folds, as if he was wearing a far too big coat, like herself. The dog stood up on his hind legs and laid his heavy head on her lap. His eyes, which were barely visible in among all the folds, instantly touched something in her and made her forget the seriousness of the situation. There was a small flash of joy in her own eyes, a glimpse. Her eyes lacked colour as well, the irises were pale and watery, and her eyebrows were thin as whiskers. She had not expected a dog. Certainly not one that would come up to her like that, devoted, without hesitation. She was not used to prompting such feeling, not from man or beast. As the beggar he was, Frank stayed on his hind legs and slavered on her coat. When she stopped patting him, he put his paw on her lap, hoping for more.

'Frank,' Sejer said. 'Lie down.'

The dog padded back to his blanket. He pushed and pulled it with his paws to make a nest. The excess kilos slowed him down, and each command from his owner had to be interpreted and carefully assessed before it was obeyed, so everything took time. He was also getting on, in dog years. His sight, hearing and movement were all much reduced.

'Let's not make this too formal,' the inspector said. 'My name is Konrad.'

He held out his hand.

'Ragna,' she whispered. 'Riegel.'

'Like the chocolate,' Sejer said with a smile. 'I used to like their chocolate when I was a boy, and a bar only cost thirty øre. Everyone could afford a Riegel.'

As soon as he had said it, he realised it could be misinterpreted, but his words made her smile and the ice was broken.

Her hand, thin and white, rested in his for a moment. He noted the lack of strength. It was warm and dry, but there was no sign of nervousness, even though she was quick to lower her eyes. Their handshake was the first step towards something inevitable. Everything that needed to be talked about, explained and understood.

She snuck a glance at him and was reminded of old, impregnated wood or a log on a river, something heavy and solid. He was a good deal older than her, tall and grey. Dressed in a plain shirt with a dark blue tie. There was a cherry with two green leaves embroidered on the tie. That wasn't sewn in a factory, Ragna thought. Someone, presumably a woman, had sat with a needle and thread and embroidered that cherry as a token of love.

'You're trying to win my trust,' she whispered. 'You won't say a word about why I'm here, not for a long time. You'll warm me slowly until I pop like popcorn in a pan. Turn myself inside out.'

'Trust would be a good thing,' Sejer said. 'Is that what you want?'

Ragna had not hoped for anything. The police wanted a confession, and when they had that, they could charge her and have the case tried in court. And concentrate on the next investigation.

'Yes,' she whispered. 'Trust would be good.'

He knew that she did not have a voice. She had lost it a few years earlier during an operation on her throat, which should have been a standard procedure, but instead had had serious consequences and permanently damaged her vocal cords. The wound had not healed well either, so she was left with a course, jagged scar that was red and clearly visible. He guessed that she often hid it with a scarf or a polo-neck sweater. She had not bothered now. Her bare, scarred neck was part of her explanation. Even though she could only whisper, he had no difficulty in understanding her. Ragna was more articulate than most. She used the muscles in her face, formed the words well with her tongue and lips. And Sejer quickly adapted to the situation. He used all his senses, read her lips and watched her expressions, something he generally did when questioning someone. It struck him that sitting here like this, facing someone who had a story to tell about fear and anger, or a dangerous opponent, or self-defence, some great accident, a burning hate, still excited him, despite his age. A childhood memory popped up. When he was a young lad and they used to lay into each other in the playground, they would then pipe up to any teacher who came to reprimand them: 'He started it.'

'Ragna,' he said in a serious tone, 'you have been held on remand for forty-eight hours now. And you will be held for four weeks, in the first instance, then for another four weeks, then it will be extended again and again. Can you cope with that?'

'Oh yes,' she whispered.

'Are you able to call the officers or make contact if you need anything? Even though your request may be refused?'

'I don't need anything. I get food and drink. I have my own duvet. A bit like Frank.'

She nodded at the dog.

'He obviously gets more than he needs,' she said, alluding to his extra weight.

This little audacity was accompanied by a good-natured smile, perhaps a small dig in return for his comment about the chocolate.

'I know that you don't have any family,' Sejer said. 'Or am I wrong?'

'I have a son,' Ragna replied swiftly. 'In Berlin. But he never comes home. He doesn't have a family either, as he runs a hotel. I usually get a card from him for Christmas and my birthday. I was only seventeen when I had him.'

'What's his name?'

'Rikard Josef.'

'And his father?'

She shook her head.

'Why doesn't your son come home?'

She shrugged and looked away. Sejer put the absent son to one side like a piece of luggage he did not need at the moment.

As they talked, he observed this quiet creature. She sat poker straight on her chair, without moving, at the ready, and was clearly in awe of the authority he represented. However, he knew that given time, a few hours or days, she would slowly thaw. She would start to move, use her hands more, shift position, lean forward and pull back, he had seen it before. Not like the loud, aggressive ones, he'd met plenty of them in his time. They tended to lean over the table, banging their fist to emphasise their words, or they moved the chair to make as much noise as possible. Some stomped around the room and cursed and swore, as they screamed those words that he had heard so often in the playground. 'He started it.'

Ragna would never be able to raise her voice. This knowledge gave her a stoic calm, kept her in her place; in a way it held her hostage. It is hard to be beside yourself when you cannot scream. She doesn't belong here, he thought. She has everything under control. An old house in Kirkelina that she had inherited from her parents. A job and good colleagues. She did not earn much, it was true, but she lived alone and did not need to pay off a mortgage. She did not look like a woman with expensive habits, and certainly did not look like someone who drank or took drugs. And yet here she was, sitting opposite him.

'Do you have any recordings from when you still had a voice?' he asked.

Her water-blue eyes widened in surprise. No one had ever asked her that before, not a single person. She thought fleetingly that this must be how it felt when a woman was allowed to talk about her dead child. To talk about the dead child for the rest of her life to someone who was not afraid to reawaken the grief.

'Why do you ask?' she whispered, and felt happy. Her cheeks reddened.

'I'm just curious,' Sejer replied. 'And if you did have a recording, I would ask to hear it. I'm trying to imagine how you would talk if you could talk.'

'I don't have any recordings,' Ragna said. 'But everyone told me that I sounded like a little girl. When strangers phoned, say a salesman, and I answered and said my name, I always got the same response: Are there any grown-ups there? It amused me every time. It became a kind of game. Embarrassing people by saying that I was nearly forty, and was alone at home, that my parents were no longer alive.'

'Amusing game,' Sejer said. 'And now that you can only whisper? Do you still like to embarrass people when they ring?'

'I don't answer unless I recognise the number on the display. I reckon that if it's important they'll phone again. If I get a text, I answer. Or an email. But I don't get many, it's mainly advertising.'

'And if someone rings at your door? Do you answer then?'

Something passed between them, like an electric current. Given everything that had happened.

'Generally I do,' she whispered, and looked down. 'I've got quite good at nodding and smiling or shaking my head, or I use my hands. And I close the door again quickly if it's not important, but then it's never important. They're all trying to sell something. But if it's a child collecting money for something, I go in and get some change. Then wave them off. I can wave in different ways. Friendly or dismissive. I can wave people off like insects. Or hold up my hand like a stop sign.'

She raised her hand to demonstrate.

'How do you manage when you're out and about?'

'Not very well,' she admitted, 'as you can probably imagine. I tend not to be out on the streets much, as there's so much noise from the traffic. And there's music in practically all the shops. Just the sound of an escalator or lift is enough. If I meet someone who wants to talk, I'm no use at all. It might be someone asking for directions, but I know they won't be able to hear my answer, and because I don't want to seem difficult or unhelpful, or arrogant for that matter, I tend to avoid situations like that as much as I can. But I do have to go out. I need to buy food and run other errands. Obviously my neighbours know, and I try to shop in the same places.'

'And what about your colleagues at work? At Europris?'

'They don't have any problem hearing me, they're used to it and have learned the technique. But we do have to be face-to-face. You'll get used to it too,' she whispered. 'I can see that you're making an effort. And your efforts are a heavy burden to carry. I don't impose myself on people unless I have to.'

'But there are lots of customers in the shop.'

'I try to solve one problem at a time. I nod and smile and point.'

Ragna lowered her head again. A signal that the ball was in his court. He wondered if she had developed exceptional hearing in the way that people with hearing difficulties often speak loudly and clearly. He did not ask. He was still astonished that she was sitting there, that she had ended up in this situation, when she was about as robust as a reed and almost inaudible to boot. He could not see her hands, as she had them hidden in her lap. He wondered how much she could lift, how fast she could run, how hard she could hit. Everyone uses whatever weapon they have to hand. It struck him that being here in this room, as they were sitting now, face-to-face, alone without noise or distraction, was the best possible situation for unpacking the truth. The conditions for lying were not optimal.

What was it his dear old mum used to say, before a blood vessel in her brain punctured like a bicycle tyre and laid her life to waste? All those memories lost – the ones that had already happened, and those that would never happen now.

'Absolutely everyone, at least once in their lives, should break down in tears of regret.' That is what she had said. And then she died. Ragna Riegel was sitting in front of him, steeled by sheer determination. Would *she* break down in tears of regret?

Chapter 2

She had had the job at Europris for many years. But
none of her colleagues had known her before the operation, and had no idea the first time she opened her
mouth. Ah, right, was all they said, and did what they
could to help her. Sometimes she sat on the till, otherwise she was out in the storeroom; there she opened the
boxes with a sharp knife, then took the goods into the
shop in a trolley, where she priced them and put them
out on the shelves. If a customer came over to ask for
something, she answered with a friendly smile and then,
without a word, went over to the correct shelf, pointed
at the thing in question and gave them a friendly nod.
Her smile was her weapon, her self-defence. If it was a
question she had to answer, she whispered as clearly as
she could, and then put her finger to her lips to indicate
that she had a handicap. The customer usually nodded
politely before hurrying off down the aisle. Many of
them were regular customers who came to understand
the situation. Several of Ragna's colleagues were of a
similar age to herself, which she was glad of. She did
not get on so well with the younger ones, as they made
her feel uncertain. She did not know their world, barely

understood their language. The meaning of the jumble of words and strange abbreviations, often in English, evaded her. One of her colleagues, Lars, who was quite a bit younger than her, often called her Ragnarokk, and she liked that. She liked the fact that he was not afraid of offending her, that he never weighed his words, and that he sometimes responded to a whispered question from her by saying, don't you stand there shouting at me!

Then they would both burst out laughing, Lars would bellow and she would laugh in her own quiet way, like a panting dog. She had kind of given her colleagues permission to tease her. But that was not true of strangers. Because she did not have a voice, she was all the more interested in other people's voices. If only they knew how much they revealed every time they opened their mouths. Some hid behind a wall of sharp noises, others mumbled and were incomprehensible. Some sang rather than spoke their melodious sentences, whereas others had voices that were flat and expressionless. And there were always those who shouted and brayed to get attention.

They worked shifts. From ten to five or from one to eight, which suited her fine. She lived alone in the house in Kirkelina and had no one else to take into consideration. Obviously being alone made her vulnerable, but it also gave her a sense of freedom and control. She came and went as she pleased, no one was waiting, no one asked questions. But she did think about Rikard Josef every day, she was glad that she had the experience of having a child, that she could be part of the conversation when her colleagues talked about their children, which they did all the time.

Not that she had a great deal to say about her son. What little she knew, she had already told them long ago, but she was happy to tell them again. Or she embellished it a bit, exaggerated to stretch out the conversation. She was proud of him, in a way, even though he had more or less cut all contact with her. Never a letter, never a phone call, never a visit. Only the usual card at Christmas, and sometimes one for her birthday on 17 June. She once got a card from Pattaya, where he was on holiday. Alone, she guessed, as there was no mention of anyone else. But it was gratifying to be able to tell her colleagues that he ran a hotel in Berlin called the Dormero, which had five stars on TripAdvisor. She had never been there, it was true – he had never invited her – but she had seen pictures on the Internet. Often, when she longed to see him, she could while away an entire evening dreaming and looking at photographs of the lounges and suites and restaurants. The large, open reception lobby with chandeliers, the bar with deep armchairs. If she was honest, it was her greatest dream: to board a plane for Berlin and to be met by her son at arrivals, then be driven into the centre of town in a big Mercedes perhaps, and shown around what had become his life's work. Eat well in a beautiful dining room, sleep in a room that he had chosen especially for her, maybe even a suite. But it never happened. And the years passed. Only the card for her birthday and another for Christmas with an angel or a star, and a formal, printed message in German. And his name of course, or just his initials, in barely legible writing. She doubted he could remember how old she was each year. He was only seventeen when he left her, full of dreams and ambitions; it had cost him nothing to turn his back. She had been thirty-four at the time, and more than ten years had passed since that dreadful day.

What if I just went there, she suddenly thought, and found my own way to the hotel, and turned up at reception with a suitcase in my hand? And asked for the manager. He would appear only a few moments later, from a door behind the reception desk, of course, presumably in a smart suit. He would walk across the carpet, with a casual elegance, and look at her questioningly. It would take a few seconds before he recognised her, she could just imagine his wide-eyed expression of surprise, perhaps even shame. She would stand there stammering, words he could not hear, to even greater embarrassment. He did not know that she had lost her voice, did not know about the catastrophe. She struggled to understand how this had happened to them, had never dared to ask. He was ambitious, it was true, and longed for adventure. Qualities she did not have. The fact that he had got a senior position before the age of thirty filled her with pride.

It was mainly her fault that things had ended up this way. Getting pregnant with a man who was well over forty, with his own family already, of course, and he had no plans to leave them – not the smartest thing to do. So Rikard grew up without a father. But how she had loved him and looked after him! How she had carried him both day and night. She was no longer interested in what other girls of her age did; she did not feel she was missing anything, not going out or seeing boys her own age, not falling in love. She was head over heels with her son and that was enough. The sight of him, the smell of him, his downy hair, his wet mouth.

She had no dreams of a big family or status. It was just her and her boy.

There were ten minutes left of her shift. She pushed the heavy shopping trolley out into the shop. There were two open boxes of things for the bathroom in the trolley itself, and the box she had overlooked, which Lars then came rushing out with and popped on top.

She started to put the toilet brushes out on the shelf; they were plastic, in three different colours, and cost nineteen kroner each, which was a bargain. When she had put them all out, with a stretch of the imagination, they looked like flowers in a bed, red, purple and pink. She knew that not everything was of the best quality. The candles they sold dripped and ran, and did not last as long as other, more expensive candles. The coffee was thin and bitter, and the boxes of chocolates were often so old that the chocolate was dry and grey. Sometimes the chocolates were covered in a white film because the box had been exposed to changes in temperature. But a lot of the other stuff was good. The plastic containers and rag rugs, ready-made curtains, cotton towels, kitchen equipment and tools. When she had finished with the toilet brushes, she opened the box that Lars had given her. She could see the word 'Malaysia' on it. It contained eight smaller boxes. She chuckled when she discovered that each box contained a ceramic skull, which was actually quite realistic, on a small base. She took one out and saw that there was a small red bulb in each eye socket. They came with two AA batteries that were to be put in the base. She opened the cover and put in the batteries, and immediately the dark sockets lit up. She then arranged the remaining seven boxes on the shelf, and put the skull with the working lights on top. She thought for a few moments about the children who might get one for Christmas and keep it on their bedside table. They would lie alone in the dark staring into the red eyes, like she was right now; in fact she stayed staring at them for some time, unable to turn away, there was something insistent about them. She wanted to show them to Gunnhild so they could laugh together.

She slotted the empty trolley back in with the others, went to the staffroom, put on her coat, picked up her handbag and whispered goodbye to Gunnhild and Lars, having first pointed out the skulls to them. It was Gunnhild and Lars that she got on best with. Some people only worked part-time or at the weekends, and she tended to ignore them. And made sure that they ignored her. Her world had to be small and manageable, because then she was in control. It was a quarter past eight when she got to the bus stop, a dark autumn evening. Four people were waiting for the bus. The others stood in the bus shelter, and she stayed out on the pavement with her back to them. For years, she had always sat in the same place, by the window three seats back from the driver. If the place was taken, she was upset. She felt displaced. Someone was encroaching on her territory. Today the seat was empty and she had a good feeling when she sat down, almost like slipping into something that fitted perfectly.

The bus took forty minutes to get to Kirkelina. She liked being on the bus, looking out through the window. Sometimes, when she was tired, she leaned her cheek against the cool glass and closed her eyes. Every time the bus passed a street light there was a flash under her eyelids. Her thoughts were always freer when she was moving, encased by the body of the bus, like a thick shell. She had come to love the journey home, her favourite time when she was still part of the world and the traffic, but protected all the same.

The street was dark and empty when she got off the bus. It was only a few minutes' walk to the house, but first she quickly crossed the road to Irfan's shop. It was always open. She liked to think that Irfan slept on a mattress out the back, and every time the bell above the door went, be it night or day, he jumped up to be of service. The bell rang as she opened the door, grandly announcing her arrival. She was met by the exotic smells of spices and other delicacies from Turkey, Irfan's home country. She bought rice and tea and tomatoes and some big home-made flatbreads that she liked to eat with cheese and ham. And four bottles of Uludag Frutti. Whenever she went into Irfan's shop, which was bright and warm, she wandered along the shelves in delight. His shop was not like Norwegian shops, it was more like a miniature market, full of colours and smells. There was a special shelf for perfume in gaudy bottles. Every now and then she would pick one up and take off the lid. They all smelt cheap and sharp, but then they didn't cost much either. Starry Night. Secret Dream. Killer Queen. He also had lots of dried fruit, biscuits and jars of interesting sauces. Nappies and soap, and fruit and veg. He didn't take away the fruit even though it had brown marks on it; the bananas could be there for ages before he put out new ones. The carrier bags were the simplest sort, thin, with no advertisements. If she bought anything heavy, she had to carry the bags in her arms, as the handles tended to break. But she only had to cross the road and then she was home. Irfan was a handsome man, some years younger than her, slim and dark-haired with golden skin. He never smiled. He had a restlessness about him, as though his body was constantly vibrating with worry. He often spoke on his mobile phone at the same time as serving her; sometimes he spoke to himself, in his own, to her incomprehensible, beautiful language. He was forever glancing out the window, as if he was looking for someone, and yet always had time to say a few words in his broken Norwegian before finishing the conversation with a nod. Perhaps he had learned that from her.

She never turned the lights off when she left home. The house would be there, bright and welcoming, when she got back from work, especially now in the autumn, when it was dark. It was a modest house, single-storey, with a kitchen, sitting room, two bedrooms and a bathroom. There was a washing machine in the cellar, and storage space for all the bits and pieces that had accumulated over the years. Her own things and things she had inherited from her parents. The cellar was cold and raw. When it rained a lot, the damp patches on the cellar floor grew larger. She had always lived in this house, even after her son was born – she did not have any money when she got pregnant and needed help. So they became a family of four. There was a small garden in front of the house, which she pretty much left to its own devices, as it was not one of her talents. She also had a neat veranda, where she seldom sat, as she found the fact that people could see her from the road uncomfortable. And with her pale skin and faded red hair, she could not take the sun. She kept the rubbish bins down by the road, next to a mailbox on a stand, and was particularly grateful for the street lamp by the end of her drive. The driveway was well lit. When she walked up from the bus stop, she liked to think that it had been put there especially for her, so she could find her way home. Playing was allowed, Ragna Riegel thought. Children are allowed to play all the time.

She had crossed the road. She had the bag in her left hand, and with the right opened the mailbox. Took out the local paper and church weekly, a brochure advertising furniture, and a very ordinary envelope. It was not often she got letters. Her surname was on the front of the envelope: 'RIEGEL'. Written in capital letters. She put her bag down on the ground. No address. No stamp. No sender. She stood under the street lamp and turned the envelope back and forth. The paper was coarse, maybe recycled, it was thinner and greyer than normal paper. Goodness. A letter with no sender. Maybe it was from Olaf next door who had something on his mind, or the Teigens on the other side of the road. Or maybe it was just another advertisement, something that had been dropped in every mailbox in Kirkelina, the street that ran from the spinning factory to the church. Immigrants sometimes offered their services that way. They washed and painted and did carpentry, tidied and repaired, and she thought that perhaps she should contact one of them about the fence. It needed painting. Or it might be something that the council had sent out to all households. But, obviously, it was not, because her name had been handwritten. She walked up the gravel drive to the house, let herself in and put the post down on the kitchen table. She dropped her bag on the floor and kicked off her shoes. Once she had emptied the carrier bag from Irfan's, she decided to make some risotto. She could use the two sausages she had in the fridge, unless they were past the sell-by date. Which they were not. She sank down onto a chair by the table and stared at the envelope. She turned it over several times, as though she expected something to suddenly appear on the back, a company name or logo, if she just waited long enough. But nothing happened. So she opened it and pulled out a folded sheet of paper, with a short message.

'YOU ARE GOING TO DIE.'

Bewildered, she stood with the note in her hand. She had jumped up in fright. Her heart was thumping. Instinctively she stared at the window as though someone would appear outside, someone who could explain what had happened. But there was nothing out there, just darkness, and some lights in the Teigens' windows. And a slight movement when she edged closer, a pale, ghostlike face that was her own reflection in the glass. Again she turned the envelope over and studied the back, but no sender's name or address had appeared in the past few seconds.

'Goodness,' she whispered, and shook her head. 'You are going to die.' It was written in capital letters, like a child would write, a smart child. The letters were clear, even and all the same height. We all will, she thought. She chose just to shrug it off and sniffed in the way her father used to whenever he felt disdain for someone, which she certainly did now. Her thoughts ran along

Kirkelina. She did not know everyone who lived there, only those closest. But many of them were her age, or older. The houses were old, built in the thirties and forties, and many of the inhabitants were alone. No families with young children. No wilful toddlers or rebellious teenagers that she knew of. But there were grandchildren, she realised. Olaf and Grethe next door had four, who often came to visit. He had put up a trampoline in the garden, she could see it from the veranda. She heard the shouting and laughter in summer. She saw the little bodies bouncing up and down, up and down inside the mesh safety netting. But she knew Olaf and Grethe, they were good people. She did not think they would have grandchildren who would even dream of sending threats to anyone. If whoever it was who had sent the letter even was a child, who went from house to house on bike or by foot. There was something alluring about the autumn dark. All the things you could do without being seen. Creep from house to house, steal through garden after garden. With rubber soles, black clothes and hood up. But was half the fun of playing tricks not seeing the effect of your mean streak? No one could see her now, as she stood here in the kitchen reading those five words. And no one would see her if she put her head in her hands in despair or ripped the letter to pieces in a rage and threw it in the fire, or cursed and swore. So, it was a prank that would have no consequences, other than that some nasty person had felt a thrill when he dropped the envelope in her mailbox and then snuck off. Ah well, Ragna thought. Some people have small pleasures. She did glance over to the window again though, where the dark loomed like a wall. It struck her that the days when teenagers roamed the streets causing trouble were long gone. They sat in their rooms now, playing computer games; they bullied each other on the Internet. None of them would even look in her direction, or be interested in her weaknesses, her universe. No one knew her greatest fear. She was simply a lonely woman who never showed herself. She would make some risotto now, enjoy it in peace and quiet, and then sit down to read the newspaper, no doubt there would be something about the local troublemakers and hopeless youth. After all, it was autumn. Yes, she changed her mind, they *would* be roaming the streets. And they would be intoxicated as well, because she guessed there was a gang of them, boys no doubt, probably in their early teens. Or they could be much younger. She remembered some poisonous girls of around eight or nine, from her own childhood. She folded the paper and put it back in the envelope, sniffed again to demonstrate her disdain. Boiled the water, diced the sausages, chopped the onion and tomatoes and chilli. She was more generous than usual with the spices. The whole time, she stood with her back to the envelope. But she could feel it through her clothes, like a sting, it would not leave her alone. It lay there screaming. She tossed her head in an attempt to cover the anxiety. To make a show in her own quiet way. To close the door that had opened into an unknown room. The kettle hummed, quietly at first and then louder. She looked over at the table again, could not help it. The envelope was as anonymous as an envelope could be. It had stopped screaming and now whispered instead, just like she did. It demanded her attention. She had never seen anything so insignificant, and yet she felt it was a threat.

She poured Irfan's rice into the pan with a knob of butter, turned down the heat and put the lid half on. Then she browned the pieces of sausage in another pan, added tomato purée and everything else, the chilli. A simple table setting, with a plate, glass and cutlery, and a jug of water. But that meant she would have to move the envelope, put it somewhere else. She swore under her breath, she wanted nothing to do with it, but then opened the letter and read it one more time.

You are going to die. In other words, backwards, die to going are you. You. The person who had written the message had good motor ability. The letters were carefully written, one by one. The sender did not want the writing to have any recognisable loops or curves. Like a fingerprint. A man, of course; a woman would never make a threat like that. Oh, so it's a man now, not a teenager, she thought. She turned the piece of paper over. The note had been written with a strong hand, and it was possible to see the letters through the paper. What if it had said 'Ragna' on the envelope, rather than 'Riegel'? Or both names. Or if it had said 'Kirkelina 7'. Then she would not have been so frightened before reading what was written, but could not explain why it should make a difference. The note was for her, without a doubt, it was in her mailbox. Her son had left home, her parents were dead. And the way the note was formulated gave the impression that she was worthless. She was just 'Riegel'. And she was going to die. It was the brevity that frightened her, just the bare essentials, merciless, no doubt. I'm hungry, she thought, confused, and folded the piece of paper again. Put it back in the envelope, opened the cupboard under the sink and pushed the letter into the rubbish bin. And there it lay among the old, rotting food.

She ate more slowly than usual, she was indignant. As though someone had spoken behind her back or started a rumour. Indignant, as she had never bothered anyone, had never stood out, had never been derogatory about anyone, neither as a child nor as an adult. She was offended. She was deeply disturbed. She sniffed again, finished her food and stood up, took the rubbish bin out from under the sink, tied up the bag, pushed her feet into some shoes and went out, carried the rubbish down to the road. Opened the bin. She saw that it was half full. She looked down Kirkelina, in case she could see or hear anyone, then she looked up towards the church. She could just make out the spire. Her neighbour Olaf appeared with his dog, walking towards the church. They were both wearing yellow reflective coats. She stayed where she was as she thought it might be nice to have a quick word with him. She knew Olaf well, they had always been neighbours. His Rottweiler, Dolly, spotted her and pulled at the lead. Ragna had never met another Rottweiler as small as Dolly. The dog still looked like a puppy and would never grow up, it seemed. She looked at her kind neighbour and longed for only one thing, that he would tell her that he had also found a ridiculous threat in his mailbox. A note that he was going to die. And only his surname on the envelope, no sender. But he said nothing about receiving such a letter, he was as carefree and happy as always, nothing was weighing on his mind. He was a man, anyway, he had a voice, some muscle even, she thought, he was broad-shouldered, and strong, and a good deal older than her. Instead he looked up at the street light by her house and said: 'I envy you that light, Ragna. It's pitch dark outside ours.'

He pulled Dolly back as she was straining at the lead.

'But I'm sure you deserve it,' he added with a smile.

Ragna wondered what he meant. Maybe he meant she needed that extra bit of help as she had lost her voice, after all, she had a handicap. Oh, I'm being mean now, she realised, Olaf is a good man. Olaf can hear what I'm saying, even if a lorry drives by as I open my mouth, he just moves closer, he listens and reads my lips.

'The Teigens are moving,' he told her and nodded to the house opposite hers. The house she could see from the kitchen and bedroom.

'Oh!' she whispered in surprise.

'A Thai family with two children have bought the house,' he continued. 'They're going to open a small restaurant in town, and apparently the wife has been given permission to run a massage clinic. At home. In one of the rooms in the basement.'

'What?' She couldn't help herself. 'Massage?'

Olaf burst out laughing when he saw her expression.

'I'm sure it's all very above board. Evidently she has a qualification from Thailand and knows a lot about bad backs. It'll probably be pretty reasonable as well, and she'll only be open every other day.'

'Will you go?' Ragna whispered.

'I expect so,' Olaf said. 'If the wife doesn't mind. They're very beautiful, those Thai ladies.'

He winked at her when he said that. The reflection of the street light made his eyes sparkle. He turned and followed a car with his eyes as it cruised past them and on up towards the church. They could just see the clock on the spire, where the pale face shone like the moon.

'The doctor says my bones are starting to look like a Christmas tree covered in snow, because of all the calcification,' he told her. 'Come on, Dolly! We need to carry on.'

He walked off with the dog behind him, and she watched their yellow reflective jackets dance into the dark. He had not had a letter. Only she had received a letter. She turned and went back up to the house, settled down on her chair in front of the television, and turned on the news channel. She had to know what was going on in the world, her own was so incredibly small, and her colleagues always discussed the night's news when they came to work the next day, and she wanted to be part of that. If anything had happened in Berlin, she paid particular attention. But the images did not hold her attention in the same way as usual. She was constantly distracted – the distraction was like a nail in her head, and it had struck something deep down. She sat still with her hands in her lap, and told herself she was a fool for not burning the letter immediately in the wood stove. She had not even torn it to shreds or crumpled it up, the letter was lying in the rubbish bin down by the road, just as complete as when she first read it. The threat still held, she had not destroyed it, it lay there screaming, screaming so loudly that the bin lid was banging, and no doubt the whole of Kirkelina could hear the noise. Hear that she was anxious and useless in number 7, a woman without a man, without even a voice. She got up and crossed the room, went out into the hall, put on her shoes and opened the door, strode down to the road, and opened the rubbish bin. Bent over. It was dark, and she had her back to the street light and she could scarcely see a thing. Which bag was it in? The one on top, or the one that had fallen slightly to the side? Some were from Irfan's shop, plain white with no advertisements, but she found a couple from Europris with the green logo. Now, try to remember, which bag had she taken out from under the sink? She rummaged around in the rubbish, squeezed the bags one after the other, trying to feel what was inside. Eventually, she pulled one out. The lid slammed into place. She was about to turn back to the house when Olaf appeared again, on his way back. He glanced at the bag dangled in her hand and she blushed.

'Ah,' he said with a smile. 'We sometimes have to dig out things from the rubbish that we've thrown away by accident too. Was it a lottery ticket? With the winning number?'

She pulled the bag to her chest and shook her head.

'Took the wrong one by mistake,' she whispered. 'I leave the bags out in the hall, and some need to go down into the basement and others out to the rubbish. I'm having a clear-out.'

'You're not thinking of moving as well, are you?' he asked.

'No, no, I'll never move.'

She turned away from him and trudged up to the house, closed the door. Her cheeks were still burning with shame. She was fond of Olaf. She could not imagine life without him, her kind elderly neighbour, who always had a good word to say and who maybe looked out for her, checked to see if the light was on in the morning, a sure sign that she was still alive. Or kept an eye out in case the house went up in flames or someone broke in. He knew that she could not scream.

Back in the house, she opened the bag of rubbish. The envelope had been pushed down and was pressed against a moist potato peeling, and some eggs that had passed their sell-by date. Some of them had broken. She plucked it out with two fingers and went straight over to the wood burner, put it down on the grey ash beside some charcoal, got the firelighter from the table. But the envelope was damp and would not burn.

Chapter 3

Her face came alive as she talked. She captivated him, despite her lack of voice. She radiated sincerity. Every now and then she held up a hand and made a gesture in the air as if to underline something, to help herself, to create the illusion of sound. Her whispering made him lower his own voice. He listened with such intensity that he could no doubt have heard a cat creeping up on its prey.

'You told no one,' Sejer said. 'Not your neighbours, or your colleagues, or Irfan in the shop or anyone else you knew. Nor Rikard Josef in Berlin. Of course the letter you found in your mailbox was a threat. That came from nowhere, like a bolt out of the blue. But you confided in no one.'

Ragna could see his face clearly in the light from the computer screen. The deep lines that ran from his nostrils to the corners of his mouth, the straight eyebrows that had once been dark but now were laced with silver. He was there the whole time, always present and near. He did not take his eyes off her, was never tempted to turn towards the screen, to see what was happening there. His phone flashed red occasionally, but he did not answer. She felt like a fish that had been caught in a net, and she lay softly against the fine mesh. There was a pile of papers on his desk, and a notepad, where he sometimes scribbled something down with such speed that she wondered if he wrote shorthand.

'It was embarrassing,' she whispered. 'I felt ashamed.'

She could see that he was considering her answer. That he did not leap to any conclusions. That he certainly seemed to understand her. What would Lars and Gunnhild and all the others have thought about the letter? What would they have said, how would they have reassured her? Other than smile about it, dismiss it as nonsense? They would never understand how much the letter had unsettled her. It must be something about her, they would think, something that had made some malicious soul choose Ragna Riegel, of all people. Point her out, without pity, tip her balance. It was not random, they would think, because nothing frightens people more than randomness. There had to be a reason, or some form of culpability. If they found no reason, no blame, then anything could happen, then any kind of precaution was pointless – hiding, keeping one's nose clean.

Ragna observed the inspector thinking. He understood the gravity of the situation, her distress, she could see it in his grey eyes. Not that she had never thought about death. Dear God, she had thought about death. But when she got the letter, she thought about it all the time, from minute to minute. She thought about the envelope that had not been franked. That meant he had driven there, or walked along Kirkelina. He had stopped at her mailbox, stared up at the house, watched for shadows in the window to check if he had been seen. Then he had hurried off into the darkening evening, or night, if it had been night, with his coat collar turned up and his hands deep in his pockets, with a plan, some intention that she could not fathom. She wondered if maybe he had tormented cats when he was a boy. The thought made her shudder.

'Did you think of anyone in particular?' Sejer asked. 'Someone you once knew or had a relationship with, or worked with or a neighbour, someone's toes you may have stepped on, a distant relative?'

'I weigh practically nothing,' Ragna whispered. 'If I stepped on anyone's toes, they wouldn't notice, no more than they would a mouse.' She pouted when she said 'mouse', and smiled at him.

'You're certainly not a mouse,' Sejer said. 'But there are sensitive souls out there who are offended by the slightest thing. I have to look everywhere, in the past as well. What about Rikard Josef's father? You haven't said anything about him yet.'

'There's nothing to tell. He would be over seventy now.'

'So you count the years?'

She felt mortified about everything again. Someone had found her in the multitude and callously turned a spotlight on her, a light she was not able to ignore. The house where she had grown up on Kirkelina, her own little nest that she loved, was now left standing in the autumn dark with all the lights on like an American weatherboard ready for Christmas. She was exposed for all the world to see. Even though she was not guilty of anything, she was convinced that the man who had tormented her had something on her.

For a brief moment, Sejer caught sight of a kind of defiance, as though she wanted to say to him, I know why I'm sitting here but I don't want to grovel. And he was not asking her to. They would go through this together, he without judging, and she without losing her dignity. That was what he wanted. It was what Ragna needed.

'Your son,' Sejer said. 'Was he the result of a brief relationship?'

'He's the result of a single night. I was at a party and I drank far too much. Even though I hid myself away in a corner, one person found me. I didn't dare let any awkward teenage boys near me. But they didn't want to be near me anyway, I had none of the things they wanted.'

'What do you think they wanted?'

'Don't ask stupid questions.'

'So,' Sejer prompted. 'One night. And then you never saw him again?'

'Oh yes, I did, a couple of times.'

'Do you ever think about him?'

'Very occasionally. But I have a big chest of drawers in my bedroom, and in the bottom drawer is a photograph that he took of me one day when we were walking through the park. A black-and-white photograph that he enlarged and wanted me to keep. He said that I should look at the photograph and know that I had been seen, that I deserved to be seen. I was never beautiful,' she hastened to say, 'not even when I was sixteen, but he somehow managed to catch me at a good moment. In a favourable light. No one else had managed that. I look like an angel in that picture.' After a pause, she added: 'He's a photographer.'

She looked down again, regretted what she had said. She had blown her own trumpet. Saying 'angel' was going too far. She blushed violently and did not want to look up again for a good while.

'But the photograph is still in a drawer? Even though it is the most beautiful version of you that you've ever seen?'

'The photograph,' she whispered curtly, 'is nothing more than pure chance. A slight mist. The setting sun. Things like that.'

'But you haven't thrown it away. What did you say his name was?'

'Walther Eriksson. He lives in Stockholm, he's lived there for years. I guess he's retired now.'

'So you do keep track, all the same?'

She looked away. He had never seen such a thin neck, you could probably break it with one hand.

'My world is very small,' she admitted. 'I don't have much to do with other people, only those from work. I spend a fair amount of time online, and there's stuff about him there. He's won a few prizes for his portraits. No, not a few, a lot.'

'So, a good photographer,' Sejer said, 'an excellent one, in fact. Good photographers don't win prizes because of chance. They have a good eye. A special kind of relationship with their subjects and good timing. They know when to fire.'

He leaned forward, and said emphatically: 'Sooner or later, that picture should be hung on the wall.'

Sometimes he chose to say nothing. Not to create uncertainty, but he did use silence as a tactic. It could trigger a body language that told him something about the person, or they might talk too much, get nervous, and give themselves away. But now it was more a case of giving her space and an opportunity to compose herself. To process and defend the things she had confided in him, things she had never told anyone. When he said nothing, her eyes roamed around the room. She noticed things, the way quiet people do, and because she had problems with communicating, she was a good listener.

'I like Grace Kelly too,' she whispered, and nodded at a photograph on the wall. 'I like old American films. They're buried together, the prince and her, in the palace. There are always flowers on the grave. And there are always people there.'

Ragna was given one of Sejer's rarest smiles.

'That's my wife, Elise. She's buried too, and there are always flowers on the grave. But there are not many people there, just Frank and me.'

'Oh,' she whispered. 'But she's like her. She looks so like her.'

'Everyone says that,' Sejer replied proudly.

'Oh,' she whispered again.

She gazed at the portrait for a while, then looked at Sejer, then back at the portrait. And again she felt ashamed that she had spoken about her own portrait in a way that suggested it was beautiful.

'Elise?'

He nodded.

Silence followed. He sat there looking at her nylon work coat; it was far too big, he could barely guess what her figure was like.

'Do you often lose control, Ragna?' he asked, out of the blue.

She laughed, a few short breaths.

'Look at me. Listen to my voice. Does it look like it?'

Her eyes met his, she was surer of him.

'No,' he had to admit. 'But you do have that most important of instincts in you – rage. Everyone does. Because at some point or other, we all find ourselves in a situation where we need it. The adrenaline, that is. It makes us strong and fast. Men have it more than women, of course; men have to go out and hunt, they're the ones most likely to encounter wild animals. But you have a bit too, don't you? That's why you're sitting here now, isn't it?'

'Yes,' she admitted. 'But women have other weapons as well, only they're not often aware of it, or just what they are capable of. Goodness, Gunnhild at work bought some pepper spray, which she always keeps in her handbag. So in that moment when she's panicking she has to rummage around in her bag. Get the lid off, aim and hit the mark, while all the time some lunatic is threatening her with a knife.'

'I can see the problem,' he nodded.

'But there's something else that will always scare an attacker,' she continued. 'Something that all women have. That they don't need to look for, and yet they always hesitate to use.'

'And what's that?'

'A scream.'

That reminded him of many cases, many women. A rape could take place in a bedroom while other people were enjoying themselves in the living room. Women had been raped in doorways while people walked past on the street. That paralysing fear. The fear that things might escalate.

'It's best to keep still. Not to move a finger. It will soon be over.'

She started to become more aware of people in a different way. She had always thought they were so similar, especially in the autumn. They all dressed the same, whether they were women or men, in down jackets and denim, black, dark blue and anonymous. Teenagers all dressed the same as well, though not as many of them came into Europris, and she was not out on the street much. But now they were no longer a homogenous mass. The troll had always had many heads, and now she could see each one of them.

She was working the early shift and was on the till. She kept the customers at a distance with a tight smile, but she nodded to the amount displayed on the card terminal, and with her hand on the box of carrier bags, looked up with questioning eyes. No one said anything when they were at the till. And practically no one looked at her either, she was simply part of the card terminal. But now Ragna studied each individual carefully. That is to say, not the women so much, and they were definitely the majority, but all the others, the men, to see if they were sending out signals, something she should notice, that extra something, be it a cryptic smile or disturbed expression. Something special about their body language, an opaque comment, or for that matter, a distinct smell, even though she realised she was no bloodhound. She could smell neither fear nor aggression. But there were no men like that, there was no one who stood out. She did not see anyone who might be the anonymous letter writer, who was maybe out to get her, or to get attention. They were no longer the same, though; despite the down jackets and denim, she saw them clearly now. She saw the subtleties and details. Even the regular customers, the ones she thought she had studied and pigeonholed once and for all, were given another assessment. No, it was none of them. Could a young father looking for a cheap toboggan, with a toddler in tow, be her tormentor? Or an older woman looking for Jamie Oliver's new frying pan, which normally cost twelve hundred kroner, but they sold for half-price? There's something I've missed, she thought, something I've forgotten, something from way back. But she didn't like to think about the past, she had enough as it was with the present, her head was full of the moment, the sounds and smells, the stream of people, it filled her completely. Everyone said that we only use parts of our brain, hah! She knew better than that. Every single cell was being used, there were no empty pockets in Ragna's head.

She let the products glide past on the short conveyor belt and was absolutely certain that her harasser from Kirkelina would show up at some point or other. Suddenly he would be standing there, staring at her, perhaps with a knowing smile. To take the game a step further, because it was a game, after all. To observe his victim close at hand, to relish her ignorance and vulnerability. Maybe say a few words that she would not understand the significance of to begin with, but then, a few hours later, it would dawn on her. Dear God. It was him, it was him! There was scarcely a metre between her and the customers when she sat at the till, and she used every second well. As a result she got more tired than she usually did, her senses were on full alert. When the long shift was finally over, she had to count the money, make sure it was right, which it always was, she was very careful. And then the minutes it took to walk to the bus stop, get on the bus, find her usual seat, the third back on the left-hand side. Relieved and frustrated at the same time because she had not picked up on anything. Her suspicion had not been aroused, she had not received any cryptic signs. That meant that she had blended into the crowd, like a fish in a shoal. She sat slumped against the bus window, with the knowledge that when she got off forty minutes later and walked the last few metres along Kirkelina, she would have to open the mailbox with 'Riegel' on it.

The street lamp by her driveway came on at dusk and she was careful not to block the light as she lifted the lid. When she stared down into the box, she nurtured the burning defiance that would turn to rage if she found another anonymous letter. But there was no new letter. She gathered up the newspaper and advertisements, a begging letter from the Norwegian Air Ambulance Foundation and an electricity bill, and when she then sat down on her chair, by the standard lamp, she read the local news to see if any of the other readers had experienced the same as her, and if they had written about it on 'My Page'. It could not just be her! If other people had received a similar message, then it would mean nothing, but if she was the only one, she could not see it as anything but a real threat. If it was a threat at all. The message was concise, that she was going to die, and that was true enough. Someone had just felt the need to point it out, some disturbed soul, perhaps. Some poor lonely person who craved attention, or someone who was going to die themselves very soon. She flicked through the paper from start to finish, and when she got to the obituaries, she read them with great interest. Strange, isn't it, she thought, I don't know anyone, no one in this town at all. She didn't want to know anyone, either. But she got it into her head that whoever had sent the message was sitting there reading the obituaries too, with equal interest, and his fingers would be black with ink, like her own, when he put the newspaper to one side. And that's the way it should be, she thought, as she made her way through the list of names. The suffering of the world should leave its mark, not just flash on a screen. She never read the news online, she liked the sound of the paper rustling as she turned the page. She remembered that when her father read something upsetting, he would sometimes shake the paper hard, without mercy, as if it were a naughty child. Then it was not just a faint rustling, it was hard and loud.

He'll get bored of the game, Ragna thought, after a while. Soon I'll be able to shake off this unease, laugh about it and forget it. It will die down, in the same way that the memory of Walther Eriksson has burned out, and my grief that Rikard Josef has gone to Berlin and doesn't contact me, other than sending garish cards with ready-printed words. That had also died down. The distance between them had become normal, a habit. That was how her life was now. She reflected on her own cowardice for a moment, it was like a cold shower. Why had she never taken him up on it, demanded an explanation? Had she neglected him, was he perhaps embarrassed about her, or was he just a man who found intimacy and contact difficult? But then what about the hotel, she thought in the next moment. A successful, five-star hotel, with all the guests and staff, he had to deal with them constantly. He would have to talk to them, care about them and serve them. Did I treat him badly? Is there something essential that I didn't give him? No! Her throat tightened. She felt irritated, she did not want to think about all this again, it was that stupid message making her so sensitive. She reminded herself that intimacy and contact were not something that was automatic in every family. Some people didn't want it, some people weren't good at it. Lots of people just upped and left, some even went to the other side of the world. They did not necessarily leave because they were bitter, or because they hated their roots. After all, Rikard Josef sent Christmas and birthday cards, and she sent him cards too, there was still a line of communication. But ringing or sending an email would be crossing a boundary; it would seem confrontational and invasive, she felt. Not that she had his email address, just a mobile number that she never dared to ring. And anyway, he had never accused her of anything, never expressed any kind of anger or hurt, and she certainly was not going to disinherit him for that. I don't have any claims, she realised, he's his own boss. Rikard Josef just wanted to live his own life in Hotel Dormero. As the top manager.

She had got into the habit of glancing down to the road whenever she passed the window. Not that she expected to catch the letter writer red-handed, bent over the mailbox, but something had come into her life that made her nervous and agitated. It was like her body was fevered. She could not help it, she kept watching what was going on in a new way, and even the planes overhead were studied carefully. There was a fair amount of traffic along Kirkelina. She heard the sound of the cars, a steady hum, especially in the afternoon. The new articulated buses that were now in use were eighteen metres long and so could not pull into the bus stop and had to stand in the road, causing a jam. She thought about the letter writer again, she thought about him more and more. He had attached himself like a burr. How pathetic, she thought, how sad. A loser, an anonymous coward. Riff-raff. And yet she could not bring herself to tell anyone, not Olaf next door, not her colleagues at work. Every now and then it struck her that he might not be an idiot at all, but a perfectly ordinary man with a wife and children, someone who wanted for nothing in his life. He just had a secret perversion. That frightened her even more. Often when she sat thinking like this, she felt her nails digging into the palms of her hands, her own modest form of anger, which she did not know how to channel, other than back on herself. Going to bed at night was a good thing. Another day without threats. She would often stand for a long time by the open bedroom window to cool down, as her cheeks were so warm. She must not fuel this flame, not at any price.

But one evening she sat down to write to her son in Berlin, all the same. Just a short letter, nothing much. He might wonder why she had written, after all, she had never done it before, and it was not Christmas or his birthday; she was not selling the house or moving, and she was not seriously ill, nor was she getting married. It was of course connected to the message, it made her behave differently, think differently. She took care to keep a light tone. The short greeting must not make him worried or signal something new, or in any way come across as a demand that he respond immediately. But she felt impelled to say hello, to remind him that she was sitting there all alone in the old house where he had grown up. And that he was still part of her daily life, in her thoughts, he must never think otherwise. But she wanted to create a space for herself in his life too, it was never too late and it was important, they were both still young. In her mind, as she sat there writing as beautifully as she could, she was standing in the lobby of the Hotel Dormero, where she had never been before. In December, the staff would decorate a tree with lovely twinkling lights, for the enjoyment of all who stepped inside. She was sure that it was her son who oversaw this. That he decided where the tree should stand, and how it should be decorated. She could just picture him, standing there directing the staff in a firm voice, pointing, dressed in an elegant, dark suit. He might even have a gold badge with 'Director' written on it. Or 'Manager'. Suddenly, she was not sure of her son's title.

Dear Rikard Josef,

Just sending a quick hello from the cold North. Christmas is approaching and I'm sure you have more than enough to do at the hotel. We are already putting Santa Clauses and angels made in China and Taiwan on the shelves, and Christmas songs play on a loop from morning to night. The grown-ups are stressed, but Rikard, you should see the children, with their red cheeks and sparkling eyes. Thinking of you at this busy time.

41

She signed the letter 'Mum' and the image of him disappeared. She felt that she had crossed a line. She was afraid he would feel guilty. Perhaps she should wait and send it nearer to Christmas.

But she put a stamp on the envelope all the same and left it on the sideboard in the hall. It was a thin, shiny white envelope that would brighten the bottom of his mailbox on Landsberger Allee when he put his hand in to fish it out. He would turn it over and see the Norwegian stamp. There was no mention of the death threat she had received. Not a word.

Chapter 4

'Things that I had accepted long ago, suddenly became an issue again,' Ragna whispered. 'Like Rikard Josef. The fact that we were not a part of each other's lives and I had never dared ask him for an explanation. That he had just left, betrayed me in a way. That I had lost my voice, and never went out. Other people with bigger disabilities were out all the time, with their sticks or in their wheelchairs. Everything was suddenly so painfully clear. Someone had seen me in the crowd, despite me doing everything I could to be invisible.'

She smiled apologetically after each confession. She was keen to explain herself, but also sorry to burden Sejer, to take up his time and space, even though that was unavoidable as she was being questioned.

'You must have looked for answers,' Sejer said. 'Did you go to bed at night relieved that you had received no more threats? Perhaps you expected nothing more to happen. Did you ever think there was something you could do?'

She put her hand to the scar on her neck. Presumably she could feel it under her fingertips like a thick thread.

'I thought about going out into town,' she admitted. 'Walking around the streets. Making myself visible. Going into shops and cafes, sitting on a bench by the market square, feeding the pigeons. I considered going to the cinema in the evening, or walking along the river. Making sure I was visible to everyone all the time. As if to say to him: come and get me.'

'But you didn't do it?'

'I lost my nerve. Didn't dare.'

'What did you think would happen if you did show yourself like that?'

She looked over at Frank, asleep on his blanket. Oh, how she envied the dog, such a simple life. She wanted to lie like that, curled up on a blanket while her master took responsibility for everything.

'Nothing would have happened,' she said. 'It would have been a pointless act. No one would have noticed.'

'But you think he would have known if you were out and about?'

'It's possible,' she whispered. 'We'd bump into each other sooner or later. It's not a big town.'

Her replies to his questions were simple and believable. It did not occur to her to lie. Or not to answer. Or to get angry. She had never had so much attention, had never felt seen in this way. Not since Walther took that portrait of her when she was sixteen. And Sejer showed no sign of impatience, judgement, criticism or scorn. Nor did she think that this calm was just one of many sides, which he used whenever he was questioning someone, to get the desired result. He had no other impulsive or unpredictable sides that only those closest to him saw, when he was happy or angry. He was a silent force.

'Frank,' she whispered with feeling, looking at the dog. 'Do you want to stay with me tonight?'

The dog heard her and opened his eyes. Despite her lack of volume, he recognised the intensity, that she was begging for something. He got up and padded over the floor, put his head on her lap, heavy and devoted. Slavered on her green nylon shop coat again.

'He's like you,' she whispered to the inspector.

'Should I take that as a compliment?'

'Yes, you can if you want to. You say the same thing. When you're not speaking, if you see what I mean. Your phone,' she said. 'It's flashing. On two lines. They're trying to get hold of you.'

'They're always trying. But I'm busy right now.'

'Do they call at night as well?'

'Sometimes. In special cases, when there's no time to lose.'

'Was I a special case?'

He pushed the telephone further away, as if to demonstrate that she was more important at the moment.

'Would you like to be a special case?'

She did not answer, just blushed deeply with embarrassment.

'We were called out in the morning,' he reminded her. 'I was already up and at work. Here, in the office with Frank. The phone started flashing, all the lines were flashing, and the call-out was on all the screens in the station, and sent to all the units close to Kirkelina. In other words, everyone knew about it. Even if it wasn't you who called.'

Ragna turned away from Frank. He went back to his blanket and lay down again, curled up and went to sleep. Some of what had happened, and the reason why she was sitting here, played through her mind like film images. The memory silenced her. She had felt so safe in Sejer's office, secure behind the closed door, with his deep voice. Not that she had suppressed what had happened, she had simply concentrated on answering his questions. Telling the truth as best she could.

'Let's talk about something else,' Sejer said. 'One fine day, or perhaps it was a terrible day, when you were sixteen, you had to walk through the door and tell your parents you were pregnant. Was that difficult for you?'

'No,' she said with a smile. 'I had nothing to be afraid of. It was a very simple message, I only needed a few words. I put my hands on my stomach and said that I was expecting a baby. In a few months' time. Can we stay here with you? I asked. Because the father lives in Stockholm, and he doesn't have space for us. My father's eyes were bigger and shinier than I'd ever seen them before. Mummy just patted me on the cheek and said, oh, Ragna, Ragna. You have your secrets, don't you? As we all do. Then we laughed a little, I think, because having a baby is something to celebrate.'

'I'm sure they had some thoughts about Walther Eriksson,' Sejer said. 'I mean, after all, he was well over forty and already had a family.'

'I didn't tell them about Walther,' she replied.

'But surely they asked? They were going to be grandparents.'

'My parents were very unassuming people,' she whispered. 'Modest and extremely sensitive. Generous. Never critical, never demanding. Mummy asked if I was happy, and I was. That was all the reassurance she needed. They were always so busy with each other, because my father was often unwell, and now finally I was going to have something of my own. She did give me a questioning look, but I just closed my eyes and shook my head in response. She immediately understood the situation. The father, Walther, was not going to play any part and so was not important. It would be just the four of us in the house at Kirkelina, no one else. So there was no need to say any more about it. There's so much talk in this world,' she added. 'About anything and everything. I had my baby. He was healthy and they were happy about it. Maybe they realised he was the only grandchild they would have. I think they felt blessed.'

'Yes, indeed,' Sejer said. 'There's so much talk, especially here at the station. But I had the impression, certainly up until now, that you wanted to explain yourself. How else could we give you a fair trial? Or do you take that for granted?'

'Oh! No.'

She looked at him horrified.

He made a quick note and then put down the pen.

'How did they react when he went to Berlin and then broke all contact with you?'

'We're still in contact!' she insisted. 'Just not very often. Rikard Josef has ambitions for his life, and thought it would be easier to do that somewhere else. People emigrate, some go much further than he has. And lots of them never come home again. He's a free spirit. A true free spirit!'

And there it was, he thought, the first sign of irritation. He had hit a nerve.

'I assume you have some photographs of him,' he said. 'From when he was a boy. And perhaps also as a teenager, before he went abroad. Is he like Walther?'

'Yes, just like Walther. He has nothing from me. Not a line, not a hair.'

'He's an adult now,' Sejer said. 'And not very communicative, only sends cards with printed messages. So I'm guessing you don't have any recent photographs of him?'

'No,' she had to admit. 'I use my imagination.'

'A long time has passed. Maybe he's more like you than you realise. Would you like that to be the case?'

'Let him be free of that,' she said. 'He is like Walther, full stop.'

'You mean, be free of you?'

Ragna stared down into her lap, at her hands that were lying there. She did not want to talk about this. It was clear that she found the fact that her son had left her hard to bear, but she had accepted it. However, Sejer also felt that she knew the explanation. And she did not want to share it with him. Or, perhaps she believed it had nothing to do with the matter at hand, and that was why she was able to put a lid on that part of her life. But everything is connected to what's happened in some way or other, he thought. Not many people would be capable of the crime she had committed. So every little detail was important.

'Shall we change the subject?' he asked.

'Yes, please.'

He pushed the water jug across the table. He had noticed that she tended to forget to drink, and when her mouth was dry, it was harder to understand her. She took a long drink, then dried her lips. He saw that she had tiny freckles on the back of her hand, and thin fingers with no rings.

'What if I were to ask you who your favourite person was, in all the world?' he said in a friendly voice.

'Daddy.'

'But he's dead.'

'Do you think I've stopped loving him because of that?'

Her reply was instant, and he was annoyed by his own stupidity. Who did he love most in the world? Elise, of course, and she was no longer there either.

'And your mother?' he asked carefully. 'Does she also hold a special place?'

'She was always so focused on my father,' she said. 'She wasn't available.'

'And are you bitter about that?'

'No, not really. I generally focused on Daddy too, he took up so much room. He was electric. Do you understand what I mean by electric?'

'A lot of energy?'

'He made the whole house light up. He heated every room. But he also short-circuited every now and then, and then everything was cold and dark.'

Sejer wrote some more notes.

'In what way was he ill?'

She did not answer for a while, looked the other way.

'Something to do with his immune system,' she said. 'He was very prone to infections. I was left to my own devices a lot of the time. Mummy was always busy, and she worked so hard. What about your parents? Are they still alive?'

'You don't want to talk about your parents any more?'

'No, you can tell me something about *your* parents now.'

He wondered what he should say about them. They were both dead, but had been hard-working, decent old-fashioned people with robust morals. They had been strict and had always expected a lot of him. Not in terms of his career, but in terms of his behaviour. They had brought him up to be polite, as they felt that was one of the most important aspects of being educated, but was not something that everyone learned. He thought through all of this, but decided to tell her about something else.

'My mother's hobby was pottery,' he said. 'She liked to make small clay figures. When they were dry, she took them to a place in town and had them fired. They turned red, like terracotta. She never glazed them. She put them on the windowsill or on a shelf, as ornaments, and there they stood. Our house was full of her figures.'

'Were they nice?'

'They were crooked and bent, and pretty awful, to be honest,' he said. 'She had no talent whatsoever. But we said nothing, my father and I, because she got so much pleasure from making them and maybe even liked them herself. Or perhaps the feeling of the soft clay in her hands helped to clear her mind. A little self-deception is a human right, don't you think?'

Ragna smiled and agreed.

'Have you kept any of them?'

'Only three. They're on the windowsill in my kitchen.'

'A mother, father and child,' she whispered. 'You're an only child, like me?'

'Yes.'

'Were they happy that you joined the police?'

Sejer's smile was wider than usual. He looked first at Ragna, then down at the table.

'My father was a reserved man who never said much. He gave a short nod when I told him, then he quickly disappeared into another room.'

'Into another room?' Ragna exclaimed. 'Have you ever wondered what he did in the other room?'

'I should imagine he went to the window, maybe even opened it. And that he stood there staring out at the garden. He probably wanted to cool down, as he was flushed with pride. Mother took every opportunity to tell people. Every guest who came to the house was met with the news: did I tell you that Konrad has joined the police?'

Ragna laughed as loudly as was possible for her. Her thin body shook.

'And your mother made a special clay figure for you.'

'She did. A big one.'

'Now I feel I know them,' she whispered.

'And your parents,' Sejer ventured, 'were they proud of you?'

'I think so,' was her modest reply. 'Of course they knew nothing about what would happen.'

Chapter 5

She had started to count her steps.

Down to the rubbish bin by the road was forty-eight steps. From the house over to Irfan's shop, sixty-four; to the bus stop, one hundred and fifty-seven. Counting gave her a sense of control, this was her territory and she paced it out precisely. Often when she went to the bus stop in the morning, she was surprised that the number was always the same. Never one hundred and sixty-eight, or one hundred and forty-nine. She looked down at her feet in their small shoes, to think that her steps were so precise. And what would she do if the number did change? Because that would mean that her overview was slipping, that her body had been knocked out of its natural, measured rhythm, that life was no longer safe. That external powers were taking over. She was walking back from the bus stop, her bag over her shoulder. It was heavy. She had taken four packets of twisted, purple candles, a goat's milk soap and some cheap shampoo from the shop. Her purchases were written down and deducted from her pay. She stopped some distance from the driveway, stood there and looked around. She saw a big removal van in front of the Teigens' house, and several men pushing and carrying. Going in and out of the old house, which was more or less identical to her own. The Thai family would be moving in before Christmas, with their own tables and chairs, and, according to Olaf, a massage table. Sooner or later she would bump into them, perhaps in Irfan's shop, and she would have to embarrass them, as was the case with most other people she met. She would whisper her name, and then give them her well-practised tight smile, and if she felt like it, tell them about how she came to lose her voice. It would take no more than a few meagre seconds, then it would be done. But it never ceased to upset her. The fact that something so minor could knock her off course in this way. The Teigens had taken down the living-room curtains, she noted, and the rooms that were now being emptied seemed unnaturally bright. She compared them with her own windows, which had a warmer, welcoming glow. My house, she thought, and started to walk again. My own house. She got to the drive and opened the mailbox. There was of course something there. In fact, she could not remember it ever being empty. She took out the newspaper first, then the plain envelope addressed to 'RIEGEL'.

She looked quickly up and down Kirkelina, to check if anyone had seen her, but there was no one there. She glanced over the road to Irfan's shop – there was still light in the windows. And there was only a faint light in Olaf's windows, so perhaps they were out. And the Teigens on the other side of the road were in the middle of moving. A car drove past, and then another, and the gust lifted the hem of her coat. She looked at the back of the envelope. The rubbish bin with its heavy lid was beside her. She should just throw the letter in without reading it. She was above all this nonsense, the letter belonged with the eggshells and leftovers, the letter was rotten. And she would slam the lid shut with such force that the removal men would think she had fired a shot. Then she would march quickly up to the house, forty-eight steps, put the newspaper on the table and demonstrate her defiance by pulling a face at whoever was trying to invade her space. Supper would be made. She would rattle around with the pots and pans and slam the cupboard doors. She would stride around the house like a general. She would read the newspaper. She had more important things to do than be scared of some idiot who was probably just bored and alone. He definitely had no friends; he was not someone who had anything to give. No one wanted to listen to him or go anywhere near him.

But what if she did all that? If she threw away the letter unread, how would she then manage to calm down? Would she just sit in a chair all night and wonder what the new message said? Would she lie in the dark under the duvet, her imagination running wild? No, she would not. She needed to keep up with him, know what he was planning. She would open the envelope, read it quickly and then throw it in the fire. Even though part of her brain said that would be basically the same as letting him in. She might as well open the door so he could step inside. She tore open the envelope all the same. She was agitated and flushed, angry and scared all at once.

The piece of paper was the same as the last one, folded double, the letters just as big and straight.

'IT'S NOT LONG NOW.'

She stood there without moving for a long time, deeply regretting that she had been foolish enough to read the message. She crushed it into a hard paper ball, so it would burn better. Then she trudged up to the house, let herself in. She threw the letter in the burner, lit a match, held it to the paper and closed the heavy door. Watched the flames through the glass. The fire devoured the paper ball with impressive speed. Wonderful, she thought. She had quite simply cremated him and all that he stood for. Nothing could annihilate like fire could. She put two big logs into the burner as though to make a statement, and stayed there on her knees until they started to burn too.

It was perhaps something she should report to the police, she thought later, when she had finally sunk down into her favourite armchair. But she had destroyed both letters, she realised, so she had nothing to show. And they were not likely to do anything anyway, it was autumn, and dark, and people were roaming the streets with all their issues and anger. Women were being beaten up and abused by their husbands, children were being neglected, the powers that be had enough on their plates. And this person had not laid a hand on her. And anyway, she told herself, I've never been the hysterical type. I'm not the sort of person to waste valuable resources on this kind of nonsense, it's below me. She put the dishwasher on, and tried to settle down in front of the television, but was overcome with regret that she had burned the letters. There would be a letter number three, she was certain of that, and she would definitely keep that one.

Number three, and four and five. And what then?
Where would it end? Should she perhaps inform
everyone close to her that some madman was after
her? What if he was one of the people in her small
circle? What did he actually want? Her fear, her life?
Better instead to curl up in a corner, turn up the volume
on the television, close the curtains and not let so
much as a strip of light in.

She went out into the hall to check that she had
locked the door and that the security chain was on,
even though the chain itself was so thin it could easily
be cut with pliers. Sometimes if the doorbell rang in the
evening, she did not dare to answer. Depending on how
late it was, and this had changed over the years. When
she was younger, she would open the door until ten,
but now she became anxious if it was after eight,
certainly in the autumn, when it was dark. Anyone who
came by car usually parked by the roadside and walked
up to the house. It was not easy to gauge if there was
enough room to turn in the driveway, especially in
winter. And when it came to clearing the snow, she was
useless, a shovel full of wet snow weighed too much for
her. She had never owned a car, so she trampled a
narrow path down to the road, and tried to clear around
the rubbish bin and mailbox as best she could.
Sometimes Olaf took pity on her and would take a few
turns on his Honda snowblower. But so far, there had
been no snow, just darkness, and the lonely street lamp
at the end of her drive. Every time she passed it, she
noted the wear and tear. Sooner or later it would come
down, but not in her time, she hoped, even though she
could see that it leaned more and more for each year
that passed.

She stood by the window. There were Olaf and Dolly going for a walk in their high-viz jackets. She noticed that he glanced up at her house, and she appreciated that. It meant he thought about her, that she was part of his universe, just as he and Dolly were a part of hers. He continued on to the Teigens' house where the removal men were still busy. Maybe he wanted to say goodbye and wish them well, which was something she had not even thought about, just as she would never contemplate going over to the house to welcome the new family when they moved in. But of course Olaf did, because he was nosy. Oh, I'm being mean now, she thought, there's nothing wrong with wanting to know the neighbours, I'm just a coward. Arrogant and uninterested. She sat down again and thought about the empty rooms in the Teigens' house. How cold it would be when everything had been loaded into the removal van, how dusty and faded. The walls full of holes and the ceiling lamps giving off a garish light – perhaps the glass covers were full of dead flies, her own were. She could not imagine anything as wretched as an empty house. The walls would have their secrets. Daylight would flood in through the bare windows and reveal all the wear and tear, all the footsteps across the floors, all the doors that had been opened and closed, sometimes with great force. Worn thresholds, discoloured bathroom porcelain that could no longer be bleached clean, the odd mirror on the wall stained brown by the years. If anything of beauty had existed between the walls, it would not be visible. Only the decay would be visible, the damage, the bad days. A bit like an old skeleton, Ragna thought, which had even more to tell about a life once lived than an empty house. Man or woman, young or old, ill or injured. Lifestyle, diet. I want to be buried when I die, like Mummy and Daddy. My skeleton will lie there with all its bumps and wounds. And in theory, it would be possible to dig up the skeleton and re-examine it. The bones would be the proof that she had once lived and she wanted there to be proof. The alternative, the burning heat, meant total annihilation.

I will never move, Ragna determined. She looked at everything around her, the pictures, the furniture and rugs, the cushions on the sofa, carefully plumped and positioned in the same way every day, and the cosy, folded blanket. The large photograph of her parents from a time when they were Hans and Signe and did not know what the future held. At the point the picture was taken, they knew nothing about Ragna, because she did not exist anywhere, she was just a possibility they had chosen to explore, and, she believed, had not regretted. Nor did they know anything about Rikard Josef at that point. She was filled with melancholy when she looked at the picture of her parents. It really was possible to be that happy for a few brief, innocent moments. She had looked after the house, and it had not fallen into the hands of strangers. She could see that it was tired, but it was old after all. Her parents had never redecorated, they did not have the means, and she had only replaced the furniture and a few other things. But it was just her, padding quietly around – no one else really came to the house. Only Gunnhild, who had popped by a couple of times when she was ill. That's how small my world is, Ragna reflected. Some travel to the other side of the world to meet new people, others make new bonds by arranging parties where they make a lot of noise, laugh, raise their glasses and spill their secrets. These thoughts made her look down at her body. She had taken the baggy green shop coat off and hung it on the back of a chair, but she was still wearing the sweater that almost reached her knees. It was machine-knitted from synthetic wool and had gone bobbly after several washes, even though she had done it on a delicate cycle. She wondered what Rikard Josef had thought when he received the letter, in an unexpected move so long before Christmas. Did he see it as a plea for contact or an accusation? Would he give something himself as a result? What if Hotel Dormero was doing badly and he was forced to find another job, would he let her know? She assumed not. If he had had a knock, he might feel ashamed and keep her at a distance. In the way that she was ashamed of the knock she had taken. Someone had sentenced her to death.

'IT'S NOT LONG NOW.'

She had thick red curtains in front of the bedroom window that went all the way to the floor. There were lead weights in the hem so that they would fall properly and look good. When she went to bed in the evening, she opened the window – be it summer or winter, she had to have fresh air. It made no difference if it was freezing cold. She liked to lie under the duvet and listen to the world outside, feel the cool air breezing in. Sometimes, in autumn, wild storms made the small cluster of trees round the back of the house into an attacker, as the wind hurled cones and branches at the wall. She often hoped for a storm. She liked it when nature showed its strength, because she found the thought that people were the only controlling force too alarming. If the sun wanted to burn out, if the ocean wanted to flood the land and drown everything there, down to the smallest beast, that was fine. She would bow to that, bow with humility. Her bed was right under the window. On occasion, she had even felt the rain on her face. Some mornings she found dry leaves on the floor that had blown into the room, and in winter, she had even woken to tiny snow drifts against the skirting. Then she would make a snowball, drop it into the toilet, and stand there watching it melt.

Now she was standing by the window thinking. It was midnight, and she was about to go to bed. She decided that she was not going to open it, that from now on she would close the world out and protect herself against everything, even nature. She arranged the curtains, puffed up her pillow and crept in under the duvet. But after she had lain awake for some time, she realised that the unfamiliar silence made her edgy. She was used to hearing cars passing every now and then, or a kind of universal hum. So she opened the window again and looked down towards the road to see if anyone was there. Kirkelina was still, and the Teigens' house stood empty and dark. She could not see Olaf's house from this side, or Irfan's shop. But the Thai family would move in soon enough and then she would have neighbours again. She lay down with her face to the wall. The cool air calmed her. Of course she had to have the window open. It was nonsense that she should change her habits because of some ridiculous messages from an anonymous idiot. And yet she was constantly plagued by questions. What would the third message say? She would no doubt receive one. She sat up in bed, gathered the duvet around her and listened to the night. She thought about how big the world was, seven billion people, cars, boats and planes, buses and trains, a deafening, thundering spectacle. But she heard nothing. That was strange. Where were they all, what were they doing, how could her little house on Kirkelina be so quiet, even if it was night? Did she live in her own little bubble? She curled up again and tried to sleep, closed her eyes tight. Had a firm word with herself, that's enough now, Ragna. The cold draught from the window sent a shiver down her spine.

She woke much later and immediately thought that her alarm clock had not rung and she had slept in. She raised herself up onto one elbow, only to see that it was three in the morning. It was stiller and darker than ever before. She was wide awake. The idea that she might fall asleep again seemed impossible, she did not feel in the slightest bit tired or heavy, but she did not want to get up at this time of night. So she lay there and listened. Something must have woken her, something outside, an animal perhaps, or a car – after all, the window was open. Or she had been woken by something inside her, a dream maybe, though she could not remember having a dream. Whatever the case, the fact was that she had always slept well, and it was rare for her to wake in the middle of the night. It must mean something. She pulled the duvet to one side and with some reluctance made her way to the bathroom. She did not need to go there, but she had to do something, walk around a bit, think some thoughts. She turned on the light over the mirror and stared at her washed-out face. The scar on her throat was particularly visible in the harsh light, like a red, twisting worm. She was at a loss. Should she go back to bed, or should she go into the kitchen and make a cup of tea, sit in the chair by the window, let time tick by until morning?

She chose bed. She lay there thinking about Rikard Josef, who patrolled the quiet corridors all day long, making sure the guests were happy. Or he stood in reception, ready to help sort out any problems, however big or small, always polite, obliging and correct. And here she was, alone, sleepless and without a voice. Even though she had carried him everywhere as a baby, even though she had given him everything and always looked after him, he had chosen to leave her. No, she turned over in bed, that was not what he had done. He had simply chosen a career in another country. He had followed his ambitions. And there was no room for her in the new life that he had built for himself, which took up all his time and energy. What did she know, little Ragna Riegel who was a shop assistant in Europris, with its horrible nylon overalls and hand-held pricing machines, and easy, undemanding tasks, what did she know about working in a five-star hotel with guests from all over the world? Nothing at all. He was of course totally absorbed by his work, he had an enormous responsibility, and lots of people to please, and some of them would complain. Perhaps they complained for no reason, but he had to smile all the same, smile and smile. And the considerable geographical distance between them had only served to widen the gap. Maybe he did not have much free time, and when he did, he did not want to spend it sitting on a plane. But she found comfort in one thing. Not once had he turned against her or behaved in a way that might suggest that he was bitter or had felt rejected. None of the Christmas cards had ever contained anything other than a friendly greeting. She got out of bed again, pulled the red curtains to the side. To her great surprise, she saw that there was a light on in the Teigens' house. She found it hard to understand. The house had been dark when she went to bed. Surely the Thai family had not got there after midnight and were now wandering through the empty house. She stood there for a while watching, because she thought that sooner or later she might see a shadow in one of the windows. Or something else, that the light might go off again, or more lights come on. She could not see a car by the house, and the external light was on, so she would have seen if there was one parked outside. Someone had come on foot. Then it struck her, someone had come to check the house was secure, of course. Still no shadows in the lit house. What kind of people were going to move in? And would they keep an eye on her home, just as she would on theirs? She closed the curtains and returned to bed. The idea that someone was walking around in the empty house at this time of night disturbed her for some time.

Chapter 6

Audun appeared one day and was going to work full-time. He did not need any training as he had worked in a building materials warehouse for a couple of years, and was quick, efficient and precise. His thin beard was plaited and dangled under his chin like a piece of rope; he often tugged at it as he moved around. His hair was gathered up into a topknot. When he arrived in the morning, it was tight and shiny like a chestnut, but in the course of a shift it started to slip down towards his neck, slowly loosening and looking more and more like a bird's nest. He had a cross hanging from his ear. Audun never spoke unless it was necessary, and had learned the same techniques as Ragna when it came to keeping people at arm's length. He smiled, nodded and carried on.

Ragna felt heavy-headed all day. She was not used to having problems with sleep, and she was so tired that everything was spinning. When the shift was finally over, she walked quickly to the bus stop. The air was raw and a mist was falling with the dusk. The lamp posts and signs looked like they were hovering above the ground. She spotted Audun some way ahead of her, walking hunched over. He did not wait for her, but she was fine with that. She mused about what he was going home to. She could not imagine he had a wife and children, he was only in his twenties. She guessed he lived in a studio flat and spent most of his time outside work on the Internet or listening to music. Black metal or something like that. It was just the two of them in the dusk, the one aware of the other, but each staying behind their own wall. These walls could of course be broken down, but they were following unspoken rules.

Ragna let him get onto the bus first. And as a result he sat down on her seat, the third to the left, and she was not prepared for that. There were lots of empty seats, but he chose hers. He made himself comfortable, leaned in towards the window as she always did. She was so taken aback that she just stood there in the aisle, unable to choose anywhere else. This was a new anxiety in her life. That he intended to take her seat every time. That he might also feel a sense of belonging, a feeling that he was in the perfect place. She sat down in a seat on the other side of the bus, where her body bristled with discomfort. She sat there looking at him. His strange hairdo looked silly. From the back, one might mistake him for a girl, with a long, white neck. She wondered if he let his hair down when he went to bed at night, and what he looked like then. When she glanced over her shoulder, she saw there were five other passengers sitting towards the back of the bus, and there were four in front of her. So there were ten of them, including her. Plus the driver, he was the eleventh. They were all going to die. And they all knew it, but you would not know to look at them. Two girls were speaking in hushed voices, heads close together; another was tapping away on a mobile phone. It looked like Audun was listening to music; he certainly had his earphones in, she could see the white wire. Why was death not visible in these fragile bodies, in the autumn-pale faces, where had they all hidden it? Death was dark, all-encompassing, a burden, but none of them seemed to be carrying anything. The driver, the eleventh of them, drove the heavy bus through the darkening, misty streets. She could not see his face, and she had not looked at him when she got on. She remembered she had once read something by Edgar Allan Poe, possibly, about an omnibus that took all the passengers to the kingdom of death. Without knowing the final destination, they had all got on and found themselves a seat, only to be slowly and surely transported into another dimension. What if that was the case now? What if the driver, whose back was all they could see, was driving to the last stop from where they would never return?

Once this thought had taken root, she felt connected to the passengers in a completely different way. They shared a destiny that she was now part of. She thought the throb of the engine was deeper than usual, that it was using more power, that the dark outside was becoming denser. She looked at the driver's broad back and imagined that he had no face. From here, he would race past all the bus stops without stopping. Would not let anyone off or on. If she stood up and went to ask him a question, he would neither look at her nor answer. Their fate was sealed. She would lose her balance, grab hold of one of the bus straps and then hang there dangling as though on the gallows. She cursed Edgar Allan Poe and all the other authors who could trigger such thoughts in her head years after she had read them.

*

Audun got off at the square. He nodded to her as he passed, which was something. She nodded back. He slipped out of the hissing door and was swallowed by the dark, so young and lithe. Of course he was shy. She felt an affection for him as a result, it was not easy to live like that, constantly having to guard your territory, being forced to be with people without feeling any connection to them, or wanting to have any connection. She put her cheek to the window and played a mind game. She pretended she knew Audun, what his home was like, what he had and did not have, what his dreams were, and his fears. That she could read him like a book just by looking at him, his topknot, his stride, his voice, his expressions. His worn, dark clothes told her what he deemed to be important and less important. But all her assumptions were based on prejudice, in the same way that others went around thinking this and that, judging everyone, throughout their lives perhaps. If we don't talk to each other and ask, Ragna thought, then we draw our own conclusions, damn and misjudge. But he had sat down in her place. Why just there, when nearly all the other seats were empty? Would she have to be first on the bus, from now on, to lay claim to what she believed was hers? Walther Eriksson popped into her mind. The way he had looked at her, that loaded, knowing look. He had understood everything – who she was, what she wanted, what her dreams were. She had drunk a whole bottle of Peach Canei that night. She had been easy prey.

When the bus stopped at Kirkelina, she went into Irfan's shop to pick up a few things.

'The dark is coming,' he said. 'You're not wearing any reflectors.'

He pointed at her black coat.

'The cars won't see you. Just look at your neighbour Skiold and his dog, they know how to look after themselves.'

He nodded towards Olaf's house.

She was surprised and touched by his concern. Did he really care about her well-being, would he be upset if she was mowed down? She had to admit she was lax when it came to things like that, but she explained that she never really walked around at night, just the short distance from the bus stop to her house. Something deep inside resisted using reflectors. It was her wish not to be seen. She put all her shopping into a white carrier bag, thanked him and crossed the road. She glanced up at the Teigens' house, which was all dark, and then it struck her that it was no longer their house. She stood by the mailbox and hesitated, staring at it for a long time. Did it not look heavier than usual? Could she not hear warning bells? She took a deep breath and opened the lid. There was nothing more than the newspaper in there. She peered quickly over her shoulder to see if anyone was watching. She was exposed now, alone under the street light, visible in the dark. And she remembered that she had stood under another street lamp in the park one evening many years ago, with Walther. He was moving to Stockholm with his family. Before he turned to leave, he put a finger under her chin and tilted her face towards the light.

'There's not an ounce of badness in you, little Miss Ragna Riegel.'

Chapter 7

Sejer noticed that her face opened up whenever she spoke about Walther Eriksson, as though she thought of him as a burning flame and immediately tried to get closer, seeking warmth. She blushed easily, often about trivialities. But she was not embarrassed about Walther Eriksson. He must have given her something important, a validity, a worth.

'Were you afraid you were going to die?' he asked. 'As you stood there under the street light and opened the mailbox?'

Her smile was forgiving.

'All the fuss about death,' she whispered. 'I don't understand people. Do you they really want to be here forever? Lots of people have died before us and they're obviously okay. I've never heard of anyone complaining from the other side.' She smiled ironically.

'So the fear you felt, what was it?'

'I was scared of losing control over my life. That I would never get it back again, that I would have to live as a prisoner or a refugee. I was used to living an orderly life where I made all the decisions, but now someone else was deciding. It didn't help if I got home and there was nothing in the mailbox, the day didn't get any better, he had a hold of me. I was constantly waiting, but I didn't know what I was waiting for.'

'And you imagined getting the third letter? Did you think about what he would write the next time?'

'When he wrote that it wasn't long until I was going to die, it somehow felt different and more serious than the first letter. He knew something about the future, he had plans. I got the feeling that he knew something about me, and I had no idea what it was.'

'Did you have anything on your conscience?'

'Not at first. But I did after a while. Because he was right. Someone had picked me out of the crowd and let me know that I had been seen. That I couldn't hide any more.'

'And that was what you always wanted?' Sejer asked. 'To hide?'

She did not answer straight away.

'I just wanted to be left in peace.'

The red light was flashing on his phone again, and because Ragna had seen it as well, there was a pause. Whoever wanted to get hold of the inspector was silently interrupting, just as the silent message in Ragna's mailbox had interrupted her life. She sat completely still on the chair. She did not appear too tired or intimidated, just very focused. There was something special about her, something he liked. A sincerity. She did not try to make herself any better than she was, nor was she defensive. She had never asked for much in life. Her son had left home as soon as he was able to look after himself. She did not blame him, she defended him instead.

'What did you think he would write in the next letter?' he asked again.

She shrugged.

'That he would give me a date.'

'A date for your death?'

'That would be the logical next step, don't you think?'

'And what would you have done then? When the day arrived?'

'Not a lot,' she whispered. 'Maybe stayed indoors, locked the door. But that's what I do anyway. You're asking about letter number three. I often imagined letter one hundred. I liked to think that by then the threats would have lost their power. I almost hoped it would happen, that the letters would pour in so I could start to laugh at them, think of them as rubbish and of him as a loud-mouthed coward. Two short messages and then silence would be harder to live with, harder to understand. I thought a lot of strange things. I often thought, if I'm going to die, I'm going to die, whether it's today or thirty years from now. But I was unfocused and they started to notice at work.'

'How did they notice? Tell me.'

'I made mistakes with the pricing. There were too many zeros or too few. People came to the till and asked if the toastie machine really did cost only twenty kroner.'

'Do you go online a lot?'

'Sometimes. I read the odd article and watch videos on YouTube, and other stories about strange things that have happened. But never for long. Half an hour maybe, then I get bored.'

'Facebook?'

'No.'

'Have you had any anonymous phone calls or threatening texts?'

'Never.'

Sejer let the silence stretch out. He mused for some time on what whispering was normally a sign of – if you were not Ragna Riegel and a doctor had cut your vocal cord with a scalpel. Lots of people whispered when they were frightened. Or if they had a secret or when they gossiped about someone, or they didn't want to disturb, say, a sleeping child, or if there was an enemy nearby and they were scared of being caught. Ragna always whispered. He had started to like it, he realised, her great stillness, her carefulness. Whispering meant that she weighed her words, did not just respond quickly, she had to make an effort to be understood. She tasted the words, planned them, formed them with her tongue and lips, used her facial muscles. He saw no self-pity there, no complaint, she would never scream at him over the table. If she wanted to make a noise she would have to start throwing the furniture. The unfortunate operation had given her a certain dignity.

He asked her if she had slept, and she had.

At first she had lain there, completely still, and listened to the cars outside the prison. There was quite a lot of traffic. She heard the trains as well, she said. They were not that far away. She told him that she had felt safe for the first time in ages, no one could reach her in the cell. So she slept better than she had for a long time. When she woke up, she was still filled with the same sense of security. The people guarding her were also protecting her; everything that was happening outside in the town seemed chaotic and unmanageable. She never heard the other inmates, no one screamed at night. No one opened her cell door to give her post.

'Is there anything you need?' Sejer asked. 'Clothes, or anything else?'

'You don't like my coat?' she teased. 'It's the Europris uniform.'

'Don't you take it off when you're at home?' he wanted to know.

'I like it,' she explained. 'I like the big pockets. The overall is proof that I have a job and don't live off social security. I have a disability, but I don't let it stop me.'

'What do you normally keep in your pockets?'

'Have you answered all your phone calls?' she interrupted.

There were no red lights flashing.

'Yes.'

'Were they about me?'

'Some of them. Does that bother you?'

She shrugged.

Sejer looked at her over the table and thought that the time of first impressions was over. That moment when he saw her for the first time, those few seconds when his brain drew its quick conclusions. Thin and insignificant in an ugly shop coat. Her eyes and hair an indistinct colour. He had moved on, his impression had slowly changed. Her white skin and visible veins reminded him of a marble statue. Her eyebrows, thin and fine as whiskers, and also without colour. Her transparency, her femininity and vulnerability reminded him of a fairy-tale elf. Of course she had been beautiful when she was sixteen, he thought, and Walther Eriksson had seen it.

'So,' he said, 'what do you normally keep in your pockets?'

She pulled a face. The inspector asked some odd questions, she thought, but guessed he had a plan, and she liked the fact that he often took detours.

'The key to the staff toilet. And to the till. Lip balm. My mobile phone, so I can get hold of the others without having to hunt around. A Stanley knife to open all the boxes, and a packet of menthol sweets. Some rubber bands. Paper clips and tape. But the pockets are empty now. I like putting my hands in the pockets, it keeps them in place. Free hands are never a good thing. I don't find it strange at all that people smoke.'

'Would you like us to contact your son?' he asked, out of the blue.

The question horrified her. She could barely answer, nor did she know whether she wanted them to or not. Her son, goodness, the way things stood, and everything he did not know. Her first response was to grip the armrests on the chair.

'It's not that easy to get hold of him,' she whispered. 'To be honest, I'm not sure what he's up to.'

'You can't get hold of him?'

'Not this autumn.'

'What do you think might have happened, as you can't get hold of him?'

'We mothers have a lively imagination when it comes to what might have happened to our children,' she whispered.

'We fathers do too,' Sejer replied. 'Would you like me to make some enquiries? You won't be able to hide what's happened from him. But we will try to break it to him as gently as possible – that you're here, that is.

And we can tell him subsequently why you're here, but that's up to you.'

She loosened her grip on the armrests.

'It would be better if Rikard Josef was allowed to get on with his life, without knowing,' she said. 'You know, ignorance is bliss.'

'But what do you have to lose?'

'The Christmas cards,' she said. 'The angels.'

Chapter 8

Someone had sent her a letter. Not the kind that she feared, this was something else, a bigger envelope with her full address and full name. It was franked in Berlin. Ragna stood by the mailbox and froze under the street light, pressed the letter to her heart, overwhelmed with joy and relief. She walked the forty-eight steps up to the house slightly faster than usual, pulled off her coat and put the letter on the table by the sofa. Big, white and wonderful, it lay there waiting for her. She wanted to save it, savour the moment. I've got a letter from my son, the hotel director, she thought. He wants to tell me something. She was fizzing from head to toe. She would have to tell them at work tomorrow, they talked about their own children all the time. Now it was her turn, her son and his career. She had gone into Irfan's and bought some food, a jar of pickled pumpkin, some habanero, a jar of garlic cloves and some spicy sauces. She put the things down on the kitchen table. She wanted to make something that would burn, first in her mouth, then all the way down to her stomach. She put some water in the espresso machine. Rikard Josef had not sent just a little card. This was a proper letter, she could feel that the envelope contained more than usual. So he must have some news to tell her, something big that he wanted to share with her. Was it possible that for the first time in years she would find a hint of concern for her and how she was? Had he realised that all was not right when he received her letter, even though she had said nothing? Was he so sensitive that he had read between the lines? Yes, she believed he was. Or was he writing to invite her to Berlin? Perhaps he wanted them to celebrate Christmas together, walk arm in arm along Unter den Linden as small white snowflakes danced in the air. She was so excited when she sat down with the letter in her lap. But there was something unusual about the envelope that made her uneasy, that she could not put her finger on. There was no sender address written on the back of this one either, but then lots of people did not bother with that, although she was particular about such things. She also did not recognise the writing on the front, she realised. But she knew no one else in Berlin. She tore open the envelope and pulled out the contents and then sat back, stunned. Inside the big envelope was a smaller envelope. She saw her son's name and address in Landsberger Allee that she had written herself. In addition, there was a blue stamp with the two words: 'Not known at this address'. The letter she had sent had been returned. She was so disappointed that she leapt up from the chair and started to pace around the room, glancing back in despair at the envelope. She was alone in the house. No one could see her, no one could hear, and yet she still had the strange feeling that someone was standing in the corner laughing at her. Celebrating Christmas in Berlin, how silly. What was she to do, what to think or believe? Not known at this address. He had been living there for years.

At first, she wanted to cry. But she pulled herself together and started to think rationally. Her letter had been returned, so what? He had moved. Well, people moved all the time. Irfan had moved from Turkey to Kirkelina. The Soi family had moved from Thailand and were now going to live in the Teigens' house. Her son had now moved away from Landsberger Allee. Nothing to get upset about. She sat down again and studied her own handwriting. It was quite fine writing, though she said so herself. Meticulous and easy to read, with tight, beautiful loops and curls. And yet her cheeks reddened in shame. A friendly nudge, this careful sign of life that she had sent out into the world had been thrown back in her face, as though she was a gift that nobody wanted. It was humiliating. She felt rejected. No one must know that she was the sort of person that was ignored. For a second, she considered opening the envelope and reading her own letter; it was innocent and simple, only it had not reached him. There were two voices talking in her head now, one hurt and dejected, the other firm and sensible. The fact that the letter had been returned meant the post office in Berlin was doing its job. They had kindly returned the letter after they had looked for her son's mailbox without finding it. There was only one thing to be done. She had to burn it. Ah well, she had not managed to get hold of him. Maybe she would never get hold of him again. Her thoughts were as black as the paper when it started to burn. Her thoughts smouldered into ash as well. She slammed the door of the burner shut, put it behind her and pulled herself together. He would send the usual Christmas card sometime in December, and he would tell her that he had moved, and he would explain why, and give her the new address so she could write back. No worse than that. What a fuss! Perhaps he had started his own family and needed more room.

She drank her espresso, which was no longer warm, and the black coffee left its mark in the corners of her mouth. Her head felt empty, the rooms were numbingly silent. They somehow felt alien too, something was missing, something she had forgotten. She sent an inspector into her brain to look for any irregularities, but without result. She switched on the television and watched the news, focused on the voices and images and after a while she calmed down again. It was not until much later that she realised she had forgotten about the meal she had planned, and immediately felt hungry. She went into the kitchen. She looked over at the Teigens' house and saw the light in the window. No, it was no longer the Teigens' house, she had to get used to the Sois. Sooner or later she would meet them out on the road. And either they would be embarrassed by her lack of voice, they might even pull back and subsequently avoid her, or they would come closer so they could hear, listen to her with a friendly and attentive expression, give her the time she needed. You never knew the way things would turn out.

After her meal, she sat and dozed in the chair. Every time her chin hit her chest, she started. She daydreamed about her son. He had been offered a fabulous opportunity at a luxury hotel in Johannesburg. Because his qualities as a hotel director were legendary. His reputation had gone before him and a headhunter had recommended him for the post, so now he had left Berlin. And had he not as a teenager talked about South Africa with stars in his eyes? Clear images came to mind like doves of peace: hotel staff in white uniforms, gardens full of exotic flowers, big glittering swimming pools with blue bottoms. All his life, he had dreamt about running a hotel like that, and he had worked hard for many years with that goal. And now, finally, his dream was reality. The negotiations had taken some time, which was why he had never invited her to the Dormero. He had wanted to wait until it was all settled. He might even send her a telegram. This thought pleased her and she got up and went to her computer. She searched luxury hotels in Johannesburg. The hotel had no less than five stars, she was sure of that, he would not lower his standards. First she found the Radisson Blue, but it was a chain hotel, and he had greater ambitions than that. But it could be the Michelangelo Hotel or the Residence Boutique. She ended up with the Intercontinental. From the photographs, it looked like exactly the kind of place he would choose. In her mind, she was already standing at reception. Perhaps there was a stuffed lion guarding the main entrance. She might need a visa to get into the country, or vaccinations; she would have a lot to organise once he had written and invited her. Reality took hold again and she recognised it for what it was, nothing but a childish daydream. She stood up, turned off the computer, her cheeks flushed. It was a good thing no one could read her thoughts.

Chapter 9

Day after day Ragna sat at the till in Europris and studied the people. She used her eyes, as she always had, to gather in details, and their aura, charisma or lack thereof. Sometimes she caught a scent of perfume or cigarettes. It was their voices she was most interested in, precisely what she had lost, and goodness, how different they were. High and deep, hoarse and sharp, sugary sweet and soft, unclear, flat or sing-song. Some only spoke when they needed to, others just chatted away. She would have done so herself if she could, in her childlike voice, which used to make callers ask if there was an adult at home. She should perhaps have told them they died a long time ago.

One day, a young man suddenly stood there in front of her, requiring her attention. He was dressed in a black suit, and had a white shirt on underneath. So far that day, she had only seen people in down jackets and denim, but here was a customer who was well dressed in a shirt and tie, with slicked-back, dark hair. On a normal weekday. He was probably around thirty and she wondered how someone in such formal clothes had found their way into Europris in the middle of the day, when he looked more like he should be at a do of some kind. A wedding, perhaps, or a confirmation, or a funeral. No one dressed like that normally, unless it was work-related. Perhaps he worked in a funeral home, and he had ten minutes left of his break from the gravity. The hearse might even be parked outside. The deceased would not notice if the driver disappeared for a few minutes. Like her, he was thin and pale, and he seemed to be a bit stressed, as though he needed to be somewhere. An estate agent, she decided, they were always smart. Or, she smiled to herself, he could be from the Secret Service. A secret agent. He noticed that she was looking at him, and gave her a brief smile, as he put his shopping down on the conveyor belt. He had bought some tools – a hammer and a small saw, the kind that could cut metal, she thought – and some screwdrivers in various sizes. He did not look the practical sort at all, Ragna thought, but that was no doubt because of the suit. As usual, she had drawn her own silly conclusions. She imagined that he was searching for something in her face, her eyes maybe, as though he wanted something more than just to pay, and she was not used to it. He put his purchases into a bag and everything clunked and jangled a bit. As he left, he gave her a last look. For the rest of the day she sat there thinking about him.

Of course it would be possible to get Rikard Josef's new address from international directory enquiries. She thought about it as she sat on the bus, to the right of the aisle, with her cheek to the window. Audun had got there first again, and was sitting in her place. She knew she had to do something, only she did not know what. The seat she was sitting on felt like it was too big for her, that it was meant for someone else. She thought about her son who had disappeared. Everyone could be traced, it would only take her a few minutes to find him. Something might have happened, something that meant she needed to get in touch with him quickly. And what could that be? she asked herself. Not much happens in my life, other than the nonsense in the mailbox. But I could fall ill. I could have an accident, the house could burn down. Would he even come to my funeral? she wondered, almost despairing. She must find out where to send his Christmas card. She did not want to blame him for anything, but she thought she had a right to know where he was. Where he was sleeping, eating and working, and if he was well. As soon as she had his new address, she would send another letter, just to let him know that she had found out that he had moved. She could ring the Dormero, of course, they would know where he was, but the idea of whispering on the phone in mediocre English, and the possibility of a bad line, did not appeal to her. She had never had her son's private number, for some reason. She would look for it now. She could at least send him a text message. He would receive it with a ping, or a drop of water in a pool, maybe even a short tune or whistle, she imagined. She had chosen the first four notes of Beethoven's Fifth on her own phone.

She felt the wind on her face as soon as she got off the bus and hurried towards the house. Olaf and Dolly came walking towards her in their high-viz jackets. She had been busy concentrating on her own steps as usual, and so lost count.

'Have you met them?' he asked, and nodded to the Sois' house.

'No, but I'm sure you have.'

He most certainly had, both the parents and children, and they were incredibly nice, he told her. Friendly and smiling, as Thai people so often are. It's like the sun comes out as soon as they open their mouths.

'Did you go to the house?' Ragna asked.

'Yes, but I only went into the hall. We stood there for a long time chatting. I did get a peek inside though and there was a lot of exotic furniture.'

'And the massage table, any sight of that?'

He grinned.

'Standing ready in the basement. And I for one will be lying on that table before Christmas. My back is so stiff,' he complained, twisting with exaggerated pain. 'Maybe she does other treatments too,' he added. She had never seen that expression in his eyes before. His words made her uncertain. He was not that sort of man, but he did not give her his usual warm smile, as he so often did when he made a joke. Instead he looked thoughtful, as though he was planning something, or had just had a good idea.

He commented on the dark, and the wind. He looked enormous in his down jacket, knitted hat and thick gloves, but she knew he was not.

'Today's rubbish hasn't come yet,' he said, nodding at her mailbox.

'What?' she whispered. 'Today's rubbish?'

'The newspaper,' he explained. 'I called them. No one in Kirkelina has got a newspaper today, and they had all kinds of excuses. Sickness, cars breaking down, and I don't know what else.'

'I won't be able to read the births, weddings and deaths then,' Ragna moaned, looking at him intently.

If it was Olaf who had sent the messages about her death, she wanted to see it in his eyes, some sort of spark, like when iron strikes iron.

'We'll have to be happy for those who are famous enough to get on the news when they die,' he said. 'I certainly won't, that's for sure.'

'Nor me,' she whispered back.

They smiled to each other like good neighbours.

Ragna opened the mailbox and peered in. No newspaper, as Olaf had told her, only a white envelope at the bottom. RIEGEL. She stood there with it in her hand as Olaf and Dolly disappeared into the dark. She withered, felt weak. The envelope slipped out of her hand and fell to the ground. She put her foot on it, muddied the white paper. When she looked over her shoulder as she picked it up again, she saw Olaf's and Dolly's yellow jackets shining in the headlights of a passing car. She hurried up to the house and let herself in, closing the door forcefully behind her before placing the letter on the kitchen table. Every time I open an envelope, she thought, he wins. She took off her coat and pulled off her boots, ignoring the letter. There was not much in the fridge when she opened it and had a look, but she had taken her coat off now, and could not be bothered to put everything on again to go across to Irfan. She had a box of eggs and decided to make an omelette. The letter could wait. It could just lie there in the meantime, until it lost all its power. She had more important things to do. She was going to have some food, find her son, send a friendly note to his new address. And then she would make a decision: whether she would deign to open letter number three, or tear it to shreds and flush it down the toilet, so the anonymous threat ended up in the sewers where it belonged, and became rat fodder.

She whisked the eggs vigorously, hitting the glass bowl with a fury, then poured the mixture into the frying pan and watched it bubble. Instead of sitting at the kitchen table as she usually did, she went into the sitting room and sat down. When she had shovelled down the simple food, she moved to the computer and searched for international directory enquiries. Rikard Josef Riegel, Berlin. Not many people would have that name, not even in a major city. To her dismay, she immediately received the message *Kein Treffer gefunden*. She stared at the screen, perplexed. There was another message underneath: Riegel 35 hits. But not Rikard Josef. He may of course have moved away, to the hotel in Johannesburg, like in her daydream. She decided to try again with his address in Landsberger Allee and this time found his name straight away, as though nothing was wrong. She struggled to understand; either he lived there or he did not. But the letter had been returned. He must have moved very recently, in which case the new address might not be registered yet. Or the post office in Berlin had made a mistake, or directory enquiries had made a mistake. They did make mistakes now and then. The larger the city, the more mistakes. Perhaps she should send a new letter to the old address, just to be sure – it might be a one-off mistake. She started to search for a mobile telephone number. But did not find that either. He must have an ex-directory number, for reasons she knew nothing about. She sat there for a long time, thinking. Then she remembered the envelope on the kitchen table. She might as well get it over and done with. Maybe he had planned something and she needed to be prepared. I'm nothing more than a slave, she thought. She went into the kitchen, grabbed the envelope and tore it open.

'I'M WATCHING YOU.'

Chapter 9

'I tried to work out whether this threat was worse than the last one or not,' Ragna explained. 'And decided that it wasn't.'

'Why was it not worse?'

'I had expected a date. That I would die next week. Or even that night, or the next morning. But instead, it was something else. I already knew that he was watching me, I had felt it since I got the first letter. That he was following my every step. I allowed myself a derisive smile. He was already starting to repeat himself, so I relaxed. Not when I was outside, then I kept my eyes peeled, but I was not as afraid any more when I opened the mailbox. Lots of people live with anxiety and distress. So I could live with a fool who was nothing more than a big mouth.'

'Did you dream about catching him? With the mailbox open and a letter in his hand?'

'Sometimes,' she admitted.

'What would you have said?'

'The only thing I was prepared to offer was a simple question. Goodness, I would say, so you can actually reach the mailbox without standing on a stool?'

She smiled and looked pleased with herself.

'Either way, I came to accept that I just had to live with it. Everyone has something. What is it that you have to live with?'

'Oh, so many things,' Sejer said. 'Goes with the job. Everything we see and experience in the course of our work. I can't just blink my eyes and it's gone, certainly not the worst things.'

'And what's that?'

'Small children. When there's nothing left of them after the adults are done. But we must be allowed to dwell on things, it's a human right,' he added. 'I often do.'

He scribbled something on his notepad. Even if she leaned forward, she would not be able to read it. Maybe he was a smoker, maybe the pen was a kind of substitute for a cigarette.

'We've found your son,' he said suddenly, and looked up.

'What?'

She sat there open-mouthed. She could not help it.

'There's a reason why your letters were returned. He had moved, some time ago.'

'What did he say?'

'He didn't want to talk to us.'

'But you said that you found him?'

A red light flashed on his telephone. He pushed the notepad to one side and looked at her earnestly, like a priest who comes to the door, Ragna thought, and steeled herself.

'He's inside. In a prison in Berlin. It's called Plötzensee. I've only spoken to the prison management.'

Ragna lifted her eyes to look at the dog. Her cheeks were tingling, she knew the blood was draining from her face.

'But why is he in prison?' she stammered.

'Embezzlement,' Sejer replied.

'Embezzlement? You mean money? When?'

'When he was working at the hotel,' Sejer said gently. 'The Dormero. He worked there for several years as a receptionist.'

'Director.' She was swift to correct him.

'No.'

'Manager. General manager!'

'He was never a manager. Nor a director. He was a receptionist. And he managed to access the hotel's accounts. He'd been siphoning off funds for a long time when things started to get a bit uncomfortable, and he bolted. We're talking millions by that stage. He eventually broke down and confessed. By then he was working elsewhere, on the other side of the city.'

'Not the manager,' Ragna whispered, close to tears. 'Not the boss.'

'No.'

'Embezzlement?'

'Yes.'

'Several million?'

'That's what they said.'

She was so devastated that he found it hard to bear.

'How did you find all this out?'

'I'm a detective,' he reminded her. 'Your son has given us permission to tell you all this. So he does want the contact, don't you think?'

She was not so sure. She could not gather her thoughts, did not know what to say.

'That's given you rather a lot to think about, hasn't it?' Sejer said. 'But what is your first reaction?'

'First? You make it sound like my thoughts are standing in an orderly queue and I can reel them off in the right order.'

'I'm sorry,' he said.

'So he knows that I'm here then?'

'Yes, he does.'

'Does he know why?'

'We haven't given him the details. We can't do that without your permission. Your case is also under investigation. But will you allow me do that when it becomes possible?'

'He'll lose his mother then,' she whispered. 'And he's never had a father. He needs to live for something when he's in prison. He should be allowed to believe that everything's fine and I'll soon be back in Kirkelina. That it's just something minor.'

'But it's not something minor, is it?'

She sat lost in her own thoughts.

'But why?' she suddenly asked. 'Surely the wages at the Dormero were enough to live off. It's a five-star hotel.'

'We have no other details,' he said. 'He might have been in some kind of a fix. Gambling debt. Drugs. That kind of thing.'

'No, never. Not Rikard. He was a very careful boy, his dream was to make something of himself. He wasn't a manager? What will they think at work? I told them all he was the boss, I told my neighbour as well. How humiliating.'

Ragna dried a tear.

'Oh, he must be so mortified,' she said. 'I know what he's like. Could I perhaps get the address of the prison so I can send him a note?'

'What would you write to him?'

'That we're not bad people, neither of us.'

'You do realise you are subject to correspondence and visit control?' Sejer reminded her. 'I'm sure you know what that means.'

'That you have to read everything,' she replied. 'Word for word. As if I care about that. I'm sitting here like an open book.'

After a long pause while she was lost in thought, Ragna wanted to talk about something else.

'Do you know what Walther once said to me? Not that we really had time to say much to each other. But, you know, he was older than me and so much wiser.'

'Tell me, what did he say?' Sejer asked.

'As I told you, we were in the park the day he took the nice photograph. The one that's in the bottom drawer. He always had his big camera bag with him. And I'm no different from anyone else. I felt silly and unsure in front of the lens, and he noticed. The microscope, he said, is an amazing invention. Because it allows us to look inside our bodies, at everything that lives inside us. A huge, invisible world. And the telescope allows us to look out into the universe. We're fine with the teeming life inside us, and the universe outside us, but we are not fine with what we see in the mirror.'

'But he said this when he was behind a camera?'

She nodded.

'The photograph I'm taking of you now, he said, is my image of you. My version. My experience. No one else can see you with exactly the same eyes. The photograph will be unique. No one can contest it. And it will always be there.'

'What made you think of that now?' Sejer asked.

'I have my own image of Rikard Josef. It will never change, no matter what happens. Have you ever looked at the stars through a telescope?'

'No, but I do look at the stars in wonder, like everyone else. I don't mind not knowing about the stars, or that the universe has secrets. I focus on the secrets here on earth. They interest me more.'

'And now you're interested in mine?'

'Yes, I am.'

'I had a dream earlier this autumn,' she confessed, 'right after the first letter. I was walking down a long mine shaft. It was dark and hot and dusty, it must have been a coal mine. I didn't know how deep it was, but I could see it disappearing further and further into the mountain, and it was hard to breathe. Then I found one of those carts, you know the kind that run on tracks that they use to transport the coal? Well, I climbed in. And then suddenly it started to move. Within seconds it was going really fast, too fast for me to jump off, and I couldn't see anything in the pitch-dark, and I didn't know how far it was to the end, or how the runaway cart would eventually stop. If it would stop suddenly, or maybe just fall over a cliff edge and disappear into the dark, never to be found again.'

'What happened when you reached the bottom?' Sejer asked.

She smiled and blinked.

'I'm still falling. And praying all the while that someone will find me and give me a decent funeral.'

She realised that she wanted to tell him another story. It was a memory she had carried for years, with wonder.

'Memory is a funny thing. Why do we remember all the small things, and forget so many of the important things? Is it the same for you?'

'Possibly,' Sejer replied. 'But our problem is not that we forget, but that we remember only too well. Our brains don't always manage to select the best things.'

'I once watched an old American film on television, a long time ago,' she told him. 'It was about a group of boys who must have been somewhere between eight and ten. It was summer and it was warm and they were wearing shorts. They were bored, in the way that boys can be. So they headed for the woods, without thinking, without a plan, and they wandered further and further away from their homes. And they were joking and jostling and bickering as boys do. I liked them,' she remembered, 'they were so full of mischief. They didn't care, had no respect for authority, no humility.'

She looked at him to see if he was listening, and he was.

'Eventually, one of them noticed that the sun was getting low in the sky, and they had been out in the woods all day. They decided to turn and go back the same way, but soon discovered they were completely lost. There was a big argument, far more serious than the usual joshing around. They all thought they knew best what to do. They discussed directions, but no longer knew which way led back, they had crossed so many paths, and the paths had forked, and there were no signs. They didn't know how far they had come, they'd paid no attention to time, but now the clock had started to tick again. It would soon be dark. They had nothing with them, nothing to drink. After a lot of arguing that got them nowhere, they set off in an arbitrary direction. They eventually stopped talking. One of them broke off a big branch from a tree, which he thrashed around. They could not bear to look at each other, they just walked. None of them wanted to be the first to cry.'

She paused, wanting to remember every detail as well as she could.

'Do you often cry?' she asked, looking up at the inspector.

'No. And you?'

'Sometimes. Yes, I do, sometimes. Lots of people say that it's important to cry, apparently it's to do with the body's chemistry. Hormones or enzymes, or something else – it's supposed to be healthy and healing. But I don't believe that at all.'

'Neither do I,' he said firmly.

She continued her story about the boys.

'One of them suddenly made an important discovery,' she whispered. 'They'd come across a railway line. They were walking on a track, and if they followed the track it would lead them to somewhere where there were people. They could be themselves again, laughing and joking. They started to walk faster, they were determined and it was still light. Even though they didn't know how far they had to walk before they found people, they were relaxed and had fun as they followed the railway line in the direction they thought was best. The boy with the stick began to sing,' she remembered. 'He whacked and hit the rails with all his might, and the others joined in the song, at the tops of their voices.

But for all that, they were tired, as they had been walking all day. And then they came to a railway bridge.'

'I was waiting for that,' Sejer said.

'One of those big, enclosed ones, you know, where the train runs through a steel construction that looks like a cage. The bridge crossed a gorge,' she explained, 'with a fierce river running along the bottom. The slopes down to the water were too steep for them to get onto the banks. And even if they did manage, they would never be able to cross the rapids. In other words, they had to cross the bridge. But the tracks disappeared around a bend on the other side, so they did not have a clear sight line. Another argument ensued. The boy with the stick had taken on the role as leader. He said that they had to keep walking. It would only take a few minutes and then they would be safe on the other side. One of the others stated the obvious, that if a train came thundering over when they were in the middle of the bridge, they were doomed. There wasn't enough room on the sides of the tracks, and the river raged below. We won't be that unlucky, the leader said adamantly. And so they ran. Halfway across the bridge, a train came hurtling towards them.'

Sejer was resting his chin in his hand, smiling broadly.

'Why are you smiling?' she wanted to know.

'Because I'm enjoying this. What happened?'

'I don't remember.'

'You don't remember? Did you not watch the end of the film?'

'I must have done, it was so exciting. I was sitting on the edge of my chair, holding my breath. The last thing

I remember is the whistle when the driver spotted the boys, and their small, terrified faces when they realised what was about to happen. And my memory has not stored the end of the story.'

Chapter 10

'What about the luxury hotel then?' Gunnhild asked. 'How's the director?'

Ragna jumped, because she was unprepared. Gunnhild had never asked so directly before, not like that, with beady eyes. Maybe she suspected something was up.

'He was never actually the director,' Ragna mumbled, and blushed furiously. 'I misunderstood. I think he's a manager. General manager.'

Gunnhild looked at her earnestly.

'Well, he's still the boss,' she said.

Ragna nodded.

'Yes, he's the boss.'

There was a brief pause, but Ragna could tell that Gunnhild was after something.

'Do celebrities ever stay there? At the hotel?'

Again, she had to stammer out an answer, a whispered lie. The humiliation – the fact that her letter had been returned, that she now did not even know where her son was – made her feel uncomfortable. Her cheeks were burning. She tried to extend time. But then the lie fell out of her mouth before she could stop it.

'Angela Merkel,' she whispered.

'Has Merkel stayed there? With her bodyguards and all?'

Ragna looked the other way. She was in the middle of unpacking a box of small rubber animals, and tried to concentrate on what she was doing, but stopped with a black-and-white cow in her hand. When she squeezed it, it made an angry squeaking noise.

'Ah, so that's your answer, eh?' Gunnhild laughed.

'Yes, bodyguards and all,' Ragna swiftly replied. 'I don't think she moves even one metre without them. Can you imagine what that must be like?' she added. 'To have someone there all the time?'

'Did they sit outside her room at night? Do you think they had a gun?'

Ragna squeezed the rubber cow again. She managed to stop the conversation in her usual way, with a little nod. But she could not look her colleague in the eye. When she held the cow up to her nose, it smelt sweet, like chewing gum.

'Why don't we go there sometime?' Gunnhild suggested eagerly. 'We could have a long weekend in Berlin. From Thursday to Sunday. I'm sure Rikard can get us a room at a discount. Don't you think he'd do that for us? He's the general manager. I've never been to Berlin.'

Ragna felt winded.

'There's not much to do in Berlin,' she objected. 'Only old museums.'

Gunnhild shook her head. She knew better.

'Not much to do? There are more shops than in London. And loads of good restaurants and fantastic galleries and posh hotels. Lots of the old Stasi prisons are open to the public now as well.'

'Prisons?' Ragna shook her head. 'Wandering around old prisons can't be much fun.'

'But it would be!' Gunnhild exclaimed. 'Imagine seeing a prison from the inside. We never get a chance here. You could at least ask. He might like to have visitors from Norway.'

Gunnhild scrutinised her with inquisitive eyes.

'He's very busy,' Ragna muttered. 'Practically never has a day off.'

She pulled the key to the staff toilet out of her pocket, and hurried through the shop out into the storeroom, leaving the rest of the cows in the box. Her heart was pounding, with shame and anger. She was embarrassed because she felt she had been caught out, and angry because she had been forced to lie. And she was irritated because she felt that Gunnhild had backed her into a corner on purpose. As though she had suddenly decided to find out the truth, as if she had the right to know. She wanted Ragna to know that she was not stupid and was not going to be fooled any more.

As Ragna entered the small room with the awful anti-bacterial blue light that always made her look like a corpse, she turned her head to avoid the mirror and slipped into the cubicle. She sat down on the toilet seat and dried a solitary tear. It was worse than standing in the corner. This was where people came to do their business, and she had nowhere else to go. She was as good as down the sewers, and there were no doubt hordes of fat rats living down there in the pipes. She shed a few more tears, clutching the key to the toilet so hard that it cut through the skin in the palm of her hand. She was nothing more than a pathetic liar, an evasive coward. Standing there talking about Angela Merkel just to save face, giving Gunnhild what she wanted to hear, quickly, without thinking. What would she say next time Gunnhild brought it up? What kind of excuse could she give then? The truth was out of the question. The fact that she no longer knew where her son was, that he had moved without telling her, maybe even changed jobs. If only he would send a letter! If only she could say to Gunnhild that they would actually have to go to Johannesburg instead, because that was where he was now, at the Intercontinental. And they could take a picture together beside the stuffed lion in the lobby, or out by the pool. She sat there for as long as she dared. Not too long, because then Gunnhild might start to wonder and come and find her. She cried until she had no more tears, balled her fists and despaired at herself, more than anything, and how pathetic she was, but also fate, which had first taken her son, and then her voice.

When she came back out into the shop, she could not see Gunnhild anywhere. Instead she bumped into Audun who was struggling with a big box of Casio watches. Every watch had to be hung on a rotating display stand by the till. Ragna noticed that he admired the watches before he put them on the stand. He stood with a watch in his hand. He was still just as quiet, even though he had been working there for several weeks now.

'Life must have been much simpler before,' he said pensively. 'Before people had clocks and watches. They got up when the sun came up, and they went to bed when it got dark. When they were hungry, they ate.'

'Would you rather live like that?' Ragna asked.

'To be honest, yes.'

He spoke without looking at her. He put the watch on the stand, bent down over the cardboard box and took out another. Every watch came in a nice white box that was lined with velvet.

'There are so many of us now,' Ragna said. 'We need a way to structure our days.'

'There are lots of ants in an anthill too,' he replied, 'and everything works perfectly well, even though there's no clock on the wall. Everyone knows what they have to do. Everyone knows their place.'

'So you would rather be an ant then?'

'Basically, yes.'

'But you've never been inside an anthill,' she whispered. 'Maybe it's completely chaotic, maybe they kill each other too. When someone takes their place.'

He granted her a brief smile, which did not happen often, but still did not look her in the eye. It was definitely a breakthrough though, the fact that he had opened up and passed a few comments, and he had not done that with anyone else, so he must trust her. Even though he had stolen her seat on the bus. And he longed for another era. She felt chosen, because he had confided in her, and she was not used to being chosen.

'I don't think things were much better before,' she whispered.

'But I do,' he replied, just as quietly.

Her thoughts soon turned back to Gunnhild's suggestion of a weekend in Berlin, and what she should say the next time she brought it up. Towards the end of her shift, Ragna resolutely walked over to the card stand by the till. What if she sent another note to her son's usual address, just to make sure that he really had moved and was somewhere else? If this was also returned, then she definitely had a problem. But she was not going to give up that easily – after all, did she not live in an orderly world? With clocks and calendars and a postal service? As well as German efficiency? She studied the cards, one by one. Most of them were of kittens and puppies, printed with 'Happy Birthday' or 'Thank You', and the others were the kind with wise words on the front. Not that it mattered. The purpose was to double-check. She picked a card of a pony. She was going to give the post office in Berlin a second chance.

When she got home, there were no anonymous letters in the mailbox. Not the next day either, nor in the weeks that followed. She wondered how much time she should let pass before she might possibly be able to see it as a closed chapter in her life, before she could take out the local paper without having to look over her shoulder, before she could walk the forty-eight steps up to the house without counting. But she could not stop. She had become one big counting machine. Everything was ticking and whirring and striking inside her.

She crossed the road and went into Irfan's shop, stood there chatting by the counter for a while. Because from where she was standing, she could see straight over to her house, with the lights on in all the windows. In other words, Irfan could see both her house and her mailbox when he was at work. She had picked up a couple of small things that she put down by the till. He had made a very simple leaflet of his special offers, and there was a pile lying there.

'There's so much paper in my mailbox these days,' she commented, watching him carefully all the while. 'Brochures and adverts and special offers. It's never been this bad before. And it's all junk mail. I just put it straight in the fire.'

She tried to see if there was anything in his eyes, if he was being evasive. Or something that resembled guilt. Or triumph. If he was the one creeping up and down Kirkelina in the dark, handing out threats. Or if he had seen a stranger with his hand in her mailbox.

He punched in the product codes as swiftly as he always did.

'Soon Christmas,' he said. 'Lots of adverts. It's up to you to take it here. You can read in the shop and then throw it away over there.'

He pointed to a rubbish bin by the door.

She picked up a brochure to be kind, and asked him to pop it in the bag.

'Do you normally celebrate Christmas?' she wanted to know.

'No Christmas tree. But we have four kids and they want presents. They learn about it at school.'

He rolled his eyes.

'But no Santa Claus?' Ragna whispered, and smiled.

'We have our own things from Turkey,' he said.

'Do you have a special meal?'

'Oh yes. I make the food.'

'Not your wife?'

'No, I'm a cook.'

'You mean a trained chef? From Turkey?'

'Yes. But I can't get that sort of work here. I tried from the start, I've been trying for years.'

There was a sting in his voice, a bitter undercurrent.

Ragna paid and took the bag that he held out to her.

'Maybe you should change your name?' she suggested.

'I've thought about it,' he admitted. 'Then I might at least get an interview. No one wants to employ someone called Baris.'

'Have the Sois been in to shop yet?' she asked. 'The new people from Thailand? The ones that have moved into the Teigens' house.'

'Been in here a lot.'

'I heard that they're going to open a restaurant, maybe you should talk to them?' she suggested. 'But perhaps you can't make Thai food.'

'I make everything,' he said. 'I'm just not being given the chance.'

Ragna wanted to comfort him. She was ashamed of her fellow countrymen. She stood there by the counter, trying to think of something to say.

'Well, your shop is wonderful,' she whispered. 'A lot of people really appreciate it.'

'If so many people like it, why have I not made more money?' he replied.

He spoke without looking at her, just like Audun. Their conversation had brought up a lot of frustration, and she was sorry.

'If I had been a brain surgeon,' he said sharply, 'I still wouldn't have got a job. A brain surgeon doesn't look like me, and the Norwegian authorities would question my qualifications. But if they did let me go to the operating table, I would use my scalpel well, believe me. On Norwegian brains.'

He tapped his temple with his finger.

She looked at him, horrified, and could not think of an answer. There was a deep resentment there that she had not seen before, like a slumbering volcano, she thought, and she tried to visualise his anger and what would happen if he erupted. She tightened her hold on the carrier bag and left, hurrying across the road. There was suddenly something strange about Irfan. He had not looked at her in the shop, but when she turned her back, she felt his eyes burning into her.

The card of a pony had been sent to Berlin. She had written the name and address in big, clear letters, so they could not be misread. Gunnhild's suggestion of a trip to Berlin had made her nervous, and she worried that it might come up again in the conversation. But at the same time, she was touched. No one else would have given her an invitation like that, an opportunity to experience something together, just the two of them. It was the sort of thing women did sometimes, when they had friends. She could suggest an alternative, Copenhagen or Stockholm or London, anything to avoid more questions about her son. Gunnhild could talk for her in noisy restaurants and shops. She could order the food and sort out anything else. She prepared some answers, memorised them until she knew them word for word, until she was certain they would sound spontaneous and unforced, if Gunnhild continued to push her about Berlin.

And still no more messages in the mailbox. So she had been a random victim, after all, and now he had gone elsewhere. He was prowling up and down some other road, hunched up in the dark, somewhere else. His short messages had unnerved others, made more and more people feel unsafe. She was sure that he only targeted women, those who lived alone. It probably gave him an extra thrill. She sat in front of the computer for a long time that evening. YouTube was her window to the world, there were lots of things that made her laugh, amazed her and terrified her. Funny films of people and animals, or surprising things, and things she did not understand – like the short video called 'The Jumper' where a man commits suicide by jumping from the roof of a tower block. She could no longer remember how she found it, or what she was looking for, only that it was suddenly there, lasted sixty seconds and took her breath away. The jumper was filmed from below, at street level, with a handheld camera, and the cameraman followed what happened moment by moment. The man paced back and forth to begin with, then positioned himself at the edge of the roof. A taut figure, dressed in black. He stood there for a few seconds, frozen like a statue, before spreading out his arms like wings. The camera zoomed in, but his face was not clear, only his body, and what he was wearing. There were no street sounds, no cars, no shouts. Then the black figure fell slowly forward in an elegant arc, crashing to the ground with terrific speed. There was a sickening, hard sound as he hit the pavement, like a heavy animal carcass. He landed on his front with one arm underneath him, the other out to the side. Blood immediately started to pour from his ears and mouth. Then there was the sound of running feet and shallow breathing. It was the cameraman running forward, to get a close-up. The lifeless body, face down. The blood. And silence, again, for a long time. Suddenly she saw a faint movement. First a hand, then an arm. Then the figure moved his head as well, very carefully to begin with, and with great effort, but he eventually managed to lift it, let it sink down, then lifted it again. And somehow, she had no idea how, he managed to get up onto his knees, and push himself up, slowly, until he was on his feet, staring straight into the camera. With a piercing look that Ragna had never experienced the like of before, as though, in some uncanny way, he knew everything that was worth knowing about her and the world and the people who live in it. Why they were in this world and where they would go after, as though he had just returned from the dead. Then he turned away from the camera, and walked calmly down the pavement, before disappearing round a corner.

The first time Ragna watched 'The Jumper', it had taken a while before she realised the film was manipulated. She was not always quick on the uptake. No one jumped from a ten-storey tower block and then stood up and walked away. Someone had had fun with the camera, someone who knew about film techniques, perhaps students from film school. And they had uploaded the result onto YouTube. She could not even begin to understand how they had done it, she knew nothing about that sort of thing. But she was hugely impressed, disconcerted almost, because it struck her how easy it was to fool people, to manipulate them, to get them to believe something, a belief that might make them do something political, for example. It was impossible to see where they had made cuts. Everything seemed to happen in one take. She studied the video again, her face close to the screen, with narrow, focused eyes. And once again she was fascinated. She thought that perhaps if she watched it lots of times she would discover the secret. Find the exact place where the film had been cut. Be certain that the figure falling from the roof was a heavy, black-clad doll. When she had had enough, she turned off the computer and looked down to the road. The light was still on in Irfan's shop. Maybe he was sitting there looking at the light in her windows as well, as he stewed over the Norwegians and their lack of openness. Or perhaps he was dreaming about a top chef job with good pay. Perhaps his books did not balance and he could not face telling his family – he might still have parents in Turkey and he was supporting them, they were dependent on him. She thought about honour and shame and fury. They might drive a person to do anything.

Ragna Riegel was sleeping.

With her face turned towards the open window that let in the cool November air. The thousands of thoughts she had had in the day that had not developed into decisions or actions, or plans for the next day, or notes in a letter, exploded like shooting stars in her brain. Her dreams were full of flickering images that made no sense, and these then filled her with fear and unease, and very occasionally joy. Of course Rikard Josef had not deserted her. She still had him on her arm, he was warm and smelt sweet, like the goat's milk soap they sold at Europris, and when she squeezed the black-and-white rubber cow, he laughed happily. But suddenly the Stasi were standing at the foot of her bed accusing her of betrayal, saying she had been weak and not taken her responsibility seriously. They had come to get her and put her in a museum. And then Irfan appeared in the doorway and he was raging, standing there in a bloody doctor's coat with a scalpel in his hand. He wanted her to think differently about things. Get into her mind. Cut important connections, so she could no longer understand what was going on, to prevent her thoughts from linking up to become realisations and conclusions. She rose and fell through all the different layers, was light as a feather and huge as a whale, a stone one moment or a bubble the next, and she could talk again, she could scream and everyone heard her, and cowered in fear.

Chapter 11

'I've been thinking about those boys on the railway bridge,' Sejer said.

The idea that the inspector had sat in his living room thinking about her and the things she had told him pleased Ragna. He had taken her home with him, did not flick her on and off like a switch; her words and stories followed him through the day and maybe even into his sleep.

She wanted to be with him in his sleep.

'In the old days, boys would lie down in between the tracks when a train was coming, as a dare,' he explained. 'Back then, the trains sat rather high on the tracks so there was plenty of room. And boys that age are thin and slender.'

Ragna's jaw dropped in horror.

'They lay there while the train went over them?'

'Yes, that's what I've heard. As I said, it was often a dare.'

'All the same,' Ragna whispered, 'if the film ended like that, my brain still hasn't stored it.'

'Then another memory has taken up that space,' he said. 'Or something you heard outside. Whatever it is was more important than the boys.'

She could not think what that might be, but nodded all the same.

'Tell me about something important that you've forgotten,' she said. The way she had formulated her request made her smile. 'That you feel you should have remembered.'

He picked up the pen again and sat fiddling with it for a while. He was constantly having to make decisions with regard to Ragna Riegel – how much he should give of himself; how much he should humour her, give her what she needed or wanted in order to push forwards. Or if he should restrict himself to building a minute-by-minute account of what had happened, writing it down and presenting it to the court. But he wanted to give her what she needed, he wanted to make this case something more than duty. Ragna was different in every way, the case was different from other cases. The connection between them was different. He was getting older. He did not have many years left in the high-backed chair from Kinnarps that he had bought himself. He wanted to have a sense of self-respect when he retired, to know that he had given everyone the opportunity to explain themselves in detail, that he had given them time, that he had listened with an openness, understanding and respect. He put the pen down again.

'For the last few days that Elise was alive,' he said, 'I had a bed beside her in hospital. I didn't sleep much, I just lay there listening to her breathing. She slept a lot. Then would open her eyes to check that I was still there, and doze off again, slipping in and out of consciousness. There were only a few centimetres between our beds, and even though the room was bare, with no sound or smell, just machines and tubes and stands, that is what we shared in those final hours. I heard her breathing, nothing more. In the last hour, she only inhaled once a minute. Her heart stopped, and started again, stopped and started, and that went on for quite a while. Then I heard nothing more. And I know it's a strange thing to say, but I was so surprised, almost annoyed that she disappeared like that, and I couldn't reach her any more. I somehow felt betrayed.'

'But you remember that final breath?'

'Yes.'

'So what have you forgotten? What should you have remembered?'

'The first night alone. I don't remember it.'

'But perhaps that's because you slept,' Ragna said. 'And didn't dream.'

'I can't forgive myself for that,' he confessed. 'That I slept. That I slept so heavily.'

'But you were exhausted,' she said. 'Of course you slept. But then you woke up the next morning. And I'm sure you remember that morning.'

'Yes, I do,' he said. 'I was the one who had betrayed her. I let her go too easily. While she lay in the morgue, I slept like a baby under a feather duvet.'

'And you're ashamed that you slept. So after that night, you didn't sleep. You didn't want to show such weakness again?'

'You're right.'

'Do you sleep now?'

'Yes, I do. And you?'

She nodded.

'Yes, at last. For the first time in ages.'

She opened her arms and hands as though she had finally been set free and could breathe properly.

He told her that he visited Elise's grave every Friday after work, and that he always had a candle with him.

'A grave candle burns for a few hours,' he said. 'I keep an eye on the time. And when I go to bed at midnight, I know that it will burn out while I'm asleep. I don't like to think about it going out.'

He changed the topic abruptly.

'How do you foresee your future?'

'I don't think about the future,' she replied. 'The only people watching me now are the guards. And they're very nice.'

'And what you did,' he said gravely. 'Does it scare you?'

'It was like falling over the edge,' she whispered. 'A natural and unavoidable consequence of a long series of events.'

'But the moment it happened is a thing of the past,' Sejer said, 'and you're in a completely different place? Are you still not horrified by what happened? Do you feel sorry for what you've done, do you wish you could undo it?'

'I don't think you understand,' she whispered. 'What happened had to happen. And now I'm here. Now, finally, I'm protected.'

Chapter 12

She had never been able to decide about her parents' grave, whether the plot they had been given was well positioned or not. They were buried behind the church, close to the wall, so they were protected from the wind and weather, and the damp that rose up from the river. At the same time they were out of sight and always in the shade. Also, the car park was behind the church and there was a fair amount of traffic, so the exhaust fumes had discoloured the wall; it was no longer red, more a dirty grey. If they had been buried in front of the church, overlooking the square, they would be bathed in sun on a fine day. But on stormy autumn nights, like now, the rain and wind would lash the grave without mercy.

Today Ragna thought the grave was protected, and well looked after. The heavy, imposing church bore the brunt of the angry winds that blew off the river. But she was soaked by the rain within minutes, and her hands were freezing. She had a grave candle with her in a bag. Her lighter was running out of fuel and she struggled to light it, but eventually managed and put on the mesh top. When she saw the small flame flickering in front of her parents' names, she felt a peace descend.

Hans and Signe Riegel.
Greatest of all is love.

Not once had she heard them say a mean word to each other, not as a child, a teenager or an adult. She stood for a while, as one does by a grave. She wanted to leave something behind, not just the candle – a kind of energy, a feeling of gratitude. She stood completely still, deep in concentration, thinking of her parents with all the warmth left in her frozen body. She hoped her thoughts would reach them like jets of warm air far down in the ground, that they would lie there glowing. That all her thoughts over the years, her longing and loss, would penetrate the wood of the coffins. There was no more she could do. Every time, it hurt as much to leave them, the connection she had felt for a short while was torn by the present, and when she emerged onto the street, the cars whizzed by and the wet gusts of wind whipped her face. With considerable force, the wind blew her back to reality, to the living. It was mid-afternoon and already dark. Frozen souls scurried across the square with bent heads hidden by umbrellas and hoods. She had to wait for a bus to Kirkelina, so she braced herself and went into Magasinet, and found herself a table in the warm cafe. It was self-service, so she was able to help herself to a Danish pastry and a cup of coffee from the machine and pay without saying a word. She sat for a while with her hands around the cup to warm them, and looked at the other customers. The cafe was full, because of the weather. Perhaps there were several of them waiting for the bus. There were certainly quite a few people with plastic bags on the floor beside them. No one looked in her direction, but she was used to that. She was used to being invisible, and had worked hard to achieve it. But she still checked swiftly to see if anyone was watching her. That was what he had written, in his third message. Perhaps he was sitting here, right now, in the warm cafe, perhaps he had followed her through town, perhaps he had waited among the gravestones, she would not have noticed him.

The coffee had been standing too long in the pot, and the Danish pastry that had looked so tempting in the display counter was dry and flaky. The baker had probably got up around four in the morning and taken the first batch of pastries out of the oven at five. Then he had loaded the day's orders into a van and driven round to deliver them all, not only to Magasinet, but to lots of other cafes as well, and that took some time. She looked at her watch – it was eleven hours since five in the morning. She ate the pastry nonetheless, listened to the hum of voices and chairs scraping on the hard stone tiles. She could see the main entrance where the doors were constantly opening and closing, and every time she felt a cold gust of air from the street.

Then she noticed someone was watching her. At first it was just a glance, but she soon felt his eyes on her again and again. She became tense and hunched. Looked over at him, then away several times, had to make sure it was her he was looking at, try to find out why. She felt edgy and wanted to leave, even though it was still some time until the next bus. There was something familiar about him, she realised, perhaps he was one of the regular customers from Europris. When people popped up in unexpected contexts it was often impossible to place them. If he was a customer from the shop, then he had never seen her without her green overall on, which might explain why he seemed so unsure. She had a black coat on, with a fur trim round the hood. Like most people, he wanted to solve the puzzle, which was why he kept staring, while his brain worked overtime to place her in the right context. A pensioner in a grey coat, eating a bun. She logged him. Lots of the customers at Europris were pensioners. His grey hair was long and unkempt, and he had not shaved for a while. The bun was probably eleven hours old as well, she thought, and his coffee as bitter as hers. She turned away. Tried to show she was uncomfortable, but he did not take the hint. She stood up abruptly and hurried towards the door. Surely that old man was not the one sending her threats? The doors slid open and she was almost blown over by the fierce wind. She pulled up her hood and took a few moments to gather herself; she had got away from her pursuer, and wanted to get home quickly now. Just as she was about to make a dash to the bus stop, he came up beside her. He was suddenly very close, and a lot taller than her, and she knew he was going to say something any moment. She noticed that he looked very meek, almost apologetic, and could not understand why. But it was her he was staring at, it was her he wanted.

'What about the boy?' he asked carefully.

Ragna clutched her handbag. She did not understand what he meant. The boy? Did he mean Rikard Josef? Practically no one knew she had a son, certainly not the customers at Europris, and she did not spend much time with other people. She dismissed him with a disconcerted shrug and hurried down the street towards the square, without turning round. The bus was standing at its stop, engine running, thank goodness, warm and bright, so she got on and walked down the aisle. Her seat was empty. Now that she was in the light, the city outside was dark and she could no longer see him. All she saw was a reflection of her own face. The rain on the glass erased her features, as though her face was running down the window. The boy, he had said. The boy. With that strange, slightly embarrassed smile.

The bus quickly filled. People were pushed together. A teenager plonked down on the seat beside her, and the proximity of a young body made her shrink back to take as little space as possible. She looked down the street one last time, at the umbrellas and illuminated shop windows. Walther, she thought, taken aback. Walther Eriksson. She had forgotten all the years that had passed. He was an elderly gentleman now. The tooth of time had worn him. He had asked about his son and she had not answered. What if he had moved back to town, what if she met him again? What if he asked for his son's address? The one she no longer had.

She fretted all the way home. He was another sign, a warning, a change. She had accepted things as they were. Now that was being disturbed. They were all in cahoots, spreading like rings on the water. You are going to die, Ragna, and it is not long now.

There was a catalogue for ladies' clothes from Wentz in the mailbox, and the newspaper. No threats, no one nearby when she looked over her shoulder. The lights were on in Irfan's shop, and in her house.

*

Was it really Walther Eriksson? That jowly, old man, unkempt and badly dressed – was it really him? She was no longer certain, back in the safety of her own house. What had become of the strapping man she once met, so tall and confident and courteous – the master photographer himself? Who had walked quietly across the floor, through a whirlwind of girls, and chosen to sit on the arm of her chair. Why? She was the youngest, thinnest and palest of them all. What had he hoped to achieve? And what should she think now, after all these years? How many girls had he photographed? Only the youngest, the ugliest, the ones with the least confidence, who allowed themselves to be seduced by his camera and big lens? The wine he had poured was sweet, on purpose, perhaps – no adult would drink Peach Canei. How many children did he have? Why was she questioning his motives at all, when she had reconciled herself with her fate a long time ago, when she had seen him as a blessing for so many years? He had given her a son. Her cheeks were burning, they were burning because she realised she was wrong, and that he was just like every other man, out to get his own way. She blushed because he had seen her at close hand today, after so many years, in the badly lit cafe; he had seen that she was not beautiful, even though he may once have thought so and caught what he saw on his camera. He had given her the photograph and she had believed what he told her. He must have been incredibly disappointed today. She had faded, every year had drained her of colour. But now he had decided to come crawling. He had asked about the boy. He did not even know his son's name, all he knew was that he had a boy. She had sent him a card after the birth, to which he never replied. No congratulations, no good luck, no thinking of you. And now, for some reason, he had come back and had somehow managed to find her. Or was it a coincidence? It had to be a coincidence. Or had his past caught up with him – was he also seeing signs everywhere? She let go of the bags in her hands, and stood in front of the mirror by the front door. Stood there in her coat. Did exactly what he had warned her not to do, and as the seconds passed, she realised she was disappearing. The older she got, the more colour she would lose. What if he came to her house this evening, with some kind of credible story, that he was visiting old stamping grounds and just wanted to say hello? That he had thought about her for all these years and wanted to know more about his son, who he had of course never forgotten. Who he had always wanted to meet, but had never found the time. Her thoughts turned nasty, her eyes narrowed. Presumably he had lost everything he had in Stockholm, his wife, children and career. And teenage girls were no longer so easy to seduce. That was why he had come back. He wanted to give it a second try, wanted to stand at her door with his hands open, his eyes begging – could he not come into the warmth, only for a moment, all he wanted was something to take with him. Some photographs, some stories about the boy.

She turned her back on her reflection and opened the front door. The only thing on the front step was a broom that she used for sweeping off the snow and autumn leaves. The wood stack was behind the house, under a green tarpaulin. She went round and got a couple of logs, held them under her arm as she wrestled the tarpaulin back into place. Once indoors again, she put the logs in the burner with some kindling. Then sat down on the floor and lost herself in the flames that she could see through the glass. Walther must have noticed that she did not recognise him. Or at least that she was uncertain. He had probably pulled his coat tighter around him and wandered the cold, wet streets, thinking about his life, or cursing it. Or perhaps he had stormed off because she had rejected him. Lonely and forgotten in his own town. Maybe he had found his way to the pub to drink away his sorrows. In his mind, he was back at the party, sitting on the arm of her chair, with his big camera bag on the floor – the weapon that got him what he wanted, especially when it came to girls. In front of the camera they became shy. In front of the camera they felt seen. The fire was burning well now, and her cheeks were hot again, only this time not from shame, but the heat of the dancing flames. The boy had done well, hadn't he? Senior management in a luxury hotel in Berlin. While all she did was put rubbish out on the shelves in Europris. She was glad he did not know about that. Or perhaps he had been there without her knowing.

For the second time, she pulled herself out of a reverie and went into the bedroom. The old glass light fitting, full of dead flies, brought to mind a pale moon. She pulled open the bottom drawer of the chest. The photograph was in a yellow envelope, which she opened carefully. She took the photograph out and carried it back into the living room where the light was better. Sat down on her favourite chair, pulled the reading lamp closer and held up the picture. It was big, about A4, she thought. There was something fairy-like about the image. She looked as transparent as porcelain, with downturned eyes. He had not included her body, there was no beauty there. She had never been shapely, or charming or confident. It must have been her childish, or rather, angelic voice, which she had now lost. He had once said that when she spoke and laughed it sounded like the tinkling of bells. There's no malice in you, little Ragna.

She did not sleep well that night. She felt like she had been caught. But she refused to get worked up about it. If she lay there without moving, she would eventually fall asleep. Perhaps Walther was lying awake somewhere, equally at a loss, his body tired and worn. He had followed her out of the cafe, which must have taken great courage. And he had identified himself, in his own modest way, and she had rejected him. She had looked at him as though he were a stranger and run away. Perhaps he thought that she was bitter, and that she would never say another word to him. Whatever the case, he could find out for himself about 'the boy'. But she had no regrets. Despite the fact that he had plied her with drink, carried her to a bedroom, and taken advantage of her as he whispered to her and stroked her as though she were a kitten. She decided she would go into town and look for him. But then she would have to reveal her handicap. And he would discover that the bells were no longer there, and that the boy had left, and vanished into thin air.

Ragna turned over in the bed, defiantly faced the wall, pressed her forehead against the cool, dry wallpaper. She lay there in the dark tracing her fingers over the flock, feeling the different patterns that she knew so well, but could not see. A lily, a leaf. She felt them under her fingertips like Braille. Was it really a coincidence that Walther had shown up now, or was he part of something bigger, a plan she knew nothing about, a pattern she could not see?

Chapter 13

As the days passed, she got to know the rhythm of the building. The main police station was full of sounds – the slamming of cell doors, the whirring and humming of lifts, the busy pulse of the place. She heard the lock turn early in the morning when they came with breakfast, or when it was her turn to go to the bathroom, and then again later on, often around eleven, when one of the guards would come to collect her for more questioning. But it was midday now, and no one had come to collect her. No one had told her that the interview had been postponed or would take place later in the day, or perhaps would not happen at all. Or that the inspector had now heard what he needed, and everything she had said was to be summarised and presented to the district court. She waited. She listened out for any movement in the corridor, sat on her bunk with her hands in her lap, nervously scuffing her feet against the floor. Any second now, someone would come. They were just late. It was winter and the guards wore heavy boots, so it was easy to hear them as they walked around in the corridor. She got up and went over to the window, stood there with her back to the door. When it opened she would turn round with a surprised look on her face.

'Oh, is that the time! He must be waiting for me.'

But no one came. It might be a tactic, she thought. They had decided they had been nice long enough now; it was time to demonstrate the gravity of the situation, what she had done, her appalling crime. She must not be allowed to believe they had forgotten it. They had noted it, discussed it and compared it with other crimes. They had given her a place in the district's history. She would be talked about at dinner tables, like some particularly juicy titbit, in homes up and down the country, and discussed over a drink or two in the evening. But for now, she had to live with the uncertainty and wait in the most humane prison system in the world, which was her good fortune. She lay down on her bunk again, with her hands close by her sides, tense as a steel spring. She normally spent the afternoon going through her conversation with Sejer in detail, but now she had nothing to go through. He was busy with something else, someone else. After all, she was not the only one, there were lots of green doors along the corridor and all day long she heard locks firing open and closed like gunshots.

It was Adde who came with her lunch at one o'clock. He was one of the guards who said little, using his eyes instead. He put down the rather unappetising tray on her desk, studied her and then turned to leave. There was something wrong with one of his eyes, it was lifeless – it might even be glass – bigger than the other and brighter, but quite definitely blind.

'Will they be coming to get me soon?' she whispered.

He did not understand, and shook his head.

'Who?'

His dead eye expressed nothing, but the other one honed in on her.

She went over to the desk, inspected the food. There was nothing to complain about – there could have been three adults in the cell and there would be enough for them all.

'Well.' She looked away, embarrassed. 'The questioning. We're not finished.'

The cell door was open. His hand was resting on the handle, his attention was actually on the corridor, in case anything should happen there. He was so calm, so secure, so strong. It obviously had not occurred to him that she could lose her mind. That she might come charging towards him with the metal fork in her hand and aim at his eye, his one good eye. She could gouge out his eye like a mussel from its shell. She could go for the pulsing artery on his neck. It bulged thick and blue under his skin, as veins and arteries often do in men who go to the gym a lot. He knew perfectly well what she was accused of, and yet he stood with his back to her, his shoulders relaxed. She took a few steps across the floor.

'I haven't explained myself,' she whispered. 'There's more.'

He turned to her and smiled, but only with his mouth. His hair, black and cropped, lay on his head like velvet. She looked at her lunch. Slices of brown bread, cheese and salami. Small dishes of butter and marmalade, some slices of apple. Half an orange and a yogurt. A hard-boiled egg. Small sachets of salt and pepper, a serviette and a carton of juice. He left, and she sat down to eat, but did not eat much. She lay down on the bunk again to wait, closed her eyes and imagined she was lying between the tracks on an old railway bridge with her arms held tight to her body. That she could feel the vibration of the train approaching. The legal system would rattle over her, but she was lying as flat as she could. That way, she would save her life.

But Adde came back. He escorted her down the long corridors to the lift, and on to Sejer's office. She hoped she would get an explanation. He had kept her waiting without letting her know why, for no reason, and now he had decided to talk to her all the same. The inspector's calm, the fact that he was so solid and unshakeable, had started to irritate her. She had come to the conclusion that he had kept her waiting on purpose, that he had a plan. Humiliation. A confession. But she was humble. She had already confessed.

She took her time to sit down, scraped the chair on the floor, was not as quiet as usual. Sejer did not notice. He gave her time to settle, waited until he had her full attention.

'Did you have any sense of time? From the event until Gunnhild let herself into the house and raised the alarm?'

Ah, so that was what he wanted, to talk about the event – then she could go along with him.

'No sense of time,' she whispered. 'Not that time stood still. But it didn't move either. It was just one second after another, and I lived every single one of them.'

'So it could have been hours, but also days?'

'Yes.'

'An eternity perhaps?'

'Yes, an eternity, or just a moment.'

'And was it a relief that someone had finally come and taken charge?'

'Yes, it was fine.'

'Just fine?'

'I knew that sooner or later someone would come. I was tired and I didn't care.'

She wanted to ask him if the timing was important. Why he was so concerned about the details and what she had thought and felt. He was presumably following procedure, even though she was in no way denying what had actually happened. Still, he wanted every link in the chain, held each one up to the light, looked at it from all angles.

'You phoned Europris on Monday morning,' Sejer said, 'to tell them you were ill. You spoke briefly to Gunnhild. Can you remember the conversation?'

'I've already told you, I remember everything.'

She tapped her temple with her forefinger, to indicate that everything was stored in her head.

'And did you go and lie down afterwards?'

'I kept collapsing. On the chair, on the sofa, on the floor. I remember I was freezing.'

'So Monday passed,' Sejer continued, 'and Tuesday. On Wednesday afternoon, Gunnhild rang to hear how you were, if you felt any better. If there was anything you needed. What you said made no sense and you seemed to be confused. Can you remember that conversation as well?'

'Yes, I was confused, which is not so strange, really. I sat in my chair and it would not stay still, I had to hold on to the armrests.'

'Can you remember what Gunnhild said?'

'She wanted to come and see me. With some food, bits and bobs, medicine. I said it didn't suit.'

'But you must have wanted an end to the situation? Did you not want it resolved, for someone else to take over?'

'Yes. But it would have to be someone bigger and stronger than Gunnhild. If you see what I mean.'

His telephone was flashing again, two lines this time. Ragna tried to ask herself what she had really wanted, but was distracted by the red lights. She was over-whelmed by the fact that he gave her the time she needed, but she was starting to feel tired. She reminded herself that she was finally safe, the inspector was not an enemy. And she had plenty of time, this would only go one way, she wanted for nothing and they fed her like a goose for Christmas. Trays of food in and out, with a few friendly words.

'The situation was already resolved,' she whispered.

'Is that what you thought?'

He made a quick note, then looked up again. It struck her that he rarely blinked, his eyes were big and open. She looked at the white notepad with blue-ink scribbles. And realised that if he wrote a message on one of the sheets, tore it off and folded it double, the note would be the same size as the ones she had received in her mailbox.

'Yes, that's what I thought. It was resolved.'

'You had solved the problem?'

She looked away and seemed to be sad.

'I was at the end of the road. I wasn't frightened of anything any more and I knew that I wouldn't get any more messages.'

'When you were brought in, you were in pretty bad shape,' he said. 'You were exhausted, dehydrated and confused. You hadn't had anything to eat or drink.'

She looked at Frank over by the window, rested her eyes on him. It was just what a person needed to relax, to watch a sleeping dog and listen to the regular breathing. After a while, she found herself breathing in the same rhythm.

'No, no food. It wasn't important. It was so hard to move around, and impossible to make decisions. Getting up from the chair, walking all the way to the kitchen, opening the cupboard, taking out a glass, turning on the tap, drinking, it was all too much. Just thinking about all the things I would have to do to get there made me exhausted. It was all I could do to sit still in the chair without lifting a finger and concentrate on my breathing. And as long as I stayed like that, without moving, I didn't need anything. I had my eyes closed for the greater part of the time. When I opened them, it was sometimes light and sometimes dark, and I realised that the days were passing.'

Sejer tore a sheet from the notepad. He glanced at the red flashing lights on his phone, put a hand to his short fringe, but not a hair moved.

She gingerly touched her own dry hair as though mirroring him. It crossed her mind that she would be grey, like the inspector, in the course of a few years. She would turn grey while she served her sentence. It would be more flattering than faded red, it would give her character. She had never had character. She had had her father, but he was dead. She had had a son, but he had left.

'Do you think you'll remember me?' she said in a tiny voice. 'When all this is over, and someone else is sitting in this chair.'

'Absolutely.'

'What will you remember, do you think? Tell me.'

She was like a child begging for sweeties.

'Your voice,' he said and smiled. 'No one else I know expresses themselves the way you do. I'm not used to people in this room, or building for that matter, talking to me the way you do. There's something special about you, Ragna. Of course I will remember you. For the rest of my life, no doubt.'

'That's what Walther said, as well,' she whispered. 'That's why I let him carry me to the bed. Ugly girls don't get many chances.'

Chapter 14

Gunnhild used a knife to cut the tape and open the lid of the thick, brown cardboard box. Inside were bags of Sloggi briefs, in packs of ten.

'Do you remember the old Direct mail-order catalogues?' she asked. 'That used to come with the post?'

'I remember them,' Ragna whispered. 'My mother and I used to sit on the sofa and look at them together. It wasn't every exciting for a little girl, mostly kitchen equipment and things like that, but I liked looking at the pictures. And they had a lucky dip, do you remember that? The surprise package?'

Gunnhild did.

'It cost four hundred and fifty kroner,' Ragna remembered, 'but the catalogues said it was worth nearly a thousand. I begged and begged for months to get a lucky dip. My mother told me it was probably just full of junk, the things they never managed to sell that took up space in the warehouse. But I got what I wanted in the end. And I've never been so disappointed in my life.'

'What was in it?' Gunnhild asked, and laughed.

'Clothes hangers, a shoehorn, cotton reels. Different-coloured combs, pens, folders and rubber bands. One of those see-through rain ponchos. And a torch that shone in different colours. Red and green and yellow.'

'I remember those torches,' Gunnhild said.

'There was also a necklace with several strings of plastic beads. I wore that necklace every day, I had to show my mother that it had been worth it. But the necklace soon broke, and I spent hours on my knees picking up beads.'

Ragna stared at the cardboard box.

'Now we get surprise packages every day.'

Ragna put the packs of briefs in a trolley and went out into the shop. They already had a barcode on them. A man was standing further down the aisle, stretching up to look at something on the top shelf. She recognised the black suit and the slicked-back dark hair. From a distance, he looked thinner and smaller than last time, when he stood in front of her at the till. It was the Agent. With his black shoes and fastidious appearance, which had made her assume he worked for the Secret Service, or perhaps a funeral home. He pulled a shopping trolley on wheels behind him. He did not notice that she was staring at him, he was not sensitive to it, because he had no enemies, Ragna guessed, he had nothing to fear. There were people like that. It was not what he was looking for, so he moved on. His suit made him conspicuous. She passed him and carried on down the aisle, and then when she was some way from him, turned and looked at him again. He had an energy about him, a nervous edge, which she did not think was compatible with working as an undertaker. He was so quick, light on his feet, obviously on his way somewhere. Perhaps he was an estate agent after all, they often dressed like that. He eventually did take something from the shelves, a packet of four suet balls, the ones in green plastic netting. So he fed the birds, she liked that. She had the same kind outside her kitchen window. And it was winter, so people often remembered to do things like that. She stayed as close as she could to him, without making it obvious, and without knowing why. There were lots of other customers in the shop she could observe. But she liked following him up and down the aisles. Keeping him under surveillance.

When her shift was finished, she took some Sloggi briefs with her and asked Gunnhild to make a note. Audun got to her seat on the bus first and sat there tapping away on his mobile phone. After a while, he stopped and started to read a book. Maybe Lars had managed to convince him and he was studying to take the forklift truck licence.

She chose a seat five rows back on the right-hand side. She looked out at the shops and parks. A kindergarten with an old fishing boat outside in the playground jogged a memory. There had also been a boat at her son's nursery that he liked to play in. Or perhaps it was more true to say that he felt protected in the small cabin. He had always been a child who liked to hide, to creep into confined spaces. Aboard the boat, he was at the helm. Suddenly she thought she saw his little face in the round cabin window, as pale and frightened as she was. After the kindergarten, the bus passed a football pitch and a shop that sold things for horses and dogs. Then lots of single-storey wooden houses, from the sixties, painted in pink and yellow and blue. She had seen everything before, day in and day out for years, because she always followed the same pattern. The pattern was imprinted like a map in her brain, and when she stuck to it, she felt safe.

She remembered the necklace again, the turquoise plastic beads, and the sound, the faint tinkle when her fingers played with the strings, the sound when the necklace broke, the beads rolling in every direction over the wooden floor. The shame she felt in relation to her mother, whom she had convinced to spend the money on junk, who never once said 'I told you so'.

She crossed the road at the bus stop on Kirkelina and went to Irfan's shop. Dolly was tied up outside, and she could see one of the Soi children in the aisle. She walked straight into Olaf. They exchanged a few words, then she picked up the things she needed from the shelves and put them in her basket. She asked Irfan if he had seen any vacancies for chefs recently, but he had not. She decided that she would tell him about her dream, when he came into her bedroom to get her brain. That she had seen him so clearly, with the bloody scalpel in his hand. But no sooner had she thought it than she was infuriated with herself. What would a man from his culture think about her confiding in him like that? 'I dreamt about you last night.' It was such an intimate thing to say, regardless of who it was. And to say it to the local shop owner was too much. She could have said it to Lars, though. Lars would have grinned happily and asked for the details. So she said nothing. When she had bought her things, she crossed the road again to her drive. Opened the mailbox, took out the newspaper, scanned the headlines. She saw there was something else lying on the bottom. Two letters. One was postmarked Berlin. The familiar blue stamp was the first thing she saw, 'Not known at this address'. The card of a pony had been returned. On the other envelope, which did not have a stamp, it simply said 'RIEGEL'. So Rikard Josef was not to be found. She could not understand it. Was Germany not a well-organised country, with perfectly functioning systems and structures? She trudged up towards the house and slammed the door shut, pulled off her coat. She tore the anonymous envelope open in a fury. She had not been chosen at random, how could she have ever believed that?

With the letter in her hand, she crossed the room and stood by the window. She wondered if Irfan would see her, if he looked out right now, see her black silhouette. The message was short and concise, as usual.

'NO ONE WILL HEAR YOU.'

She sometimes got up in the middle of the night and pulled the curtains to one side, stared over at the Sois' house, and at the church spire and pale clock face further up the road. After a few restless turns around the floor, she would creep back down under the duvet, and make herself as small as possible. No one had seen her, no one knew what she was thinking. Often when she lay awake like this, she thought of Walther Eriksson. He had probably gone back to Stockholm, and she had not given him anything. But then, she had nothing to give. And even worse, a postman in Berlin had once again stood in Landsberger Allee with a card of a pony in his hand and not known what to do with it. There was no longer a mailbox with the name Riegel on it. But it was Christmas soon! His card would come as always, she was sure of that, and she would mention to Gunnhild, almost in passing, that the Christmas cards were flooding in. Got one from Berlin today. Goodness, my boy has so much to do!

She lay awake and listened to the dark. Stretched herself out as far as she could, then curled up like a prawn, tossed and turned. The night was no longer silent, she could hear the seven billion people who lived on this earth. They were breathing like an enormous beast, cackling and screaming and wailing. She remembered that she had once heard about a man who had stayed in a completely soundproofed room for twenty-four hours. He explained that it was like an immense pressure in his head that kept building and building, until it was impossible to think. Like being cast in concrete. Imagine that silence, Ragna tried, it must be like death. She looked at the alarm clock – ten past four. Not much left of the night, but not yet morning. She got up and went to the bathroom. The window was covered by a plastic blue curtain, which she pulled aside as well. There was a thin strip of grass at the back of the house – or rather, it was more weeds and heather, frozen and leached of colour. The woodpile was also below the window, under the green tarpaulin. She had a pee, and then went back to bed and curled up.

She thought that she should ring Naper, her GP, to get some sleeping tablets. Finally, at six, she got up again. She put her feet down on the cold floor, put on some clothes and then went out and switched on the light in the kitchen.

*

Three days later, she sat on the bus on the way into town and planned her modest plea. She did not like to beg, but Naper had never actually refused her anything. He had never questioned her, never been authoritarian or arrogant. Quite the opposite, in fact, there was an air of melancholy about him that she identified with, that made her feel a connection. With his grave face and heavy jowls, and hands as big as bear paws, he reminded her more of an ageing lumberjack than a doctor. When she got there, she explained that she was not sleeping, and had not done so for some time. That the tiredness made her heavy and slow, and she could not shake it. She often had a headache when she got up and things flickered in front of her eyes. He wanted to know if anything had happened. If she was worried about something, or had experienced a loss. Or was she afraid of something. She looked uncomfortable, as one often does at the doctor's, pale and apathetic, with her hands in her lap. She shook her head. Imagine bothering a busy doctor with trivialities like the letters in her mailbox, she would never do that.

'I guess it's part of getting older,' she said, without looking at him.

She was sitting quite close to him, dressed in her green Europris shop coat with her handbag on her lap. She whispered her request. He looked at the screen, scanned through her medical history over the years – plenty there, she was well over forty, after all.

'I'll give you something gentle,' he said, 'that's non-addictive. But be careful all the same. It's usual to have sleeping problems for periods of time, but they generally pass naturally. But you're not one who's prone to complaining, Ragna, you're very patient.'

He wrote out a prescription, and she heard the printer hum.

'Do you have any good nights in between, when you sleep well?' he asked.

She was struck by how friendly he was, despite all the complaints he must have heard over the years, all the expectations and demands, sickness and death, all the people he could not save.

She nodded. 'I do have some good nights.'

'Are you bothered by nightmares? Lots of people develop sleeping issues if they have bad dreams over a longer period of time. They dread falling asleep.'

'I don't dread it,' she responded. 'All I want to do is sleep. Sleep through the night. If that's possible.'

She had the prescription in her hand and noticed his signature, which was illegible.

'And your son?' he asked, all of a sudden. 'He'll be coming home for Christmas, I suppose? Or are you going to Berlin?'

The question was so out of the blue that she started to stammer.

'We've not decided yet.'

He said nothing for a while. It was a sore point for her, he had seen it before.

'Come and see me again,' he encouraged her.

She folded the prescription and put it in her handbag. Closed the door quietly behind her, and went out through the waiting room. There was something sad about the people sitting there, she thought. Perhaps none of them were sleeping either, maybe they all had aches and pains, maybe it was them she heard at night, complaining, breathing and wailing.

She handed the prescription in at the chemist, and when she came out again, she opened the box and pulled out the tray of tiny pills. They were no bigger than a grain of rice. It was hard to believe that something so small could really help her sleep. She had no idea what they contained, as she had not asked. One summer, a long time ago, she was on holiday in the Algarve with her parents, and in one of the villages they saw a man sitting on the pavement selling grains of rice. He claimed that the whole of the Lord's Prayer was engraved on each grain. They were in glass pendants on leather thongs, and people bought them and wore them around their necks, believing that they carried a prayer, that they would be protected. She had not bought the grain of rice. She did not believe in what she could not see. She held the packet of pills tight in her hand, noticed the red warning triangle. She liked the triangle, it must mean they were effective. But as she did not drive or operate any heavy machinery, it did not apply to her. Now she had a defence. A switch. She could turn it on and off, sleep or not sleep; it was a choice, some form of control over the night. Wake up when the chemicals had left her body. Choose the day, and then choose sleep. Keep the demons at bay.

The pills were protection against intruders, her equivalent to Gunnhild's pepper spray that she had bought on the Internet and always kept with her.

She wandered aimlessly through the city centre, window-shopping. Popped into Magasinet and had a quick look in the cafe, in case Walther might be sitting at one of the tables, watching her. She decided to have a look in the pet shop, as she sometimes did, because she liked the smells and sounds. They had aquarium fish and parrots, hamsters, guinea pigs and rabbits. There was a macaw called Papa Doc that had been in the shop for years, and she never tired of admiring him. His cage was always open, so he could go in and out as he pleased; in other words, he had a standing offer of freedom which he chose not to take. Maybe he thought there were too many people out there, too much noise, too many staring eyes and pestering fingers. So he sat there on his perch where he felt safe. Ragna stood quietly and watched the bird. He stared back at her with bright eyes, tried to gauge what sort of person she was, if she had good intentions. She whispered some words of affection and he sidled closer. She wanted to touch him, stroke his feathers. But a sign said that Papa Doc should not be touched, and it was clear that he could bite off your finger. His red feathers had a moisture to them, and his eyes had a twinkle. She knew that he could talk, but today he had nothing to say. She leaned closer, tried to tempt him. 'Beautiful boy,' she whispered. 'Beautiful boy.' But he was not going to be fooled into imitating her. Another bird in another cage started to whistle in a seductive manner, which raised her spirits. When she closed her eyes, she could pretend she was a real stunner walking down the street, with people clamouring all around. As she was leaving, without having bought anything, she passed a display of postcards and stickers and other bits and pieces, all with pictures of animals. But it was something else that caught her attention. On the wall above the display was a metal sign. It was A4-size and had on it a picture of a snarling Rottweiler with a studded collar. A hole had been drilled in each corner, for screws. And under the picture it said in big letters: 'BEWARE THE DOG!'

Ragna's eyes widened. She had never seen a dog like that, nor canine teeth like that – it certainly was not like Dolly. This was a predator, trained to attack. She rose up onto her toes and took down the sign to look at the terrifying beast more closely. The sign was meant to be hung on a wall, or a fence, or a gate, and it was solid and heavy. She went over to the counter and opened her purse with rare determination. Someone had sentenced her to death. Now she had protection.

'Do you have one?' the assistant wanted to know. He put the Rottweiler in a bag and watched her tap in her pin code.

'No,' she whispered. 'But I need one.'

He was taken aback by the fact that she whispered, but thought that it was maybe her way of flirting. She had lowered her voice to make herself more mysterious, and he was charmed.

'With that on your wall, you won't need an alarm,' he said.

She thanked him and left, hurried down the street to the square, with the sleeping pills in her bag and the Rottweiler in a plastic carrier. Once she was sitting on the bus, in the third row on the left, she took the sign out of the bag. It weighed a lot. She could not stop staring at the snarling dog. She could hang it the wall of the house with those nails she had lying in one of the kitchen drawers.

As soon as she got home she put her plan into action. She hammered hard and furiously with all her might and continued long after the nails were embedded in the wood, one in each corner. The hammering was a warning to the whole neighbourhood, Ragna thought, as she stood there banging away. The woman who lived here knew how to defend herself. When the sign was in place, to the left of the front door, she stepped back and admired the dog from a distance. Then she went down the steps and onto the gravel driveway. It looked like the dog was following her with his eyes, no matter where she stood in relation to the door. She moved sideways to the right, then to the left, to the bottom of the steps, all the way down to the road, keeping eye contact with the dog all the time. She saw the red wetness of the dog's mouth, the yellowish teeth that could pull and tear.

The real Rottweiler, the one she did not have, that she might have called Attila or Saddam, that weighed more than seventy kilos, was right inside the door; the one that she wanted visitors to imagine, when they had seen the sign, would attack given the short whispered order 'Attila, go' – especially if that person had ill intentions.

But what about the children, she thought, the ones who came to sell raffle tickets, small and hopeful with rosy cheeks and frozen fingers? They would also lose their nerve, and they did not have much before. They would turn on their heels and run as fast as they could, raffle tickets in one hand and some cold coins in a plastic bag in the other. Ah well, she shrugged, swings and roundabouts. She went inside again, locked the door and put on the security chain.

There was a raw chill to the dark November days. When she went to throw out the rubbish, with no coat on, the snow whipped round her and pinched her cheeks in the short distance down to the road. She did

it as quickly as she could, then shuffled back to the
house, bent double like an old lady. The cold was evil
and chilled her to the bone, she felt that it was out to
get her, that it was significant in some way. She decided
to buy a pair of sheepskin mittens. The cheap, synthetic
mittens were not good enough, nor were the boots.
She had no fat on her body, so she was easy prey.
When will I learn? she asked herself. I've lived in this
country all my life. The Eskimos, they knew how to
dress. For them, the cold was a given, something they
lived with, constantly. The frost killed any bacteria,
so the food kept longer, everything was clean and
sparkling white. She associated Eskimos with something pure, fresh.

But it was warm on the bus, and her favourite place
was empty. She spared a thought for the driver, who
sat there bouncing in his seat, and was bombarded by
a cold gust from the street every time the door slid open
with a wheeze. She was nearly home. What should I eat
tonight? she wondered. Maybe some of Irfan's flatbreads with ham and a hot sauce. She felt her face
lighting up every time they passed a street light, even
when she closed her eyes. It was snowing, but the
snowplough had not been out yet. She trudged along
the road in her thin boots. There were salt marks on
the leather and her toes were numb. She felt something
was amiss. But it was the cold, she was walking with
her head bowed, did not look up. She quickly crossed
the road, then stood there, at a loss, looking around. It
was darker than normal, quieter, colder; something
essential was missing from the street, as though it had
lost its pulse and was dying. She walked faster, no one
was following. When she finally got to Irfan's shop, she

saw that the light was not on. That was strange. She stared at the dark window in surprise, then noticed the sign.

CLOSED. HAVE MOVED.

The notice, which he had made himself, on a piece of cardboard with uneven writing, had been taped to the door.

Ragna clutched her handbag to her chest. In it was her purse, and the money she was going to use to buy flatbreads. She felt like a little girl with a coin in her hand who had come to the sweet shop too late. Irfan Baris had moved. Without telling her, without preparing her or any explanation, without thanking her for all the years she had been a loyal customer. And there was nothing on the sign to say where he had moved to. For all she knew, it might be somewhere south of the river, where she seldom went. Or even worse, he might have moved to another town. It was almost like losing a lover. Irfan was a handsome man, with eyes as brown as chestnuts. He always listened to what she had to say, and sometimes surprised her with thoughtful comments, like she should get herself a reflector. And what about all the praise and enthusiasm she had showered on his shop? The interest she had shown in his well-being, his family, how they celebrated Christmas, and more? All the money she had contributed to his business over the years – she shopped there all the time – did it mean nothing? Was it not even worth him telling her that he was going to move?

Without thinking, she looked around for Olaf, he would know. She peered up the road and down, looked back at the dark windows, the empty shelves. How could this have happened? And so fast, it took time to move. There must have been more of them, she thought, maybe they worked all night. While she lay sleeping, they had packed everything into boxes and loaded them into a van. She was overwhelmed by a sudden sorrow, felt worthless, forgotten, ignored. Standing there alone and freezing in the dark, as though she had been robbed. Well, there would be no flatbreads and ham, as she had planned. No longer could she wander around in her living room looking over at the lights in his windows, lights that had become a part of her life, and the street. No doubt someone else would open a shop there, the place could not be used for anything else. But right now, there was nothing, no wonderful smell of exotic spices, no fruit that he was selling cheap because it had been there too long. She tried to remember what she had in the fridge and it was not much. He could have said something. He could have prepared her. She pushed the door hard several times, to relieve her anger. She swore in the dark, a whisper that no one heard, some-thing mean about foreigners who had no manners, had no understanding of common courtesy. She turned her back on the shop and stormed across the road.

There was nothing in her mailbox.

Every time she looked out of the window she was filled with an indefinable fear. The whole street had changed, she thought, the lighting outside was different, it was intruding into her living room. She found herself going over to the window again and again in the hope that she was mistaken, that suddenly the lights would be on in Irfan's shop as though nothing had happened.

Long before he came to Norway with his family there had been a newsagent's there called Sweet News, and before that there had been a small hairdresser's with only one chair. Her father went there occasionally, though generally he let his hair grow. But she remembered the nice smell of shampoo and hair tonic. And the scent of leather from the chair her father sat in, which could be lowered and raised and swivelled round. Sometimes, if she asked nicely, she was allowed to sit in the chair herself. The hairdresser pretended that they were at the fair and swung her this way and that, before her father had his hair cut. And now, black windows. The miserable sign was scarcely visible, no more than a pale square on the locked door.

Then suddenly she noticed a man. She did not know where he had come from or how long he had been standing there, she had been so focused on the closed shop. He was standing under the street light at the bottom of her drive. The first thing she noticed was that he was standing absolutely still. He was dressed in something long and dark, but as far as she could see had nothing on his head. And he was staring at her house. His head was big and round, and his body was long and thin. Because he was standing under the light, she could see him quite clearly even though it was dark. She stepped back into the room. It was just someone out for a wander, who happened to admire her house as she looked out, because the warm light streaming from the windows made it welcoming. If she went and looked again now, he would be gone, perhaps on his way up towards the church. But that was not the case, he was still standing there. And his arms, those long arms, were not hanging loosely by his side, but were pressed against his body as though he were carved in stone. Perhaps she should close the curtains and turn off all the lights? Instead she collapsed into the armchair, sat there for some time and watched the clock on the wall as time ticked by. She could hear the small click each time the minute hand moved. Felt with her whole being that he was standing there, felt his eyes.

She had to get up and check again. He had not moved. It was cold and he was unsuitably dressed, no hat or gloves. He seemed oblivious to the dark and the snow. His posture was defiant, like he was making a demand, or waiting for something, only she had no idea what. She stepped to the side of the window, hid behind the curtain. But he had of course seen her silhouette through the glass. What if she waved to him – would he wave back? Would her hand act as a signal to set something in motion, something over which she had no control? She huddled up behind the curtain, held the thick fabric tight in her hand. A car drove slowly by, the white headlights dipping, but the man did not move. She tried frantically to find a way to deal with it, she could not simply ignore him, he was standing in her drive, he was staring at her house. She should probably walk those forty-eight steps down to the road and ask what he wanted, if he was waiting for someone or something, if he was looking for an address. But he might then answer, nothing, and I'll stand here as long as I like. I'm within my rights. Which was true. So she tried to ignore him, did not dare go out, but hit the wall with her fist to vent her anger. She would not do much more than produce vapour in the cold air, and words he could not hear. And if he was suddenly gone, did that mean he had come up to the house and was standing on the top step right now, laughing at the Rottweiler, because he realised she did not have a dog, or, even worse, he knew, because he had been watching her for a long time? Instead, she turned on the television and sat down in the armchair, stared at the flickering screen without taking anything in. She resisted the temptation to close the curtains. Then he would probably think that she had seen him and was frightened, and she did not want to give him the pleasure, if it was the thrill he was after. Ragna thought she could hear him, standing there by the lamp post, growling. She could hear him over the sound of the television, as though he was right outside the window. Or was it Olaf using some electrical equipment in his house, a drill perhaps? She decided to wait for half an hour, and if he was still there she would ring the police. It was definitely time to get someone else involved. The clock on the wall ticked by, she could hear clearly. So she turned up the volume on the television, but she could still hear him. When those long thirty minutes had finally passed, she peeped quickly out through the window – he was still there. So she gave him another half-hour. Tiptoed out into the kitchen, made sure always to keep her back to the window. She brewed a cup of tea, and stirred in the sugar. Snuck back into the living room, bent over so she was under the radar, and watched the minutes pass on the wall clock. He was still there.

She rang the police on her landline. A female officer answered. She was polite, but not particularly interested or helpful.

'Duty officer. How can I help?'

Ragna tried as hard as she could to make herself understood.

'There's a man watching my house,' she whispered. 'He's standing down by the road staring up at the house and he's been there for a long time.'

Silence. Perhaps the officer was writing it all down, or maybe she was rolling her eyes to a colleague.

'So he's not in your house?'

'No,' Ragna whispered.

'He's standing down by the road?'

'Yes.'

'Well, why are you whispering then? It makes it very hard to hear what you're saying? Could you speak normally, please?'

There. She heard the first hint of irritation because she was not like everyone else.

She swallowed and tried to explain, managed to stammer that she did not have a voice because of an injury. Again, there was silence on the other end.

'So he's hurt you?'

'No!'

Another silence. Ragna could feel the pressure in her head; her throat tightened.

'He's been standing there for over an hour,' she whispered. 'He hasn't moved, he just stands there staring.'

'I'm sorry, can you repeat that?'

'He's been standing there for over an hour!'

'What's your address?'

'Kirkelina 7. Riegel.'

'And you don't know who he is? You don't know him?'

'He's sent me some letters.'

'I see.'

A pause.

'So you're drawing your own conclusions here. You've received some letters, and now there's a man standing outside looking at your house. Are you sure it's the same person?'

'I think so.'

'You think?'

The officer did not say anything for a long time, but Ragna could hear some mumbling, as though she was conferring with someone else. The mumbling lasted for some time, and then she was back.

'Is there a bus stop or something like that on the road?'

'No, that's further down.'

'And you're sure that he's looking at your house? He's not standing with his back to you? It's dark, after all.'

'His face is pale,' Ragna said. 'He's standing under a street light at the end of my drive. He wants me to see him.'

'Is he doing anything other than standing there?'

'No.'

'Have you recently broken up from a relationship?'

It was Ragna's turn to be silent. But then she realised what the officer was thinking.

'No, I haven't.'

'No ex-husband or ex-partner?'

She thought about Walther, who had suddenly popped up after all these years, but then dismissed the idea.

'No,' she said firmly.

The officer asked her for more information about the letters. It dawned on her that she thought of Ragna as disabled, as people always treated her in that special way. No doubt they got lots of calls from confused and sick people, who shouted and screamed and made a fuss. The switchboard was probably constantly flashing red with incoming calls.

'But he's done nothing to you?'

'He's just standing there.'

'He hasn't shouted or threatened you?'

'No.'

'Then I'm afraid there's not a lot we can do,' the officer explained. 'Not unless he's on your property. And as you said that he's down on the road, I'm afraid he has every right to stand there, unless he threatens you.'

Ragna was really running into problems now. It was getting harder for her to express herself clearly. She desperately wanted to slam the phone down, but decided to try once more.

'How long do I have to wait then?' she whispered in desperation. 'What if he stands there all night?'

'Sorry, can you say that again?'

'What if he stands there all night?'

'That's not very likely,' the officer said. 'We don't have any cars available in your area at the moment, I'm afraid. You'll just have to try your best to ignore him. It's cold out there,' she added. 'He'll be freezing soon enough, but that's his problem.'

Ragna guessed that the officer was smiling. At herself and the elegant way in which she dealt with the public, the kind of smile she used when she wanted to end a conversation. The officer was of course very good at discerning what was serious and what was nonsense. People's constant need for attention. Old ladies were the worst.

'But the letters,' Ragna whispered in desperation. 'They must mean something. I've had three of them. He's threatening me!'

'In that case,' the officer said, 'you should bring them here so we can have a look.'

Ragna threw the receiver down. She could not bear having to admit that she had burnt them.

She stomped to the bathroom, without even glancing at the window, and started to run a bath. As she could not scream, she had to find other ways to make a noise. She sprinkled a handful of peach-coloured bath salts into the water, which were supposed to have a 'relaxing and revitalising' effect. Not that she believed it, but she had nothing else, not even a drop of red wine. There was good pressure in the old pipes and the water gushed out of the taps, so the bath was quickly full of cascades of calming foam. She took off her clothes and left them lying on the floor like an abandoned nest. The foam meant that she did not need to look at her own skinny body in the water, and she lay there without moving, and with her eyes closed. Breathed slowly and evenly. She had understood how important it was to breathe properly. She had even heard that some people went on courses to learn the art, and that the right breathing could remedy all kinds of ills, including anxiety and stress. She decided to lie there until the water had lost most of its warmth. The man would be gone by then. Tired and blue with cold, he would finally have slunk off. Slowly she started to relax and both she and the room smelt good. She had heard that you could get high from bath salts, and that it is a powerful and destructive rush, which surprised her. Bath salts were available everywhere, even young children could get hold of them, and old ladies were given them for Christmas. The warm water had made her so heavy and relaxed that she felt quite dizzy when she stood up and got out. She was smooth and pink like a salmon. The mirror had steamed up so she could only see herself as a shadow. I've always been unclear, she thought, that's nothing new. Before she left the bathroom, she opened the window to let out the steam. She went straight back to the living room. The man had gone. He really had gone! She peered up and down the road, no one was standing under the street lamp staring. She thought that he might have moved on to the next house to terrorise them, Olaf or the Sois, or someone else. And the officer she had spoken to would still be on duty, answering the phone. There would be red flashing lights on the switchboard all night, and the next day, and she was just one little red light that they could turn off whenever they liked. One of seven billion. One of the complainers.

She felt hot as a poker straight out of the fire and her clothes were sticking to her. She checked again to see that the man had gone, leaned against the window that immediately steamed up, so she drew a smiley face. Turned on her computer and searched for 'The Jumper' on YouTube. She never got tired of watching the weightless dive from the tall building all the way down to the ground. Never tired of the resurrection, when he stood up and walked towards the camera. His eyes, black, inscrutable, that said so much. You hadn't expected this, had you? A spark of triumph. Or perhaps, his eyes were challenging her, as though he wanted to tell her something or get her to do something, as though he had seen her, Ragna Riegel from Kirkelina 7. She went to the window again, the man was not there. Irfan's shop was still dark. She cautiously went out and round to the back of the house to get some wood from the pile under the bathroom window, pulled the tarpaulin into place. The November air was sharp and cold, but she was still warm from the bath. Her blood vessels that had been opened contracted with such speed that her cheeks prickled. She was no longer heavy and slow, she was sharp and alert. She went back in and put the wood on the fire, sat on her knees in front of the glass door until it was burning well. Turned down the volume on the television and sat there staring at the flames. The door had beautiful cast-iron latticework, so she watched the flames through several small, arched spaces, a bit like a stained-glass window in a church. Why do flames have such a powerful effect on people, almost hypnotic? They were enough, she needed nothing else. And by the sea, one needs nothing apart from the waves that roll in and break on the shore. It must be something to do with endless repetitiveness, the dancing flames, the swell of the waves, the sense of some-thing that has always been and always will be. The eternal. She found that she wanted to meditate, but did not know how. Was it not a case of closing out the world and focusing on a small space, for example the blue at the centre of a flame, which she had heard was actually cold? If she chose one of the small windows in the door, and only looked at the flames through that one alone, everything around her, the room, the house, the street, would disappear and her tormented soul would find peace. But she found no peace.

She took four sleeping pills before she went to bed. They had no effect, no matter how many she took, but she swallowed them all the same, she might as well use what she had, and she was all too familiar with the power of imagination. She closed the bathroom window, and wrestled the hasp back into place. It got harder with each year, as the wood expanded with the humidity. The mirror had cleared and she glanced at herself. And immediately regretted it, as she saw nothing to cheer her. It was so quiet in the house that the silence had its own sound, a steady hum. Or in fact, she realised, not steady at all, it swelled and subsided, rose and fell. When she lay in bed, the hum got louder. She knocked her knuckles gently against the wall seven times. Stopped, then knocked one more time. No one answered. The hum was still there. It made her think of a leak. A poisonous gas seeping out of a large container.

Chapter 15

On the day that Ragna told Sejer about the man standing under the street light and her conversation with his colleague, who had dismissed her, he pondered long and hard when he got home in the evening. He also felt solidarity for his colleagues who received an endless torrent of phone calls day and night, an enormous amount of which were gibberish from lunatics or drunks, or pranks from children.

He pulled his chair over to the window and sat there in the half-light thinking. From the twelfth floor, he could look out over the town that sparkled and twinkled below him with the lights reflected in the river. Some important buildings were floodlit, like the theatre, the old fire station and the brewery, and the strings of lit streets reminded him of Christmas lights. He liked to see the city from above, as he had an overview and it gave him a sense of distance and control. The nights must have been so dark before electricity, he mused, pitch-black and overwhelming. Only the moon bathing the river in its cold light. Frank was asleep at his feet. He took a sip of whisky. He sometimes smoked a cigarette, just the one, in the evening;

the tobacco was dry and strong and made him dizzy. He tried to imagine the fear that Ragna must have felt when she saw the man by the street light. Dressed in black, immobile, staring at her house. There were clear rules when it came to communication between people, and staring was not the done thing. Eye contact could easily switch from being open and inviting, flirtatious, an expression of interest, to being threatening, a serious precursor of aggression and violence. The man had stood there like a statue. That in itself was puzzling and unsettling, a form of aggression. If he had been pacing back and forth, just glancing up at the house every so often, then he might have been waiting for somebody there, by the lamp post. Someone who never showed up. He snapped out of his reverie and took Frank out for a walk, his steps light on the newly fallen snow. They met nobody, the streets were empty, and all the windows bright and warm. It's inside the four walls of the home it happens, he thought, the abuse and betrayal, threats and slavery. It often went on for years, and no one knew anything about it. The same defence mechanisms in people that made them avoid anything uncomfortable, also kept them alive. It was a paradox that had always bothered him. He studied the windows one by one, as he passed, saw figures moving around inside. Perhaps some were sitting looking out, as he so often did himself. But here in the denseness of the dark, the bright windows looked inviting. It would not be long now before there would be stars and wreaths in nearly every window in anticipation of Christmas. He carried on at a steady pace. Other dogs had left their signatures by the roadside. Frank knew them all, they walked the same route between the blocks every night. They never went particularly far, as Frank was fat and found it hard to breathe. Sejer himself was lean and resilient, an ascetic on the verge of undernourished, some might say. He liked being that way, alert, sharp and clear. Hunger, not for food, but for everything else.

And he liked the dark. The biting snow on his cheeks, the cold that made his eyes water, the snow crunching under his boots – it was so clean and cold that everyone and everything left a mark. A sparrow weighed no more than a few grams, but still left a trail. On other continents far away, the sun was blasting the landscape, breaking down heaths and forests, drying out riverbeds, destroying harvests, forcing people into the shadows, where they sat and begged for mercy as they dreamt of a cool paradise and longed for soothing rain and glittering rivers. He tried to imagine living in that heat, working in it, struggling in it. He would never manage that.

He looked up at the stars that were sparkling clear in the cold. He knew the obvious constellations, like the Big Dipper and Orion's Belt, and usually looked for the Dog Star. He loved its brightness that outshone all the other stars, and reminded him of a boat. It was actually two stars very close together, he knew that, which was why it sparkled more than other single stars. But as soon as he had found it and confirmed it was still there, he looked down again. On the whole, he was a man who concerned himself with what happened on dry land. There was more than enough to keep him occupied there. And he could neither understand nor move the stars, and he liked to keep things moving.

Frank picked up a plastic chocolate milkshake cup from the side of the road – so that was tonight's trophy that he would take home. Sejer allowed him this, it was a dog's instinct to take home prey, after all. Once he was home he would heave his heavy rump up onto the sofa, which he usually managed on the third attempt, and then bury the quarry under a cushion. To hide it from other predators so it could be eaten some other time. There was something about this simple ritual that touched Sejer. Frank continued to be Frank, an ageing hunting dog, even though he got food in a dish twice a day, and the occasional sausage or biscuit. With misgivings. Twice on the short walk the dog did his business, turned his back on the result and kicked snow over it. He moved slowly on the way home, was out of breath. It's all my fault, Sejer thought, as he tugged at the lead. You'll have to stop dribbling in front of the fridge, Frank, you mustn't look at me with those black eyes, I'm an old man.

When he had turned off the light that evening, and Frank had buried the plastic cup under the cushions and fallen asleep on the mat by his bed, Sejer lay awake thinking about Ragna. And the fact that she was alone in a cell, on a narrow bunk. With bars in front of the window and a toilet bucket in the corner. There was something very appealing about her that was slowly growing on him. This delicate woman with tiny cinnamon-coloured freckles on her hands and a rare mix of shyness and pride. She would often not look at him, and yet came across as determined. She was sad, but she was not ashamed. She was patient and grateful for all she got, she never complained or fretted. He was still not sure how much she accepted responsibility for what had happened, they were not at that point yet. There were moments when he felt that she was glad of the situation, not with what she had done, but with where she found herself now, that someone else had taken charge of the catastrophe. That she was being looked after. For her, something was over, the problem was solved. And would not disrupt her life again. He had not seen much despair, or defiance. He did not know if she understood the magnitude of her crime, or if she was at all concerned about forgiveness, if she thought about things like that – they had never discussed it.

If he was honest, he had never really understood what forgiveness was himself. What it entailed, what it might mean to those implicated. Could one forgive and then later regret it, like giving a present one couldn't really afford? He suspected that the one who forgave had a motive for doing so, in much the same way that the guilty party had a motive for the crime. Was forgiveness something that the victim or those affected gave out of pure magnanimity, a generosity of almost divine proportions, or was there an egotistical need to be better than the offender? See this insurmountable divide between us? Well, I'll just make it bigger. You'll never reach my level, that is your punishment, you will never deserve it. You will have to carry my forgiveness for the rest of your life, and it will be as heavy a burden as the crime you have committed. It is binding, and will hold you forever. If you break this pact we have made, through my forgiveness, you will be eternally damned. He realised they were not particularly charitable thoughts. Mean, in fact. And as a result, he could not sleep. What did he know about forgiveness and supernatural goodness? Of course it existed. And Ragna Riegel would need it.

Chapter 16

'I seldom ask for anything,' she explained quietly. 'It's too much effort. I always have to explain something, and I hate explaining myself to strangers.'

'But you seem quite happy to explain yourself to me,' Sejer said.

'I have to.'

'You don't have to, you've chosen to. Lots of people sit in that chair and refuse to explain themselves, often on the advice of their lawyer. What you don't tell us, if you so choose, cannot be used against you, but the case will continue all the same. And what you stand to lose is a healthy portion of old-fashioned goodwill from those who will judge you.'

'So that means I'll have goodwill? Because I'm giving my version?'

He nodded.

'Goodwill is worth a lot more than people realise, it can take us a long way. Tell me about the night you discovered the man standing under the street light. Did you sleep at all?'

'Only in short snatches. I had horrible dreams and woke up, then went back to the dream. There were points when I just lay there dozing, neither asleep nor awake. I really don't like that grey zone,' she said, 'because nothing is certain. I hear something outside and it might be real or it might be a dream, the sounds criss-cross that boundary and create all this confusion. But I did manage to sleep for about an hour in the morning. And then I dreamt that he came back. That he snuck up the drive over to my bedroom window, which was open. That he was standing there, breathing into the room. I could hear his breathing so clearly, it was heavy and had the slow rhythm of a huge animal. But when I woke up, I realised it was just the wind. It sometimes catches the branches on the tree at the back of the house. When I got up and came into the living room, I almost didn't dare look out the window, but he wasn't there. An hour later, when I went to catch the bus, I pulled open the mailbox, but it was empty. I couldn't understand it. He had been standing there by the lamp post, I was convinced that he had left a message and that it was something dramatic, as he'd wanted to make a point with his presence. As though he wanted to say, I'm here now. I kept looking over at the closed shop while I waited for the bus. I still felt bitter that Irfan had not said anything, I was a good customer, one of the best. I bought all kinds of things in his shop, even things I didn't need, because I liked being there and looking at what was on the shelves. Once I bought a bottle of liquid soap that I poured in the bath. It had these tiny bits of glitter in it that stuck to my skin. You don't get things like that in Norwegian supermarkets. But then, I'm childish. And I would have to find somewhere else to buy food, and it wouldn't be as convenient, because

I would have to drag all the heavy bags with me on the bus. Shop for a week at a time, not just pop over the road on impulse. I've never been much good at planning in advance.'

She sent him a pleading look.

'Can I write to Rikard Josef? If you read the letter?'

'What do you want to write?' Sejer asked.

'Just a few lines. That I'm thinking about him and don't judge him in any way, that he must have been in a very difficult situation, and that I was too. That's what we people do, find ourselves in difficult situations. Goodness only knows what's wrong with the people who never do.'

'They don't exist,' Sejer assured her. 'Tell me more about how you feel about your son.'

'He's a good boy. But then, all mothers say that. I wonder if he'll come to my funeral, it might not be long now.'

'What makes you say that?'

'You never know, things like that. It's not written anywhere that I'll wake up tomorrow morning, it's not a given. Do you take things like that for granted?'

'I think everything will be all right.'

'You think so?'

She smiled a little.

'If Rikard were to die while I'm in prison, would someone tell me?'

'Of course.'

'Would I be able to go to his funeral?'

'Why are you talking about his funeral? Do you think he's ill?'

'Maybe. I couldn't get hold of him and you didn't talk to him directly when you rang.'

'I'm not the only one who decides things like that,' Sejer explained. 'I'm just a small cog in a big wheel.'

'No,' she objected. 'You're a big cog in a small wheel. If he dies, I want his body to come back here. I want him to be buried beside my mother and father. I've reserved a place for us both. As far as I know he has no one else, he's certainly never mentioned anything. And if he's defrauded the hotel, like you say, then his colleagues will have turned against him. Oh, that's so awful, I almost can't bear thinking about it. I thought he was so successful.'

She reached for the jug of water that was always on the table, and he noticed that she spilled a little.

'But you can make friends in prison as well,' she added. 'They might even become best friends. You can't hide in prison, people know the most terrible things about you.'

'What was your thinking in the days that followed, after you'd seen him watching you?'

'I tried to keep control. Like when you're out walking alone at night. You hear someone following, you hear their footsteps. And you know that if you start running, your fear will explode. If you manage to stay calm, you can keep hold of the knowledge that it's just someone else out walking, like you. I did sometimes pull the chair over to the window so I could keep an eye on the road. And I would sit there for hours, looking up and down, studying each car. It helped me to feel I was in control, that I was prepared. But it was a miserable life. Having to be at the window the whole time was a compulsion. I wanted my old, simple, quiet life back, with no intruders, but I'd lost it forever because someone out there had decided to destroy me. Slowly.'

'Then there was a long period when nothing happened,' Sejer said. 'No letters, and no one watching you.'

'It was so strange,' she whispered. 'I was on my guard all the time, listening and looking. It was a relief to be at work, as I could relax there. I would have worked double shifts if possible, but we were well staffed so there wasn't any need. But I watched people all the time, and I noticed that if I stared at them, they stared back. All those little mechanisms are amazing – it actually only takes three seconds to pick up signals, for example, fear or scepticism or interest.'

'You weren't sleeping much,' Sejer said. 'How did that affect you?'

'I was irritable, obviously. I've never been quick-tempered, but I couldn't deal with things in the same way. I needed comfort and security, at the same time that I pushed everyone away. Only Gunnhild stayed. She was the only person I had, and I knew that she was keeping an eye on me. She was waiting for something as well. For me to break down or collapse, so they had to carry me out.'

'Is that what you wanted?'

'Yes.'

'But you're sleeping well here?'

'It's like coming home. Like being a child again. I go to bed, but the adults are still up and look after me, I can hear them moving around. You, doors opening and closing, footsteps, muffled voices. Do you remember that feeling from when you were little?'

'I do,' Sejer replied. 'I also remember another feeling I sometimes got, if I was awake after the adults had gone to bed. When I heard nothing, just my own breathing. I didn't like that much.'

'One evening on my way home from work,' she continued, 'I got off the bus in the centre of town. I had a rucksack with me as I was going to do some shopping, then take another bus back to Kirkelina. I walked slowly down the pedestrian street on the way to the supermarket, looking in all the shop windows. And then I came to a dress shop, and I stopped. It's an expensive shop, and I never buy anything there, far too pricey, and I'm actually happiest in this old overall.'

She pulled at the sleeve, and gave a resigned smile.

'You probably don't know the shop, it's called Ladies Choice.'

'I do know it,' Sejer said.

'Well, anyway, they have some beautiful dresses, and we're allowed to dream. So I stood there like a little girl admiring them, but I had to laugh. I would never be invited to a party, so what good were beading and sequins to me?'

'But if you were invited to a party?'

'Then I would decline. I don't know if you go to parties, but for me, it would be impossible. The music and voices and laughter and clinking glasses and chair legs scraping on the floor. You can imagine. I'm hopeless in situations like that.'

'I am too,' Sejer admitted.

'And when I'd had my little daydream, it was time to move on,' she said. 'I turned away from the expensive dresses a little too abruptly and stepped back on the pavement, and a man who was passing walked straight into me. We collided with such force that it left me dazed. He got just as much of a fright as me, poor thing.

He was an Englishman, about my age, well dressed and totally horrified. He put his hands on my shoulders and stammered, "Oh, I'm so sorry, darling! I'm so sorry!"'

She watched Sejer to see if he was listening. She saw the small changes of expression in his face and eyes, as the images she was giving him flicked by.

'He stood looking at me for a few moments,' she whispered. 'And then I couldn't stop myself, I just burst into tears. In my awkward way. Can you imagine?'

'Why do you think that was?'

'No one has ever called me darling,' she said. 'No one, not even my mother or father, or Walther, or Rikard Josef. None of my friends. No one has ever looked at me like that, put their hands gently on my shoulders or talked to me with so much care and concern. He asked if I was all right, if maybe I was hurt or wanted to say something. But all I could do was cry, which is pathetic, and, well, I'm not very charming when I cry. His hands on my shoulders got heavier, and even though I was wearing a coat, I could feel their warmth. They were very warm. And he looked at me closely. "Is there anything I can do?" he asked. But I pulled back and just wanted to run away. My ridiculous crying was bad enough, I did not want him to know that I didn't have a voice, that would only make him more concerned, and I couldn't bear that. There's a limit to how helpless a person can be. I managed to force an apologetic smile before walking as fast as I could down the street and out onto the square, and when I finally turned the corner and knew that he couldn't see me any more, I bawled my eyes out. It didn't matter, no one would hear me anyway. Care and concern, I thought, from a complete stranger. Darling,

darling, and his warm hands, the weight of them on my shoulders, I could still feel them. My life took a turn. Something I had not seen before had been revealed to me. When the bus pulled away from the square, I realised that I had forgotten to buy food. My rucksack was empty and I had nothing at home. So I cried a bit more, then laughed in my stupid way, and I didn't care what people thought. The man sitting next to me must have thought I was mad.'

She rested for a while in the cell, on the foam rubber mattress with a plastic cover. Once again she was a little boy on the railway track. The steel was singing, she could feel a fine vibration through her body, she was quivering like a string. She liked the feeling, someone had touched her that evening by Ladies Choice. The Englishman had touched her. At home in Kirkelina she had often sat in front of the burner and stared into the flames, tried to meditate her way out of her sad life. Stop time, hide away in a small, secret space. But she had never managed it. Here in the cramped cell, however, she could slip away to almost anywhere. It must be the thick walls, she thought. No one could reach her in here. And because the room was safe, it also felt big, much bigger than eight square metres, more like a beautifully lit, big hall with an arched window. That is what it felt like, even though she knew it was not true. After a while, she turned over to face the wall. She remembered the encounter on the street, relived it over and over again. It was only when she was back home again in the warmth, and had taken off the empty rucksack and her thick coat, that she started to question the whole experience. She could recreate every detail in her mind, even though it had all happened so quickly. The force of his strong body that had so swiftly changed to gentle concern. Perhaps it was not a coincidence after all, she had thought. His friendliness and worried eyes had been overwhelming. He might have been waiting for her, he may have waited a long time, been standing around the corner keeping watch. And no one dressed like that, not on a normal weekday in November, not in her town. The man had been wearing dark trousers, and an elegant winter coat, which might have been wool. She had seen a white shirt and thin tie. He had short hair and nothing on his head. She had not had time to notice what he was wearing on his feet. But he was a sign. Someone had sent her something good. She should have answered his question.

Is there anything I can do?

But what should she have asked for? Should she have clung on to him and begged for help? Tugged and pulled at his expensive woollen coat, can you teach me to scream?

She was woken by a quiet click, and knew that it was one of the guards looking in through the peephole. Then there was another click when it was closed. It was Louise who came in and pulled her out of her dreams. Louise spoke to her in a friendly voice, the kind an adult might use to talk to someone with special needs. Ragna could read the signs, she was used to them. Even though Louise was at least twenty years younger than her, she spoke down to her and pronounced everything clearly. There were many reasons for it. Her own unattractiveness, the fact that she was sitting in a cell and was fragile as a bird. And that she did not have a voice. Louise wanted to know if everything was all right.

Ragna had a sudden urge stand up for herself. She did exactly what Louise had done, she was patronising. She whispered that nothing was all right. She was awaiting a trial that presumably would leave her utterly exhausted, and then she had to face years in prison. And after that, the rest of her life, carrying a burden that was so heavy it was almost impossible to bear. Was everything all right?

'You know what I'm accused of?' she whispered. 'And the sentencing framework?'

Louise had to admit that she did.

'Then don't ask silly questions.'

Louise reacted in the same way that the other staff did when they did not know what else to do, she rattled her keys and turned on her heel. But Ragna would give her one thing. None of the others locked the cell door in the same quiet way. She clearly had no need to underline the obvious difference between herself and Ragna.

Chapter 17

She remembered that it was night, the room was dark and the alarm clock emitted a green light. The sound of the doorbell made her bolt up and to her horror she saw it was three o'clock. Someone was on her front step, wanting to get in. Someone who was not afraid of the snarling Rottweiler. She did not turn on the light. Her heart was pounding, and her breathing was far too fast. Were there not more sounds too, a kind of rustling at the door, a faint banging on the wall? It was hard to work out what was going on. Were there more of them? What did they want? She owned nothing in the world, did not want to own anything. The only thing of any value she had was her son. She was sitting up in bed and did not dare to move the duvet, he would hear it, the person standing at the door breathing. If the duvet rustled she would give herself away, and it would only incite him. To what, she did not know, but surely something terrible, because no one with good intentions would ring the doorbell in the middle of the night. She sank back down into the bed as carefully as she could, not a breath must be audible, not a heartbeat. She fell into a state of petrified apathy, she had reached a point long anticipated in her thoughts. The moment had arrived, something awful was about to happen, he was on his way in. He had threatened her, had stood there under the street light and watched the house. She curled up, making herself as small as possible, and imagined that she was lying in a shell, an impenetrable, protective skin. Nothing happened inside the shell, no one could reach her there, she did not actually exist. She grabbed a corner of the duvet and held on to it as hard as she could so she would not drift away. In her mind, she ran through the construction of the front door and the lock. It would be easy to force it open with, say, a crowbar, as the wood was old and rotting. The security chain on the inside was hardly a problem, no thicker than a chain she might wear round her neck. Or had she imagined it all? She was so vulnerable at the moment. Was the shrill sound in the house no more than the remnants of a dream? She did not dare take any chances, did not trust the voice of reason. It was best to lie there without moving and wait for whatever it was outside to give up and wander back down to the road and then disappear into the dark. Was a catastrophe unfolding – if, for example, her house was on fire and she had not noticed, then surely he would ring the bell again? He would shout and bang on the door as loudly as he could. If he did not, then something else was afoot. But it couldn't just be her imagination, she thought, the doorbell had a loud ring, an unmistakable, shrill signal. Her mother had chosen it, as she was hard of hearing.

A minute ticked by, two, then three minutes. No more sounds in the silent night. She lay there, still curled up in her shell, which hardened as time passed, hard as bone, hard as stone. She was unbreakable, nothing could get into her core. She needed nothing in there, not even food. How close would he come, what was his intent? It was a long time since he had sent the first threat. Well, not sent really. It had not gone through the post. He had been in her vicinity right from the very start. She waited for the next signal. Another ring would be the death knell, catastrophe a fact. No one would hear her. But it was as quiet as a grave now. That may of course mean that he was prowling around the house, peering in the window. Her breathing was short and shallow like someone in the throes of death. She reprimanded herself. Everything was locked. There was nowhere he could get in. She moved a hand very slowly, then a foot. She did not want to leave her shell.

Her head was boiling, she could feel it, as she often did. Her cheeks were burning and feverish, her forehead and hands sweaty. She felt her neck and stomach getting hotter and hotter, the heat spreading like fire. She was sweating as though she were in a furnace. Perhaps the house was burning after all? She could not smell any smoke, could not hear the crackling of flames, nor the chirping of the smoke alarms installed in each room. She kicked off the duvet. Her whole body was cooking, her insides were bubbling and seething, something terrible was happening to her brain, it was melting, she could feel it. It melted and poured out, down the brainstem, down her backbone, all her memories disappeared. Her mother and father and Rikard Josef were all washed away by the searing brain mass, like a raging torrent. What would cause such a sensation, this intense heat, the trickling in her head and down her neck? A brain haemorrhage, she thought, a massive brain haemorrhage. The explanation was obvious, she had heard so many stories. It was of course the blood she was feeling, bursting out and destroying vast tracts for good. She was gripped by panic in the extreme. Was it this that was going to kill her? She had never even considered it.

She wanted to get out of bed, but could not move. With enormous effort, she eventually managed to reach out her hand for her mobile phone that was lying on the bedside table, so she could ring for help. Yet she felt that she was numb in the mouth and realised that she would not be able to do anything other than gasp for breath. Her fingers would not do what she wanted either, she was not able to tap in the number of emergency services. She was burning all over. She moved the little that she could and suddenly realised that she was dressed, tightly swaddled in thick clothes. It was like lying in a cocoon. She could not remember the evening before. Something terrible had happened to her that she could not understand; no one would find her here, not for a long time. As she lay there in this red-hot grip, like an iron in the flames, held by something she could not free herself from, she suddenly remembered the Englishman on the street. As soon as she remembered him, he was standing there clear as day. He came to her like a saviour, full of care and concern, darling, he whispered, darling, is there anything I can do? She wanted to touch him but could not raise her arm, it was heavy and immobile. Why did she remember him and no one else? Perhaps because the others had poured out of her head. There was nothing left in her skull, it was as dark and echoingly empty as Irfan's shop. She lay there, completely still, petrified and hot. She had no idea for how long.

After an ocean of time, there was a change. The feeling that her brain had melted was replaced by something else. It congealed and rose up her backbone, found its way back to the brainstem and back to its original home inside the membrane. As it gradually regained its original form, she heard a crunching sound, something safe and familiar, like walking on snow. The thought of snow was cooling, the snow lay right outside her house in beautiful white banks. She regained some movement, she could formulate words again, she thought, and she was no longer so hot. She lay there quietly and breathed, slowly in and slowly out. When she was finally able to sit up again, she discovered to her surprise that she had not gone to bed with her clothes on after all. She was wearing only a vest. She put her hands to her head, it felt solid and fine. Perhaps it was a nightmare after all, one of the worst, and now it was over. Then she remembered the doorbell. The doorbell had been real, had started the whole thing. The alarm clock showed five past four, so an hour had passed.

She lay awake until the morning. Did not dare fall asleep, just felt immense gratitude that her brain was intact and that she could move, her fingers, her mouth, everything. I can, she whispered in the dark, I can! She put her feet gingerly down on the floor, slowly stood up, had to make sure that everything was all right and she would not fall over. But she was fine, absolutely fine, supple and mobile as a child. When she was dressed, she went somewhat reluctantly out to the hall, stood in front of the door for a long time, wanting to open it. Someone had been standing out there at three in the morning, someone who wished her ill. She was sure that he had left a message, a white envelope, most probably on the doormat. Her heart hammered as she opened the door, and looked wildly around for a sign. But she saw nothing, and all was quiet.

She had the day off and so took her time with everything, had breakfast sitting by the kitchen window. She looked over at the Sois' house, where the lights were on. It looked nice. The house was probably full of laughter and love, and so it should be, they had two children. She still had not spoken to them, only seen them from a distance. Soi had driven up in a van one day and stopped by their mailbox. She had studied him carefully, a small, compact man with short hair. How easily he picks up the post, she had thought, not a hint of anxiety. Well, that was certainly how it looked. No one was out for Mr Soi and his lovely family, no one had reminded them about death. Her brain still felt fine, everything seemed to be in working order. The memories of her mother's busy hands, her father's ravaged body and Rikard Josef's round cheeks, it was all there. She could pull them up and put them away again whenever she wanted. She thought about the Englishman again, he had not left her. Perhaps he was still in town, perhaps he walked down the pedestrian precinct at the same time every evening, on his way to some event or meeting that required smart clothes. What if she took the bus into town and wandered down the same street at the same time as before, around seven o'clock? She could stand in front of Ladies

Choice, and if he really did walk by in an elegant coat, she could do the same manoeuvre, turn suddenly and bump into him. She dreamt of being seen again, being held by those gentle hands, being spoken to with such care. He would call her darling, he would be concerned. Ask if there was anything he could do. She chewed slowly on the crispbread, the noise filled her head. Now that she had started to listen, the noise got louder, and she realised there was nothing for it but to put the food to one side. What was it her mother used to say when she had a stomach ache or toothache? You should not pay it so much attention. She picked up the plate, cup and knife from the table and carried them over to the sink, where they clattered and clinked when she put them in the washing-up bowl. The fridge was humming as well, and as she normally did not hear the sound, she wondered if it was about to give up the ghost. A heavy trailer drove past on the road and she felt the vibrations in the kitchen floor. This was what it must be like to live with poor hearing all your life, and then suddenly get it back. The noise of the world. She stood by the sink, felt anxious, put her hands over her ears. Then she heard her blood, rushing like a waterfall, behind her eardrums. She did not know whether she could bear to live with all this noise.

It was half past six when she took up her post at the end of the pedestrian precinct. She had put lipstick on and she had done her hair and sprayed it, to keep it in place. Her ears were cold. Behind her was the square with all its lights and chestnut trees, in front of her the shops. She stood under some eaves and kept her eyes peeled for the Englishman. There was a chance that he would show up, that he had a fixed route, something that he always did at this time, it wasn't an unreasonable thought. Tall, straight-backed and purposeful, he would come striding down the street. From where she was standing, she had a good overview of all the streets, she could see the river and the promenade, the fire station and the church. She could also see Erotica, and all the strange things they had in the window. And Ladies Choice, of course. And slowly, it sank in. She had of course been deleted from the Englishman's memory. What he had said were just phrases, something he said all the time, whenever he bumped into someone. He said darling and love and sweetheart to everyone, she knew that, that's what Englishmen were like. She felt like an idiot, standing there in the cold, and yet, she kept an eye on the time, and watched out for him, minute by minute. At ten to seven, she walked the last steps to the dress shop, positioned herself and studied the window, all the expensive dresses, turning round every now and then to look up and down the street. She stood there for a long time, freezing, had never felt so alone, even though there were people milling around on the busy shopping street. Her feet got cold, her cheeks and fingers, and still she waited. When the clock showed a quarter past seven, she realised how ridiculous the whole project was. What was she thinking, how naive could you be, how pathetic? Wandering the streets in the November dark, chilled to the bone, in the hope of bumping into a complete stranger?

Her feet were leaden when she walked back to the bus stop. The bus came after twenty minutes, and when she had settled in her regular place, she tried to fold herself in so she would take up as little space as possible. She did not want to be near to anyone, did not want to see or hear them, and no one was to see her. That was her punishment for being so stupid. Good God, if only folk knew. But even then, as the bus pulled out, she looked down the street one last time – he might have been delayed. Once they had left the centre and the warmth had returned to her body, she felt more reconciled with herself. She was allowed to dream, to yearn, wish and hope. Everyone did, at one time or another, or constantly, if they were desperate. They dreamed of bumping into someone. She put her cheek to the window, as she often did, closed her eyes and slipped away. Where was he now? she wondered. Yes, he was good company. He was with friends, he was on top form and elegantly dressed, as he was when we bumped into each other by the shop. Where in England was he from? Oxford perhaps. No, London, of course, she was sure of that. Mayfair possibly, or Kensington, where he had an exquisite flat. She would love to know what he was called, George, or Michael or William. She decided he was William. It fitted with Walther. The two men in her life, two brief encounters. She stored William in her mind alongside Walther. Her brain was now firm and wrinkled as a truffle.

Night after night she lay awake, despite the sleeping pills. Was her head not awfully hot, did her arms not feel heavy, like two clubs that she could not lift? She had no idea what Naper had given her, probably small sugar pills, she thought. She took four, six, eight, and still lay awake. On her right side, on her left side, on her back, curled up or stretched out. She was always more anxious around three in the morning, in case someone rang at the door, but all she heard was a rising and falling hum. She made another appointment with the doctor, sat in the waiting room and thought about what she would say. He nodded gallantly when she came into the room, but did not get up from his chair. He was extremely overweight which meant that not only did he find it hard to move, he was also very generous with patients who asked for relief, especially if it was something self-inflicted, as he could hardly point a finger himself. And Ragna liked him for this. He was on her side. She told him that she was still not able to sleep. And when she did sometimes fall asleep in the early hours, she had terrible nightmares. She told him that her brain had melted, that the content had spilled out of her skull and down her spine, that she had not been able to move and had lain there as though caught in a fox trap, and could not even reach for her mobile phone on the bedside table.

Naper looked at her for a long time. Much longer than usual and with greater gravity.

'Did you have a temperature, perhaps?'

'No, definitely not.'

'That was not a good dream.'

'No, it wasn't,' Ragna whispered. 'And it all happened in my body, if you see what I mean. Not in flickering images, as dreams normally do.'

'Well, there's nothing to stop you taking two tablets,' he said.

'I take four,' Ragna explained, 'and still can't sleep. Sometimes I take six or eight, and that doesn't work either. What's in those pills? They're suspiciously small.'

He winked at her, as though he had been caught out, and turned to the screen to scan through her notes.

'Well, you're certainly not an addict,' he said. 'I'll give you something stronger. But remember, you're getting older. And we lose a lot of things over the years. Like the ability to relax. Our beauty, our radiance, our mobility.'

'Beauty?' Ragna had to chuckle. 'I've never had that to lose, so that doesn't scare me.'

She sat there patiently while he wrote out a prescription. She was only scared of her own fear when she lay awake hour after hour, and her thoughts spun through the dark to terrible places. And people rang on the doorbell at night and wanted to get in. Maybe Naper could not sleep either. She wondered if he had anywhere to go with his complaints, or if he spent the afternoons writing out prescriptions for himself.

'I'll give you some Apodorm,' he said. 'But you must go to bed as soon as you've taken a tablet. They're very strong and can cause memory loss. It is possible you might forget anything you do after you've taken one.'

Ragna smiled.

'That's absolutely fine,' she said. 'I don't do much in the evenings anyway. Certainly nothing that's worth remembering.'

'You will definitely sleep now,' he promised. 'But you'll probably be very heavy-headed when you wake up.'

'I'm heavy-headed anyway, from lack of sleep,' she said. 'Thank you.'

Again, he looked at her long and hard.

'And was there anything else?' he asked.

She shrugged. What did 'anything else' mean? Was he after her secrets? She knew that 'anything else' was an important sign, an open door, but she did not dare go in.

'There must be a reason why you're having these unpleasant dreams,' he prompted, giving her a friendly nod.

'I spend too much time on my own,' she admitted. 'In my head. My thoughts go wild.'

'You need someone to distract you,' he said.

'And would that be a man, perhaps?' she whispered, and raised her eyebrows.

'Perhaps.'

She thought about the letters. About the dark figure that had stood under the street light. About the doorbell that had frightened the life out of her at three in the morning. She had a chance to say it out loud, that someone was after her, things might be easier if she confided in him, they could maybe laugh about it together. But something stopped her, the fear of what might happen if she admitted she was scared. She did not want it recorded in her medical history, there was too much there already.

'Don't drink alcohol when you're taking Apodorm,' he instructed.

'Why not? What happens then?'

'It will wipe you out completely.'

'That's what I want,' she said. 'That's why I'm sitting here.'

There was a long silence.

'You're trying to escape from something,' he said.

'Aren't we all?' Ragna retorted.

'No,' he replied firmly.

Then he said no more. She stood up to demonstrate she had nothing on her mind.

'Just call me, if there's anything,' he said.

He stood up as well, albeit with great difficulty. Put his hands on the armrests and pushed himself up. This simple movement left him breathless. The look he gave her as she left reminded her of the look in William's eyes.

She went to the chemist to get the pills, then took the bus home. Opened the mailbox, but it was empty. Suddenly she was furious that there was nothing there. She panicked when there was a letter there, and felt very uncertain when there was not. As soon as she got through the door, she looked up at the electric wire that was connected to the doorbell. It came out of a hole in the wall, ran along the coving and then disappeared into the wall again. But so did the wire for the outside light, so she had to get it right. She wanted to keep the outside light at all costs, so the Rottweiler was as visible as possible next to the door. Full of purpose, she marched into the kitchen and found a sharp knife, before going down into the cellar and switching off the main fuse. She pushed a stool in to the wall, climbed up, hesitated, got down and opened the door, studied the bell. And the outside light. Went in again and stepped up onto the stool. One wire was thinner than the other, and as far she could work out, she had to cut the thinner one. She cut through the wire, with her teeth clenched and her heart in her throat. She went down into the cellar to turn on the main fuse and then looked out the front door. She had light. But no sound. She was glad when she knew for certain that the connection had been cut forever. For the fun of it, she put her finger on the bell again and again, and was childishly delighted when there was no shrill ring. He would have to knock instead now. Until his knuckles were bleeding. No one else came to see her anyway, so if someone knocked, it was him. Her stalker. After locking the door and fastening the security chain, she returned to the kitchen and opened the packet of Apodorm. She read the instructions several times. Naper had given her a hypnotic drug. She liked the sound of that. The list of possible side effects made her smile; they were almost endless. Dizziness. Headaches. Nightmares. Memory loss. Aggression and confusion. Breathlessness. And then, of all things, drowsiness. Fancy that, she had been given sleeping pills that might make her drowsy! She would have howled with laughter if she could.

Whenever she moved around in the house, she glanced through the window down to the road, in case anyone was standing there staring. There was a constant battle going on inside her: it's over now, she thought; then, of course he's not going to stop. No doubt he was planning the next move. What did he want from her? Did he want her to run out of the house and attract attention with her confused behaviour? She had tried. She had called the police. No one had come.

She went into the bathroom and put the packet of sleeping pills on the shelf under the mirror. Apodorm. Dormero. There was a connection. If only it was night, then she would crawl into a cave where no one could find her. The doorbell was broken. She had chemical protection and a snarling dog.

She closed the red curtains and turned off the light. When she was lying under the duvet and had swallowed two pills instead of the one recommended on the packet, she wondered about Rikard Josef and what could have happened. When the chemicals lulled her to sleep, she dreamt about him. It started with a strange dragging sound across the floor. She could not understand what it was, could not imagine what kind of creature would move like that. She wanted to sit up and have a look, but once again had problems moving – her arms were heavy, as were her legs and head. She could feel a band tightening around her forehead, a ring of steel. But eventually she managed to haul herself up halfway and rested on her elbow. She saw her son on the floor, tried to whisper his name, but nothing came out. He edged closer awkwardly. He had lost a leg, and was holding himself up with crutches, the kind they had during the war. They were made of wood, with thick cushions under his arms. He was moving his mouth as well, but she heard nothing, and she realised that he had the same affliction as her. He did not have a voice. So he had nothing to say to her, and she could not ask where he had gone. Then he dissolved into the dark. But she heard his crutches all night long. They thumped on the floor like two sticks. She heard the one foot he still had, the heavy tread of a hard boot; she heard his effort, his struggle, his exhaustion, his breathing. He was restless like her. When she woke after a long night, she was heavy and exhausted, just as Naper had said she would be. She felt unsteady and shaken, as though she had been knocked over. The band across her forehead was still there, and still quite tight. She remembered the dream. She was certain that something terrible had happened to her son, and she could not help him. She threw the duvet to one side and got out of bed, was scared she might tumble, used the bedside table to support herself, and then the wall. She hoped that her stalker had come to the door, and had left again when the doorbell made no sound. The pressure across her forehead persisted. But when it finally eased, she felt rested.

Chapter 18

'Daddy always went to bed first,' Ragna explained, 'and early, as a rule. In summer he would go to bed when it was still light, without even closing the curtains. If the sun wanted to shine on him, he took it as a sign. He would be showered in gold, he believed, and if he could then gather enough sun energy, he would also be able to shine on others. The lights in the bedroom were always on, in both summer and winter. The ceiling light, the reading light above the bed and the lamp on the bedside table. It has a red shade, like a toadstool. I still have it. Daddy always lay next to the wall. My mother would go to bed a couple of hours later and always wore an eye mask. The bulb in the ceiling light was sixty watts, the one in the reading light, and the one in the toadstool were both twenty-five. Like an interrogation room.'

She smiled at the inspector.

'Daddy would often lie and knock on the wall,' she whispered, 'with his knuckles. As though he were sending secret messages to the room next door, which was my room, and later Rikard's room. My bed was next to the wall, which was no more than cardboard between us. In the evenings I lay awake and listened, there was something he wanted to tell me, and he obviously thought I could understand his secret code. That only he and I understood. He would knock lightly with long pauses in between, or he would knock hard and fast in a set rhythm, or without any rhythm at all. Sometimes he found a pattern that he would repeat over and over. And even though I understood nothing, Daddy's tapping on the wall was an important sign. It meant that I was part of a pact, one of the chosen few. We had our own language. Daddy was trying to teach me the language, that was what we were doing every night. As time passed, I started to know some of the signals that he repeated and was able to answer back. Some were very short, others consisted of several phrases. But every time I learned a pattern, he found another. I spent a lot of time awake, befuddled by all the knocking and what it might mean. I so wanted Daddy and me to have our own special language that no one else understood. Sometimes when I was bored at school, I would sit tapping gently on the desk to see if anyone reacted. If someone else knew the special code, if someone would look up and send me a nod of acknowledgement, a sign that he belonged to the secret pact. You know what a lively imagination children can have. But no one did.'

'And you never found an explanation? You never understood any of the signals?' Sejer asked.

'Yes, there were a few I understood,' she whispered. 'Every evening when we had been lying there tapping for a long time, he always finished with a short signal. Four sharp knocks. Then a pause, then five more. GOOD NIGHT. You see?'

'Do you still knock on the wall?'

'I knock on the cell wall before I go to sleep. An old habit. Like when people who have said an evening prayer all their life suddenly lose their faith and decide to stop. Then they can't sleep. My knocking is a message to myself that it's night.'

The inspector looked at her for a long time.

'What about his immune system?'

She started, and seemed somehow to regret sharing these secret signals with him.

'Yes, it was the infections that killed him,' she responded swiftly. 'Just think what it must be like to carry all those aggressive microbes around in your body all the time, it would drive you mad.'

'Are you saying that he was mad?' Sejer asked.

'I've never known anyone as wise as my father.'

He could see that her thoughts were elsewhere, beyond the office, beyond the city and time, seeking something that was no longer there, something she could not return to but remembered vividly.

'Daddy was just skin and bones in the end,' she said. 'He weighed no more than fifty kilos. Any fluid he had in his body gathered in his feet. Elephant feet, he used to say. He would press his thumb against his skin, and it would leave deep depressions that lasted for ages. He could have put marbles in them.'

Sejer had a clear image of the sick man.

'At his funeral, when it was all over,' she continued, 'when everyone had said what they wanted to say and we had dried our tears, I went and stood beside the coffin. I had to move one of the big wreaths. And in the silence of the church, I tapped our secret signal on the top of the coffin, wishing him good night.'

'What do you think people made of that?' Sejer said with a smile.

'No one dared ask.'

Her story about her father and the knocking made a deep impression on him. The ill man who slept with the light on. Who let the sun fill him with energy in the hope that it would benefit others. He was moved, because Ragna had shared this with him, without embarrassment, but what she had said about her father had also set him on a new track that he chose to keep to himself for the moment. He did not want her to withdraw or censor what she told him. Until now she had not tried to cover up anything. He did not think she was avoiding something, holding something back or exaggerating. If some of the information was lacking, it was because she had forgotten it or she had remembered it wrong, in which case he would find out later. It was more usual for the accused to embellish their stories. Some liked to be in the limelight, and they flourished with the attention they were given during questioning. Some liked to play, others avoided eye contact, they kept things back and lied. They blamed their genes or the support systems that had failed them, they had never got what they needed, had never been understood. They had a brutal father or a cold mother. They were misunderstood souls. And often it was true. But in front of him sat Ragna Riegel. Every now and then, he remembered in a blaze the crime she had committed, and every time, the thought horrified him. Her whispering voice followed him to sleep some nights.

When he was alone in the office, he sometimes studied the photographs from the crime scene. In some ways, they did not compute with what was happening in his office. The aerial views of Kirkelina, the driveway with the mailbox and rubbish bins. The gravel up to the house, the front door with the picture of an aggressive dog. The small living room with its sparse furniture, television and Jøtul wood burner. And what they found in Ragna's kitchen – he would never be able to delete it from his memory.

'If I was to ring the prison in Berlin,' he said, 'and Rikard Josef was willing to come to the phone, would you talk to him?'

Ragna put her hand to her mouth.

'But I don't have a voice,' she gasped, distraught. 'Speaking on the phone isn't easy. You'll have to tell him what's happened first. About the operation and everything. So that he's prepared.'

'Of course I'll do that.'

She had tensed up and shifted position.

'Tell him that I don't expect anything, no explanation or apology or anything like that. He doesn't have to beg for forgiveness. He's never done me wrong. If you got him on the phone, so I could just hear his voice again, I would be eternally grateful.'

'He might say no,' Sejer said.

'I'm sure he'll say no,' Ragna replied.

She did not ask when he had thought of ringing. Or when his shift was over. So now she just had to wait, alone in her cell. She checked her watch every few minutes and saw time slipping away, that it was not on her side. Slowly she processed what might actually happen. Her son's voice on the other end of the line, after so many years. It scared her. What if she was confronted with bitterness and accusations, what would keep her alive then? How would she manage to get through what she was now facing? She prepared a few short sentences, friendly and neutral, that would not offend him, in case they only had this one conversation. If they had a conversation at all. What was the point of her sitting here preparing when he would probably say no when asked? Maybe one of the guards, say Adde with the dead eye, would open the door with a bang and give her the short message that her son had declined. So that would be that. No new line of communication, no link between him and her. She regretted it all. The hope she had built up, which would only open the wound again if it was lost. She would lose him for a second time. But what if the inspector suddenly came in with a cordless phone in his hand, and said that he had to be present when they spoke and that she should keep it short? What if a miracle happened? She lay on the bunk and waited, with her hands cupped under her head, her eyes wandering over the ceiling, along the walls. Listening to what was going on out in the corridor with the same intensity as a hunted hare. What are you doing right now, Rikard? Has someone official come to tell you that your old mother is in prison, and that she is on the telephone begging for contact? But that she now has a handicap that will make conversation very difficult? But I'm not that old, Ragna thought, I'm only forty-six. I've never asked for anything. But what's happened to us now means we belong together. That's all I want to say.

Had Sejer forgotten her? She checked the time again. It was passing so quickly, his shift would soon be over.

Had he forgotten his promise? Had he got caught up with other things? It was taking so long. Of course, there were things in his life she knew nothing about. Perhaps someone else had committed a crime that was far worse than hers, a crime that would take up all his time. And involve far more interesting and exciting interviews than the ones he had with her – the investigation, press conferences, meetings. Every now and then, she dozed off. But she still listened intently, with an aching heart, for footsteps. After only a few days locked in the eight-square-metre cell, she had become adept at visualising what was going on outside. The corridor, the control room, the staffroom, the toilets, the kitchen and exercise yard. And beyond that, the street, where she could no longer walk, and would not do so for many years to come. Everyone talked about the importance of fresh air, but she was perfectly fine with the air she breathed in her cell. The exercise yard, the light and movement, it was a change to be fair, and of course she had gone for some walks, but there was a limit to how much she could get out of it, walking in big circles underneath barbed wire, under the gaze of the security camera, the guards, the tower, under the pale sky. She eventually fell asleep again, and had a dream. The same thumping sound of the crutches on the floor, the dragging foot. Her son loomed up at the end of her bed to show her that he had lost a leg. She pulled herself up and stared down at the foot he still had, the one in the brown boot. She noticed that the laces were not tied and she immediately wanted to help him. But when she reached out to him, he slowly slipped away, his eyes trained on her, as though he wanted to say 'look how damaged I am'.

'Ragna,' she heard, 'Ragna!'

There was someone standing by her bed with a cordless phone. A guard who she had not seen before had come into the cell without her hearing, which was unusual.

'Berlin,' he said. 'We'll give you a few minutes.'

She sat up so suddenly that she felt dizzy. The cordless telephone was surprisingly heavy; she was breathing like a frightened animal and knew that her son would hear it all the way to Berlin.

At first there was some crackling on the line, perhaps it was tapped, but she did not give a damn. She had enough to cope with trying to regulate her breathing and stop her heart from running wild.

'*Mutti?*' she heard. '*Mutti. Wie geht's?*'

Oh, that voice! It was Rikard's voice, coming out of the receiver like a warm embrace, but it was much deeper than she remembered, much wiser and warmer. The last time they had spoken he was an angry boy, impatient to get out into the world. Now he was a twenty-nine-year-old grown man, tall, she imagined, with muscles, who had experienced both the good and the bad. And as the breathless seconds passed she realised that he was like Walther now. It was the same voice, deep, considered and friendly, there was something reassuring and inviting about it. Her grip tightened around the phone, she pressed it closer to her ear so he would be nearer. She remembered the day he was born, how she had held him, with the same feeling she had now. She would never let him go.

'*Alles ist gut,*' she whispered. '*Alles ist gut.*'

She was immediately overcome with embarrassment at her choice of words and lack of voice. Then, quietly and cautiously: 'Do you have everything you need?'

'Yes, yes,' he assured. 'Christmas soon. I have friends here, you know. So, we're in the same boat, you could say.'

Yes, he was in a boat. He had always liked to play in the old fishing boat at nursery. That was why he used that image, she guessed. He had felt safe in that boat. A hiding place from where he could watch the world through a porthole. He sounded happy. Content, at least, not broken or lost or humiliated. She was filled with a tingling joy. It rose from her feet to her cheeks, warming her, and she glanced in desperation over at the guard who would tear the phone from her hands in only a few minutes. She was sitting on the edge of the bed, leaning slightly forwards, eager as a young girl.

'Yes,' she whispered. 'Many of us are in that same boat, Rikard. I wrote to you. To Landsberger Allee. Everything was sent back.'

Her son said nothing for a long time. Perhaps he felt ashamed after all, perhaps he was fumbling to find an explanation. She would not pressure him.

'Sorry, I didn't hear you,' he said. 'Can you try again?'

The line crackled, it irritated her, this was the world's most important conversation between a mother and her son.

'My letter,' she whispered. 'It was sent back.'

Another pause, and then a deep sigh.

'I don't have that flat any more.'

No, she knew that. That he had lost everything, his job, his position, his home. And the respect of others.

She did not want to cry, but could not help sniffling.

'*Kann ich etwas tun?*' he asked, all of a sudden.

She was pulled back in time to the pedestrian precinct and Ladies Choice and the Englishman William who had asked exactly the same. How strange it was that everything was connected, there was a meaning to everything. He was definitely like Walther, he had the same warmth, the same intelligent sensitivity and care that she had fallen for, that had made her feel safe.

'Write to me!' she whispered. 'I'll be here for a long time.' She said each word with as much force as she could. Used everything the speech therapist had taught her, every muscle, every breath. 'Can you hear me?'

'Yes, I can hear you. I will write to you,' he promised.

'Write whatever you want,' she whispered back. 'You don't need to explain yourself.'

'*Du auch nicht,*' he said.

Her throat tightened and her eyes welled up, and she was glad no one could see her. The officer who had been standing over by the window, coughed. She continued to clutch the telephone, to press it to her ear, which was now burning.

'They will read everything, you know,' she whispered.

'That's the way it is,' her son replied.

The golden moment was over.

'They're saying I have to go. I'll write!'

His last words. She wanted to thank him with all her heart. But she was so close to crying that she could not get the words out. All she managed to give him in parting was a little sob. Then she nodded several times, as she normally did when she wanted to finish a conversation. She nodded even though he could not see her. Then the line was cut.

'He promised to write!' she whispered, and beamed at the officer. She was reluctant to give the telephone back, as if he was still in there, lived there, and was now being carried away by unknown hands. But the air was full of glitter. A shower of golden glitter, like the stuff she remembered from her childhood that you could buy in long plastic tubes, that she loved to put on her drawings and home-made cards, and Christmas decorations, and sometimes even in her hair.

'You'll have to read it,' she said to the officer. 'The letter.'

'Don't you worry about that,' he said kindly. 'We don't pore over every single word. Most letters say the same thing,' he added.

Ragna stared after him, dumbfounded, as he disappeared through the door. The same thing? Most letters? What kind of a statement was that? Every letter was a unique document that related to a unique person in a unique situation. No one else had experienced exactly the same, in the same way, and no one else felt the same love that she felt for her son, because there was only one of him. Idiot, she said to herself about the officer. You've obviously got no children.

It was only a couple of minutes later that she really grasped the fact that they had spoken. He had been seventeen when she last heard his voice. He had come to the phone now, of his own free will, and spoken to her. She started to shake, her whole body was shaking. She wondered what the inspector had said when he rang to set up the call. He had said the right things, he knew how to touch people. But he had not mentioned their crimes, neither hers nor his. She felt another rush of joy through her body, her hands and feet were tingling, she had to stand up, pace back and forth across the cell. His voice, so mature and calm, evoked a very clear picture. He certainly did not have crutches. And he still had both his legs. 'What about the boy?' Walther had asked, in the dark outside the cafe. The boy, she thought with pride, as she stood in front of the window in her cell, her face to the light. The boy is wonderful, and I've just spoken to him.

Chapter 19

Lars tapped in the six-digit number 007007, which he had chosen, to turn off the alarm. The red light stopped flashing and he opened the doors to the shop.

He liked being the first one in. It made him feel like the boss, which strictly speaking he was not, but the truth was that the others behaved as if he was their superior. He was strong and confident and well spoken, and a good head taller than the ladies, all obvious advantages of being a man. He turned on the lights, opened the till and then did the morning round, first through the shop, checking the well-stocked shelves, then out into the storeroom. They always set mouse-traps at night, so he checked them next, but there were no dead animals. There were periods when he picked up dead mice like windfall, as there were plenty of biscuits and chocolate to be had. He started the coffee machine, looked over all the unopened boxes and crates that were piled from floor to ceiling. He checked the pricing machines, that there were enough labels, and if there was anything lying on the floor he picked it up and threw it away in one of the containers. Though, to be fair, there never was anything on the floor. Both

Ragna and Gunnhild tidied up after themselves and kept things in order, the way women do. Audun was also learning the ropes. He stroked his thin beard as he walked around. Ragna came in without a sound. He noticed that she had not done her hair, the dry wisps of indeterminate colour were going every which way, and her shop coat was stained. Lars said nothing, but Gunnhild did, as soon as she came to work.

'There's a clean overall in the staffroom,' she said, looking Ragna up and down. 'I'll get it for you.' And then she added, eyes sharp: 'Did you sleep in today?'

'I'm on the till today anyway,' Ragna mumbled, embarrassed. 'No one will see the stains when I'm sitting down. I think it's coffee.'

She turned away and tried to do her hair with her hands, but only made it worse. She felt rested, but quite out of herself too, and a bit fuzzy, as though she had drunk a few glasses of wine. However, she put on the clean overall and went to the till. She had taken Apodorm for several nights in a row now, but they were not so strong after all. She had swallowed six tablets the previous night and still not managed to sleep, lying there feeling the cold draught from the window and listening for footsteps. And when she did manage to sleep through the night, it felt as though she had been on a long journey to a foreign country when she woke up. She almost did not recognise her own room and it was hard to get going.

The person who was after her, who she called her stalker, remained silent. She did not know what he was thinking or planning. This made her angry and frustrated, and she started to walk around with clenched fists. She remembered that aggression was listed as a possible side effect of the pills, and that made her even angrier. She noticed that Gunnhild was watching her more closely, which she both liked and did not like. No one else cared, but it made her feel she was being watched, and work was where she had felt relaxed until now. She could breathe easy in the shop and she felt looked after. The fact that the large, brightly lit shop always had six security cameras on had never bothered her in the slightest. The lens was like a dead eye, it did not really see her, it only registered her movements without judgement. But Gunnhild made her own judgements.

In all the years that Ragna had worked at Europris, she had never stolen so much as a paper clip. She was not the sort to horde things she did not need, she was not greedy, and she got by with very little. But the others stole things, she was sure of that. And they covered for each other. She didn't think Audun did, though – the fact that he never spoke meant that she felt a connection, and so she thought the best of him. She wondered if Rikard Josef was an introvert, if he had inherited that from her, if that was why he never got in touch. But it was finally December! She could expect a Christmas card from him any time now. With his new address. She fantasised about a Christmas card from Johannesburg with a picture of the hotel on front, maybe a swimming pool in the foreground and lots of lush plants around the entrance. Only once had the card not come until after Christmas, but instead of being upset about it being late, she was over the moon because the card had been particularly nice that year. An angel with glittering wings.

*

She had not been sitting at the till long when the first customer came through the door. It was the Agent in the dark suit. Today he really was in a rush. He looked neither left nor right and hurried down the aisles with a big shopping trolley, pushing it in front of him, in his good shoes. He had obviously planned his visit as there was no hesitation, no hanging around. He picked up washing powder and a sack of sand in quick succession. Ragna imagined that the sand was for his old mother, who he looked after. No one clears the snow for me, she thought, I just have to make sure I keep upright. She felt so tired and heavy. She was aching everywhere and her eyes were dry. Her mouth was dry as well, and the skin on her cheeks and hands. When she had a moment, she got herself a glass of water and drank from it whenever she could, otherwise she would not be able to say anything in the few situations where she needed to. It was the tablets that gave her a dry mouth. One of the side effects. More customers came in, December was always busy. They bought little Santa Clauses and angels and lights, and all the other Christmassy things. The Agent was out of sight for quite a while. In the brief moments when no one was standing in front of her waiting to pay, her mind wandered, but it met resistance. It was like walking down a long corridor and constantly being stopped by closed doors, then having to find another way round, with more closed doors. She barely saw the others all day, and when she did, she only saw their backs as they filled the shelves as fast as they could, pricing and stacking. Gunnhild had this suffering expression on her face, which she always got in the run-up to Christmas, when they were all busy, underpaid and tired. And still at the bottom of the social ladder without even the right to strike. Her pricing machine fired like a machine gun.

The Agent came into view again. His dark suit made him stand out among all the down jackets. He stopped by the stand of Casio watches, which was only a few metres from the till. He turned it round slowly, studied the watches one by one. The whole time, goods were passing her on the conveyor belt. The customers were all a bit fuzzy today because she was so tired, but the Agent held her attention. He stood trying on the watches without realising he was being studied. She could see that his trolley was full, and he only had practical things. No angels or Santa Claus, not even candles. Perhaps he did not celebrate Christmas, not everyone did. Suddenly, Gunnhild was in front of her with a cup of coffee.

'Just want water,' Ragna whispered.

Gunnhild gave her a stern look.

'You look tired,' she said. 'You need something to perk you up. I'll get Audun to buy you a bottle of mineral water, as the tap water here is horrible. In the meantime, drink some coffee.'

She disappeared again, and Ragna saw that the Agent had made his choice. He walked towards the till with the watch in his hand, pushing the full trolley in front of him, and got in the queue. He stared at the Casio watch, admiring its impressive range of functions. The face was big and full of various displays, and the strap was smart. When it was his turn to put his purchases on the conveyor belt, he held on to the watch, and only when she had scanned everything else, did he hold it out for her to take. He had very dark eyes, she noticed, and they were deep-set. There was a twinkle in the darkness, a reflection of the shop lights. Ragna bent down and took a white box with a lid from the shelf below the till. The box was lined with blue velvet and contained a small Casio brochure. She put the watch in the box, closed the lid and scanned it. He paid by card and she gave him the receipt.

'The guarantee,' she whispered, and pointed to the receipt. 'Don't throw it away.'

He looked up in surprise, had not understood her. Automatically leaned in towards her, as there was so much background noise in the shop.

'The guarantee,' she repeated. 'One year.' She pointed at the receipt that he had in his hand, and then at the white box that slowly slid towards the end of the counter. When she had made sure that he finally understood, she looked away. She could not bear his astonishment, wonder and curiosity, she had seen it all before, for years. She clammed up. She glanced quickly at all that he had bought and pulled out three big bags, and he moved down to make room for the next person in the queue.

Then he was gone. The doors slid shut and she forgot him. She listened to 'White Christmas' and 'Santa Claus is Coming to Town' as they droned out of the loudspeakers. A short while later, one of the customers – an older man – discovered the white Casio box that had been left behind at the end of the counter. The Agent had packed his things in a hurry, and had missed it. Ragna opened the box and stared at the watch he had chosen and paid for. Perhaps he had not noticed yet, he had other things he needed to do, and was carrying three bags. Only when he got home and emptied all the bags would he notice that the watch was missing. And panic for a moment. But then he would realise it was still in the Europris shop and they would of course have put it to one side. Ragna put the box down on the shelf below the till and told the others about it. She described the Agent in detail, it was easy.

'Suit? Surely he doesn't wear that all the time?'

'Yes,' Ragna said. 'He really does. He's been here before, and he'll come back again, in a black suit. Believe me. I told him to keep the receipt.'

For the rest of her shift, she sat there, looking out for him. Her eyes were constantly drawn to the entrance, which opened and closed all the time. But he did not come back. She was afraid that he had not understood his oversight, that he had looked in the car, if he had come in a car. Or that he had phoned the bus company, if he had taken the bus. But if he needed a watch, he would come back again for a new one. Only Europris sold them that cheap. Before walking to the bus after her shift, she checked to make sure that the watch was still lying on the shelf.

No threatening letters in the mailbox. No card from Rikard Josef. Still dark in Irfan's shop. The mean, succinct sign was still there on the door. But the Christmas card would come. It was advent, and no doubt busy in the hotel, she would give him time. She could just imagine him hurrying along carpeted corridors in expensive black shoes, dealing with the constant questions from the guests and staff. She took the paper and carried on up to the house. Then it struck her. She had not walked forty-eight steps as she usually did, but had done it in thirty something.

She looked around, bewildered, and stared down at her feet to see if they looked different. How was it possible? She looked back at the mailbox, which seemed to be closer than usual. She saw her tracks in the snow, a narrow trampled path. The problem, her uncertainty, could of course be resolved. She could go back down to the road and count again. But she dismissed the idea. I've just taken slightly bigger steps than normal, she thought, because I'm tired. How silly! Resolute, she turned and went inside, and banged the door shut. Thirty-something steps, well, well. Tomorrow it might be fifty-something, and so what? She was tired and could not walk any other way, sometimes she was slow, other times fast, and that affected her stride. Again, she cursed Irfan Baris. She often could not face going to the supermarket in town after work, so she had to use what there was in the fridge. She found some out-of-date eggs, but eggs lasted for months. She whipped them up and poured them into the frying pan, added some bits of hard cheese, salt and pepper. She had the omelette with a piece of bread and an espresso, to keep her awake. She must not fall asleep in the chair, the nights were bad enough already.

There was no one by the lamp post staring up at the house. As there was nothing interesting on television, she read the newspaper, but only the headlines. She sat in the armchair staring at the dark windows, trying to order the day's events, thoughts, conversations and observations. To see if she had missed any signs. The Agent stepped into the spotlight, he had to be important in some way or other. He must have discovered by now that the Casio watch was missing. He was annoyed. He had gone through the day in his head, had looked in all his pockets and the car. He had planned the following day so he could pop in to the shop and ask if they still had it. And she would give him a friendly smile and hand him the white box from the shelf below the till, and make him happy. It would be a perfect moment. And she did not have many of them.

Then she fell asleep in the chair, despite her efforts to stay awake, with her chin on her chest and her pale, freckled hands on the armrests, still wearing her green overall. A lonely, conscientious soul with hopelessly dry, undernourished hair. Not even a sparrow would live in such a terrible nest, she often thought, whenever she caught sight of herself in a mirror. And time slipped by, and no one woke her. No one rang on the bell or knocked on the door, as she no longer had a doorbell, only a terrifying Rottweiler, ready to attack.

When she woke up, her mouth was dry, and she was so angry she could have wept. She discovered it was late in the evening, about the time she normally went to bed. She was stiff after spending a couple of hours in a crooked, uncomfortable position on the chair, and her neck ached. She turned on more lights, struggled to clear her head and looked to see if there was anything worth watching on the television. She was hungry again. She went into the bathroom and started to run a bath. The water gushed out of the taps. She got undressed. Got it into her head that she had forgotten to lock the front door, that anyone could walk straight in, open the bathroom door and find her here, naked, and utterly devoid of beauty. She shrugged and was blasé again – of course she had locked the door. The small movement, turning the key to the right every time she crossed the threshold, was automatic. She filled the bath nearly to the brim, and sank into the hot water, letting her hands float up. They were small, like those of a child. It was a very quiet night on Kirkelina. All she could hear was a drip from the tap. She closed her eyes and breathed deeply. It was as if she was weightless. If only she had been a fish or a sea anemone, or a jellyfish with long tentacles, how delightful life would have been. She floated around with the fish for a long time. But then suddenly came to when something broke the silence.

She heard several hard blows echo through the house, as though someone was trying to get in. She flailed around in the slippery tub, managed to sit up, but then slid down again. As she panicked she swallowed the soapy water and it went down the wrong way, and she remembered that she had put two handfuls of bath salts in when she was running the water, and that American teenagers had been using it for years to get high, and now it would enter her blood system and go to her head, and terrible things would happen. She would lose her grip on reality and maybe hallucinate; she might even start to gnaw at her own flesh, she had heard stories about that. She held on to the edge of the bath and listened. She heard knocking and hammering some- where in the house, at a door, not a window. Someone was using a lot of force, a person with a special strength. This was no knuckle rapping on the window. She had lived in the house all her life, and she had never heard anything like it, not even on those rare occasions when her father was well and decided to sort things out. To hang up pictures, do some repairs, move the furniture, as instructed by her mother. The warm bathwater was now on its way down to her bronchial tubes and left a disgusting taste in her mouth. She wanted to cough it up, but it was too far down. She heard the knocking again, with the same force. She stared at the bathroom door, petrified – she had not turned the key, had never done that, not even when she was a pregnant teenager. Her mother and father had never invaded private moments, like when she sat on the edge of the bath, naked, with her growing belly. She coughed violently and spat the vile taste out of her mouth, sitting bent forward in the warm water like an old man about to die.

There was more knocking, but it was less intense this time. When it finally stopped, she gave herself a stern talking-to, with the voice of reason. The person knocking on the door was presumably some sort of salesperson who had tried without success to ring the doorbell. It might be the fishmonger, who came by every fourth week and parked his white van outside. Maybe he had come to sell her some Greenland prawns, or halibut or cod or fishcakes. But they always came in such big bags, and she lived on her own. She had once tried to explain to the fishmonger that she did not have a freezer, just a small icebox at the top of the fridge, with enough room for a loaf of bread. And she would never be able to eat five kilos of prawns, even if she took a year, but it would be nice if he could do what van Gogh once did when he needed money for absinthe. He had painted some tempting pink prawns and had a potential buyer who desperately wanted the delightful crustaceans, but he was not rich and could not pay. So van Gogh said he could sell him half the picture, and he cut two of the prawns out of the canvas with a sharp knife; he got his coins and absinthe, and the buyer got as many prawns as he could afford. Might that be a solution? But the fishmonger had never heard of van Gogh's prawns, and he was not willing to open a packet and sell her half a kilo. But he had given her a smile before he had returned crestfallen to his van and driven on to Olaf's house.

But now everything was still as a grave, the old house resting undisturbed on its foundations. She had not heard a car door shut or an engine start. She had managed to cough up most of the soapy water, but her throat was still burning. She regretted slightly having cut the wire. Presumably the poor soul who had been standing out there, no doubt a shivering salesperson, or a child collecting money for the school brass band, or a deaf-and-dumb student from Lithuania with some not very good drawings, had moved on. She allowed herself to sink back down into the water. She had no idea what time it was, and she was exhausted, but not sleepy. She remembered it was December. People would come knocking at the door until Christmas now, selling smoked salmon and Christmas biscuits. Beware of the dog, she thought. Whoever had been at the door was not afraid of dogs.

The water was cold and opaque. Ragna opened the window so the steam would evaporate, put on her clothes and crept into the hall, where she turned the key as quietly as possible and opened the door. The air was ice cold. She looked to see if a folder or brochure had been left on the step. 'We came, but you were not home. We would like to remind you of our services and hope to see you next time.' But there was nothing there. She looked down at the road. Maybe whoever had been at the door had left something in the mailbox.

She went back in, locked the door, and attached the security chain. She should be tired and relaxed after the hot bath, but she felt agitated. She swept through the house, turned on the television and the computer and all the lights and lamps, and looked out at the street light on the road, but there was no one there. She popped four Apodorm out of the tray and swallowed them, then four more. What did it really matter if she was awake or asleep, or something in between? The time would pass all the same, the days, weeks and years, until she was with her parents again. She actually longed to be there. As she washed down the pills with some water, she laughed silently, at herself and her own indifference. She laughed at all the others too, all the effort and fuss they put into being something or getting noticed, and living as long as possible, please dear God. If only she could make a noise, just once. Go out onto the veranda and cup her hands round her mouth and wake all of Kirkelina, screaming so loud that the windowpanes exploded. But if she tried, it would be no more impressive than a snake's hiss. She took off her clothes again and turned in. The pills had an immediate effect, and she barely managed to find a comfortable position before she was hurtling down a deep shaft, falling and falling, her arms and legs out in every direction like a cat that had to land on its feet at any cost. As she fell, she dreaded the moment she would reach the bottom, as she had never fallen at such speed from such a height, and she did not believe for a moment that someone would be there to catch her.

There was nothing in the shaft. It was dark and hard to think, and it got narrower and tightened into a funnel. There was barely room to move, she had to press her arms into her body, she was caught, the shaft closed in around her, until she finally stopped. There was not a sound, not a glimmer of light that reached her. The dark was damp and green, like a well, she had no feeling of time, could not feel her own body, the only thing she registered was that something was preventing her from moving, a clamp or a band. A week passed, a month, a year. A whole life passed. And then finally, she started to rise again, slowly to a higher level, and gradually there was more space. It was no longer so quiet, there was more and more noise. A clanking, rattling and banging in her head, and she rose and rose. After an eternity she broke the surface, but the ascent did not stop, she continued to rise up into a tower to new, dizzying heights, and the sounds that reached her were no longer in her head, they were outside. It was the traffic on Kirkelina. A bus, someone honking their horn. And broad daylight.

She discovered it was eleven o'clock and there were three missed calls on her mobile phone. Gunnhild had rung. Slowly she recalled everything that had happened. She was in a new day and everyone else was far ahead of her. She realised that in the hours that followed she would pay for falling down that shaft and climbing the tower. The price would be a heavy head, and a body that she could barely drag across the room. The silence and dark had enveloped her in a protective embrace where no one and nothing could reach her, not the shrill ring of the alarm clock, not her mobile phone and Beethoven's Fifth Symphony. But it did not last for ever. She had forgotten to open the bedroom window and the air in the room was saturated with her breath and fear. She turned over on her side and for a moment hung over the edge of the bed, staring down at the synthetic rug with a Persian pattern. Decisions had to be made. Messages had to be answered. Lights had to be switched on. Somehow or another, her feet had to get to the floor and she had to take those arduous steps to the bathroom. She had never weighed more than fifty kilos, but now it felt like she weighed a hundred. Most of that weight was in her head, she reckoned, her brain was like a solid block of cement. Even her spinal cord fluid was thick and infected, like the bathwater the evening before, and there was no longer any contact between her brain and body. Not so strange then that her feet were not behaving. There was no earthly reason to get up. All the day would bring was either an empty mailbox with no card from Rikard Josef, or a mailbox with a threat. So she turned back to face the wall and closed her eyes. In her head, she heard scornful laughter, directed at her, Ragna Riegel, the Ugly, the Miserable, the Persecuted. The Lonely, the Abandoned, the Wretched. The coward who could not get out of bed, who crept around like a thief. She was also very thirsty. She had never been so thirsty. The tablets had dried out her mouth and tongue, she would not be able to say a single word even if she had to. She turned on the bedside lamp, the poisonous red toadstool with its 25-watt bulb, and pushed herself up onto her elbow. And then she saw the folded piece of paper. Someone had left a note, there, at the foot of the toadstool. A message. She lay for a long time staring at the piece of white paper. Closed her eyes and opened them again, but it was still there. She did not touch it. Instead she tried desperately to remember what had happened the previous evening. She froze in that uncomfortable position, resting on one elbow. Looked around the room to see if there was anyone there, if the door out to the hall was open, anything. But she saw nothing, heard nothing, not even a puff of air. She had been lying in a well all night where no sound could reach her, not the alarm clock, not her mobile phone. Someone had managed to come into the house, into her bedroom, while she lay at the bottom of the shaft and was deaf and blind. He had stood by her bed and looked at her in the dark, listened to her breathing. He had perhaps noticed that she was breathing heavily.

The connections in her body short-circuited again. The orders from her brain were not getting through. Her hand would not listen. It took a long time before she finally managed to pick up the piece of paper and read the message.

'I AM CLOSER THAN YOU THINK.'

It did not matter that she had no voice, she would never have dared use it anyway. She was more concerned about listening to what was going on in the room, outside the door, in the hall.

If he was still there. All she could hear was the noise from Kirkelina, the steady hum of cars heading towards town, and every now and then the heavier throb of a lorry or bus. Her eyes moved around the room, looking feverishly; nothing had been moved, no one had touched the curtains, the bedroom door was shut, as it should be. She tried to work out how he had got in. She understood why she had not heard him, she had taken eight Apodorm. All the same, breaking open a door or window would make quite a noise, even if he did have good tools. She was sure that she had locked the door and that the security chain was on, as usual. He might still be in the house, maybe he was standing in a corner waiting, in the living room or the cellar. She had another thought, an important one. She remembered the telephone conversation with the police officer on duty who had not believed her. The note, the handwritten note that she was holding in her hand, was indisputable evidence. Someone was threatening her. And he was becoming dangerous. The thin paper was presumably covered in the secretions from his fingers, his unique loops, whorls and arches that no one else had. If the fingerprints matched any of those they already had on record, they could arrest him. Confront him, punish him. She held the note with great care, was not going to destroy it or burn it, but instead take it with her. Go to the police station and put it down on the counter.

That was the most important thing she had to do. The other was to let Gunnhild know that she was ill, that she had taken some sleeping pills and had therefore not heard the phone. She got out of bed, and tiptoed over to the door, opened it, stood there, listened. Nothing, bar her own breathing, her own heart. She tiptoed to the bathroom door, peeked in, and immediately felt the freezing cold air. Slowly, it all came back to her. She had had a hot bath the night before and had as usual opened the window to let out the steam. But she had forgotten to close it again, it had been open all night, fixed only by the hasp, which was easy enough to lift. When she was in the bath she had heard a hammering on the door. She went over to the window and looked out. Of course, he had climbed up onto the woodpile, and from there it was easy to swing up onto the window ledge and lower oneself onto the floor. He had stood there listening to the house, the smell of bath salts still lingering in the air. He had then opened her bedroom door very, very carefully, and stood there looking at her, the little he could see in the dark.

He had written and folded the note in advance, so his errand was done in a moment. Then he crawled back out of the open window, lowered his feet onto the woodpile. Jumped down into the snow and disappeared.

She struggled a bit with the hasp, it was tighter than usual. She had no strength in her fingers and she was shaken. She eventually managed to close the window and, with trepidation, approached the living room, then went on to the kitchen. She studied the windows. They were intact, everything was in its place. She looked into the hall, made sure that the door had not been tampered with and the security chain was still fastened. Then she threw on some clothes and ordered a taxi. She hurried down to the road to wait, stood there freezing, with the folded piece of paper in her hand, and her handbag over her shoulder. She did not open the mailbox, as he had left his message on her bedside table. She waited and waited and got colder and colder. The taxi would come from the left, she thought, from the rank by the square. The cold made her clear and sharp, and with this clarity, came rage. She was going to put a stop to this nonsense once and for all. She wanted her life back, the security and peace, a good life where she knew what was happening and was in control. She noticed a car that was driving slowly, some way down the street. She stepped out into the road and waved, saw the indicator blinking. Got into the back seat, the note still in her hand. The driver turned and looked at her, a familiar face. It was Irfan Baris. She wanted to smile, but then remembered she was angry with him for moving without saying a word. So she leaned forward between the front seat, her face close to his.

'Your shop,' she whispered, 'the new one. It's probably much bigger and nicer than the one you had here.'

Yes indeed, he told her, it was.

'But now you've closed that shop too, so you can drive taxis?'

'My cousin is in the shop. We run it together.'

She leaned back.

'But when do you have time off then?'

'I don't,' he said. 'Where are you off to?'

'The police station.'

'Oh.' He looked surprised.

He kept an eye on her in the rear-view mirror, and she felt his usual nervous energy, eyes constantly looking around, fingers drumming on the wheel.

'Why did you have to close the shop on Kirkelina?' she asked resentfully. 'Did it not make any money?'

He hesitated, made eye contact in the mirror.

'Someone from the tax office show up,' he explained. 'They wanted to look at the accounts.'

'And they weren't in order?'

He said nothing, just looked at her. It crossed her mind that he was looking at her more than the road.

'I suppose someone called them,' he said.

'Someone called them? And reported you, you mean?'

'Why would they otherwise suddenly show up?' he replied in a bitter voice. 'They had never come before.'

There was silence for a while.

'Has someone stolen something from you?'

It struck her that that was not the case. Not even a bicycle had been taken. Not that she owned a bike, the traffic on Kirkelina was too heavy and there was no cycle path. She closed her eyes, she was cold, tried to plan her entrance to the police station, going to the counter, what she would say. She had to assert herself, somehow.

She leaned forward again and whispered in his ear. 'Could you wait outside? Could drive me home again afterwards?'

He nodded. He nodded several times, his eyes either in the mirror or looking at the taximeter, which showed 149, then 150.

'Cold today,' he said. 'Very cold.'

He pretended to shiver, hugged his slim body. Flicked some switches on the dashboard and she heard a fan starting up, then a current of warm air reached her face. She closed her eyes, listened to the engine, liked the feeling of being on her way somewhere, of taking action. Finally something was going to happen. She was no longer someone who curled up in a corner. She knew her rights, and she would demand support.

Irfan kept his beautiful, alert brown eyes on her in the rear-view mirror. All the way to the market square, over the bridge to the south side of town, then up along the river. After about fifteen minutes he turned into the street where the main police station was, a big red-brick building with lots of glass. It was not possible to drive up to the entrance, as this was guarded by some large blocks of stone, a bit like a row of teeth, so he stopped a short distance away and explained that she would have to walk the rest. He pointed down the street to a kiosk that sold coffee and newspapers.

'I'll wait for you there,' he said.

She started to walk towards the entrance. She walked with a determined step and her chin up. She felt his eyes on her back. Was he one of the people who had sought refuge in Norway, who lived well on all the benefits, but who hated Norwegians? Some of her rage gave way to fear, perhaps she would not be able to report her case with as much authority as she intended. When she got to the double glass doors at the entrance, she noticed the cameras high up on the wall. So, they had already seen her. She stood looking at the cameras for a while, one to the right of the entrance, the other to the left. There was no one else there, the area in front of the building was empty. The row of stones, or teeth, had swallowed her, and she was in. To her surprise, the door slid open as she walked towards it, and she came into a large reception area with several counters, and a seating area with sofas and chairs. The counter for passports was to the left, beside the lift. And to the right was the station duty officer's desk, in a closed room, but the walls were glass, so she could see in. The uniformed officer who was inside looked up and she mustered her courage. She looked around for a queuing system, just to make sure, but it seemed they only had one for passports. She went into the small glass room, holding the note tight. The duty officer was a slightly older man, who was bald, well built and presumably strong, but not particularly friendly. Strong in a physical sense, she thought, and because he represented an indisputable authority. All she registered, however, was indifference and a total lack of interest, as though she was interrupting something important. And even though there was no one else there, even though there was only the two of them in the glass room, he sat hunched over some papers and let the seconds tick by. Her knees felt weak and like jelly, and she was unsure of where to start. How to begin, would he help her, was he not there to help her, is that not what they learned at police college? Eventually, he looked up. His attention did not last long, as if she were something he just happened to notice, a passing insect. She put the folded note down on the counter in front of him.

'This note,' she whispered, 'was lying on my bedside table when I woke up today. Someone was in my house while I was asleep.'

The seconds passed again, good God, they went fast, ticked by as fast as the numbers on Irfan's taximeter. The officer took his time, his eyes gave nothing away, and he did not touch the paper. First he had to establish who she was and why she was whispering. She valiantly straightened her back, wanted to show him that she was clear-headed and sober, that she was all there, in every way.

'Is there any reason for you to whisper?' he wondered.

She swallowed, pulled the collar of her blouse to one side and pointed at the red, jaggedy scar.

'You've been assaulted?' he said.

'No, no. The doctor made a mistake,' she whispered.

He stared at her white neck with curiosity.

'Do you have any ID with you?' he asked.

She nodded, taken aback, nodded and nodded again. Then she fumbled around in her bag to find her Visa card with the awful photograph. It certainly had not been taken by Walther Eriksson, but rather one of the photo booths in the post office. He studied it, turned it over, looked up at her to compare.

'And who was in your house?' he said.

'Don't know.'

'Was the door forced?'

She shook her head.

'He came in through the window. It was open all night.'

'Open? In the middle of winter?' His mouth fell open. 'Do you know how cold it was last night? It was well below minus ten.'

'The bathroom window,' she stammered. 'I forgot to close it before I went to bed.'

He had not even looked at the note. She could not understand why he would not read it. She heard a powerful, steady hum in the background and realised the lift was moving. She turned round and looked out through the glass. There were more people out there now. Several who wanted a passport, and others who were waiting to come in here, who wanted the officer's attention, while she stood there, bewildered.

'Has anything been taken from the house?' he asked. 'Any valuables?'

'I haven't checked properly,' she had to confess. 'But that's not what he's after.'

'I see.'

'He's after me.'

He made no reply, just raised his eyebrows.

'He's been after me for a long time,' she added. She tried to lean forward on the counter to make him understand how serious it was, but could barely reach with her elbows.

'So we're talking about someone you know?'

'Not really,' she said.

She felt herself shrinking. She could hear that she was making a hash of it, could see it in his eyes. And he was talking more loudly than he needed to; he automatically thought, like so many other people, that she must be hard of hearing as well. She tried to think of another way of saying it.

'He leaves things in my mailbox as well,' she whispered, 'Threats and messages. He's been doing it all autumn.'

The officer was silent for a long time. There was something disconcerting about the way in which he looked at her. Her heart started racing and her cheeks were hot even though it was cold.

'And do you have these other messages with you?'

'I've burnt them,' she said. 'I only have this one that I found this morning.'

She put her finger on the folded paper in front of him. Finally he picked it up and studied it carefully.

'On the bedside table?' he asked.

'Yes.'

Were the corners of his mouth not twitching?

'So, did someone stay the night with you? And maybe left before you woke up?'

Ragna was so stumped that she almost burst into tears. At the same time, she knew that she had to keep her composure, that she had to get this uniformed, arrogant oaf to understand how serious it was, and if she started to cry he would assume that she was anxious and depressed and advise her to see the doctor. Not that that was entirely untrue.

She leaned as far forward on the counter as she could and rapped the woodwork with her knuckles.

'Read the note!' she begged.

He read it.

'I want to report it,' she said with determination.

'You want to report it? This?' He waved the note.

'Breaking and entering,' she whispered. 'Harassment.'

He hesitated, then shrugged. Turned round, picked up a form from the shelf and put it down on the counter in front of her. Then found her a pen.

Ragna studied the questions on the form, there were a lot of them. An endless list. The lift started to hum again. She glanced over her shoulder, some people were coming in, others going out. The reception area was full of people and there was a constant babble. But it was her turn now. She wrote as precisely as she could. She had worked herself up into a great fury and her hands were sweating, but she wrote. Filled in the form and pushed it back over the counter towards him.

'Will you send someone out?' she wanted to know.

He read through the form, carefully, from start to finish.

'You say here that nothing is missing and the door had not been forced. Was the window broken?'

'I told you, I left it open.'

He nodded.

'And otherwise, there was nothing that was broken, no overturned furniture, or anything like that?'

'No.'

'That doesn't give us much to go on,' he told her. 'Initially, at least.'

'But he left that message!' she whispered. 'That's proof! He was in my house last night, surely that's a break-in?'

'Who was in your house?' he asked in a calm voice, looking straight at her.

'I don't know. That's why I'm standing here now!'

He studied the handwritten message for a third time. Again, she saw a smile tug at the corners of his mouth.

'I'll attach it. It would be good if you could go home and make sure everything is there and intact. And contact us again if anything else happens. Then we'll investigate more closely.'

'More closely? He can't get any closer. My bedroom!'

A sob escaped, which she quickly swallowed.

'He was standing at the side of my bed,' she added.

The officer said nothing more, just gave her a short nod to end the conversation, in the same way that she did. Ragna saw her report and the folded note disappear onto a shelf.

But she stayed where she was. She thought, I have to stay here until he asks me to leave the station. But then she collapsed, was drained of any strength. These people saw everything in the course of their work, rotting bodies, raped women, abused children, car accidents, charred people. And here is Ragna Riegel. No one has laid a hand on me, it's just an evil game, and I'm too sensitive. She turned and snuck out like a guilty dog, slowly crossed the reception area towards the door. But then she straightened her back, and was pleased with herself after all. She had reported it. She had followed the rules and the officer had not chased her off. Her case had been given a place in the system.

She found Irfan's taxi a bit further down the road. He was reading the newspaper and the car smelt of coffee. She settled in the back, and the car swept through the city, the river to the left of them now, with all its currents, eddies and waves. Irfan watched her in the mirror again.

'I've got the heating on full blast,' he said.

She nodded. Ran a hand through her hair. Had she even brushed it today? Goodness, what must she look like, what was she wearing, and why was he staring at her like that?

'I didn't phone the tax office,' she whispered. 'I don't know anything about your accounts. But I liked the food. Now I have to go to the big supermarket in town.'

He did not reply, just continued to watch her. She looked at his hands. They were golden brown, the right index finger tapping impatiently on the wheel, whatever that meant.

'So now there's two of you doing the sums,' she said. 'Two of you sharing.'

'What did the police say?' he asked, curious.

'Papers,' she mumbled. 'I had to fill in some papers. They weren't very interested, but they put the form on a shelf. I've always been on a shelf,' she added. 'Just drive me home.'

Chapter 20

Justizvollzugsanstalt Plötzensee
Friedrich-Olbricht-Damm 16
13627 Berlin

Liebe Mutti,

As promised, I am writing to you now.

*I have not written Norwegian for many years, so
please bear with me. I speak German, think German
and dream in German. I quickly became part of this
country and of this city, Berlin, which I love so much.*

*The inspector told me about your throat operation
and the terrible consequences it had for you. He told
me I would have to listen carefully on the phone, which
I did. It was not very easy, but I will learn. It is so sad
that you now have this disability, I remember when
you spoke to me as a child, your voice was like that of
a young girl, high and bright. I can hear your voice,
and I remember your laugh too, tumbling out like
sweeties from a bag. And now your voice is gone
forever. But I listened hard and I understood.*

*So, a catastrophe has brought us together again.
After so many years of silence. A silence that was*

wanted – intended. Here I sit in my cell. Things went so wrong, even though that was never my intention. I embezzled huge sums of money over a long period of time. It was quite easy, no one noticed, the accounts at the Dormero are so enormous, so I continued month after month, closed my eyes and ears to what I knew would eventually happen, a little bit here, a little bit there, until eventually it amounted to millions. A slippery slope, you know, you start slowly at first, and then faster and faster, and you know you will end up at the bottom. But that is no excuse for my crime, no excuse. To begin with, I imagined I would pay it all back, it so often starts that way. There is a problem to be solved, and then you will pay it back. But the figures grow and grow, and eventually I went under. I ran away and hid in another part of town, in a poor neighbourhood where I thought they might not look. So I stayed there and waited. The inspector cannot tell me why you are in custody without your consent, but he said it was serious. I don't understand, Mutti, I really don't understand. Were you driving a car? Did you hit someone? Were you driving at monkey speed? Here in Berlin that means driving over the limit. Can you tell me what you have done, or not done? Are you innocent? I am not.

Everything started so well here in Berlin. My first job was at the Gasthaus, do you remember, as night security, when I was seventeen. People came stumbling in drunk late at night, they could not stand up and had lost their keys. So I helped them, let them in with the master key, and they gave me tips because they were so glad to be finally going to bed. The money was not great, but I had my own room and board. I studied hotel management every night. Sat alone at reception, often without interruption, except for the odd guest looking for matches, or a beer, or a schnapps. Being the only one awake in the whole building, reading in the light of a single lamp, while I followed the clock hour by hour, until morning, made me feel like a lord of the night. The others slept, and I watched over them. They were wasting their time, I was using mine well. Then after a while I got a job at the Dormero, as a bellboy. You should have seen the uniform. I often stood in front of the mirror and saluted. I was there to serve. When I think about it now, I smile like an old man. It was red with gold buttons and cords, and very dashing. I polished my shoes every morning. The wages were still not anything to write home about, but the guests were wealthy and I got lots of tips. Not just coins, big notes too. They gave me whatever they had in their pockets, without looking, as the light was usually dim. At night especially, when they came back from the restaurants, and I took them up in the lift to their rooms, opened the door and showed them in, as I had done in my previous job. I carried on with my studies, and did my best to get noticed. When I finally got a job as a receptionist, having studied hospitality management, I took out a big loan and bought a flat in Landsberger Allee. Oh, I wish you had seen it, Mutti. Two big balconies and a view over Berlin. And a BMW in the garage.

It is hard to explain, really, why that was not enough. I wanted more, I always wanted more, it was so easy. Everyone liked the blond Norwegian, the polite, hardworking receptionist, they were blind as bats and could not believe it when my fraud was discovered. But by then, I was gone. I worked in a small hostel on the other side of town, where the pay was pretty poor, but I got a room. The guests were largely men and women without means, tarts and escorts. I spent twenty-four hours a day at the hostel, never went out. I changed the beds, washed the toilets, never asked any questions. Oh, that I had fallen so far. Day and night, I waited for the police. I knew they would come. I could not sleep and I barely ate. Every time the door opened and someone came in, I started with fear. Every time I passed a window, I looked out, if only you knew how it feels to be tormented in that way, the feeling that everyone is after you, it is unbearable. So when the cars finally drove down the street and I saw the navy uniforms, all I felt was relief. I breathed easy and I walked out with a straight back and got into the car. I think I may even have smiled, though I am not sure. You might find that strange, no doubt you think I should have gone out with my tail between my legs. But I didn't. Coming into the cell was like coming into the light after too long in the dark. Can you understand that?

There are twenty men in the unit here, but there are 570 inmates in the prison. Everyone in my unit, which is called Erstemal, is a first-time offender. You know what that means, don't you? They have all made a mistake, like me. Peter is the youngest, he is only eighteen. Travelled frequently to Colombia to get cocaine, then suddenly one day no more. It is a blessing, of course, that he was not caught down there. Can you imagine what the prisons are like? Erstemal is no doubt very different and we live well here. Helmut is sixty-nine, and he was a little too fond of children, so they caught him. He tends to keep himself to himself and we just let him be. Full of remorse, of course, as they so often are. I also like to be left alone. Have spent so many nights working and studying while others sleep. So time passes slowly and the days are long, but they are good, and without fear and torment. And in a few years, I will be released. Everyone here, the guards and men and women alike, is friendly. They ask me about Norway, everyone has heard how beautiful it is, with all the waterfalls and mountains. I have no visitors, but I have my music, my computer and training. I have some muscles now, Mutti, you should see them. The thin boy who left Kirkelina is no more, and my muscles are not only useful when there is something heavy to lift, in a way they also help me to carry all that I have to carry now. And then there is Wilfred, the priest, who also comes to see us. We all suspect that he is gay, and think he is in love with young Peter. He frequently goes into his cell and stays there for a long, I mean a long, time. We hear their hushed voices and sometimes it is strangely quiet. Then our imagination runs wild, but nothing is said out loud. But we do think, Helmut and I and the others, that the priest is serving a sentence too, he does not dare come out of his cell. Peter is very pretty, almost like a girl, and the priest's eyes are always shining when he has been in Peter's cell. If I want to, I can work in the kitchen or laundry, or one of several other workshops. I am no pleb, Mutti. But, my cell is my castle, it is quiet here. Everything is neat and tidy and no one is after me. Lots of time for thinking, and I often think of you. Not so much regret, it is simply not there, all I did was take the opportunity, a golden opportunity. But am I a bad person for it? I do not think much about the future. Perhaps I should, one has

*to find one's place in the world, after all. I should never
have lied to you, I should never have given you the
impression that I ran the hotel. But I wanted you to be
proud of me, and to think that I was doing well and
that I was the boss and earning lots of money. I thought
I was the bee's knees in my dark suit behind reception.
I liked being in the limelight, I liked having lots of staff
under me, the cleaners and the chambermaids and
serving staff. And the lie just lay there and festered,
grew bigger and bigger by the year. It was always there,
like the black box on an aeroplane, they have to find it
when the plane crashes to discover the truth, if the pilot
was drunk or there was a storm. So, now I am writing
to you. The inspector will no doubt read it all, but we
can forget that, Mutti, let it just be me and you. To
think that we are now both sitting in a cell, in different
cities. My cell is twelve square metres. How big is
yours?*

Your son, Rikard. The Swindler. The Lost Son.

Ragna did not care that unknown hands had opened
this letter from her son. That they had left greasy finger
marks, smiled or yawned with boredom, or been indifferent to the whole thing. She read the letter with rever-
ence and a pounding heart, she read it again and again.
And one last time, as slowly as she could, word by
word, sentence by sentence. She looked at every letter,
she noted his stroke. In some places she felt a trembling, a tiny vibration in the loops and curls, or she
noticed that the thickness of the ink varied; in some
places the letters were lighter, as though he was weak
and unsure, only to get bolder and darker when he felt
strong and secure. But equally, it could be that he just

had a bad pen, one that was about to run out. She sniffed the paper. There was definitely a scent there, the paper had been lying somewhere, on a shelf or in a drawer, and soaked up all the surrounding smells. Her son had held it and folded it a couple of times before carefully inserting it into the envelope. More than anything, though, it was the writing that touched her. She recognised it from his schoolwork, only it was even more elegant now. Not many had such fine hand-writing, so even and beautiful. She was sure he had got that from Walther. The artist.

'Mutti'. He had written 'Mutti'! The word was so full of love and devotion. And every bit as beautiful as 'darling'.

Her throat felt tight, but she did not cry. She was so full of happiness and joy that she felt she might lift off from the floor and float up to the ceiling and stay there, look at the world from a new perspective, from dizzying heights. And the guards would come in and not see her anywhere and think that she had escaped. She folded the letter and put it back in the envelope, sat there with it on her lap for a long time. Then she looked around the cell for a suitable place to keep it. There were not many options. There was a simple desk by the window with a single drawer, and she put the letter from her son in there. There was nothing else in the drawer. As soon as she closed it, she had to open it again – the letter was still there, she had not been dreaming. The letter was hers. A personal and private document no one could take away from her. And over time she would get more letters, she imagined a whole pile. Only when the initial rush of joy at hearing from her son and the swell of warm emotions had subsided, did she go and stand by

the window and lift her face to the light, with her eyes
closed. The light played on the thin skin of her eyelids,
in a shifting pattern of red. She wanted to open herself
up to something, she wanted to confess. She realised
that she was standing there in her green Europris shop
coat, which was probably covered in spots and stains.
She had been so tired this autumn and had not coped in
the way that she normally did. Had not looked after
herself. Goodness, what if her son was to see her like
this! He was sitting in his cell in nice, clean clothes, she
was certain of that. She would ask him about it. She
would write back to him, straight away. She would ask
what he got to eat, how his cell was furnished, all twelve
square metres. What he dreamt about at night, what he
longed for, what he missed. She knew he did not long
for his mother, and it never occurred to her to demand
or ask for anything. She would thank him for every
word, every line, every confidence, and would never,
ever take it for granted. For the first time in years she
felt a connection between them, an open line of communication. She was still standing by the window in the
light. The gratitude she felt was so deep that she had to
open her eyes and look at the sky outside, even if it hurt
her eyes. Mustn't ruin anything now, she thought, must
keep the connection alive, tread carefully, whisper back
to him.

Chapter 21

His wife Elise had often commented on his eyes, she said that only small children had eyes like that. Life's ups and downs, the big dramas, were recorded as spots and flecks on your eyes, and the gradual leaching of colour as you got older. But even though he was close to retirement age, and he had seen some of the most terrible things you could see in life, his irises were still as clear as ever, untainted by illness, fear and the ravages of time.

He looked at Ragna.

'Someone had come into your house,' he said. 'He had stood and watched you while you slept, and left another threat on your bedside table to demonstrate how close he could come if he wanted, and that you had no chance of escape. How did you feel when you got home again, after you'd been to the police to report it?'

For the first time, Ragna was not wearing the Europris shop coat, she had thrown it off like a dry snakeskin, and thus changed colour. Underneath she had on a black sweater with a slight rib and buttons at the neck, which made her look even paler. But it was a very definite change for the better, she was like a new woman. He noticed the shine in her eyes; she had read the letter from her son.

'My mind was blank,' she remembered. 'Nothing in the house had been touched. He didn't want to steal anything. He wasn't looking for valuables. He was looking for me.'

He gave her a kind smile.

'And you are not valuable?'

'Don't be stupid,' she whispered.

Sejer was pensive, and then scribbled something down.

'But you are,' she swiftly carried on. 'You represent something valuable.'

'I agree,' he said calmly.

'How can you be so sure?' she asked.

'Because the people around me tell me that I am. My family. My colleagues. It's hard to feel valuable when you're alone in a cave.'

She looked at him with something that resembled defiance.

'I went to work,' she told him. 'I was with people every day. Customers and colleagues.'

He made another note.

'But did you show yourself to them?'

'There's nothing to show,' she said, sounding tired. 'No beauty. No wisdom. No experience.'

'Or,' Sejer suggested, 'are you just mean?'

She was so astonished by his question that she did not reply immediately.

'I'm not mean,' she mumbled eventually. 'I don't have anything to give.'

'But you want to write back to your son?' he said.

'Oh yes,' was her prompt response. 'I'm going to answer. I'm going to write a thousand pages.'

'So you do have something to show? Something to give a selected few?'

She grinned sheepishly, and was happier again.

'Yes, a selected few. But that's allowed, isn't it? How did you get him to ring?' she asked. 'What did you say to him?'

'The voice is a powerful tool,' Sejer said. 'And you've lost yours. I used mine for all it's worth.'

'And no one dares say no to you?'

'Oh, they do, believe me.'

'You're always so friendly. Have you ever been nasty to anyone?'

'All the time. Being nasty goes with the job.'

'Tell me more,' she said.

'If you only knew how often I have to get people in for questioning in connection with a murder. How many times I've had to sit at this table and look a person in the eye, knowing that he or she is probably innocent, but I still have to ask all the questions. Where were you? What were you doing that night? And if I don't find anything, I strike them from the list, obviously. But they still have to endure that for the rest of their lives – that they've been questioned in connection with a murder. And will be judged for it. I think that's nasty.'

Neither of them said anything for some time, but they did smile at each other. Frank was the third living being in the room, and, somehow, he balanced them. The silence was not uncomfortable, however long it lasted, because they could hear him breathing, and the odd grunt and growl, which meant he was dreaming.

'When you read the messages,' Sejer said, 'did you imagine a voice? One that you'd never heard.'

She pulled at her sweater, which was a little too short.

'I imagined and thought lots of things. Maybe he didn't want to use his voice, because then I might recognise him, if he was someone I'd known in the past. There was a reason why he didn't threaten me by phone. I fantasised that maybe he didn't have a voice at all, and that was why he had chosen me. That he was bitter about his handicap and was therefore spitting his venom at someone like himself.'

Sejer quickly wrote something down, just a single word, she thought, which made her curious. The letter from Berlin had given her a boost, she felt more courageous, and this made her lean forward, as though she had new rights.

'What did you write?' she asked.

'Just a reminder.'

'But what?' she insisted. 'Tell me. You sit there writing notes day after day, and I have no idea what.'

'You wouldn't understand it anyway,' he said. 'It's a way of thinking, an association technique that helps me remember what we've talked about.'

'Tell me,' she said again.

He gave in and pushed the notepad over the table towards her, let her read the one word: resin.

'Resin?' She pulled a face. 'That doesn't make sense.'

'I told you. It's just a prompt to help me remember. There are lots of different techniques you can use.'

'So you do it to help you remember the interview.'

He nodded.

'But resin?' She looked puzzled. 'How can the word resin make you remember anything we've talked about?'

Sejer pushed the notebook and pen to one side.

'We were talking about feeling valuable,' he said. 'And how other people see us. Which made me think about all the valuable things that have not been discovered yet. Which then reminded me of a story from 1905 in Pretoria.'

Ragna liked listening to his deep voice. He was telling a story and it made her feel like a child again.

'A miner was out doing the rounds one evening. He had a lantern with him, and decided to go and explore a cave. There he discovered a big, dirty, greyish-yellow lump on the rock face. It was not like anything else he'd seen on his daily rounds, and he thought it might be resin. And as resin can be used for quite a few things, he tried to cut it out, but it was far too hard, so he had to use a pickaxe to dislodge it. It turned out to be a 3,000-carat diamond.'

Ragna's eyes popped out of her head. 'Three thousand carat?'

'Or six hundred grams, if that's easier for you to understand.'

'Diamonds look like resin?'

'When they're not cut, yes.'

'He must have had a good eye,' she said.

'It was cut up and divided. The biggest stone is now part of Queen Elizabeth's Crown jewels.'

'Ah, well,' Ragna sighed. 'I'm certainly no uncut diamond. And you won't need a pickaxe to discover me.'

'True, you're opening up of your own accord. But the story says a lot about how random life can sometimes be. And shows that hiding in a cave is not always the answer. But sometimes being curious is worth it.'

Chapter 22

Dear Rikard Josef,

To think that you've written to me! A proper letter, and a long letter at that. After all these years of cards with printed messages. You have no idea how much it means to me. I could fill a thousand pages describing how I feel right now, because when I write, I don't need a voice, and I can be bold and strong. And you will hear me, loud and clear. Finally, I have some new pictures of you in my mind. And these images are made all the more vivid by your voice, which is much deeper now, and your breathing, which I heard on the phone so clearly, as though you were in the room with me, as though I could reach out my hand and touch your face. I no longer carry you in my arms or push you around in a pram, but you are so close to me now. And I can see from your letter that you are a mature man. When you talk about the priest and Peter and Helmut, you do it with such respect. I can see that I managed to teach you the important things in life, that people should be allowed to live in peace and be who they are. I may not have managed other things so well.

You have lived a long life since we last saw each other, and I have too. You say that you wanted to be something, that you studied while you worked night shifts, that you wanted to make me happy and proud. So you exaggerated and told me you were a manager at the Dormero. And I was happy and I was proud, and I told everyone at work, and Olaf, my neighbour, and the man in the shop over the road. But don't let's dwell on that now. I would have been just as proud if you were still a bellboy in a red uniform. And I can't tell you how happy I am now! Even though you, like me, have gone off the rails. But what does embezzlement mean anyway? Your only crime is that you fiddled some numbers, and as a result, people feel bitter and betrayed. They felt you had let them down, but you have not hurt anyone, no one lies sleepless at night because of you. And nor should you, or I, for that matter. You will do your time, and people will forget your crime. But I will be in prison for the rest of my life, until my heart beats for the last time. What I have done is so terrible that people will talk about it for generations.

So, I told everyone that you were the director of the hotel. Lars and Gunnhild at work, and anyone else who wanted to listen. You know how everyone talks about their children, about how clever they are and where they work and what they study and how much they earn. I wanted to boast about you, show you in a good light. In my world, you are still the boss and you still shine brilliantly. You must never believe anything else.

I was not driving 'at monkey speed'. I can't drive at all, you know that, I have never had my hands on the wheel. I take the bus to work every day and always sit on the third seat to the left, by the window. And apart from that, I don't have much to do with other people. You know what I'm like. And what I have done is so much worse than driving 'at monkey speed'. I will tell you more when I have mustered the courage. But please don't sit there in prison in Berlin and worry about me, somehow I will cope.

Everyone here looks after me well, especially the inspector. He makes no grand gestures, and when we sit together and talk, his big, heavy hands are always still, never twitchy. I have not met any of the other inmates, and that suits me fine, I think so much better when I am alone, and I have plenty to think about. I'm sure you do too. Or have you done all your thinking and are now focused on serving your sentence, so you can hold your head high again? How do you get on with the prison staff, do you like them? Are they friendly? Do they treat you with respect? The officers here are very correct, they never overstep any boundaries, and they are never facetious or patronising. When they are in my cell, they are friendly and give me all their attention, but I know that as soon as they are out the door, they forget me. They blow me out like a match, because they are going into the next cell, and there are quite a few of us. But there is one exception, and his name is Adde, and he has a blind eye, or what we call a glass eye, even though it is probably made from plastic or acrylic, I have no idea. I often sit looking at that eye, the one that doesn't look back. I think his glass eye is more beautiful than his real eye, it is bigger, and the colour is clearer. There are even tiny, thin red vessels in the white, which were presumably painted on by hand. Sometimes I play with the idea that it is that eye that sees me and the other that is blind.

I have never had a man in my life, Rikard. Since you went to Berlin, after my parents died, I have lived alone, and I have chosen to live alone. I was a little in love with a man I met not so long ago, called William. He was from Mayfair in London. But nothing will ever happen between us, because I am sitting here now. Please don't ask me about William, as it just upsets me.

You heard my whispers on the phone, and perhaps it made you think. You may have read about people who have lost their voice box talking with the help of technology, in a distorted, mechanical voice. The sort of voice that frightens small children and gives them nightmares. Other people learn a technique whereby they swallow air, and then release it with a burp to create the sound of a word. I don't want to talk with a voice like that. Even though the doctors encouraged me to. I have never been a beauty, but I did not want to make things worse by having a hideous voice. When you speak like that, using either air or a talk tool of some kind, people step back in alarm. But when you whisper, they lean in so they can hear. But I was talking about Adde, and he can only see me with one eye, but my goodness, does he stare. And I both like it and don't like it. I don't know what he sees or thinks, because he says nothing. But I can tell that he has drawn his own conclusions, even though he knows nothing about me. And I think I can safely say that I could surprise him.

You said you were in a big prison, with nearly six hundred inmates. I know the Stasi had many prisons in Berlin, is yours one of them? You must tell me all about your days, and nights as well. Tell me what you eat, tell me more about Peter and the priest. You must all be kind to them. Be kind and wish them well, and maybe they will find each other. But I know that you are kind, Rikard. I now keep the letter you wrote safe in the drawer of my desk, by the window. I often go over and open the drawer, just to make sure it is still there. I hold the envelope up to the light, and see your writing shine through. I will treasure your words like jewels and take them with me wherever I go. Not that I am going anywhere for a while, it will be a long time before I am allowed to walk the streets again or catch a bus, but your words will be with me in my dreams. From now on, let us think about each other every day, in the morning and evening. My dear boy, I only have eight square metres, but what more does a person need? A desk and a bed and a window, so the sun shines in on a good day. The cell makes me feel safe. I know where I am. It is impossible to get lost in eight square metres, but equally, it is impossible to hide. Now I am out where everyone can see me, like you. Tell me what you can see through your cell window. If you can see a patch of sky, then remember that I am serving my sentence under the very same sky.

With love from,
Your mother

Chapter 23

Out of the blue, Lars suggested that they should all go to the pub one evening.

'Saturday, sometime after six? Just the four of us? I'll book a table.'

Audun smiled politely and Ragna looked the other way.

'It's your birthday,' Gunnhild said immediately.

Yes, it was, Lars admitted. His fortieth birthday, and the celebration he had had with his family, with tapas and red wine and speeches, was not what he had wanted.

'I'll pay for everyone,' he said quickly. 'Fish and chips.'

The shop closed at six o'clock on Saturdays, so they agreed to meet at Kongens Våpen at seven. The pub was on the south side of the river and very popular. It had a good reputation and was busy most nights. There was never any trouble, no fights or drunks, so they did not have a bouncer, and as far as anyone knew, the police had never been called. Lars had asked for a quiet corner, he assured them, glancing at Ragna, who smiled without looking at him.

Considerate, always so considerate. She was just a burden. She could imagine the noise level in a pub on a Saturday night, and it was also the kind of place where they were likely to be showing a football match on the screen. She would not stand a chance. So she said no.

'Yes,' Lars said forcefully.

'No,' she whispered.

'Yes,' Gunnhild ordered.

Audun said nothing. He accepted the invitation with a small nod, but Ragna was distraught. She would not be audible in a pub where they played music, perhaps even sang Irish drinking songs. But if she said no again, all eyes would be on her. A no would make her colleagues even more worried about her, and she did not want that either. She could perhaps say yes and go with them for a short while, and then go home early. They would accept that.

On the bus, on the way there, she had several conversations with herself about what she might say that evening. The odd comment now and then when she could easily catch their attention. Everything was going very well for Rikard Josef. He had a lot to do at the hotel right now, in the run-up to Christmas. No, he wasn't coming home, it was impossible for him at this time of year, given his senior position and responsibilities. Did he have a girlfriend? Were there any grandchildren on the way? Not that I know of.

And then she would look down at the table, abashed.

He's only thirty. He doesn't have time for that sort of thing, he has to do the accounts and wages in the evenings, and contact people high up in the business.

That was the kind of thing she would say, and her words would fall as lightly as that evening's snow, with its big beautiful snowflakes. She also had a present for Lars. She had gone into Magasinet, the department store in town, and bought him a book, *1000 Proverbs and Sayings*. On the title page, she had written: 'YOU HAVE A VOICE. HERE ARE THE WORDS.'

She had been dreading it all day. Had huffed and puffed and sighed like a martyr facing an enormous challenge. She had tried to keep a smile on her face, but failed; she was worried about what might happen, was her head not a bit warm, was her brain about to melt again, would it escape, because then she would lose what little language she had. Would someone break into her house while she was out? Despite having locked and closed everything, she imagined her stalker would find a small opening somewhere, a crack or a gap where he could slip in like a poisonous gas. She had not heard anything from the police. Nor had she contacted them. Her report and the threat had no doubt been forgotten, they had other more important things to do. She would love to be able give them that – something spectacular that they had never seen before, but as she was not spectacular, she did not know how.

Gunnhild met her at the bus station on the other side of the bridge, and greeted her like a close friend, which she was not. But Ragna did soften. The enormous snowflakes landed on her shoulders and she did not brush them off, but left them to melt into her coat. She pretended that the crystals shone like glitter against the black material, and she definitely needed decoration. She loved the stillness of snow, it was compact, dense, and strangely cosy. She heard better and could be better heard herself.

'I've never had fish and chips,' she admitted to Gunnhild, speaking into her ear.

'It's good,' Gunnhild said. 'And the chef at Kongens Våpen is English, so he knows what he's doing.'

Gunnhild hooked an arm through hers and pulled her along. Ragna had never been so close to Gunnhild. Had never felt her body in this way. They walked close together, hip to hip, through the streets, past all the low, wooden buildings which were warped and crooked, and not particularly well maintained, but all the more charming for it. Ragna knew that Irfan lived somewhere around here, it was cheaper than the other side of the river. And she presumed that his new shop was somewhere nearby, the one he had opened with his cousin, after the tax office had gone through his papers. Now there were two of them to keep the accounts. She was unfamiliar with the area, but now that she was walking through it, she understood his choice. This was where all the immigrants lived, and they would want to go to Irfan's shop. She missed the flatbread that was so fresh there was condensation in the bag, and the jars of spicy sauces. Ragna could tell from the way Gunnhild was holding her arm that she felt responsible for her. On the one hand Ragna wanted to let herself be led like a child, but on the other, it annoyed her. I can walk, after all, she thought, and I can see, and I can hear. Then she regretted these thoughts and smiled happily at Gunnhild and brushed some snow off her sleeve. She thought of it as a caress, and could not remember the last time she had caressed anyone. Why had she not seized the opportunity to give William from London a sign of affection, a hand on his arm, when they stood so close on the pavement and she had the chance?

The entrance to the pub was on the corner of one of the town's beautiful old streets, and they could hear the noise from some way off, the usual hum of voices that rose and fell and sometimes erupted in a roar. Ragna had a sudden urge to turn. Gunnhild felt her arm twitch with reluctance, and tightened her hold.

'There might not be a football match tonight,' she said optimistically.

'There's always a football match,' Ragna whispered. 'You can hear there's a football match on. Don't play the fool.'

'They only last ninety minutes. I'll sit beside you,' Gunnhild promised. 'And there's no obligation to say anything anyway, it's not as if you have to talk non-stop, there's enough people with big mouths in the pub on a Saturday night. You can look and listen, think of it as an experience, a memory to take with you. I tell you, there's a few of us who could do with keeping our mouths shut more.'

'But you'll never know my thoughts,' Ragna whispered. They both laughed.

And they really were given a quiet corner.

At the back of the pub, with two high-backed benches that faced each other to create a booth, and a coarse wooden table with scars and notches, and carved letters that were still legible, an A and an R and a K, and even 'I love you'. No attempt had been made to sand down the surface and give it a new varnish. Ragna sat on the inside, next to the wall. From there she could look out into the room, at the big screen, which was showing a match, just as she had predicted, red and yellow strips against the neon green of the grass with its white, chalked lines. Every time one of the teams scored, a jubilant roar from the other customers broke over them like a wave. They did not play any music when the match was on, and she managed better than she had feared, the high-backed benches acting as a kind of sound barrier. It was just the four of them, close together. Lars and Gunnhild, Audun and herself, their faces soft in the candlelight. The low light and warmth meant that she soon relaxed. She leaned forward, then back, rested, looked at the others one by one, followed the conversation, watched them – just as they watched her, making sure she was all right, because she needed them more than they needed her. They know me, she realised. They listen and read my lips, wait patiently while I shape the words, nod when they've understood, ask me to repeat it when they haven't, like I'm someone important. And the fish was good, hot and white inside the crispy golden shell, with thick, home-made tartar sauce and fat chips with salt. She ate greedily until she was full, and her mouth was greasy. She washed it all down with cold beer. Not bad, she thought, we've never sat like this before.

Gunnhild had given Lars a printed T-shirt. She had ordered it online; it had a picture on the front of a man on a huge forklift truck, and underneath it said in bold letters: 'LARS IS THE BEST'. Audun sat there clutching a white envelope, as though he did not want to give it away, but eventually he pushed it over the table to Lars. It was a gift voucher for Paul's Tattoo, where he could now decorate himself however he wished. And they had plenty of suggestions.

Audun added quietly that he could also choose a piercing, if he preferred that.

'A ring in your nose,' Ragna whispered, teasing him. 'You're such a bull.'

Lars promised he would go to Paul's Tattoo. He would think carefully about what kind of statement he wanted to make, as it would be for life. Gunnhild told them about a documentary she once saw, about people living with HIV in Los Angeles. One woman had a big tattoo across her chest: 'I AM HIV POSITIVE'. That way, everyone knew without her having to stammer over the truth.

They raised their glasses.

Lars opened the book from Ragna last, and read out some of the sayings and quotes in a theatrical voice. '"It is hardest at night, said the blind man, because then it is so dark."'

Ragna held the beer tankard with both hands. Took a sip every now and then, laughed when the others laughed, absorbed everything. She studied the other people in the pub, wondered what kind of houses they had and what was waiting for them at home. Yes, it was hardest at night. You could never be sure of anything in the dark, your hearing and smell took over, but most of all your fear and treacherous imagination. Regardless of whether you were blind or not.

'"He who speaks ill of others will swallow his own tongue,"' Lars quoted. 'Do you speak ill, Ragna?'

He winked at her across the table.

'But wait,' he said. 'You can say whatever you like, because no one will hear you anyway.'

She tried to think of this as cheeky and amusing, as she usually did when Lars teased her. He was the only one who dared state the obvious. But a bell was ringing somewhere, maybe in her head, or in one of the dark corners of the pub, which reminded her of something else.

For a while she said nothing, sat and looked at the walls, which were covered in old weapons. They looked real – they might even have been used in a war, or two. Maybe there were traces of blood on the woodwork and rusty metal. Had someone really used that sword, that knife, that axe? she wondered. Had heads rolled and limbs been severed? There was an old axe hanging on the wall not far from the booth where they were sitting, it was a terrifying weapon. The handle was longer than usual and the blade was double-edged. She thought it might be an execution axe. She could happily have kept one of those under her bed. But then, she would probably not be able to lift it. How much strength would it take to separate a head from its body, she wondered, with all the bones and the muscles in the neck? A lot, no doubt. In addition to will and determination.

She realised the others had forgotten her. She had been quiet for a few minutes, lost in her own thoughts. They had forgotten her because she had not said anything, had not looked at them with pleading eyes, look at me, listen to me! But as the noise level had increased, it would not be possible to hear her anyway. The match was over, someone had put the music back on, and people were starting to get drunk, so they were screaming and yelling. She had guessed it would end like this. She knew that she would not be able to sit there much longer, and she dreaded the moment when she had to raise a hand and say I think I'm going to go home now. Most of all, she dreaded the guilt in their eyes because they had forgotten her. It was not as if they owed her anything. It would perhaps have been easier to be in a wheelchair, she thought, then they would all squabble about who was going to push her. There was something honourable about pushing a wheelchair, and all you needed was a bit of muscle.

Gunnhild followed her out onto the street, where they huddled together in the snow and waited for a taxi.

'Well, well,' Gunnhild said after a while, 'that's life. It always gets noisy later on in the evening, you know what it's like when people drink. Did you know that alcohol affects your hearing as well?'

She looked at Ragna. The flames from the lanterns by the door cast a flickering light over her face.

'But you had a good time, didn't you? A good memory to take home with you. And it's always nice to get home when you've been out. Whether someone's waiting there or not.'

The corner of her mouth twitched, and her eyes drifted as though she yearned for something far away, something unobtainable, something that was lost. It occurred to Ragna that she had always assumed that Gunnhild's life was perfect, that she wanted for nothing and never felt different, or left out. That what waited for her at home was wonderful. But what did she actually know about Gunnhild? She only knew the side she saw in the shop, the effective and energetic Gunnhild. Now she was watching out for a car in the dark. And even though they had just called for a taxi and it was probably still some way off, she seemed impatient. The noise from inside was too distant to lure them, but the odd wave of laughter did ripple out to the pavement, particularly when the doors opened and someone came out for a smoke. Ragna squeezed Gunnhild's arm, leaned in towards her.

'You're going back in, aren't you?' she whispered.

There was only the two of them, together in the dark and the snow. No one could hear them out there.

'Guess I have to play the game,' Gunnhild said. 'I've got no excuse. No one asks why you're going home early. If it was me, they'd have me up against the wall demanding an explanation.'

Gunnhild had had a few beers and was confiding in her more than usual.

A number of uncomfortable questions raced through Ragna's mind. What if Gunnhild was actually deeply unhappy, what if her husband no longer loved her, what if she was suffering from a fatal or painful illness that was not visible, MS or arthritis or something else? I spend so much time trying to keep people at a distance that I don't actually see them, she had to admit.

'It's your choice,' she said. 'If you do actually want to go home.'

'There's rules you have to follow,' Gunnhild said. 'It's a game. You've got your moves, I've got mine. We've got another round to go in there.'

Then she said nothing more. She turned round and looked at the old building, as though fascinated all of a sudden, as though she had never seen it before. When the taxi pulled up, Gunnhild opened the door and helped Ragna in, making sure her coat did not get caught in the door. She looked at the driver and said, 'Kirkelina 7, please,' so Ragna did not have to tell him. Ragna watched Gunnhild out of the side window for a long time, saw the white hand waving. Followed her with her eyes when she turned and went in again. She had hoped that Irfan would come and collect her, but the driver was an older man with a red turban. Her head was singing with all the beer. My moves, Gunnhild had said. And your moves. The game between people, the assumptions. On the inside. On the outside. It was still snowing heavily. The snow was on her side. If anyone had walked the forty-eight steps up to her door while she was at the pub, she would see the tracks. She wanted to lean forward between the seats and ask the driver with the red turban, who was no doubt from India, why he had willingly left the sun and warmth and that exotic beauty, to come and live in this cold town. She could tell him that she wished she had a beautiful, wine-red turban like his because her hair was so awful. No doubt he had long black hair that reached halfway down his back and did not need to hide it at all. But she said nothing. Something small tickled her cheek. It was winter, surely she did not have to swat away a fly. She pulled off her glove and felt her cheek. Maybe it was a little beastie that had got under her skin, a sand flea or something. And the sand flea would penetrate deeper and deeper and infect her, leaving an open wound that would weep and ache. The driver spoke to her, but she could not hear. And if she answered him, he would not be able to hear her. It was best just to keep quiet. She imagined that he had said something beautiful about the snow.

Not so much as a cat had been there. She was the only one to leave tracks, and when she turned and looked at her own footsteps she felt visible again after the hours in the pub, when they had forgotten her because she was quiet. Her footsteps were clear in the light from the street lamp, the characteristic zigzag pattern of the soles. There was something recognisable about them, she thought. Whoever was following her would notice. Then he would see her tracks everywhere, find her anywhere. The snow was no longer on her side. It fell silently and steadily, but it would betray her.

It's not a sand flea, she thought, when she was sitting in the armchair by the reading light, and her cheek was still tickling, like someone was stroking the right side of her face with a feather. It also felt warmer than the left side. She had drunk a beer and was a little tipsy, but whatever it was needed closer investigation. It certainly didn't feel like a caress, more like a strange and unsettling irritation. She went to the bathroom and positioned herself squarely in front of the mirror, then leaned in closer, despite Walther Eriksson's insistence that she should be wary of her own critical eye. She stared at herself now, her face close to the glass, and immediately saw something that had not been there before. It looked like a small white worm. And it was crawling out through her skin. She stepped back in horror, but then leaned forward again, she was not mistaken. Only she realised it was not crawling, or creeping, in fact, it was not alive at all, it was just a piece of thread. She managed to get hold of it with her index finger and thumb, but then lost it time and again, as it was slippery like spaghetti. But she persisted and eventually caught it between her nails and with wide eyes started to pull. The hole was no bigger than a pinhead to begin with, but as she pulled at the thread it got bigger, she could not stop what she was doing, she was completely absorbed by what she saw in the mirror, no longer aware of the room around her, it was just her and the white thread. The hole slowly grew, to the size of a corn kernel, then a grape, then a plum, the thread got longer and longer, there was no end to it. Of course she had to keep on pulling until the thread came out, if that was midnight or the next morning. After a while, the thread started to curl, she noticed, it reminded her of unravelled wool. Her mother had often knitted new things from old garments, and she let Ragna unravel them. Her face was unravelling like an old sweater. She could see the red muscle tissue underneath. She could also see some of the white sinews and a thin layer of yellow fat. She was disintegrating. The long white thread gathered in the sink like a big nest of pasta. If I carry on pulling the thread, Ragna thought, I'll get down to the bones, and soon there will only be my skeleton left. What's the point of saving it anyway? Even Rikard Josef has disappeared, is there anyone other than me who asks about him? Does he even exist?

She let her arms drop. There was no thread left. The hole was now so big that she could put her fist in it. She went and lay on the bed as though someone had laid out her body. She had not taken any sleeping pills, turned off the lights or opened the window. She stayed there until morning, staring at the ceiling. She noted every single crack in the old wood, and a considerable amount of fly shit that she had never bothered to wash off. She got up at half past six and then remembered it was Sunday. Lots of people would be happy about that, like Irfan or the Sois or Olaf. She personally thought that Sundays were dead days, to her they were like a dirty room with sharp lighting. Everything was slow, both outside and inside her body. There was not much traffic on Kirkelina, people were outdoors doing different things. She found her clothes in the bathroom, but avoided the mirror, did not dare to see if the hole was still there, if her bones were still shining through the red mass. I can't look, it's not true, she thought, and snuck out again. In the living room, she realised that the windows were actually rather dirty and the light in the room was grey. She had not noticed it before. She looked down to the road, which was empty. She went to the kitchen window, looked up to the church spire. It was still dark in the Sois' house. She imagined them all sleeping together, curled up like puppies in a box. She still did not dare to touch her cheek, but hoped that the hole had healed in the course of the night. She pulled some faces to test it, reasoning that she would feel it if there was still an open wound. She felt nothing. She remembered it was advent, a time of expectation. She had not yet lit the purple candles from the shop, they were still in a drawer. She wondered who had moved into the flat in Landsberger Allee. People do not just disappear. She could not understand it.

She decided to go for a walk along Kirkelina. This was not something she normally did, but she had had the window closed all night and needed some air. She hoped that Olaf might be out with Dolly. When she got to the bottom of the steps, she was seized by uncertainty. How many steps would it be down to the road today? Could she walk without counting? Her whole system relied on her measuring the distance down to the mailbox, thus defining her own space and exactly how big it was. She was not able to break the pattern. She took a few hesitant steps. The damned counting in her mind started immediately, and after ten steps, she took four back. Then she walked forward for eight and back for five, then thirteen forward and three back. When she had completely lost count, she started to walk faster, it was only a few metres down to the road. She had outmanoeuvred her own system. Triumphant, she turned round. The footprints looked like a horde of people had been playing in her driveway.

She set off towards the church, with her hands deep in the pockets of her coat. She met no one. Every now and then a car drove past, but they were also going slower than normal, it was Sunday, after all, there was no need to rush. The cold air on her cheeks felt good, but was the right cheek not extra cold? Had the hole not healed as she had hoped, it felt like the chill was in her bones. She stamped her feet hard on the ground, to make her presence known. Of course it cut to the bone, she had no fat on her body, and the wind was coming from the right, blowing the bitter cold from the river that ran through town, all the way up to Kirkelina. A taxi came driving towards her, the light on the roof was on, perhaps it was Irfan. The shop would be closed today, and he might want to earn some Sunday fares. But it was not Irfan, she discovered. The driver looked at her directly as he passed, possibly in the hope she would wave him down. She carried on. Huddled over as she was freezing now, but she liked it, liked walking briskly up the road without meeting anyone. After some time, she lifted her head and looked around. To think that she had walked this far, time had stood still, no ticking either inside her or out.

*

Later, she sat at the kitchen table and drank some hot tea from a large cup with two handles. The window here was dirty as well, covered in a grey film. It would not be easy to wash them while it was cold. She could not remember them being like that the day before, but that's often the way with things that happen slowly, she reflected, like the division of cells in the body, never the same as before. Was anything happening in there at all, she wondered, or were her organs in fact in the process of shutting down? One machine at a time, until the whole biochemical factory lay cold and deserted? She leaned closer to the window and spotted a mark that she could not work out at first, until she noticed a small feather quivering in the wind. A bird must have crashed into the window, perhaps it was lying dead in the snow below. She stood up, opened the window and looked down. But she could not see a dead bird. Either it had been eaten by a cat or it had just got a terrible fright and flown away. She closed the dirty window, went over to the computer and sat staring at the screen as it sprang to life.

On YouTube, she found 'The Jumper', but a thought struck her before she pressed play. The young man who jumped from the building, hit the asphalt, then got up and left the frame was remarkably familiar. She had seen him before, no, not just seen him, she felt that she knew him, or had known him once a long time ago, because there were some strings in her that resonated every time she looked him in the eye. It was of course a ridiculous thought, the video was not even Norwegian, and she did not know any young men, apart from Audun. And he certainly did not look anything like Audun. The video only lasted a minute. But those sixty seconds always seemed to stretch on for much longer. There he was, on the roof of the building, only a few steps from the edge. He was slim and dressed in dark clothes. A black jacket that sat neatly on his hips, but was not buttoned. He stood there for a long time without moving, preparing himself for the great fall, then he stepped out to the edge. Not a sound to be heard. No music, no traffic from the street below, no shouts or screams. That was perhaps why the images made such an impact, because of the silence; everything had stopped, everyone was holding their breath, just as she was holding her breath. Then he spread out his arms so he looked like a cross, or a figurehead. And in fact, he did not jump at all, he fell forwards into a swoop, as elegant as a swallow. His jacket swung open and fluttered around him so he looked like a flying squirrel. The noise of the body hitting the ground was the first sound on the video. He immediately started to bleed from his ears and mouth, and the person with the handheld camera stormed across the street to get a close-up of him, she could hear his footsteps and shallow breathing. Time started again. Ragna took a deep breath and waited. Any second now he would slowly move one hand and lift his head, muster his strength and manage to pull his body up until he was standing, then he would start to walk, staring straight at the camera, at her, Ragna Riegel, with that inscrutable expression. Only this time it did not happen. He stayed on the ground, and the pool of blood expanded and grew, as though the lifeless body was emptying itself of fluid. He did not move so much as a finger. The seconds ticked by and she waited, touched the screen with her finger, poked him. A minute passed, and another, had the computer frozen? She knocked it a couple of times to jolt it into action, but nothing happened. Four point seven million people had watched this video and now it was over. The screen went black. But still she waited, she knew that it automatically went back to the beginning, it would play again and again, on a loop, until she decided to watch something else. But the screen remained black. Even though the blue light was still flashing to show that the computer was on, she could not find 'The Jumper' again. It was just another trick, they had fooled her once more. She could not believe anything any more, everything was fixed, everything was a trick. Everything that happened outside the windows, everything that happened inside. She lifted her hand and studied it carefully, imagined the blood flowing through the tiny veins that coloured the tips of her fingers pink, imagined the cells that were constantly renewing themselves to make her fingers sensitive. Divide, for God's sake, divide! she thought. She came abruptly to herself when someone knocked hard on the door.

Chapter 24

The relationship and atmosphere between them had changed, but Ragna could not put her finger on when exactly it had happened. Even Frank, who was lying by the window, was on his guard. He had pricked up his ears when she came into the room and was full of expectation when she went over to say hello. She looked at Sejer with a more critical eye, saw every wrinkle and line in his serious face. She thought he was less sympathetic and spotted something new in his slate-grey eyes, a doubt that had not been there before, a different attitude. She said nothing. She sat as she always did during these interviews, like a schoolgirl, with her hands on her lap.

But now the silence unsettled her, which was also something new.

'Is there a letter from Berlin?' she asked.

Sejer did not answer immediately. She could not understand why he was so reserved, which she found disconcerting. Three seconds passed, and then twenty.

'Yes, there is,' he replied reluctantly.

'Have you read it?'

'Yes, we have.'

'But I can't yet?'

'You'll get it soon.'

He immediately wrote something on his notepad. She could see that it was more than a keyword this time, was in fact several sentences. She did not want to ask what he was writing, she was not really bothered anyway, all she cared about was the letter waiting for her, maybe even in the inspector's desk. But she held her tongue. She had some rights, and he had not said that they would hold the letter back.

He put the pen down and scrutinised her face. More closely than before, Ragna felt, they were obviously no longer going to be friends. It was serious now. For some reason he had decided to be mean. The room felt different, the light was sharper. He was willing to throw the trust she had built up overboard, she was now going to be pressed into a corner. Time was running out, perhaps; he wanted to close the case, to move it on through the system. She had never for a moment believed she would get away with it. And she did not want to either, she just wanted to explain herself properly.

She could not bear the silence any longer.

'Do you think Rikard Josef could get a temporary release?' she whispered hopefully. 'So he could come and visit me?'

'I doubt it very much,' was Sejer's short reply. 'Be happy with the fact that you've been allowed to receive a letter and read it, despite correspondence and visitation restrictions. We've done a lot for you. And I'm afraid I don't know anything about the rules for leave from Plötzensee Prison.'

'So now you don't want to do any more for me.'

When he did not answer, she made another attempt.

'Why are you looking at me like that? What is it?'

'That's what I'm trying to find out myself,' he said. 'I'm trying to understand what actually happened.'

'Who have you been talking to?' she asked nervously. 'What did they say?'

She pulled down the sleeves of her sweater to hide her hands.

'What are you frightened they've said?' Sejer asked. 'An uncomfortable truth?'

Ragna put a hand over her throat, as though the scar might give her away, and she had to avoid that at all costs. She did not like the direction this conversation had taken. She had told the truth, she had laid her cards on the table from day one. She had a feeling there was something she had forgotten, and that her desire to cooperate was no longer appreciated. What was the point in continuing? Maybe she should stop talking for good now, and let him work it out himself. Lots of people did, they said nothing, on the advice of their lawyers. She had been given the same advice too, but ignored it. She crossed her arms and sent him an injured look. They were clearly in a new phase now and were going to fight with different weapons. It struck her that they had not fought at all, never used any weapons, the words had just flowed, from her to him and back again. She thought about her son and felt anxious. Maybe they wanted to punish her, for whatever it was she had done, by not letting her see his letter. Only Rikard was important now, and everything they were going to say or write to each other. She felt effervescent joy at the knowledge that he was thinking about his mother, and that he called her '*Liebe Mutti*'. She wanted to know more.

'I can see that things have changed,' she whispered.

He nodded in reply.

'I've spoken to the people who know you,' he explained. 'It's routine to question them, people who have been in contact with you for some time and know something about you.'

'The people who know me? That can't have taken much time.'

'There's more of them than you think,' Sejer said.

She reached for the water jug, but he was quicker and poured a glass, pushed it over the table towards her, seemed kinder again. She left the glass standing there, her hands were shaking too much and she did not want him to see.

'They can't have had much to say,' she said faintly. 'I've never been particularly chatty, for obvious reasons.'

'Our eyes provide us with a lot of information. I'm sure you know what I mean. And as you don't say much, I'm sure you keep your eyes open when you're with other people.'

'So what have they seen then?' she asked truculently.

Because she was annoyed, she had stopped shaking. She picked up the glass and drank down the water in great gulps, then banged the glass back down on the table.

'What are you frightened of hearing, Ragna?'

'No one knows anything,' she exclaimed. 'It's all guesswork and assumptions. Everything we think we know about each other is wrong. I don't know what you want, I don't know what you're after – I've put all my cards on the table. I've not held anything back. It's you who is keeping things back.'

'Sometimes we have to.'

'We?' She looked around the room. 'There's only you and me in the room. So from now on, you're going to be tactical, is that it?'

'Yes, that's what I thought,' he replied calmly.

'I'm going to get that letter from Rikard,' she whispered with determination. 'I'm not going to say another word until I get my letter, it's my right.'

'Strictly speaking, it's not,' he said.

They looked at each other for a long time, and in the end, she had to look away.

He stood up and went over to a shelf where Ragna's letter was lying, pushed it over the table to her.

'You opened it with your fingers,' she complained, 'as though it were just advertising.'

She held the torn envelope up to show him.

'You could at least have used a letter opener,' she said. 'This is a valuable document.'

She could not sit still; she waved the envelope in anger and had trouble expressing how she felt.

'Yes, we should have,' Sejer conceded. 'You're right.'

'We?' Ragna said again. She sounded bitter.

'I,' Sejer corrected himself. 'It was me who opened the letter, and I opened it with my finger. I am very sorry that I did not show greater respect.'

He looked her in the eyes when he said this.

'I want to read it in my cell,' she demanded. 'I want to read it now. I want to go back.'

Chapter 25

Liebe Mutti,

All I see through my window is the prison wall. It is eight metres high. On top there are great rolls of barbed wire, which remind me of nests that no bird wants to live in. And I can see the tower, of course, where the guards are on patrol 24/7. The top is made of glass and is a bit like a diamond cut with six surfaces. They walk slowly, their eagle eyes looking out over the enormous prison grounds. I often sit here watching them, while I try to imagine what they think as they trudge their set round, always in a circle, as though they were in a running wheel. I can also see a small patch of sky, it's not very big, really too small to get any sense of the weather. I have to go out into the exercise yard to do that, but I'm out there every day, as a rule in the afternoons. But I'm not that bothered about the weather, as I'm neither a farmer nor a fisherman.

Yes, of course we are serving our sentences under the same sky, even though sometimes, as a child, I wondered if we actually lived in the same world. We now have something in common, something that unites us, which might be a good thing and lead to a better under-standing. A new openness. But I don't expect much, I've learned not to, I was worn out by everything that went on at home, that I escaped from. But it feels good to write to you, it's new to me. When Helmut passes down the corridor with the post, I go out and call after him, as there might be something from you in the big pile. The others get letters, and now I'm no different from them.

There's a small cafe in the prison that we call Plötzen which is open for a few hours in the evening. I don't often go there, but every now and then I go down to get a cup of coffee, or something else I can take back to my cell. The cafe is run by a girl, and there aren't many of them in the unit. Not that that particularly bothers me, but sometimes it does good to hear her voice, which is high and bright, like I remember your voice was. I realise that young Peter also has quite a high, girlish voice. Just like all the other inmates, he's found a survival strategy, you have to. He's the youngest here, and the thinnest, so the most vulnerable. He thinks before he speaks. Behaves like an angel, is quick to lower his eyes. No one lays a hand on him. There are not often fights, more verbal disagreements, which blow up out of nowhere, but then subside before they turn into violence. None of the men in my unit are violent. Most of them have something that gnaws at them, they have secrets, but then we all do. You too, Mutti. It's a human right to have secrets. Something we carry deep inside, that we will carry to the grave, and that's the way it should be, I think.

I don't know what you must be thinking as you read this. Maybe you hope that one day I'll come home, or come to visit you in prison, if I get out before you. But I will never move back to Kirkelina, you must understand that there is nothing for me to come back to. And as for us, well, the future will tell, but we won't ever share that future. Is that what you sit there dreaming about, and now I'm crushing your dream?

It's nearly dinner time here. The chef is good, a Chinese man, but he doesn't beat the chef at the Dormero. As staff, we used to eat in the kitchen whenever we had the chance, we'd lean against the metal counters and worktops and help ourselves to the heavenly food. But those days are long gone. So much belongs to the past now. So, I'm going to go down to the canteen and find myself a place. Maybe you eat on your own in your cell. As I remember you, you would probably prefer that.

Greetings from your son,
Rikard Josef

Ragna folded the pages and held them to her chest, over her beating heart. She tried to feel her son's pulse in the thin paper, to hear his breathing.

She had a very clear image of him sitting in his cell at a desk by the window. He was sitting there writing to her. But she could only see his back and neck, not his face, she could not get hold of it, had no idea of what his face looked like as a grown man. When she played in her imagination, she saw brief glimpses of her father, his straight nose, his thick, black brows. Or she saw Walther's square jaw and high forehead. She was certain that Rikard had thick, beautiful hair and was not stuck with her wispy thin bird's nest. He would be tall and broad, she reckoned, with muscles from all the hard training.

Goodness, he must be so handsome. She sat for a long time with the two pages to her heart. They nourished her soul. The words penetrated in through her skin, passed her ribs, joined the bloodstream and flowed straight to her heart, she could live on this for a long time, a long time! But after a while, other thoughts started to jostle for attention, his words echoed in her head.

'If we actually lived in the same world. It's a human right to have secrets. You would probably prefer that.'

She suppressed these thoughts that were clamouring to be heard, put the letter in its envelope and stowed it in the desk drawer with the first letter. She wished she had a ribbon or a cord that she could tie round them, as the number grew and became a pile, because she knew that they would. Valuable letters should be held together by something, preferably a ribbon, if only she could get hold of one.

When she had her dinner a couple of hours later, she was reminded of the Chinese chef at Plötzensee Prison. She imagined that he was small and round, with smiling eyes and square hands.

There were a handful of pale meatballs on her plate, floating in a cream sauce, with boiled vegetables and mashed potatoes. There was a glass of water, too, and a small dish of lingonberry jam.

'Who makes the food here?' she asked.

The guard had to think, and then remembered that it was a woman called Gerd.

'Do you like it?' he asked.

'It's all right,' she whispered, and looked up. 'But the only thing that tastes of anything is the lingonberry jam.'

She gave a humorous smile – after the letter from Rikard, she could afford to.

'Not everyone is happy,' the guard told her.

He obviously remembered something and grinned.

'We've had some people here who threw their trays against the wall,' he told her. 'And others who didn't dare eat because they thought the food was poisoned. Or full of ground glass.'

He roared with laughter.

'Believe me, they often had good reason to think that someone was after them.'

He winked at Ragna and went over to the door.

'But I guess there's no one after you, so you can just enjoy it.'

She heard the irony in his voice and flushed with anger. The door slammed shut and his steps retreated.

She stabbed a meatball with the fork and considered what he had said. Sooner or later she would leave this cell and have to eat with all the other inmates at big tables. She did not know if she could face that, as there would be a lot of noise: voices, and the clinking of glasses and cutlery. No one would hear her. Not that she would have anything to say. She would much rather be where she was and eat at the desk. This was how she wanted it to be.

Chapter 26

Whoever it was outside continued to knock. At first it was just one knuckle, but then he used his whole hand. He was insistent. Why did he not draw the conclusion that she was out? To be fair, he would have seen from the road that all the lights were on, but still, when no one answered, there was a reason. It was a Sunday, so he was not a salesman. Ah, she thought, maybe it was some children selling raffle tickets, it was soon Christmas. She might win a cake or some smoked salmon. But a child would not hammer on the door like that, it had to be an adult. A man. Who was not going to give up. He stopped at intervals for a few seconds, then started again. She would just ignore him. This was her house, her castle, and he was not even a friend, she had no friends. And the people who did know her would never show up unannounced on a Sunday. But he kept knocking. It might be the minister. What if Rikard Josef was dead? Perhaps he had been killed in a car accident in Berlin – that was why she had not been able to get hold of him. Strange that she had not thought of that before. A cold hand gripped her heart and she found it hard to breathe. She tiptoed into the hall; the man out there must not hear her, must not hear her heart that was pounding as loudly as he was knocking. She could see a dark shadow through the frosted-glass window. When he knocked again, she thought it sounded weaker. Perhaps he was about to give up. But if she did not open the door, he would only come back, she was sure of that, maybe later in the day or the following day, or the following night. He was out to get her. She could open the door, look him straight in the eye and ask what he wanted, in a sharp, deadly voice. She had to laugh at herself. She could never come across as sharp and deadly. She put her hand on the door handle and wondered if he could see her shadow through the glass, as she could see his. She guessed so, he had stopped knocking and was waiting now. She thought about the minister again. Perhaps he had come to tell her that her son had had a heart attack and that he was in intensive care. It was not surprising really, given how much responsibility he had in the hotel. She opened the door ever so slightly. She hardly dared look out through the narrow gap allowed by the security chain. She would let him say what he wanted first, then she would shake her head and wave him off. She would close the door with a bang, just to make the point. He moved closer and tried to make eye contact through the gap. She could not see any white around his neck to show that he was a minister. He was definitely dressed in black, a young man in a good suit, with pale skin and short hair. It was the Agent.

'The dog,' he said with a nervous smile as he pointed at the Rottweiler. 'Will it bite me?'

A flood of thoughts and suspicions rushed through her head. Her mind was working overtime to make everything fit, a logical explanation for what was happening, for all the things that had been happening for a long time now. There had to be a logical explanation. That face, she thought, those black eyes, she had seen them before. Not just in the aisles of Europris, she had also come across him in another context. Her hand kept a firm hold of the door. She saw that he had a folder under his arm, that must be where the explanation lay. She undid the security chain and opened the door a bit further. The Agent took a step back. And a new explanation overrode everything else in her head. She realised why he had come. He had forgotten the Casio watch at the till. Perhaps he thought she had taken it home with her. Had he come to collect it? But then how did he know where she lived? She opened the door a little wider, it was almost halfway now. He took a step closer again, looked past her and into the hall for the Rottweiler. She wanted to tell him that the watch was lying in its white box at the shop, but he spoke before she could.

'I have good news for you,' he said.

He was very enthusiastic now, the half-open door had encouraged him, and there was a vigour to his young body and a light in his eyes.

'News?' She frowned. Had something happened to Rikard after all? Her letters had been returned, and she was quite sure something was going on down there in Berlin. She did not open her mouth, but just stood there staring. He would have to do the talking.

'Do you have a minute or two to spare?' he asked. 'I have something important to tell you. But the dog ...' He squirmed. 'Does it attack people?'

He pointed at the Rottweiler on the wall again, and forced a laugh, but she held her mask.

'Only if I ask him to,' she whispered.

Her cheeks were getting cold. The snow was drifting into the house and, as she breathed it into her lungs, she felt every cell in her body freeze. He was no doubt cold too. He had no winter jacket on over his suit, which actually looked rather cheap close up. The material was shiny with wear in places, and it was too big for him, the sleeves were too long. The jacket was not buttoned. He did not appear to have much muscle and he was no taller than her. But those eyes, she thought again, so deep in their sockets, they wanted something. She had seen the same inscrutable look so many times when the Jumper stood up after his fall. She realised that he would never get up again, that the last jump had been too much. She studied the Agent in more detail. There was a unique intensity to his voice, a faint trembling, and his hands fidgeted as he held the brown folder. His nails were incredibly long, she had never seen a man with nails like that, they were thick, yellow and pointed. She had revealed her secret now, the fact that she had no voice. She was not sure he remembered the moment when she gave him the receipt for the watch and whispered that it was also a guarantee. She guessed he was like most people and would continue to talk nervously when there was no response, there was something intimidating about people who did not speak. Those who just watched and waited. It dawned on her that she was wearing the green overall from Europris. She often hung it on the back of a chair and put it on when she could not be bothered to look for anything else. Her grip on the door handle was so tight that the tension spread up her arm.

'News?' she said finally. 'What kind of news?'

He leaned forward in order to hear her better, he was now less than a metre from her face. She had asked a question – that was an invitation, he could go on.

'It's cold,' he said, and shivered.

It was obvious that he wanted to come into the warmth. Ragna stared at his long nails, his unbuttoned jacket. If he jumped from a great height, it would flutter like the wings of a bird.

'Your watch,' she whispered, 'we kept it to one side.'

He did not understand, shook his head.

'Watch?'

'The Casio watch you bought at Europris. You left it by the till.'

'Oh yes,' he exclaimed. 'The watch!'

He nodded several times and suddenly seemed like a normal, polite young man with no hidden intentions.

'The watch was a Christmas present for my brother,' he explained, 'I've been looking for it all over. I'll come and get it tomorrow.'

She immediately regretted mentioning it. Now they shared something, the start of a conversation, there was recognition. It would be hard to interrupt that now. She should have closed the door straight away, or she should not have opened it at all.

'Your doorbell doesn't work,' he said, nodding at it. He had obviously pressed the bell several times. 'Something must have happened to it. A broken wire, or something. Or is it battery-powered?'

She did not answer. Just stood in the doorway and waited.

'I've been here a couple of times before, and it worked then. But you didn't come to the door.'

'I know you've been here before,' she said.

'So you heard me then? Well, I guess it doesn't always suit. You're not obliged to open the door to everyone.'

She wondered if he thought he was more special than others who might ring at the door.

'What's your news?' she asked again.

She closed the door a touch, felt he was taking too long to say why he was there.

'Why don't I come in for a moment?' he suggested. 'It's so cold outside. I've got the papers here.' He pointed at his folder. 'We could look at them inside.'

'Papers?' she said.

He made a show of shivering, his cheeks were white with cold. Goodness, it could absolutely be the case that Rikard was dead, she thought again. The Agent was a lawyer, of course, he had come to tell her about the will. The flat in Landsberger Allee and perhaps some other things she knew nothing about.

'What's in the folder?' she wanted to know.

He did not hear her and she had to try again.

'Your folder?' she repeated, and pointed.

'A unique chance,' he replied, full of enthusiasm. 'A fantastic opportunity!'

'Opportunity? Are you selling something?'

'Not at all!'

He shook his head.

'This is something you can have for free.'

Dear God, his black eyes pinned her to the spot. Ragna pulled her overall tighter, held the slippery green material close to her body. She put one foot out on the step, so that he would pull back, then peered down towards the road.

'You don't have a car?' she said.

'Oh yes, but I parked it further down Kirkelina, at the turning place. The snow wasn't cleared here.'

She tried to think quickly, looked down towards the road again. No cars, no people, no one had seen him standing there at her door. A fantastic opportunity, he had said, a unique chance. And it was free.

He followed her in. Down the hall and into the kitchen. He was extremely polite, bowing and grovelling like a servant. He had said he was not a salesman, but he behaved like one. He had something to offer, good solutions, intelligent suggestions as to how she could change her life, possible profits, wise investments, or a product that would give her improved health, or supplements, or a share in a house in Spain, her imagination ran away with her. The fact that she had invited him in did something to him. The besuited young man seemed to change gear, his movements were quicker, filled with a new energy. He had had a plan all along, she realised, and now he was going to put it into action.

'And the dog?' he asked, again, as he glanced nervously into the living room as they passed.

'He's sleeping,' Ragna whispered. 'He'll come if I whistle.'

'Let's hope you don't whistle then,' he said.

'We'll see. He's well trained.'

'Can I sit down?'

He had already pulled out a chair, but he was still standing holding the brown folder that contained the news, the unique chance. She suddenly noticed that he only had long nails on his right hand, and that the ones on his left hand were short. Perhaps he played the guitar.

'What's your name?' he asked, with interest.

'You already know,' she responded.

He gave her an apologetic smile.

'Yes, of course,' he said. 'Riegel. I forgot, you have a nameplate on the door. Ragna Riegel. Why don't you sit down, Ragna?'

He nodded at the empty chair on the other side of the table, talked as if she were a guest in her own house. So she remained standing in protest, at a slight distance, leaning back against the worktop with her eyes on him all the while.

'So,' he said, with the same intensity as he pulled out the chair, which scraped on the floor. He put the folder down on the table and put his hand on it, as if to emphasise the importance of the contents. 'So, Mrs Riegel, you know what kind of times we're living in.'

She raised her thin eyebrows.

'The signs,' he said, and looked at her. 'Have you seen the signs?'

Signs? She thought about the letters she had received. The anonymous letters, the note on her bedside table.

'What's your name?' she asked, staring at him.

'Bennet,' he quickly replied.

'Yes, Bennet,' she nodded. 'I've seen the signs.'

He seemed happy with this answer. He nodded several times as though she had confirmed something important – his own importance in the world, perhaps, or the value of what he was about to show her.

He's here now, Ragna thought, in my kitchen, just a couple of metres away. She had lost most of the feeling in her lips, as she often had on the rare occasions she had had too much alcohol, like the night with Walther Eriksson when she had drunk the peach wine.

'Then you know what I want to talk to you about,'
Bennet said. 'Then you know why I'm here.'

It was Ragna's turn to nod. She could feel a drawer
knob in the small of her back, it cut through the thin
material of the overall like a sharp edge.

'I'm sure that you're looking for the truth,' he said.
'Having stumbled around in the dark for so long, you
deserve some answers. Good answers.'

'Yes, I do,' she whispered.

She was like an eagle, alert, ready. She pressed herself
back against the drawers, her heart racing, her blood
pumping, everything working together.

'Well, I have come to tell you the truth,' Bennet said.
'And I can see that you're searching. That's why you let
me in. Perhaps you've been waiting for me.'

The truth, Ragna thought. Everyone is searching for
the truth. But she was no longer so sure that she wanted
it. She did not nod, she did not smile, instead she
listened to his breathing and realised they were in
rhythm. She heard the rustle of the cheap suit fabric
when he shifted position on the chair, it sounded like
her own nylon overall.

He leaned forward over the table.

'We have to start with an uncomfortable fact,' he
said, 'but I can tell that you're prepared. You have
thought long and hard about many things.'

He folded his hands on the table.

'Fact?' she whispered.

'That you're going to die, Ragna,' he said in a grave
voice.

She felt the drawer knob again, it was sharper, it
dug into her back like a claw. She felt the adrenaline
surge, and the fury – this man had invaded her life

and destroyed her mind, caused her brain to melt so that it ran down her spine. He had robbed her of sleep, he had made her face unravel like an old sweater.

'And so are you,' she replied. 'You are going to die. And it won't be long.'

Her response took him aback. It was not what he had expected, not what he was used to hearing. So he was lost for words, and needed a moment to plan his next move. He chose to smile. They were in a part of the world where a smile could disarm an enemy.

But she gave him no more chances. She turned her back to him, and opened the top drawer, studied the contents, rattled among the plastic and metal. She ignored the spoon and the ladle. She considered a big pair of scissors for a moment, but then chose a knife instead, with a long, jagged edge. Pulled it out of the drawer, gripped the handle and turned to look at him. His eyes started to dart this way and that when he saw the knife. In the blink of an eye he abandoned his role. He had no strategy for dealing with this. She liked the fact that he said nothing. He scrabbled with the folder, with his right hand, the one with the nails, as though that might protect him, grabbed it and held it up like a shield. It did not occur to him to run, out of the kitchen, out into the snow.

'My name is Ragna Riegel. I don't threaten people anonymously. Do you hear what I'm saying?'

The Agent nodded. For some reason he was still smiling, and it made him look like an idiot. While his mind worked furiously to understand the situation, he looked at her properly for the first time. But he did not get up and leave.

'The news,' she said as she approached him with the knife. 'I want it now.'

He raised his hand to ward her off.

'If you would just listen to me a moment.' It was his turn to whisper now.

'Oh,' Ragna continued. 'So you've lost your voice now as well. Then you know what it's like. Now I'm the one sending the messages. No one will hear you.'

Finally he felt the urge to get up and leave. But doing so would only make the situation worse, and he suspected that the woman in front of him was totally unpredictable. He chose to stay in character. Do what he had come to do, cling on to that remnant of control. But his strength failed him, and all Ragna could hear was a faint mumbling.

'I've come to offer you a place in the Thousand Year Reign,' he stuttered. 'Before it's too late.'

The Thousand Year Reign? She was still holding the knife, pointing it towards him. The tip was no more than a metre from his torso. She took a step forward, then another. She thought it was strange that he remained seated, that he didn't push the chair back and try to get away. He was holding on to the folder for dear life. When she suddenly leaned forward and thrust the serrated knife into his stomach, he looked astonished. But he was still only concerned with staying upright on the chair, as though falling over would be an admission, a final defeat. She pulled the knife out again. It was not easy as it had gone in all the way to the handle. He fell forward over the table, one hand still holding the folder, the other over the stab wound. It looked like he had completely forgotten her. He turned his face to the window, where the low winter sun shone in. She heard a faint wailing, then all was quiet for a long time. She did not like the fact that he was still sitting on the chair. It meant that she had not asserted herself enough, she wanted him on the floor. So she stabbed him again, and again, randomly. Then she heard a long, hissing sound and she knew that she had punctured his lung. He must have had a lot of air in his lungs, because the noise went on and on. He started to cant to the side; she pulled back and waited for him to fall to the floor. He was bleeding heavily onto the linoleum, which was cream-coloured, and she was amazed at how quiet it was. Finally he fell all the way. With a great sigh, he lay curled around the table leg.

She was still clutching the knife so hard that she felt it all the way up to her shoulder. She turned away from him and went over to the worktop, dropped the knife in the sink, turned on the tap. The blood and water disappeared down the plughole and she washed her hands, which were clean and white again in an instant. She turned back and looked at him. The Agent. Bennet. It was all so clear now. He was the one who had jumped from the roof of the high building. He was the Jumper. She could see that now, it was him; he was wearing the same clothes, his black jacket open. Now he would never get up again, never look at her with those inscrutable eyes. The sign she had been given so clearly only moments ago. He had jumped for the last time, and now he would stay on the ground. He had forgotten his watch at the till. She had held his time in her hands. She knew that the watch had stopped now as well, lying in its white box, she was absolutely sure of it. She nodded to herself as she had these thoughts, and reflected on all the obvious signs. Of course there was a pattern, an order.

She dried her hands on the dishcloth and stood looking at the bent body under the kitchen table. The fluorescent light on the ceiling was reflected in the blood and it looked shiny like oil. His body was no longer receiving signals from his brain, and now he looked like a broken doll that someone had thrown away. She watched him in silence, the fluid pouring from his wounds, spreading out into a big pool. She realised that she had to do something. She came up with a temporary solution. She walked resolutely into the hall, pushed her feet down into some boots and went round to the back of the house, to the woodpile under the bathroom window, and pulled off the green tarpaulin. When she gathered it up into her arms, she could feel the cold seeping in through her overall. It was covered in frost and snow. She carried it back into the kitchen and started to spread it over him, tugged at the corners. She covered him as well as she could, made sure that the water-resistant fabric covered everything, his head, hands and feet. So she did not need to look at him. What cannot be seen does not exist. Sometimes you had to buy yourself time.

When she had finished, she realised how thirsty she was. She turned her back on him and opened the fridge, found a bottle of Uludag Frutti that she had bought from Irfan before he closed the shop. She ignored the Agent and took the bottle with her into the living room. The lemon drink was cold and sour, just as she liked it. She took small sips, swallowed and closed her eyes. Oh, she was so tired, so tired of it all. She could not even think. Not back, not forwards. Despite what had happened out there in the kitchen, she felt calm. She had erupted, and now she was sitting in the ash rain. The great machinery that had whirred in her head all autumn had finally fallen quiet. It felt so good just to sit still in the chair, with her hands in her lap, and drink the cold Turkish lemon fizz straight from the bottle.

When she came to herself again, her head was heavy and her feet were numb. She had fallen asleep, or perhaps just dozed, she was not entirely sure, she only knew she had been far away and now, with a jolt, was back again. She reluctantly opened her eyes and had the vague feeling that something terrible had happened, which scared her. But it may not have happened at all; she had had terrifying dreams before. The first thing she saw was the clock on the wall. She remembered something, but pushed it to one side. What was the last thing she did before she sat down in the chair? She leaned forward and looked at her knees. Her body felt remarkably disconnected, as though all her joints had come loose. When she tried to stand up her legs would not hold her, her hips felt dislocated, but she pushed herself up with her arms, forced herself to stand upright. After a few unsteady steps, she found her balance. She saw the empty Frutti bottle on the table. Why had she been so thirsty? She had exerted herself, she had been terrified. Or furious, or distressed, the adrenaline had dried her out. She crossed the room and went into the kitchen, where the light was still on. Everything was clear and sharp. Something had happened out here, she realised, but her brain had not stored it, her brain often made strange choices. She saw the green tarpaulin. It looked like she had carried the whole woodpile in and stacked it on the kitchen floor. But then she recognised the shape of a human body under the tarpaulin. So that was it. The Agent had knocked on the door and she had let him in. Bennet, he had said, that could be a first name or a surname, not that it mattered now.

She put her hand to her heart, stood there looking at the mound on the floor. She did not feel much. Mostly just amazement that she had ended up in this situation. It was hard to think, so she used her eyes instead. She stretched out a hand and supported herself on the worktop. Was that not a slight movement under the tarpaulin? She had not expected that, she took a step to the side, felt that her hips were not in place, held on to the counter with both hands. He was moving. Her eyes had not played a trick. It must be a hand, because there was no movement where she knew the feet were; if she remembered correctly, the hands were under the table. She heard no sounds – there was not much life left in him – but there, she saw the movement again, it was obvious now, he was scratching at the floor with his long nails. It was the right hand. She had heard his lungs collapse. How was that possible? She could not understand, or was it perhaps just death cramps? She had heard about things like that. Headless chickens that ran around the yard. It annoyed her that he would not lie still. It meant there was still life in him, and if there was life in him, it made everything a lot harder. She would have to make some decisions and think through what had happened again. And she could not face thinking about it. She had finished something, it could not start again, not now that everything was so blissfully still. She turned to the sink, picked up the knife she had left there, with its shining, clean blade. Then she bent down over the tarpaulin and thrust the knife through the green fabric, not caring where she stabbed him. There was absolutely no movement now – she stood watching for a while to be sure. She dropped the knife into the sink again, the sound of steel against steel, and turned on the tap. More blood and water washed down the drain. She looked over her shoulder to check on him, she did not want to see even a tremor. And there was none.

She paced back and forth on the kitchen floor, stamping like a sulking child, she had to get her hips sorted, get the joint back in the socket. She thought she heard a click, and then another, and everything fell into place and she could move freely again. She washed the knife properly with the washing-up brush and liquid, then put it back in the drawer. It was a good knife, and useful for so many things. She noticed the folder lying on the table. He had not had the chance to open it. And it held the truth, he had said, the good news, the unique offer. It was a brown leather folder, no, not leather – she held it to her nose and it smelt of plastic. She went back into the living room and sat down with the folder in her lap, she could feel there was some weight to it. It belonged to her now, she had the right to its contents. She had just won a long battle, and this was her plunder. It had a solid zip, which she opened and then pulled out the contents, and rested them on her lap while she threw the folder down onto the floor. A pile of magazines, lots of them, maybe as many as twenty, and they were all the same. On the cover was a colourful picture of a woman and a small boy. Mother and son, Ragna thought, mother and son! They resembled one another, both had dark hair and skin, and brown eyes. The mother was wearing a beautiful headscarf and the boy had a blue hat on, which might have been crocheted. The photograph had not been taken in Norway, but in another country, at the market, there were stalls with colourful fruits, piles of baskets and lovely fabrics. The boy had an orange in his hand, and he was running for his life. Behind him came an angry man, shaking his fist, and the woman, the mother, had her hands to her cheeks. Ragna understood the picture immediately. The boy had stolen an orange from the fruit seller and was trying to run away. Only now, after she had studied the image, did she read the title.

AWAKE!

She opened the cover. The magazine was published by the Jehovah's Witnesses and this was the December issue. The topic for the month was parenting and criminality. She carried on, reading snippets here and there, running her eyes down the pages. One article was about Armageddon and Judgement Day, and there was another about the Thousand Year Reign and the Chosen Ones. All the signs, the truth. The man lying on the kitchen floor, the man with the long nails, was a Jehovah's Witness. She felt leaden and utterly exhausted. She had clearly misunderstood. She let the magazines fall to the floor, there were so many of them, and they slid out into a colourful fan. There was so much to take in, so much she had to sort out. She should probably ring someone and explain, but she had no energy left and no one could hear what she said on the phone anyway. All she wanted to do was sleep. And the man out in the kitchen was not going anywhere. So she went to the bedroom and collapsed on the bed. Oh, the air coming through the window felt so good, it cooled her down. All she had to do was wait. Someone would come. They would know what to do. It's impossible to do everything alone, and I have no voice. I have to rest. You must rest, Ragna.

She closed her eyes. Her heartbeat was calm and light, because her heart did not know what to do, and carried on with its job of keeping her alive, without judgement. The boy had stolen an orange. Did that mean that the mother had failed, she wondered, or did it mean that in some faraway land that she knew nothing about, a juicy orange was such an irresistible temptation for a poor boy that he could not stop himself? Would they chop off his hands, did he live in a country where they did things like that? She lay for a long time thinking about the picture. In her imagination, she was the woman and Rikard Josef was the boy. He had once, when he was eleven, stolen a big hunting knife from a sports shop, but the staff caught him red-handed. She had had to go and collect him and apologise on his behalf. She remembered the shame. She had had to promise the shop assistants that she would give him a serious talking-to, and she tried to recall what she had said. That he must never do that again, that he was not that kind of boy and she was not that kind of mother. And when she asked him why he had stolen it, he said that it was a good knife. I wanted it. Did the Agent know that? Was the picture a sign? The topic of the month was parenting and criminality.

She changed position several times before she finally settled and fell asleep. She dreamt that she was walking through an exotic market in a foreign country, buying fruit. And it was Irfan who owned all the stalls. Irfan stood there in a long white tunic, and she stopped and talked to him for a long time, she had a voice, and it was bright and clear as a bell, and Irfan clapped his hands in delight. He gave her a basket for the fruit and she picked out all the things that tempted her, plums and apricots and dates and other treats. She paid for an extra orange, the one her son had stolen, and put the coins in Irfan's hand.

She did not know how long she had slept, curled up in the dark room. Maybe one hour, maybe four, time stands still when you sleep. But she thought it was still Sunday, and through the gap in the curtains she could see that it was still light. There was not a sound in the house, she could hear no traffic on the road, where was everyone, had everything stopped? She got up and walked slowly to the bathroom, as though there was something wrong with her legs. Not even Walther Eriksson would have been able to find anything alluring about the face that stared back at her from the mirror, not even with the best camera in the world. She thought her eyes looked darker, like the eyes of the woman at the market, the mother of the orange thief, a mother who had perhaps not fulfilled her duties as a good parent. She had not managed either, she realised, as Rikard Josef had just vanished. She looked around for some clothes but could not find anything other than an old nightgown that had been thrown on the floor. It had thin straps and a lace trim around the neck. She pulled it on over her head and went into the kitchen where the Agent was lying. She gasped when she saw the tarpaulin, as she was sure it had slipped. While she was asleep he had moved again, the mound was a different shape. This time he had without a doubt moved his arms and legs in an attempt to get across the floor, perhaps even to stand up. She went over to him, bent down and listened to see if he was breathing. She kicked his body gently, then again, and a third time, with no result. The initial gentle nudge with her foot became hard kicks, she had to be certain. He was down and she kicked him all the same, as people have always done. She was no different from anyone else, no better, and it was easier than when someone was standing.

She needed to put some more clothes on, she felt that it was cold. And she should put some wood in the burner. The woodpile under the window at the back of the house was no longer protected from the wind and weather, as the tarpaulin was in front of her on the floor. She looked up at the clock and discovered that she had been asleep for hours. Her hand-knitted cardigan was hanging on the back of the chair by the computer, she put it on, wrapped it tight around her and turned on the television. She switched to the news channel, sat on the edge of her chair and stared at the flickering screen. Perhaps they knew already. Maybe Agent Bennet had been reported missing. Could she stab someone with a knife without anyone noticing, could she cut a string forever, not just the thin thread of a conversation, but an entire physical entity, without any consequences? No, she could not. There were cameras everywhere on the street, maybe even in her own house, someone would have noticed something. She looked around and saw the two smoke alarms on the ceiling. They looked like beautiful UFOs, plate-shaped with a small mesh that looked like a window.

They might have tricked her and installed a camera there instead; that was what society had become, everyone was being monitored. She noticed a small flashing red light in both of them, which she had not seen before. This made the UFOs even more alive, somehow, as if they were inhabited. She remembered there was also a detector installed in the kitchen, and if that was actually a camera, then the whole thing had been filmed. She went out and stood under the detector; the red light was flashing. That could be a sign that someone was sitting in the control room up there at this very moment watching her on a screen. Little Ragna Riegel in her nightgown and cardigan. She raised her hand and waved. Looked down at the green tarpaulin, smiled at the camera again, waved and pointed, waved and pointed. Then she pushed her bare feet down into a pair of boots and went round to the back of the house to get some wood.

The logs were covered in a fine film of frost, in beautiful tiny crystals. If she was going to do all that she had to, she at least needed some warmth, and perhaps also some food. And she did not want to greet people in her nightgown, even if it did have a lovely lace trim, and everything had to be in order when they came. As she knew they would, several of them. Or would they? Had she not already asked them for help several times, and yet no one had come? She got angry again. She stacked as much wood as she could balance on her arms and went back in, put it in the burner. When the fire was blazing, she sat down on the floor and stared into the flames. Her cheeks got even hotter, and her shoulders and chest. What need was there for anything else when you had a fire? The flickering tongues transported her elsewhere, they crackled and danced, became a living being that she had to keep alive. As long as the fire burned, time stood still. For a while she looked at one log, then at another. The glittering snow crystals had long since melted and evaporated, the living room was as hot as a baker's oven, she had to take the woolly cardigan off. She did not want to hear another sound from Bennet now, but snuck out to the kitchen to make sure, tiptoeing closer. She thought once again that the green nylon fabric had changed shape – now the mound was spread out over the floor like some great, formless single-celled organism, an enormous amoeba. Her father had explained this to her when she was little, that this happened to all of life. And it would happen to her, she too would take on another form. She would die and then she would come back as something else.

'As what though?' she had asked. With her small hand in his big one.

'A small animal, maybe,' her father had replied.

'Oh!' she had exclaimed. 'Can I choose which animal?'

'I'm sure you can,' he had said.

She had squeezed his hand and said that she hoped she would be a small squirrel, and he said that he could picture that squirrel perfectly. Quick and bright, with a shiny coat, just like her. He winked at her, and she asked if it took a long time to change shape, and come back again. Oh yes, he thought, it took a long time. It takes a thousand years. But the trees will still be here, so you can play in them and hunt for nuts.

'And what about you, Daddy?' she had asked. 'What do you want to be when you come back?'

'I want to be your father all over again,' he had replied. 'I want to be your father until the end of the world.'

'Father to a small squirrel?'

'I can carry you in my inner pocket,' he had said. 'The pocket here, closest to my heart.'

Since then, she had never feared death.

She opened the fridge and looked in to see if there was anything she could eat or make quickly, but there was not much there. She took out a packet of salami and ate a few slices, which of course made her thirsty. She did not have any more Uludag Frutti, just a bottle of juice that was mouldy. She could not understand why her fridge was so empty. She went over to the sink and drank some water straight from the tap, even though her mother had often told her when she was a little girl that she risked getting a tape worm that could grow up to several metres long in her tummy and steal any food that she ate, so she would be thin as a rake. And I always have been, she thought suddenly, so the worm has always been there. Once she was back in front of the wood burner, she thought she could feel something wriggling inside her, demanding space, it twisted and turned like a metre-long piece of spaghetti. But she had worse things to deal with now than a worm in her stomach.

She went out several times to collect wood. In and out in nothing but her nightgown, in the end she could not even be bothered to put on her boots. It was actually all right to walk barefoot in the snow, she had never done it before. She spent some time and a good deal of care piling the logs up on the floor, it might be a while before anyone came to her assistance. She would rather not have to go out and get wood in the dark, so she stockpiled enough now to last her until morning. Every so often she glanced at the TV, which was still on. She reckoned that sooner or later the Agent's face would look at her from the screen, because he had been reported missing, or, even worse, her own face would appear. No, how on earth would that happen, no one other than Walther had any photographs of her. But she had to follow what was happening, she had to be prepared. She kept the fire going in the burner until the glass was black with soot and she could barely see the flames, only a few glowing points in the depths of the burner. She needed to rest again. She turned down the volume on the television and curled up on the sofa, pulled a blanket over her, and listened out for footsteps and voices, or cars pulling up outside and doors slamming. Looked up at the UFOs' red flashing eyes.

The fire had died down a long time ago, and there were only a few embers glowing in the blackened logs. She saw the Agent's magazines scattered on the floor, they would burn well. So she got down on her knees in front of the burner and tore off the pages one by one, and watched the young orange thief being eaten by flames. The boy's body curled up as it would in a crematorium oven. As she sat there staring into the flames, she realised that it would probably be a long time before she had the opportunity to visit her parents' grave again. She had always enjoyed going there, and no one could say it was not well looked after. Which would not be the case with her own, when the time came, and that might be soon. But it was Sunday, she remembered. No shops would be open so she could not buy flowers or candles, and she could not go to the grave empty-handed, in the same way that one does not go to a party without a gift. She closed the door to the wood burner, steeled herself and ventured out into the kitchen to see if she had anything suitable. She avoided looking at the Agent. She might have something she could give them that would look nice on the white snow. She rummaged through the drawers and cupboards. She found the twisted advent candles that she had not used yet, but they would blow out straight away. Eventually she found a packet of serviettes that were cream-coloured, with pink roses and green spiky leaves. They were exceptionally beautiful, she thought. She popped them into her handbag. Then she put her coat on over her nightgown, found some gloves and pulled on a pair of wellies that were standing in the hall. They were not warm, but they were closest to hand.

When she opened the door she discovered it was dark outside. Perhaps she would need a torch, but then she remembered all the spotlights in the graveyard, and one of them was not far from her parents' grave. She did not bother to lock the door, did not know whether it was evening or night, as she had not bothered to look at the clock. But there were still lights on in Olaf's house. As soon as she was out on the road, she realised how slippery the boots were and how cold it was. She was not wearing tights and her coat was short, so her legs were bare. Struggling to stay on her feet – as there was ice everywhere and the gritters had obviously not been out – she looked to the right and the left, then crossed the street. She walked quickly past the closed shop and remembered once again that it was Sunday, so there were not many buses. She never took the bus on a Sunday, but guessed there was only one an hour, or two if she was lucky, and she was never lucky. She waited and listened. The bus had a special drone that she would hear long before it appeared. She kept looking in the opposite direction, where she knew the police would come from when they got the message. But she saw no blue lights. She tried to curl her toes in the wellies, stamped up and down on the icy road, to keep the blood circulating in her body. Olaf's house looked so warm and inviting. She could clearly picture Dolly, curled up in front of the fire. After a long wait, the bus came rumbling up Kirkelina, it was almost empty and she slipped into her usual seat. When the bus passed her house, she looked up at the light in the windows and found it hard to believe that it could look like such an ordinary house. No one knew anything about the Agent under the green tarpaulin, all they would see was the light, which they might associate with warmth. She opened her handbag and took out the packet of serviettes and admired them through the plastic. Her mother had taught her numerous ways to fold a serviette, she could make a fan or a rose, a bow or a heart, a lily or a pyramid. But she noticed these were three-ply and soft. The more expensive the serviettes were, the harder they were to fold.

Her cheek against the window, her bag in her lap. No flashing blue lights coming towards them, and she could hear no sirens. She looked up at the black sky over the town. They all believed that it stretched on for eternity, whereas in reality, the atmosphere was as thin as a bride's veil and the sky stopped just beyond the tallest skyscraper, or after twenty minutes in a rocket. Twenty minutes, she thought, and then nothing. Beyond was just dark and cold, and beneath the veil, tiny people lived inside a glass cloche.

She slipped several times on the narrow path up to the church. The ice lay like a clear film on the paving stones and she moved as carefully as she could, bent over like an old lady. The boots were too big because she had no tights on, and the soles, although ridged, did not provide much grip. She turned to the left by the entrance and followed a well-trodden path round to the back of the church. When she saw her parents' grave up against the wall, illuminated by the nearby spotlight, the sorrow sank through her like a heavy stone. It weighed her down. The feeling of loss was more acute than ever. Here they lay, as close together in death as they had been in life, but it was only she who thought of them, only she who offered kind thoughts. If I was God, she thought, I would breathe life into them again. But there was no God, not up there, nor down here. She fell to her knees, no longer cared about the cold, the snow on her bare skin was nothing. She glanced quickly over her shoulder to see if anyone else was around, but there was no one there that cold Sunday evening, she was alone with the dead.

She opened the packet of serviettes, felt the soft paper, and considered her options. What could she make with these? She ran quickly through the steps that she had learned as a girl, and then started to fold a swan with beautiful tail feathers. She had not forgotten how to do it, the folds were in her fingers. Despite the soft paper, the magnificent bird with its long neck stayed upright. She folded another one, identical to the first. Put them down in front of the gravestone, facing each other like two lovers, because they had loved each other, for better and for worse, though often it had been for worse. No, not worse, it had just been difficult. What is it about us? She felt miserable. Why can't we cope? What is the point of that? She kneeled in the snow for a long time looking at the swans, they were proud and beautiful, just like her parents. The wind would catch them soon, and the snow, maybe even the same night. They would be blown away and chased from grave to grave until one of the workers noticed them and picked them up because he thought they were rubbish, just some wet paper, not a declaration of love. She stayed there for a long time. She burned the image into her mind, until she was sure she could recall it whenever she needed it.

By then she was stiff and cold. She managed to stand up and was about to leave when a gust of wind raced through the graveyard, lifting up one of the swans. It flew a couple of metres and she ran after it, but just as she was about pick it up, there was another gust of wind, which was stronger than the first. She felt desperate as she watched the bird disappear between the gravestones, into the dark where there was no spotlight. She went over to look. She checked behind each grave, went to the right, then the left, further and further into the graveyard. It could not just disappear like that! She continued to search, walked in the other direction, towards the front of the church, even though that was not the way the bird had flown. No one saw her as she wandered around bare-legged, no one would understand her desperation, it was just a serviette. Then she suddenly found it, it had settled next to one of the rubbish bins by the wall. Relieved, she took it back and placed it in front of the grave again, listened to the wind, which had dropped. When she came out onto the slippery path down to the square, she lost her balance and fell forward, and her right knee hit the paving with force. Tears sprang to her eyes as the pain shot to her head and she let out a despairing howl, which no one heard. For a moment she lay there and tried to move her leg. Maybe she had broken her kneecap, maybe she would never make it down to the square, and if she was not able to do that, she would freeze to death. No one would come to the church until morning. She scrabbled around for her bag, got hold of it and pulled it to her, then managed to get up, and gingerly put some weight on her right leg to see if it would hold her. It was extremely painful, but she hobbled slowly down towards the bus stop, dragging her leg behind her. All she wanted now was to get home and sit down in the chair in front of the stove. Maybe someone had been to her house and sorted everything out, given that the door was open. While she stood waiting, she put all her weight on the left leg. The injured one throbbed and ached intensely and she was afraid that she would not be able to get onto the bus as the steps were so steep. When it finally came and the doors slid open, she grabbed hold of the handrail and used all her strength to haul herself up. Once she was sitting in the warmth and light of the bus, she pulled up her coat to look at her knee. It was very red and much bigger than the left one.

She was surprised when she opened the unlocked door and went into her house, limping in the heavy wellies.

She thought it strange that no one had come, that she was back in the same incomprehensible situation. This was her own little world; the others were all elsewhere. But she was happy. She thought of the swans as good work. Her mother had taught her a lot about duty, dignity, patience and humility. Her father had taught her many other things, but his was a wisdom she could not put a name to. It was all about being in the moment, opening your senses. Taking each second as it comes, not fighting it. She was in the moment now. Her bare legs were blue with cold and her knee was red and swollen, but she was still in one piece. Her bones were rattling, she could hear that, but she managed to cross the room. There was not even an ember in the wood burner now, just soot on the glass. She stood in the kitchen doorway to check the tarpaulin. There was no noticeable change in the shape, but she thought that the fabric was vibrating with life. Perhaps the warmth in the Agent's body had been transferred to the tarpaulin, where it had woken to life thousands of microorganisms. Maybe, given time, they would eat him up. In her mind, she set fire to it all. Bennet with his long nails and prophecies of death. It occurred to her that the tarpaulin might not burn as it was synthetic, and would probably just melt into his cheap suit, and deposit chemicals on his pale skin. They would have to bury him in it, a hard, synthetic shell that could not be removed.

She put some wood in the burner. It was dark outside, and there was no traffic on the road. She thought about the night ahead, and the day that would follow, Monday. Because it was Monday tomorrow, wasn't it, or had she got confused? She thought she had an early shift. Gunnhild would phone as soon as they opened, if she did not show up.

I feel so heavy, Ragna thought, my joints feel loose, and my knee hurts. There's a great stone inside me, I'm cold and I haven't eaten and I don't know why all this has happened. I just know that it started a long time ago. I can't wander around in the aisles at Europris with the pricing machine in this state. It was not the bones in themselves, she realised, it was the ligaments that held them in place that were about to snap. I'll come apart at the seams like a ragdoll. The fire was soon burning merrily and she felt warm and peaceful. She saw some white letters on the TV screen. She had forgotten to turn it off before she went out. There was no picture any more, just a message that appeared when the television had been left on for too long.

NO SIGNAL.

She turned it off, and then on again, and got the picture back. It was good to watch the news, to see how everyone else was living their lives. The seven billion people beneath the veil that she would soon be cut off from for a long time. From now on, she had to live each minute in her own head. As if she had not always done that anyway.

She spent the night on the sofa. The pain in her knee kept her awake, but she was all right with that, she wanted to be awake when they came to the house. With the daylight came a message from Gunnhild, asking if everything was all right.

Ragna thought about the Agent in the kitchen. She did not want Gunnhild to come to the house. Someone else had to come, a man, several men, people who would not lose their heads, who would act according to set procedures, who had been into similar kitchens before. She sent a message back to say that she had all she needed, that she just wanted to rest. But after a while she got up all the same, dragged her sore leg behind her. And sat down to wait. She had pulled the chair over to the window, so she could see them as soon as they came. Every now and then she cried a little when she thought about what lay ahead, all that she would have to explain, without a voice. At other times she was overwhelmed by exhaustion and dragged herself back to the sofa, and when it started to get dark, and still no one had come, she went to bed. She wanted it to be Tuesday, because she was sure they would come then. She ate nothing and drank nothing, she was so weak it was almost like being intoxicated. She rose and sank, hovered and floated, there was a rushing in her ears. She thought about the two serviette swans, saw them clearly in her mind's eye and was glad that her brain had stored that important memory. She thought about the empty flat in Landsberger Allee, where Rikard Josef no longer lived. She thought about the young orange thief and the pictures of him she had burnt in the fire. Who was to blame for him stealing, was it anyone's fault at all, and what was guilt, and what should one do with guilt, could it be washed away or forgiven, was it a coating that would always stick with her?

After long periods of rest, she got up again and sat by the window, as patient as an old woman who had nothing to wait for, other than death. There was a steady flow of traffic outside, but no one stopped by her house, only the Agent had stopped and he had not

had good intentions. All her life she had watched the
world through this window. When she was little, she
had had to stand on a stool to see out, but the picture
was always the same. Only the colours were different.
The street light was still on, so her helpers would be
able to find their way to her house. What is the first
thing you remember? they would ask. Daddy, she
would say. He saw me clearly. He saw everyone else as
well, the vultures. The predators. Daddy was always
frightened. He died from it, he died from fright. I'm
going to die from fright too, and that's fine, because
then I'll end up in Daddy's inner pocket, the one next to
his heart, and that's where I want to be. And your
mother, do you remember her? She always got up early,
long before the rest of us, she had to be ready. Each
morning she put up her long hair, she dressed nicely
every day, there were so many authorities to deal with.
They all came to our door and confronted her with
everything we were unable to do, everything we struggled with. Our duties, tax, the bills, which were not
always paid. Rikard Josef and his upbringing, Daddy's
illness. They were constantly coming to get Daddy,
they took him away without a word. He was not big
and strong, he was thin as a fencepost. He did not eat
much, there were more important things to do in life.
Why did they come to get him? her helpers would ask.
Because he knew so much, he had his own vision, an
intuitive understanding that the rest of us shut down,
because we cannot take it all in – we have to lie, to
ourselves and to others, to adapt and survive; the space
we operate in cannot be too big and bright, because
then we lose control. But Daddy went out and was
open to it all – that was why they came to get him. All

they could see was a madman wandering out into the road to stop the traffic.

It was me who found him, she would say. He had hanged himself sitting down, from one of the handles on the cupboard door, all he was wearing was a pair of old underpants. His legs were as black as ink, the blood had sunk and gathered at the bottom. He sat stooped with his chin on his chest, it looked like he was praying, but I know that he didn't pray. What did you think? they would ask. That he was right. That we were all frightened, deep down, of life, that is. Of every day. Just not the last day, not for what would come after it.

Following this long sequence of thoughts, she came to herself again. She wondered if she had heard something out in the kitchen. The sound reminded her of the scratching up in the loft at night, when the mice were scurrying about. If only he could lie still out there, she had no more energy. But she hauled herself up and limped into the kitchen. She took hold of one of the corners of the tarpaulin and lifted it to one side. The Agent's eyes were open. He was staring at something in the distance that she could not see. She was sure that it was the Thousand Year Reign, that he finally had a place as one of the chosen few, and that was what he had wanted. But if that was the case, if he was staring into the Thousand Year Reign, it was not a beautiful place. The Agent looked horrified, disappointed, terrified. She put the tarpaulin back with care, waved to the camera again to show them she was still waiting, and pointed towards the hall to indicate that the door was unlocked. Then she returned to the sofa and rested for a while. She could feel that her body needed food and water, but she could not face it. She was floating, rising up to the ceiling, was light as a feather. They could come and lift her up, carry her away, lock her up, if only they could find her son and let him know. At regular intervals, she tottered out into the hall to make sure the door was still unlocked, opening it and looking down to the road, and then closing it again. There was another message on her mobile phone from Gunnhild. This time she could not bear to answer. She no longer checked the time, only noticed the light fading, then it was dark, then it got light again, then it was dark, as the days passed. It must be Wednesday now, or Thursday. Her tongue felt thick in her mouth and everything, not just her knee, ached now. There was a flickering in front of her eyes, like a fluorescent tube just before it breaks. She struggled out to the bathroom to get some paracetamol, but all she found was the box of Apodorm. What did it matter if she was asleep when they came? They just had to wrap her up and carry her out. And she so desperately wanted to be carried. She pressed the tablets through the foil, took out another tray and continued until she had a handful.

She was lying at the bottom of a boat, she could feel the movement of the sea, and it was stormy. She rolled back and forth on the long, heavy waves, her body knocking against the sides, sometimes soft, sometimes hard. No, it was something else. Someone was shouting and shaking her, she wanted to answer but her mouth was dry and she could not form the words. All feeling had run out of her in the same way that the blood had run out of the Agent. She just wanted to be left in peace on the rocking boat. But whoever was calling would not give up, the voice was right next to her ear, she could feel the breath, it was warm.

'Ragna! Wake up!'

She wanted to open her eyes, but they were dry too. Wake, awake, there was something familiar about the words. She had heard them before, read it somewhere. Gradually her sight returned, but all she could see was her hand, which she lifted shaking to her face.

'I've hurt my knee,' she managed to whisper.

'Did you faint?'

It was Gunnhild.

Ragna realised she was lying on the floor and was wearing only the nightgown.

'He's lying in the kitchen,' she said.

'What did you say? Maybe we should call a doctor.'

'No, he's dead.'

There was a short silence.

'Not Rikard?' Gunnhild asked. 'Has something happened to Rikard? Has someone called from Berlin?'

Ragna would have given her arm to be able to scream. To scream from the bottom of her lungs, the depths of her life, a scream that would shatter windows. But she could do nothing but repeat herself in a whisper.

'I think he's dead. Can you not smell it?'

Gunnhild went reluctantly out into the kitchen and stayed there for a long time. Ragna crawled across the floor to the sofa and hauled herself up. When Gunnhild came back in again, she stood there with her hand to her mouth, her eyes wide with horror.

'Who did that?' she asked.

'Me.'

'No,' Gunnhild said, petrified.

'Yes,' Ragna said. 'I had to.'

'Have you killed him?'

'I think so.'

Gunnhild collapsed into Ragna's favourite armchair.

'But why?'

She did not get an answer. She went to the telephone to ring. She did not say much, she had to give her name, that she was at Kirkelina 7 and it was in connection with a death. She opened the veranda door and let in the freezing air, then stood by the window, staring down towards the road.

Ragna propped herself up on her elbow.

'Did they believe you?' she whispered.

'Who?'

'The police.'

'Of course they believed me.' Gunnhild looked bewildered. 'Why would they not believe me? Who is he?'

Ragna sat up straight on the sofa, leaned back against the cushion.

'Don't know him at all.'

'But,' Gunnhild stammered, 'why did he come here?'

'He's been pestering me all autumn.'

'Pestering you? Why?'

'I don't know.'

Gunnhild glanced down at the road again.

'Did he come here to get you?'

'I think so,' Ragna said. 'Will they be here soon?'

'It won't take them more than ten minutes,' Gunnhild said, 'they're just across the river. We mustn't touch anything,' she added. 'Have you touched anything?'

'I live here. Of course I've touched things.'

Gunnhild went over to the sofa, found a blanket, and laid it gently over Ragna's knees.

'But why didn't you ring anyone?'

'I've tried several times, but no one comes. You don't know what it's like.'

Gunnhild went back to the window, watching just as Ragna had done all autumn.

'I can't get hold of Rikard,' Ragna said.

'Why not?'

'I can't find anyone. Everyone just disappears.'

'Not everyone, surely?'

'Walther,' she whispered. 'Mummy and Daddy. Rikard Josef. William. And Irfan.'

'Irfan?'

Ragna pointed at the window.

'He had the shop over the road. I went there every day.'

'Have you taken anything?' Gunnhild asked. 'Pills? Why do you have that picture of the dog by the door? You've never had a dog.'

'You're asking too many questions,' Ragna complained. And then she wept. Time had started up again – she noticed that the second hand on the wall clock was ticking.

Chapter 27

'Do you believe there's an afterwards?' Ragna whispered.

'After death? There's nothing after death,' Sejer said.

'Yes, but if. Only if. What would you want it to be?'

'I don't want anything after death.'

His words were followed by a smile, which Ragna reciprocated.

'There's someone you miss,' she said, and looked up at the photograph of Elise.

'Yes, there is. I will never see them again.'

'But if you saw them,' she insisted. 'Would you not be happy?'

'I've never been that bothered about happiness,' Sejer said.

'You're so stubborn,' Ragna exclaimed.

'So are you.'

'What are you interested in then?'

'Right now, I'm interested in you.'

They smiled at each other again. They had made a secret connection. Sejer was like a mountain, an unconquered rock face. But she saw something else as well, she saw it every time he glanced over at Frank by the window. She saw the devotion shared by the long grey man and the small fat dog.

'Are you particularly fond of Frank because he can't talk?'

'Perhaps,' Sejer had to admit. 'I have to use all my senses to know what he wants and what he needs. When he's gone, it's his eyes I'll remember, and the smell of him. But when people we know die, it's their voice that stays with us.'

'People talk too much,' Ragna said. 'Too much importance is put on words.'

'That's how we solve our problems,' Sejer said.

This reminded her of something she had once seen when she was out walking.

'It was shortly after the fateful operation,' she explained. 'I was looking for a way to come to terms with what had happened. So I went for a walk, but being alone in town on a grey day only amplified my feelings of grief. For everything that I had lost forever. I walked for hours, and gradually there were fewer and fewer houses. Eventually I was out on a country road with hardly any traffic. I passed a paddock with two horses, one brown and one black. Just then, as I stood there looking at them, it started to rain. It was not a fine summer rain, but one of those sudden showers that turned into a downpour. I huddled up by the electric fence. It was raining so hard that it was pummelling my shoulders. I had nothing with me, no raincoat, no umbrella, and there was no shelter anywhere nearby. So I stood still and thought, ah well, I'll get wet. I continued to watch the horses, because something had happened. First they lifted their heads to the rain. Then they moved slowly towards each other and the brown horse put its heavy head on the back of the black horse. And they stood together in the rain, as close as two steaming big animals can. There was something so simple and heart-warming about it, something so natural. Yes, I thought, there's far too much talk in the world. It's better to do, to take action. I turned round and walked home again and was really quite happy.'

'And what are your thoughts on what comes after?' Sejer asked.

'I have so many thoughts about death. Some people think of death as a personal insult.'

She smiled briefly as she remembered an article she had read somewhere.

'If one fine day, after a long and arduous life, I find myself weightless and suspended in space, without knowing what's up and what's down, without seeing or hearing, and I don't know how long I'm going to be there, and can't understand why I'm hanging there and no longer know who I am, well, then I'm dead. And because I'm dead, I'm free. But if, after a few years, or maybe a few thousand years, some patronising creator comes and picks my free soul out of eternity and forces it into another body of flesh and blood, I don't know that I could face that.'

They were allies again. The acknowledgement passed from him to her and then back again.

'What about the squirrel?' he asked.

'The squirrel, yes,' she whispered. 'It's a lovely story. The kind that a father should always tell his children. What do the newspapers say about me?' she asked, out of the blue. 'Has the case been given a name? Most big cases usually get a nickname. I want to know what mine is.'

Sejer shook his head.

'The Riegel case?' she suggested.

'No.'

'Is it something with Jehovah perhaps,' she said. 'The Jehovah case, or the Jehovah killing?'

'You'll be spending a lot of time on your own in the years ahead,' Sejer said. 'And you'll get access to newspapers and the news soon enough. Now, I want to ask an important question. You'll be asked the same thing in court when you get there. Think carefully before you answer.'

'Okay.'

'When Bennet came into your kitchen and sat down at your table, and told you why he was there, did you feel your life was in danger?'

She thought carefully about this, exactly as he had said she should.

'I just wanted the torment to stop.'

'Did you feel your life was in danger? Yes or no?'

'I wasn't sure what would happen.'

'So you wanted to beat him to it?'

'I wanted to be on the safe side, to be sure.'

'Is that what you will tell the judge? That you killed Bennet to be on the safe side?'

'I'm answering your question as best I can!' she stammered. 'It was foolish of him to come alone. Jehovah's Witnesses never come alone.'

'The other person couldn't make it,' Sejer told her. 'And Bennet was a conscientious young man.'

'He could have said that,' she mumbled. 'He just came into my kitchen and said I was going to die.'

'And when you stopped him from carrying out his mission, whatever you thought that might be, how did you think then?'

'I thought about you,' she said.

'Us? The police?'

'I saw what was on the floor, and knew that finally you would have to come.'

Chapter 28

Dear Rikard Josef,

Have you ever thought about how difficult it can be to know the truth about things? The definitive, most detailed version of an event? Or how difficult it is to answer questions properly, or to be sure of anything at all? Is it possible to be entirely truthful? Of course not. As soon as a thought takes form in the brain, it sparks into action and sends out a signal that turns into words, which are shaped by the journey from thought to speech, coloured by fear and assumptions, and the desire to be seen in a good light, when you have been eclipsed. Sometimes I think that everything that has happened to me over the years has taken place underwater. Whenever I think about people I have known, their faces are like pale anemones floating on the currents of the sea. Perhaps I am still underwater. Everything seems to unfold so slowly. Reality is only visible in glimpses, like the flickering of the sun on the surface of the water.

Sejer asks me questions and I answer as best I can. It was like this, I say, these were my thoughts and fears

– I have to formulate and express them, and it feels right. Then, when I am back in my cell at the desk by the window, I think I should have given a different answer. More truthful. Better. Is that really how it was, how much of it was my imagination, my pathetic attempt to share the blame? But try to see the truth, Rikard. Do you think we would recognise it if we were to find it, in the same way that we recognise lies? Lies sound like nails falling into a tin. But the truth is more of a rushing sound, I think, like waves breaking on the shore. The truth takes us to an enormous door, and when we confess everything, when we assume responsibility and lay all our cards on the table without flinching, the door opens and we can pass through into the sparkling light. And once we have passed through, once we have confessed everything, no one can touch us. We are naked perhaps, but also unassailable and pure. What did you say when they asked you about all the money you had embezzled? Did you talk for a long time about how difficult everything had been? That you felt you had to get away from Kirkelina because you had great dreams, that you got to Berlin and suddenly you were alone in an unknown world, that you fell for temptation and could not resist because you were damaged, perhaps by drugs or gambling? Even good people, those with high morals, dream of the chance to change their lives, and perhaps those who never find that chance are the lucky ones. Did you tell them that you had become a slave to something, that you had to serve a mighty lord, or did you simply say that you discovered what you would describe as a golden opportunity? I was greedy, maybe that was your answer, I am a thief, plain and simple. Perhaps you did

not say that at all. Your defence lawyer told you what to say, he advised you on the details and you listened to him. I have chosen not to have a defence. We will sort out all the formalities, of course, there is a lot of information, but I have made it clear from the start that I am guilty. That I am not at all interested in being acquitted, or getting as short a sentence as possible. I just want to be understood. I want the court to follow my journey step by step, so they can understand that there was no other way. My lawyer says, of course, that he feels almost redundant. I may not have a voice, but I have managed alone for all these years. I'm like a dog, I can look at people, and the sensitive ones pick up on my signals straight away. The inspector always does. And one person is enough, Rikard. If there is one person who is willing to listen, just one who is able to understand without judging, I see it as a privilege that very few experience. I chose the inspector. When the day and time come for me to go to court, and I have to give my statement, which practically no one will be able to hear, so everything will have to be repeated over a loudspeaker, I will be brief and accept what I am given. This cell is eight metres square, and I can watch the sky, the odd cloud drifting by, or the migrating birds. I would love to be part of a flock like that, third place on the left, following a strong leader to warmer climes. And the rain, Rikard, let it rain, and remember that every drop that falls is a beautiful snow crystal a few kilometres up, where it is always cold.

Once, many years ago, before you were born, Mummy and I went to London. Daddy was in hospital that spring, and Mummy was tired. When he was in other people's care, she could rest and relax because she knew he was in good hands. And she was like a girl again. We walked and walked and explored the city and watched the people, arm in arm, as if we were best friends. We went to the theatre and to the market and to the wax museum, and I could have walked the streets of London forever. We had no worries, and we took everything that fell from heaven with a smile. It rained every day. But instead of huddling up and looking for shelter, we lifted our faces to the raindrops and enjoyed all there was to enjoy. On the day we left, we took the train out to Heathrow, and were standing in security fumbling with our bags and cases when suddenly two security guards asked us to step to one side, out of the queue, and to go through a scanner. We both giggled nervously, Mummy and I, but we did not have even a sugar lump more than we should, only cheap things that we had bought at Camden Market, plastic jewellery and glass and some second-hand clothes. So we went through the machine, one after the other, turned round with our arms out straight, head high and legs apart, and I remember seeing a peculiar image of myself on the screen, a shining, orange figure, an alien version of my body, naked and transparent. It was oddly liberating that someone could see all there was to see. It felt good to stand there, I had nothing illegal to hide, no secrets. When Mummy and I had gone through the scanner, we walked arm in arm to the gate, laughing like two hysterical teenagers. We were both euphoric. I will never forget that moment, it taught me that the truth is bright, honesty casts its own light. People can see through us to our bones, and it feels good. Nothing frightens us humans more, but nothing feels better than letting it happen. Now, I am in that scanner again. I twist and turn so that everything can be seen, everything I have collected through the autumn. Everything that has happened in our house in Kirkelina is being revealed.

Do you know what I dreamt the other night? That you had a little girl somewhere, who you knew nothing about. That you once had a girlfriend, but you split up, and she had the baby afterwards, and didn't tell you. A daughter that lived somewhere in Berlin, without a father or a Norwegian grandmother. What if it were true? Some people's dreams come true, and it was so real. What do you think she is called, Rikard? Maybe a name that is more usual in Germany. Helga, or Hildegard, or Heidi? If it is true, and you were to find out about it, would you be happy?

Liebe Mutti,
I don't have a little girl anywhere. Nor a little boy. I don't want you to dream things like that. I don't want my blood to run in anyone else's veins. And if your dream was true, I would not want that little girl to know anything about you or me. For God's sake, we're both in jail! Our branch of the family must be chopped off, it has to stop with us. Walther is living his life in Stockholm, a life we know nothing about. I may even have been fatherless for a long time. Not that I would care, I have always been fatherless.

The priest came to see me yesterday and we talked for ages about lots of things. It strikes me that priests have thought about almost everything, they always have an answer, and if they don't have an answer, they have a quote from the Bible and if they don't have a quote, they say that our minds are not capable of understanding God's long-term plan.

Don't think so much, he kept saying, don't question everything. Be in the moment, be where you are right now. In your cell, with the light filtering in through the window. The heart that beats in you is a good heart. I know that it is good, he told me.

For a moment I was tempted to mention Peter. To look him in the eye and say straight out that if there was something he had not managed himself, it was to be in the moment. With Peter, who he adores and presumably desires. They will never find each other, not here inside the prison or outside its walls. They will each be locked in their closet for the rest of their lives. But the rest of us who wander around in the corridor watch them with a little smile, and I think they can feel it, they know they've been rumbled. They burn like torches, both of them, if you see what I mean. The truth, the light, as you put it in your letter, streams into our corridor like beams from a brilliant sun whenever they walk side by side to Peter's cell, the old and the young, for an important conversation, apparently. You can see it on their faces and in the priest's blue eyes and Peter's dark eyes. But you should know that the truth can also kill, as it has done since time immemorial. In my mind, I see Peter falling to his knees and confessing his love to the priest, who is duty-bound to reject him, given his vocation. He is a Catholic. Later, the officers will find Peter in his cell, he has hanged himself. It has happened before, it happens all the time, you know what I'm talking about. So, Mutti, I do not have a little girl. I would have told you if I did. Would that have made you happy? Would that have given you the purpose in life that you feel is missing? Once again I have to disappoint you. I left you and I will never provide you with a grandchild.

I still don't know anything. Why are you in prison? Did you harm someone, lose control? I have been living here in Berlin for twelve years and I have always wished the best for you. But lots of things are coming back to me now, memories from when I was little, and when I started to understand as a boy, and finally as a teenager decided to flee. I chose the path of least resistance, a coward's solution. And I'm not proud of that. Perhaps you remember some of it as well, or you have tried to forget. But ever since the inspector called and told me that you were being held on remand for a very serious crime, it's as though someone has opened a chamber that had been closed for years.

There are lots of things I want to ask you about.

Do you remember the time you took me to the nursery on Kirkelina, but never came to collect me? It was summer, and I had a half-day place, from one to five, that was paid for by the council. They had to ring you several times. Granny was visiting Grandad in hospital, and we had no contact with the neigh-bours, for obvious reasons. While I waited, I played in the big boat, the one with the pirate flag and small cabin, do you remember? I would often sit in the cabin and look out at the world through the porthole, because I felt safe in there. I wasn't that old, you know, but I remember it well, how the grown-ups looked at each other, the murmuring and raised eyebrows. They often talked like that, in hushed voices. The other children were picked up one by one, the cars drove out of the parking place and disap-peared, and silence fell on the playground. The adults discussed what to do with me, who they should contact. And I sat quietly in the cabin, and if any of them had asked me, I would have begged in a feeble voice to go home with one of them, possibly the one called Britt who was so kind. Stay the night with her, sleep in her bed, in a house that held no uncomfortable surprises. But they didn't ask me what I wanted. They were more interested in getting rid of me, they wanted to go home to their own children. But you came in the end. Suddenly there you were in the doorway, and all you had on was your underwear and some old wellies. I crawled out of the boat and walked across the grass, and you looked at me with glassy eyes, as though I were a stranger.

'Who do I have to pick up?' you said. 'Is there someone asking for me?'

There are tears in my eyes as I write this to you. And I wonder what telling you all this now might lead to, when you are obviously in a very difficult situation. And need something quite different. But I'm going to continue all the same. That was a random example. I have lots of stories like that, a sea of strange events that frightened me and confused me. Just as you were always frightened and confused, and Grandad too. The kids at school used to ask me about life in the loony bin on Kirkelina. Or they shouted after me that they'd seen my mum naked. Or they pointed and laughed and screamed because they'd spotted Grandad in the middle of the traffic, where he stood shouting and waving his arms until the police came to get him. Everyone's going to die, he'd shout, everyone's going to die. I have problems sleeping, Mutti. I'm constantly afraid. But I guess you know all about that.

Granny was always so tired. Exhausted by the fear that you and Grandad would be sectioned, that social services would come and get me and that I would be handed over to strangers, and that she would be left on her own. In her own heroic way, she managed to keep the family together, she managed to show us in the best possible light whenever they turned up unannounced, and she assured them that she was in full control and knew what was going on at all the various levels. When I think about Granny, it warms my heart, but it also makes me sad. She had no life of her own, she had more than enough to do looking after us. I used to get up at the same time as her, you know, always very early, she had to be ready, always prepared. I sat in the doorway to the bathroom and watched while she put up her long hair, and fastened it, one hairpin at a time, practised to perfection, until her silver locks were all gathered in a big bun. How she took her time getting dressed, always in a dress or skirt and jacket, always good shoes, even when she was indoors, because then she was in control, and goodness knows, she needed to be. I loved our time together in the bathroom, it was sacred, just me and her, and the house was quiet and normal. Grandad had not got up yet, or you. The madness had not begun, it was just Granny and me. Our eyes met in the mirror. We smiled and winked at each other in our special way, we had our own signals, our own language. We were the only ones in the world who understood anything at all. We never spoke about our mornings in the bathroom. We did not have much peace in our house, I could only listen to my own thoughts at five in the morning. Granny was a queen, Mutti. She was a queen.

And you are being held on remand, Mutti. Which means that you didn't just stop the traffic on Kirkelina or predict everyone's death and destruction, or stand on the square ranting. You didn't wander the streets in only your underwear. You have destroyed something or someone. My imagination is running wild here in my cell. I have always been so afraid that this would happen.

Your son,
Rikard Josef

My darling Rikard Josef,

What can I tell you, other than that I am well! I have been very well for a long time now, but you have not kept in touch, you left. Year after year I have managed alone, I have a full-time job with good colleagues, and get on with all the neighbours and the man in the shop over the road (although he has moved now). But this autumn I have been at war, I have been the victim of a cruel campaign and have for a long time been receiving anonymous threats. I asked the police to help me on several occasions, but my request fell on deaf ears. No one bothered to come and see me, no one heard what I said. And now you write to me about things that happened a long time ago. That is all in the past, there is no point in opening up old wounds, and that is what you are doing. You must remember that I had a lot to deal with when I was young. Your grandfather and his illness, financial problems, the authorities, who were constantly on our back. Social services who would turn up unannounced, come in and ask personal questions, while they checked that everything was clean and there was food in the cupboards and clothes in the drawers.

And there always was, to say anything else would be a lie. I carried you in my arms, do you not remember? And you know that I've always been susceptible to infections. That day you mentioned, when I was late in coming to pick you up from nursery, I had a temperature and was feverish. It turned out to be a lung infection and I was on antibiotics for two weeks. But you know that our family is prone to infections, that our immune systems are not strong, all families have their weaknesses. So when they called me from the nursery, I ran out of the house to come and get you, and was confused. You know how hot and bothered a fever can make you. The only thing I could think was that I had to get there before social services, I knew they were watching us with beady eyes, and that they would take note of the slightest thing. Do you know what I have often thought? That you went to Berlin because you were ashamed of us. You were ashamed of me and your grandfather, you were ashamed because we did not have much money, and you wanted so much more. We were the family you did not want to introduce to others. If that is what you thought, I would like you to tell me. The truth will not kill me, just so you know. The worst thing is not knowing. But now we're talking again, you and I. So let's just continue and see where it gets us.

Your mother.

Mutti,

I have read your words very carefully. I have read them again and again, and I hope, of course, that you are in good hands. That they understand what you need and that they have the support network that you will need when the case is over, and you have been sentenced.

And I hope that you accept their help. I was not ashamed, Mutti, I was tired and confused. I tried to find a role for myself in the circus that was our family, but couldn't. I was always superfluous, I just rattled around, hid away in the corners. Grandad was unpredictable, you lived in your own world, I never knew what to expect. I tiptoed around, with my eyes peeled and my ears open, in case something was about to happen, a terrible storm, a landslide or an earthquake. The doorbell scared the living daylights out of me, I imagined that big strong men had come to tear me away from the house and throw me into a car and whisk me off to some strangers in an unknown house and that I would never see Granny again. I also remember good days, when Grandad ran around in the garden trying to catch sunbeams, and Granny sat in the shade knitting, while you cooled down in the paddling pool that we always had out. You were always too warm. But the atmosphere could change just like that. Grandad might spot a bank of clouds approaching at speed that would take away the sun and lower the temperature. Preparations had to be made. Everyone had to go inside and hide in the bathroom. I have no idea how many times I sat there on the hard floor, close to Granny, waiting for it all to pass. Those few hours at nursery were a relief, my time off. The small cabin with the round porthole was my space, my own little world where I was king. There were kind, predictable adults there to help us. But the things that happened in Kirkelina had nothing to do with immune systems and fevers – I didn't understand that when I was little, but as I got older, I did. I'm going to write something important now, and I want you to believe me. I always think of you with great affection, and I think of Grandad with great affection too. And of course, Granny. But I'm not the first person to have left the people they love. The unpredictability was just too much, living with the derision of others, and the feeling that anything could happen at any moment. Loneliness and predictability became the better option. Even though I made some bad choices. The officers here never get excited about anything, they behave in a certain way and it's the same, day after day. And there's something about the cell, you know, the walls keep me in place. My cell reminds me of the small cabin in the fishing boat, where I felt safe and could look out on the world. The way you look out on the world from your cell window.

You, too, should read these words again and again.
Your son in Berlin

Chapter 29

'It was you who found him, wasn't it? Your father.'

'Yes, it was me who found him. All he had on was a pair of old underpants. And they weren't clean either, that was how far things had gone. He was in bed most of the time. We often heard his voice, like a radio in the next room, as he lay there and read the news. Messages and warnings that he received from foreign stations that were inaccessible to us. Messages from the enemy.'

She smiled sadly.

'He couldn't be bothered to get dressed in the morning, and he couldn't bear the thought of food. He had more important things to think about, he said, we mustn't bother him with trivialities.'

'But he was allowed to stay at home?' Sejer asked.

'My mother insisted. She could see that he didn't have long left.'

'Tell me what it was like,' Sejer said. 'How he died.'

'He had tied a lamp cable round the handle on the cupboard door, and hanged himself sitting down. It would have taken a while for him to die.'

'Were you frightened?'

'Just sad. We knew it was going to happen one day, Mummy and I, we were well prepared. But to hang yourself is not a very dignified way to go, if you know what I mean, it's not a pretty sight. I'm sure that you know what I'm talking about, that you've seen it yourself. No one should hang like that, we should die lying down.'

'Yes, I have seen it,' he said. 'Did he leave a letter?'

'Not a letter, as such, just a short message. "Feel free to laugh."'

'"Feel free to laugh"?' Sejer realised that deep down he actually liked Hans Riegel, this father he had never met.

'Were you ever worried that you might inherit your father's illness?'

Ragna frowned.

'Oh, I have some of the same problems. I often overheat, especially at night. It's possibly my internal thermostat,' she said with a smile. 'But that's more to do with my age.'

Sejer tried again.

'Schizophrenia is often inherited. Your father was a paranoid schizophrenic.'

'Inherited?'

She looked away.

'I don't know very much about things like that,' she muttered.

'You don't? Were you ever frightened that you might develop the same illness?'

Sejer's office had never been so still. Another line on his phone started to flash, a door slammed further down the corridor, a car on the road outside hooted its horn. Sounds that they had been unaware of until now suddenly filled the room.

'I'm not ill,' Ragna whispered, without looking at him. She shook her head.

'I'm not ill,' she repeated.

'It was just a gentle question,' Sejer said.

'Who have you been talking to?' she asked immediately.

'Your GP, Dr Naper. You have a long history, Ragna. Some people would say that you are seriously ill. And that you have been for a long time. Your medical file is extensive, and it goes way back. To your teenage years, in fact.'

'I don't want to talk to you any more today,' she said and fidgeted on the chair. She lifted her right hand to stop him.

'Do you feel threatened?'

'I'm just saying that you're wrong. My head,' she said and laid a hand across her brow, 'my head is perfectly clear. It's tidy and ordered and always has been.'

'Apart from when your brain melted.'

'That was a nightmare. Don't you use my dreams against me.'

'Don't forget I've read your letters from Berlin. There is a reason why your son left, isn't there?'

Another silence. They were no longer allies, they no longer had eye contact.

'Schizophrenics often have a sensory system that goes beyond what other people experience,' Sejer said. 'The constant stream of impressions, of sounds and smells and images, can sometimes get too much. Because there is no filter in relation to the world, and it becomes difficult to sort out what is important. Is that what happened this autumn, Ragna, did things get out of hand?'

She jutted her chin out.

'I am a level-headed person,' she said. 'And I have no idea what you're getting at.'

'You closed yourself in more and more. You locked all the doors and found a dark corner where no one could reach you. But Bennet managed to get in, nonetheless, all the way into your kitchen. It's fine to be in a cell, you can cope there. No one can get to you, no one asks you to come out, and there aren't too many impressions. And in that situation, you seem to be perfectly well.'

'Oh, for goodness' sake –' she looked at him with indignation – 'that's ridiculous!'

'We have to talk about this, Ragna. And for your own sake, it would be better if you helped us, rather than withdrew. I have tried at all times to follow you and to understand your thoughts and actions, and why you acted in the way you did. We are going to have to go down this path, and if I can't get you on board, we'll draw our own conclusions without you. Is that what you want?'

'Draw conclusions?'

She filled her lungs with so much air and was so fierce in her defence that he could not help but think of a pufferfish, the kind with poisonous spines. This little woman was a force to be reckoned with, after all, but he continued.

'Does it frighten you?' he asked. 'The idea that you might be ill?'

'I'm just saying it's wrong.'

'I can show you what we've found,' he said.

'I've answered your questions,' she whispered. 'I did what I did for obvious reasons, which I've talked about at length. For days, in fact. So I think we can agree that I've lived in fear and desperation all autumn. And that I spun a web to catch the intruder. And when a fly flew into the net and got stuck, and shook the whole fragile construction, I thought it was a poisonous wasp and stamped on it. There is no need for you to try and find another angle all of a sudden, what is the point of that?'

'Everything has to be correct,' Sejer said. 'That's the way our system works.'

'I have never, in my life, explained myself as carefully, and in as much detail, and with as much honesty, as I have in my conversations with you,' she snapped. 'And still you're not satisfied.'

He searched for the right words. What had he expected? That she would turn to him, innocent as a child, and whisper, oh, is that what's wrong with me? I didn't know, but that explains everything.

'At some point in the future,' Sejer said, 'you will look back at everything that has happened. And you will be able to see it with an objectivity that is not possible today. Your experience will stay with you for the rest of your life. Now think carefully, are you willing to live with a lie?'

'But I'm not lying! My intention all along has been to tell the truth.'

'You have chosen the version that you can live with,' Sejer said, 'and that is perfectly understandable, that is how we are made.'

'Then you're living with a lie too,' she said.

'Yes,' he admitted. 'But I have not been accused of murder.'

Whatever it was that was growing in Ragna's head was not a tumour. The thin, viscous branches that were spreading across her brain tissue could perhaps be treated with poison, or preferably a scalpel. This intruder was of a different nature. A misconception. Perhaps it had always been there, like a seed from her father. And it grew and it grew. An enemy had invaded her life. The enemy had watched her and terrorised her for a long time, robbed her of her sleep and of her senses, made her come undone. Ravaged her body and camped outside her house. Ragna had looked for him everywhere, she had looked for signs, and she had found them.

Sejer was crossing the pedestrian bridge over the river; he stopped halfway and stared down at the swirling current. Frank spotted a puppy and scrambled desperately to get closer, but Sejer held him back, and then walked swiftly on. Ragna Riegel filled his head and heart. They had possibly just had their last candid conversation. He had destroyed her trust in him by intimating that he doubted her reality. Like her illness, he had invaded her and confronted her. There was not really anything worse you could say to a person. She had refused to talk any more, and that was her right. Everything he had seen and heard throughout his working life ran through his head. The ones who made excuses, the ones who denied the crime, the ones who could not remember. The angry, the damaged and intoxicated, the mean and brutal and dull, the cynical and the less bright, the indifferent and the cowardly, the ones who blamed others, and there were plenty of those. Ragna was none of them. With her disability and history, she was both unique and vulnerable. The enemy had managed to get into her kitchen and press her into a corner. She had defended herself. To be on the safe side. Because she knew that finally someone would listen.

Sejer and Frank walked along the promenade to the main square. He thought about justice; there was not much of it in the world, and there was no order, no plan, no purpose. No reward in heaven, no green pastures. Just a swarming mass, where a few were granted happiness, but most were not. The believers prayed to God, and sometimes were heard, but more often they were not. Very few questions had clear answers, and as for the truth, well, it could be stretched like a rubber band. Ragna Riegel had attracted an enemy because for years she had lived in fear of having an enemy. Because she carried a heavy burden. Because she had a disability. Because she had seen her father sleep with the lights on and press his meagre body close to the wall. Because the authorities had been on their backs for years. Her father chose death. Because to him it seemed a safer place. And he was probably right.

They came to the square, with a thousand small lights in the chestnut trees, shining like diamonds. Everyone talks about the light, he thought, that's where they long to be, that's what they dream of. But some want to be in the dark, to remain unseen – that is where they feel safe. And yet, because they are not seen, they fall apart, they fall into their own trap, as it were. He heard music from somewhere in the distance, it sounded like sleigh bells, and he realised it would be Christmas in a few days' time. He crossed the main bridge over to the south side of the river and walked all the way back to the station, with the river on his right now. He felt the icy wind on his cheeks as he passed the fire station, a northerly wind, sharp as a knife. It cut him to the bone and his face felt stiff and tight, and if anyone had seen him at close quarters, they would have thought he was a bitter man. He walked faster, they still had a lot to get through, if she wanted to continue at all. As he walked he mused on his own fate. He should have chosen another role in life, the role of defender. Instead, he was the one who held people accountable, who pushed and prodded and confronted. To make them confess, give evidence and repent. How different his life would have been if he had spent his days in court, thundering with clenched fists, as he fought like a lion to prove that his client, who was guilty, had had no alternative. That was what he wanted to do now. To stand up for Ragna Riegel. To be that lion. But I have never been a judge, Sejer thought, and I never will be. I understand people too well. Or, it occurred to him, I'm too much of a coward.

He shivered and walked, shivered and walked, his eyes trained on the icy pavement.

Chapter 30

Dear Rikard Josef,

Here I sit by the cell window and think of you. And about myself as well. How far do you think words can lead us? Can they bring us together again, will we meet again? I am not asking for much. But if I neglected you and did not give you what you needed, and in that way drove you from home, I ask for your forgiveness a thousand times over. I beg on my knees, because I am truly on my knees now. And if you cannot forgive me, that too I will bear, because I had not expected you to make contact at all. But you should know that I will never judge you, I just want to understand, in the same way that I hope to be understood. Everyone has their reasons, their motives and despair. All this talk of people having a choice. What does it mean? Does it mean that every person, in every society and in every situation, truly has a choice? And that they can make the right choice? Would it not be easy then to navigate the legal system? Would it not be easy to pass judgement and hand out punishment? Why then does the concept 'extenuating circumstances' exist at all, which allows for certain crimes to be judged differently or even dismissed? Does that not amount to an admission that many people do not have a choice?

If this is the life I am to have, this cell with its narrow bed, and a small desk by the window, then I will accept it without complaint. It is still light in the morning and dark in the evening. I fill my lungs with air, and my heart, which is also good, continues to beat. This is a life, too. But I am not making any plans, do not want to think ahead. It is the curse of mankind that we live our whole lives in fear. Of what might happen, tomorrow or next year. Or we live in fear of old sins, a mongrel that snaps at our heels, and that sooner or later will catch up with us. Instead of walking out of the house when the sun is high, lifting our faces and feeling its warmth on our cheeks. Your grandfather often did that. And it gave him pleasure enough for one day. I have always been content with little. When you came into the world, you were a treasure I never dreamt I would have, which is why I held you so tight, and carried you in my arms. I often stood at the window watching you, when you sat on the lawn playing, or in the snow with your pompom hat on, and snot running out of your nose. I kept an eye on all the cars that drove past, to see if any of them slowed down – I studied everyone who walked down the road. And if they looked at you for too long, or stopped to say a few words, if you were making a nice snowman for instance, I would come rushing out. And I would stare hard at them to demonstrate that you were mine and that I was responsible for you. That is probably why you had to cut free in the end.

Perhaps I got what I deserved.

What can I say in my defence? If you never have your own children, you will never be able to understand how hard it is to do everything right. I hope with all my heart that your days pass well. And the hours, and minutes, and all the dark nights.
  Mummy

Chapter 31

To Sejer's surprise, Ragna wanted to continue. But she did not talk in the same focused way as before – she was more on her guard and watched him with keen eyes. She knew that something unpleasant was coming and she was steeling herself. In the end, she chose to beat him to it.

'I know what you're going to say,' she whispered. 'So just say it.'

Sejer weighed his words, as he always did with people who had been hurt.

'After all that we've talked about, after all this time, do you still think it was Bennet who sent you the anonymous threats?'

'Is it so strange that I came to that conclusion?'

She saw the compassion in the inspector's eyes.

'You came to that conclusion when he was sitting in your kitchen. I am asking what you think now.'

'He said I was going to die,' was her prompt response.

'But have you, even tentatively, ever thought that perhaps you attacked the wrong man?'

She looked at him with scepticism.

'Are you going to tell me that you've found some brat who went from mailbox to mailbox, and half the town received the same threats? I don't believe you.'

'That's not the story I was going to tell,' he said. 'No, that's not what we've found. No one else has reported receiving threats, like you. But before you got that first letter in your mailbox, had anything happened? Something difficult that might have triggered the whole thing?'

'Are you saying that it's my fault?'

Again, he gave her a sympathetic look.

'I was fine,' she said. 'Everything was fine and normal. I like working in the shop, I like putting nail brushes from Taiwan neatly on the shelves, with the right price. Sometimes I build small pyramids for fun. The others laugh at me when I do that, I know it's childish. I like sitting at the till as well, as I don't need to speak. No one notices me, they leave me in peace.'

'Would you have liked someone to notice you?'

She looked insulted, and did not answer.

'Would you have liked to be noticed in the way that Walther Eriksson noticed you? To be seen in that way?'

Her cheeks were red now.

'Yes and no.'

'But it happened, all the same,' Sejer said. 'You got a message. Someone had seen you.'

'Lots of messages.'

'But you didn't keep them,' he said. 'You can never take them out and read them again. I will never be able to read them either, and they can't be used in court as evidence of the reign of terror you say you went through.'

'I say I went through? What are you trying to suggest?'

She snorted angrily a couple of times.

'You wouldn't have kept them either,' she said. 'No one would. By burning them, I felt I was ignoring him. Destroying him. Denying his existence. I did what I thought best. And when I saw him standing down by the road, watching the house, I rang here and asked for help. I talked to a policewoman, but she didn't want to send anyone round. And it's not easy for me to make demands,' she added, 'given my voice. I can't make a fuss on the phone. I can barely be angry at all.'

Sejer doodled on his notepad.

'You didn't ring, Ragna,' he said quietly. 'Are you aware of that? We never received your call. All calls are meticulously recorded and saved, and we can't find your call anywhere. And I can promise you, we've looked.'

Ragna sat there and held her breath. At first she wanted to laugh, but then she saw his eyes, his grey eyes. She had never felt such compassion from anyone before, not even William, the Englishman.

'I did!' she whispered.

'No,' Sejer said.

'It was a female officer,' she insisted. 'I remember her well. I remember what she said, word for word.'

'But there is no one who remembers you.'

Her mouth was so dry that she struggled to formulate the words.

'You make it sound like I don't exist.'

'Oh, you exist, Ragna, I can see you clearly. And I hear everything you say, every single word. But the telephone conversation that you told me about is not recorded in our archives.'

She looked over at the dog that was lying by the window.

'You're forgetting one important thing,' she said. 'I came to the police station in person and filed a report. And I handed in the last message, the one that he'd left on my bedside table, with that report. I told you, I took a taxi here, and it was Irfan who came to get me. Irfan Baris.'

'We have spoken to Baris,' Sejer said.

Again, that unshakeable calm.

'Then he can confirm that he drove me here. That I came into the reception on the ground floor.'

'And he has. He picked you up at Kirkelina, you were standing in the road waiting, and he drove you to the police station, but he parked a bit further down the road and sat there reading the newspaper. He knows nothing about what you did after you got out of the car.'

'Then you must find the report straight away. Go and find it now!'

'We have not received a report about a break-in at Kirkelina 7. Nor the message that you say you found on your bedside table. The two documents were never submitted.'

'Yes, they were.'

'We can't find them.'

'Then you've lost them,' she said in despair. 'Now that what's happened has happened, you're denying that I asked for help, because then you could be held responsible.'

Sejer felt awful, as though he had clubbed a child. He had asked her to be honest in her evidence, had said he was willing to listen, and for days he had listened. Ragna had taken him into her lonely world, and now he had rejected her version. He was questioning her perception of reality, he had utterly betrayed her. And everything between them, the trust he had so carefully managed to build, would be ruined.

'You seemed to be confused,' he said calmly.

'Confused? Who said that?'

'The people we've spoken to. Baris said that you were standing in the road, in the freezing cold, with practically nothing on. Your neighbour has seen you poking around in your dustbin on several occasions, and carrying the rubbish back into the house. People have also seen you wandering up and down your drive, down to the road and back again in a very agitated fashion.'

'But I've explained all that!' she whispered. 'I was trying to lose count of the number of steps. So I could regain control.'

'You were confused, Ragna. What came first? The confusion or the threats? Think about it for moment.'

'I am not ill,' she said flatly. She started to cry, without a sound, and did not wipe the tears away, just let them fall.

'It's not up to me to judge how ill you are,' Sejer said. 'Someone else will do that. But if that is the case, it would explain everything that has happened. And it's an explanation that the court will believe, so the outcome will be different, and far better for you than prison. You will serve your sentence on different terms, you will be treated in a different way, and you will probably be released much earlier. That is why I am telling you all this, because I want the best for you. Because I want you to be somewhere where you won't be judged, where you will be treated with care and understanding.'

It seemed that she had suddenly thought of something, a memory she could use.

'You've got security cameras here. By the main entrance. And in reception.'

There was no change in Sejer's expression when she said this.

'We have looked at all the recordings,' he said. 'We have gone through them several times.'

'Then you know that I was here, and you've seen the documents.'

'No,' he said. 'We have not seen the documents.'

He turned his laptop so the screen was facing her.

'You can see the recordings for yourself. Would you like to?'

She nodded, but had no idea where it would lead. When an image of the entrance to the police station appeared on the screen, she leaned forward in anticipation. There were the wide glass doors, there was the paved area in front, the sign on the wall, the symbol of a standing lion bearing an axe. But no movement, not a person in sight. Everything was filmed from above, she was looking down on everything, just as the camera had looked down on her. Then a figure appeared.

'There!' She pointed triumphantly. 'I'm waving as well, do you see?'

Sejer remained silent. He was not looking at the screen, he was looking at her.

'Now I'm inside,' she whispered. 'Can you see that I'm inside, at reception?'

She saw herself, standing in the middle of the floor, bewildered, clutching her handbag. She was wearing only a pair of leggings and a thin, short-sleeved blouse.

'Tell me what you see,' Sejer said.

'I'm not wearing very much,' she admitted. 'But I left the house in a rush, so it's not surprising that I'm a bit stressed.'

She watched the screen closely. The woman moved to the right of the picture, towards some comfy chairs by the wall, where she sat down and put her bag on the chair beside her. She sat there for a long time. With her hands in her lap and staring at the door into the duty officer's room. There was something helpless about the poor woman, she could see that clearly herself. Was that really what she looked like, so wretched and timid? Was that how other people saw her? The minutes passed. She glanced at the digits in the bottom right-hand corner, two, three, four minutes. The woman stretched out her hand and picked up one of the leaflets from a pile on the table. For a while she sat reading the brochure, looking up every so often.

'What was the leaflet about, Ragna?' Sejer asked. 'Can you remember?'

She thought about it and looked at the screen again.

'I think it was about love.'

He nodded.

'What did it say about love, Ragna?'

She struggled to dredge up the memory.

'Something about violence.'

'That's right,' Sejer said. 'Real love is free of violence. You were reading a leaflet from the Women's Shelter.'

'But I'm about to go in and talk to the duty officer now,' she whispered eagerly. 'I had forgotten how nervous I was, I had forgotten that I sat there for so long drumming up courage.'

As soon as the figure stood up, she was fully alert. She was going to file a report now and hand in the message as evidence. But then she realised that the only thing she had in her hand was the leaflet she had been reading from the Women's Shelter. She crossed the reception area and went in through the glass door to the duty officer, where another camera started to film her, from another angle. Without saying anything, she put the leaflet down on the counter. Real love is free from violence. Then she gave the officer a firm nod and walked out.

The camera on the outside wall caught her as she left the building. She walked towards the semicircle of stone blocks, then started to walk faster and eventually ran down the street to Irfan's taxi. The screen went black. Sejer struggled to find the right words in the silence that followed. She had lowered her head, did not want to look him in the eye. Her hands were in her lap. Her narrow shoulders sank in resignation, and even though he could not see her face, he was sure that she was flushed with shame.

'It must have been the skulls from Malaysia that started everything,' she whispered. 'The ones that Lars wheeled out into the shop. I put batteries in one of them and the eyes lit up. It was as though they were looking at me, as though they wanted to tell me something.'

'What did they want to tell you?'

'That I was going to die.'

Chapter 32

She was sailing on the ocean. The boat was no bigger than the little paddling pool that Rikard Josef had when he was small, and the sail was the size of a tablecloth. There was a mild breeze blowing. She saw no other boats, no people, no masts. She was not concerned about her direction or position as she bobbed peacefully towards the horizon where the sun was shining gold. But she never got there, the sun changed colour to peach then pink and red. The light started to fade. The night fell and it got colder. In the dark, she heard the seagulls that would no doubt eat her if she drifted for too long. And when they had pecked her to pieces, the lack of beauty she had always lived with would no longer be a problem. She had been told that they went for your eyes first. But then daylight came again, and she saw some mountains in the distance, great blue and purple mountains. The little boat drifted in the right direction and she sat on her knees with a hand shadowing her eyes. Soon she saw the cliffs and the white surf. The rocks were so sharp and jagged that the little boat would be torn to shreds. She closed her eyes and prepared herself for the impact, raising her arms for protection. She curled up in the bottom of the boat and waited.

She had been asleep for a hundred years or more, or so it felt. She had been to another country, another continent, another dimension, a world she could not enter or leave as she pleased, it was just there. The medicine she had been prescribed, once the experts had confirmed that she had lost her mind, and the doctors had concluded she was suffering from a hereditary mental illness, was the same that her father had taken all those years ago. There were a number of unpleasant side effects that she recognised from her father's complaints – he had often refused to take the pills, to her mother's despair. Her mouth was so dry that it was sometimes hard to make herself understood. Her head was full of cotton wool, and not much else. When she moved it was as though she was stuck, as though something was pulling her back. Her peripheral vision was reduced, but she could see clearly straight ahead. And when she tried to free her thoughts, when she needed to escape, she could not find the white beaches, or deep green forests. She struggled to link her mind with words and images, and was quickly exhausted. Too often, she gave up and sat in a shapeless fog.

She knew that she had to write to her son and tell him the truth. Or what the police claimed was the truth. But she had no idea why she should trust them, why they had stripped her of her credibility. And they would disappear out of her life soon enough. She would be left alone with a diagnosis as destructive as a wrecking ball. They said she had inherited the mental illness from her father. That she had been ill for a long time. That she had never been terrorised, that there was no stalker, that she had never asked the police for help. This terrified her so much that she clung on to her own version for dear life, for fear she would stop breathing. The Agent had come to her house to offer her a place in Paradise. They said that was his only errand. But only she had looked him in the eye and heard his voice. You are going to die.

Ragna always woke up early in the morning, and was given her medicine in her cell, in a little plastic cup. She had to swallow the pills while the officer watched: Zyprexa morning, noon and night. It was humiliating. Her father had said that Zyprexa could kill you, he had heard of several cases. But she did not mention it. But she got into the habit of studying the officer closely while he or she waited for the empty cup.

They had robbed her of her life. They had forced another reality onto her that she did not want. She cried a lot in the period that followed. Did madness provide some form of mitigation – what sort of reasoning was that? She found it incomprehensible. She wanted to take responsibility, she wanted to serve her time. She was no longer friendly to the prison guards, and peered at them with narrowed eyes, as she saw more clearly then. She seldom spoke, and sat by the window for hours, keeping watch on the light, making sure it behaved as it should, that the sun rose and set at the right time. She had to accept their awful claim: that what she had seen did not exist, and what she had heard had only happened in her head. But she could not. She was, of course, exhausted after a long autumn of terror; she had balanced on a knife edge and seen signs of her tormentor everywhere, and her desperation had given rise to some strange thoughts. It happens when people are under a lot of pressure. But madness was something else. In a sudden flash, she remembered sitting in the kitchen beside the body, waving at the smoke alarm. The memory made the blood rush to her cheeks. She stood up so abruptly that the chair fell over. No one waves to their smoke alarms – why had she done that? Then she pulled herself together again. Fine. It was perhaps a little over the top to accuse the authorities of surveillance, but she was suffering from lack of sleep – it affects your mind, and you see things everywhere. The next thing that popped up in her memory was the sound of the Agent's hand when he knocked on the door. The feeling she had at that moment: he is here now. I have known he would be for a long time. It was almost a relief when he followed her into the kitchen and they stood there face-to-face. He was a person of flesh and blood, not a ghost, not something she had imagined. And then he had repeated the same message, only spoken this time. She remembered rummaging around in the drawer, her hand between the spoons and rolling pins and ladles. She wanted to assert herself once and for all.

She sat on the bunk with her face in her hands and recalled every single second. His eyes, so astonished. His nervous hands that were itching to open the folder and show her the truth.

She let this torrent of memories pour over her, tried to accept them one by one, tried to see them in a new light. In her mind, she composed the letter she wanted to write to her son, where she told him everything. What would he think, what would he believe? It would not lead to anything positive. He may even fear that he had inherited the illness. He would never come home now, he would think she was contagious, that she too would die sitting down with a cable round her neck, as his grandfather had done, the blood gathered like ink stains at the bottom of his body. In all these years, she had received nothing from him except a few mean cards, and yet he had always been near. And now, after the event, he was even closer than before. If she wrote the letter she wanted to write, she would frighten him away forever. All he would feel when he thought of his mother was shame and horror. He would deny her existence, never mention her to others, not even the prison priest. My mother, he would say, no, I have no contact with her, nor do I care what she does.

Ragna cried again, tasted the salt in her mouth, felt desperately sorry for herself. She looked around the cell for an escape. The first thing she spotted was the green metal cupboard, with an even more solid steel handle. Then she looked over to the window and the multicoloured curtains made from a coarse material that would be impossible to tear. Her nylon shop coat would not work either, and she did not have any shoelaces or a belt. She reached out to check the quality of the sheet, but it was synthetic, they had thought of everything. All this talk of the truth as something bright and pure. She had to adjust to it now, bow down to it, grovel. A defiant rage surged through her and she decided to write to Berlin anyway, to give him her version of the autumn's events and then the police version, which was not the same as hers. Her crime in all its horror. The fear and anger. The admission of guilt, which they now wanted to deny her, which they thought she did not need to assume, because she was ill. They believed they were saving her, and clearly did not understand her sincerity, her future. All doors would be closed when people read her papers, when it was written there in black and white – what medication she had to take, what it did to her head and body. They had cast a different light on everything that had happened. The only part that was real was the murder. Bennet slid down from the chair, slowly like a doll, first his head dropped, then his arms, and finally his feet gave way, as he floundered for something to hold on to and found the table leg.

She chewed on the pencil for a long time, as she used to do when she was a child. The wood softened and had that peculiar taste that she liked so much. Then she wrote with determination, word after word. And as she wrote, she felt calmer. This was a hugely important project. There was nothing left to lose when your reason had been taken from you. According to the doctor, the medication would keep her in the real world where everyone else lived. The chemicals would, in effect, stop any attempts to escape to another reality, she would see the same things as everyone else, hear the same things as everyone else. They would strip her to the bone in court, revealing everything about her behaviour over the years, and various other events. The newspapers, she wrote, would devour her like vultures, as though she were already a corpse, contaminated by something that stained her whole family. She underlined certain words, or she scribbled them out and found better, more precise formulations. She dried her tears. She wrote faster, she worked herself up into a sweat. As she progressed, she remembered her father, everything he had said, and now she understood it all. Ragna, he had said, you must always be the master of your own life. That is what Ragna means, goddess or master. You must never let anyone force another reality onto you. You are one of the gifted. You are one of those who can see where we are going.

And yet here she was, she had surrendered to them. They had shown the evidence. They were many and she was one. She cried again. Then she thought about the seven billion people living in the world, who went to bed at night and dreamed secret dreams in secret places. People were only together for brief moments in time.

The police would read this letter before they sent it on to Plötzensee Prison. She did not care. She would not see their faces as they read it, would not hear their thoughts and what they said to each other. She wrote page after page. Do you remember the time ... ? My face was always so warm, I thought it was a fever. I stayed indoors a lot, I was afraid of the sun, I burnt so easily, and I was scared for you too, you had inherited my white skin. Red hair. Every time my cheeks got hot I thought it was a fever, that I had an infection and that it had gone to my head. There were so many signs. I interpreted them as well as I could, and interpreted them wrong.

I apologise a thousand times over.

She paused every now and then to gaze out of the window. She searched for something to rest her eyes on, a bird, or a fluffy cloud drifting by, or a treetop blowing in the wind. When she felt she had told him everything – thoughts, words, deeds – she pondered on how to finish this long letter. She feared it would be the last. She did not expect him to reply, she did not dare to believe that he would accept her crime and her madness. He would pull back, slam the door, deny her forever.

My dear Rikard,

I value you so much. If you deny yourself a child, you will never be able to experience the love I have for you. You wrote that you do not want your blood to run in anyone else's veins, but there are no guarantees when it comes to children. Your child might be sickly or healthy, he or she might live a long life, or die young. A child can be your pride and joy or your greatest anguish. You cannot control these things. Life has its surprises for us all. Here I sit in a cell, but I have been blessed with a healthy son. My blood does run in your veins, but only the good blood, and I am good. If only you remember these words, and reflect on them in rare moments, I can ask for nothing more.

Your devoted mother

Chapter 33

She had confessed and pleaded guilty, on the basis of the doctors' assessment of her mental health. She had described her crime in very few words, but in enough detail; her head was clearer now, something had been released. The cell seemed bigger than eight square metres. She felt the great door of truth had been opened. But the signs were still there, the connections she had seen – they forced their way in, whether she wanted to see them or not. The messages, the forgotten watch, the Jumper who did not get up from the ground, but lay bleeding from his mouth and ears. The Agent who had hammered on the door and wanted to come in, who had talked of an imminent death, which would prove to be his own. There was a connection, a logic. Or was it all random, was everything in life random? Forces from above and below pulled and tugged at her, each championing their own agenda. The brain always looks for a pattern, she thought. It either finds what it is looking for, or makes it up, as she had done. The prosecuting authorities wanted to replace her version with their own. This is reality they said, come here.

She lay down on the bunk and, when she eventually fell asleep, dreamt that she was standing on the roof of a tall building and wanted to jump. Rikard Josef was on the street below, waving at her. Without a moment's hesitation, she dived, opened out her arms and felt as though she were floating. It went on forever. It was not so strange that people jumped, not so strange that many chose another way. She woke with a jolt before she knew if anyone was there to catch her. No, she was falling too fast, no one was strong enough to catch her. Louise came in and picked up the letter, which was of course not sealed, as they still had to read it. With her eyes, she followed the white envelope as it left her cell. With her mind, she followed her confession, the long, detailed letter full of sorrow, regret and anger, all the way from her cell to Berlin.

Chapter 34

'Have you sent the letter?' she whispered. 'I hope it's not been left on a shelf somewhere, under a pile of paper, and won't get there until summer, it's happened before. I'm asking, because I haven't had a reply, and days are passing. How long do you think it takes for a letter to get from here to Germany?'

'Three or four days, I reckon,' Sejer replied. 'Yes, Ragna, we have sent the letter. It was franked and put in the tray for outgoing post, and it's no longer there. Rikard will have received your letter a while ago, but you have to give him time.'

'I will have to believe you,' she whispered bravely.

She poured herself a glass of water.

'I had problems sleeping last night,' she said. 'Do you know what I was thinking about?'

'Tell me,' Sejer said.

'I lay awake thinking about Joan of Arc.'

'The Maid of Orleans. Why were you thinking about her?'

'She was burned at the stake,' Ragna explained. 'And now I'm going through the fire too.'

'The fire? You mean Rikard's judgement of you and your crime?'

'Exactly,' Ragna nodded, happy that he had followed her thought process. 'I lay there staring at my window, just as Joan of Arc stared at the small opening in her cell wall in the hours before she was burned. They kept her prisoner in a tower. She had to find a way through the pain and suffering. The flames would lick at her, scorch her black. She needed a sign from God, proof that she had His mercy and would remain in His grace after death. So she prayed. She prayed and watched for a sign, but it was pitch-black and she could see nothing and hear nothing. She continued to pray, for hours. And then something strange happened. The moon slipped out from behind a cloud and its light shone in through the small opening that had two metal crossbars, one vertical and one horizontal. When she got up from the bed, she saw that the white light had transformed the bars into a cross on the stone floor. It was a sign from God. And Joan fell into a deep, peaceful sleep, and went to the stake with dignity.'

'A beautiful story,' Sejer said. 'If it's true.'

'It's a beautiful story, regardless.'

He had to agree.

'You have presumably not prayed,' he said, 'but you are looking for a sign.'

'I suppose so. But I can't find any because I'm full of chemicals. Before, my mind was a labyrinth and I could play in there for hours, happy as a child, but now lots of the paths are closed. My brain can't find the same solutions that it used to, if you see what I mean.'

Sejer looked serious and nodded.

'Do you know what?' Ragna said. 'Once when I was a baby, my father tried to sell me on the market square.'

Without thinking about it, Sejer laughed, but she was not offended.

'I was only a few months old, but I could sit up in the pram, and before he left home, he made a big sign. "New screaming baby for sale. Great potential. Offers accepted." It was autumn, there were a lot of stalls and the market was full of people. My father positioned himself between the fruit, berries and fresh eggs, and held up the sign in his hand. A constant flow of people went past. They looked at me, some people made offers, old ladies in particular, they laughed and smiled and discussed their bids. But Daddy shook his head and said, too low, far too low! We're talking about something quite unique! We stayed on the square until the sun went down. Then he tucked the sign under my blanket and pushed me home again, all the way along Kirkelina from the church to number 7. My mother said he was extremely happy when he came through the door.'

She drank some water.

'Mummy told me the story when I was older. I was hurt at first, obviously, but then I realised that Daddy thought I was extremely valuable, and not for sale at any price. That was what he had wanted to tell the world.'

'There is a lot of wisdom in madness,' Sejer said, 'if we only look for it.' He made a note and pushed the pad across the table so she could read it.

'Great potential. Offers accepted.'

When he later accompanied her back to her cell, the letter was lying there, shining white on the desk by the window. She did not see it until the inspector had left, and the first thing she noticed was how carefully the letter had been opened. He must have used the sharpest knife in the building. She stood looking at the letter for a long time, then took a few steps forward and inspected the envelope closely with her eagle eyes. Was it thick or thin, did it contain a single sheet of paper or three or four, had he dismissed her in a few words, or given her more, something she could comfort herself with and live with? How could she bear to read it? She snatched it up and cradled it in her lap, wanting to know how much it weighed, if it warmed her through her clothes, or if the dry paper conveyed no understanding. How silly I am, Ragna thought. Everything is too late anyway, I will never get over this.

My dearest mother, my confidante,

Your letter was lying on my bed when I got back from the gym today. I have never trained as hard as I did today. I pushed myself beyond the pain threshold, only to discover that pain is uncomfortable, but not dangerous in any way. Everything that streams through my body makes me warm and happy, I am stronger, I can cope with more and I enjoy the respect. People here call me Sef. They ask why I wanted to come to Berlin, and I tell them what I've always thought about the city, that Berlin has a weight and authority to it, and a long history of pain. That is why I feel at home here, and I really do. I saw that the letter had been opened, as usual. I pulled out all the pages and sat down by the window, with my head to the glass, with the same anticipation I had as a child when you and Granny gave me a bag of sweets on Saturday night. Do you remember those sweetie bags? They were never the same. Every week you found something new, and even though it sometimes included things I didn't like, like salty liquorice, I ate everything. I would have to wait a whole week until the next one. I am still sitting by the window. Sometimes I look up, to draw more light into the room. And I am crying now as I write to you, as you perhaps cried when you wrote to me. I am weeping with sorrow and horror, but I am also weeping with relief. Your letter contained things that I did not like and that shocked me, but gradually it is sinking in, and I am accepting it, little by little. Like when you drink hot tea, sip by sip, and burn your lips, and it takes forever to finish the cup. I don't want to be the one who destroys this fragile connection we have started to build together. We're building a bridge, I think, that will need strong foundations. I wrote to you that the truth kills, and you wrote that it is bright. It is shining on me now. This is what I have longed for all my life, for you to see yourself in terms of your illness – that was why you had to live at home, so Granny could look after you. I hope that you are willing to accept help, that you will take the medication the doctor has prescribed, even though it has side effects. Granny and I had to endure the side effects of your illness. I hope that you will accept the diagnosis and choose psychiatric care, if the judge gives you that choice. That you will stay there as long as required, that you try to create a life with others in the same situation, or as we have previously talked about, in the same boat. If that is how things unfold, then I promise you, dear Mother, that as soon as the trial is over and you are settled wherever you are going to serve your term, I will apply for leave to come and see you. On the grounds of illness in the family. I'm sure I will get help with the application. I could perhaps ask the priest to write a letter of recommendation, as men of the cloth are often good with words. Of course I carry with me much of what is good in you, Mutti. I remember all the times you carried me out to the paddling pool on those hot summer days, and the water was so cold it took my breath away, because the hose was attached to a tap in the cellar. Then afterwards I would lie down on a big towel and you would wrap me up, so not even my head was showing. You said that I was the most precious gift, and that we should go inside and give the present to Granny. You carried me in your arms those few steps across the lawn. I must have looked like a little mummy. And Granny slowly unwrapped the towel and clapped her hands in delight because I was the best gift she had ever been given. I have lots of memories like that, and now I am reliving them.

As for me, I am a simple thief, and I am deeply ashamed. I am serving my time with other simple thieves. There is something dirty about my crime, is it not the meanest of them all? Emotions like fear and hate and jealousy set everything else in relief. And the person standing in the dock before the judge becomes so clear. A thief is just a thief. I can't explain my crime in terms of confusion, or sickness, or desperation. I was just plain greedy and I have to live with that. I saw a golden opportunity and I grabbed it. Going to work at the Dormero and fiddling the accounts became an exciting game, an addiction. And all the time, I was super nice and friendly to my colleagues, more chatty *than usual, accommodating, warm and generous. They had no idea that I was laughing at them inside. But then the mood changed. At first it was barely notice-able, but then their eyes started to turn away whenever I came to reception, and there was a coolness I had not felt before. And I've told you the rest.*

And now I want to have a big heart, dear Mother, just as you have opened your heart to me. You talk about children and love. I am perhaps a bitter man, but I am not old. You have opened a door for me, and I will open a door for you, so now it's the two of us against the world. We have to stick together. Please keep writing to me! Tell me about your days and weeks, and of course the trial, when it happens. I will wait for you here, I'm not going anywhere for a long time, and please believe me when I say there is nothing I need. I do not want you to suffer. Bennet's family and friends will grieve for the rest of their lives, but they will also hear your side of the story in court. Perhaps they will understand your fear and feelings of persecution, and that you acted out of desperation in a threatening situation, even though that battle was in your head. The Jehovah's Witnesses are people of faith, and they might understand and forgive you, in the way that I understand and forgive you. Perhaps they can see Bennet taking his place in the Thousand Year Reign, together with a host of white angels, if that's what it looks like. Perhaps his nearest and dearest will gather together and read about forgive-ness, there is so much about it in the Bible, and pray for you. And you know, they say that time heals all wounds, so the morning will come when you wake up and are able to look people in the eye. Take it day by day, a little at a time, and you will slowly move forward and see if it works. Think of insects on the surface of the water, Mutti. The film is not visible to the human eye, and a water skater does not weigh much, but because it moves carefully, it stays standing. You know all about that, with your whisper. Don't be so hard on yourself. Just surrender to the care of those who wish you well. And put your trust in me and what we have started to build.

Your devoted son,
Rikard Josef

She read the letter again and again, until she knew it off by heart. To think that he had given her such a gift, such comfort and understanding, and so many promises. She sat on the edge of the bed for a long time, with the letter in her lap. She could not bear to put it away in the drawer; instead, she stuffed it under her clothes, and felt the dry paper against her skin. At regular intervals, she put her hand on it to reassure herself it was not a dream, that it was not her sick mind playing a trick. The letter was real. The words came from her son's heart, and they had travelled all the way from Berlin to her cell. The letter would last forever, it would exist after her death, and perhaps a grandchild might read it one day and see their father's greatness.

She wept silently. Tears of both sorrow and joy. How lonely and bewildered he must have been as a child. She folded her hands, but she did not pray. She walked happily round the cell, to the window and back, unable to sit still. When Sejer paid an unexpected visit some hours later, he stood in front of her, solid as a pillar, almost two metres tall with silver-grey hair, and she was as bashful as a girl.

'Did you read it?' she whispered, breathless. 'The letter from Rikard?' She put a hand to her chest where the envelope was hidden.

'Yes, I read it,' he said.

She could see that he was slightly embarrassed too. Ragna suddenly realised that he was not in his office and therefore not in the role of interviewer. He was not going to cross-examine her any more, pressure her, question everything she said. Not that he had ever really done that. But now he was as a guest in her domain, and he behaved as a guest should.

'I don't know where I'll end up,' she told him. 'But I will never forget you.'

'I certainly hope not,' he said.

'I take my medication now, three times a day. My head feels so confined, but what happens from now on is reality.'

'Reality is not the worst that can happen to a person,' Sejer assured her. There were certain things that could be documented, that was all. He did not have much more to say. He had wanted to show her sympathy, to show that he knew what was going on in her life, and that he understood only too well what her son's acceptance meant to her. He bowed and made to leave, but then stopped in the doorway.

'I won't forget you either. Meeting people like you makes my job worthwhile. People who have something to give.'

She was so bowled over that she blushed furiously, as she often did. She could not imagine what he felt he had got; she had given him nothing, only some tangled thoughts. But he obviously appreciated them, she could see that.

The heavy metal door did not slam as normal, as he closed it gently behind him. All she heard was the small click, and in that way, he showed her his respect. And then his footsteps disappeared down the corridor. He walked slowly. A man who had his own steady rhythm, who could not be pushed or thrown off balance. Like granite, Ragna thought. Shortly after, the doors started to slam again, one after the other in quick succession. It made her think of gunfire, but she knew it was the food trolleys making their way down the corridor. She heard the hatch open, the little click. Then Adde came into the cell and put a tray down on her desk. She gave him a friendly look, and smiled at both the glass eye and the healthy eye. There was a small card on the tray with a number, the number of her cell, 706. There was a jug of water, a bowl of fresh salad and plate of something that looked like tortilla wraps.

She decided that she actually liked this officer. Today she could afford to, she felt generous and she would not have much more to do with him anyway. She would soon be in psychiatric care and, perhaps, could go for walks in a beautiful garden under leafy trees. There might even be a pond with water lilies, and there would be a small bridge over the pond, where she would walk with her son. Adde went out. She took a bite of the tortilla and chewed it well. The food was surprisingly good, much better than normal, and so spicy that tears sprang to her eyes, and her head heated up and her nose started to run, and she laughed as though she were drunk. Goodness, she had never tasted anything like it. She drank some water, it was cold and refreshing. The second tortilla was a disappointment, dry, tough and tasteless, not like the first. She took another bite and felt something strange in her mouth, something like sausage skin, which the cook must have forgotten to remove. She pulled it out of her mouth and opened the wrap to remove whatever was left. Inside was a folded sheet of paper. It was damp and limp and yet so recognisable. Someone had sent her a message. In here, behind the walls, in her cell.

The shame flared up so fast that it took her breath away. The spices made her burn and the humiliation made her burn and her heart was racing. How naive could she be, how incredibly stupid, to believe that it was finally over, that whoever it was who had been after her all autumn had given up. She had not been so naive since that night with Walther. But then she remembered that her pursuer did not exist, and she sat for a while with her face in her hands, as she battled with her conflicting thoughts. She held the soggy piece of paper up in front of her eyes. She could not understand what he wanted from her, what kind of threat he had written in his usual, evil way, but she could see the big letters through the paper.

She got up and paced around the cell with the message in her hand. This time, she would show them once and for all who knew the truth. But then she was floored by uncertainty again. She wanted to read it, but resisted at the same time. If she read the message, it would be real, and it would be the same as letting him in, just as she had throughout the autumn. Time and again, she had read those messages, time and again she had allowed herself to be destroyed. No, she would close the door on that forever. She scrunched up the message into a greasy, soggy ball. She wanted to throw it away, but did not know where. There was no toilet in the cell, otherwise she could have flushed it down the drain. She only had a bucket with a lid, but she might be tempted to pick it out and read it. No one must see the message. She had chosen which side she was on – she had abandoned her illness, and was now somewhere in between, caught in a clamp. She carefully opened the paper ball, ripped it into tiny pieces and put them in her mouth one by one. Chewed, swallowed, drank some water, chewed, swallowed, drank some water. I am swallowing it all, she thought, my illness, everything. I will pretend this is not happening! After a while it became hard to swallow. The pieces of paper were lying in her stomach like a thick mass of porridge, and it was swelling. She drank more water. It was so hard to breathe, but soon her stomach acid would dissolve the mass and it would disappear forever. The acid would erase every word.

She sat slumped at her desk for a long time. After a while she heard the doors slamming again, and knew that they were coming to collect the tray. Or did they have another errand, and who was going to come? She stood up, hiding the metal fork behind her back, and stared at the door that was about to open.

Adde came in.

'Wow!' he exclaimed. 'You've drunk a litre of water. Some of the others complained too,' he laughed. 'Some people couldn't even eat it, it was so spicy.'

Ragna stood there staring. He stood with his legs apart, like her. Then he walked over to the desk and picked up the tray, not noticing that anything was missing.

'New man in the kitchen,' he explained. 'That's what happens when a taxi driver from Turkey gets a job as a prison chef.'

'Taxi driver?' she whispered, terrified. 'Turkey?'

There was something about his eyes. They both seemed to be dead and glassy now, she thought. He had never seen or heard her, no one did. She only had herself. And the fork.

'Your eyes are watering,' Adde said. 'It must have been spicy.'

Ragna felt the paper ball growing again, becoming heavier and heavier until it filled her belly. It pressed against her lungs and tried to force its way up her throat, wanting to spew out of her mouth for the whole world to see. She touched the prongs of the fork with her fingertips. They were sharp.

As Adde walked towards the door, Ragna started to make strange sounds, as if she was trying to cough something up, or was crying, or perhaps even laughing. He turned round but could not understand what was going on or what the strange expression on her face meant. He had heard the stories about Ragna Riegel, but never noticed anything.

'Is everything all right?' he asked, looking at her closely.

Ragna took a few steps forward.

'Yes, Adde,' she whispered. '*Alles ist gut.*'

Karin Fossum's critically acclaimed novels have won numerous prizes. She is two-time winner of the prestigious Riverton Award and has also won the Glass Key Award for the best Nordic crime novel, an honour shared with Henning Mankell and Jo Nesbo, as well as the Los Angeles Times Book Prize. Her highly acclaimed Inspector Sejer series has been published in more than forty countries.